DEAD STOCK

KATE IOLA

HAMMERSMARK BOOKS • HARTLEY

Hammersmark Books
PO Box 4, Hartley IA 51346

Visit our website at www.HammersmarkBooks.com

For information about special discounts for bulk purchases,
write to: sales@HammersmarkBooks.com.

First edition
2 4 6 8 10 9 7 5 3 1

Library of Congress Control Number: 2006926571

ISBN: 0-9776878-0-5

Book design by Jennifer Cizek

Author photo © 2006 by Michael Fischer

Knife by E. Carroll Hale III

Printed in the United States

For Maureen Kampen

FOREWORD

You don't have to be a journalist to know what makes news. Conflict, threat, timeliness, drama, emotion, disaster, proximity, suspense, prominence, progress, and consequence are a few of the defining elements you'll find in any Journalism 101 textbook.

A good story only requires one or two of those elements. Kate Iola uses all of the elements above to elevate *Deadstock* to a compelling message that is more than just a good story. Here's how *Deadstock* impacted me, and what it made me ponder.

• I couldn't stop reading. I'm an early-to-bed, early-to-rise kind of guy. But *Deadstock* kept me up several nights far beyond my bedtime.

• I couldn't help but tell others about this book. What we initiate in conversation probably best describes what's on our minds and what we find important.

• Everyone loves a good story. Try to read a book-load of scientific facts and numbers—no matter how important—and our minds often go to sleep. Boring. But intersperse the same facts into a good story and our minds fully engage. We can't resist a good story.

• We learn through stories. For much of time, oral stories were nearly all we had to convey our culture and history to the next generation. Whether oral or written or visual, a good story of the right elements commands our attention. In *Deadstock*, we are entertained as we learn about the consequences of deadly animal disease, the work of our nation's security and defense system for food safety, and the vulnerability of our food to terrorist attack.

• Scientific facts and a big imagination create an irresistible story. Kate Iola exploits the full potential of fiction to tell a vivid, detailed and powerful story about a foot-and-mouth disease (FMD) outbreak in livestock based on scientific fact.

• *Deadstock* touches the lives and livelihoods of every agricultural producer. Proximity, as a news element, means how close the reader is to the story's theme. The consequences of a FMD outbreak would be economically devastating to many segments of our agricultural industry. Consumers are directly impacted, too. Everyone who eats, whether meat lover or vegetarian, by reading this book will better understand the threats to our food security.

• The ultimate message from *Deadstock* for both producers and consumers is that America must be relentless in protecting our food system. In our abundance and comfort, we must not ignore increasing risks and vulnerabilities. We must invest in research to learn more about deadly diseases and food safety. I know you will enjoy *Deadstock*; I hope that while you are entertained, you also will more clearly understand what is at stake with our food system and why we must protect it.

Loren Kruse
Editor-in-Chief
Successful Farming magazine
Agriculture.com

DEADSTOCK

For Donna
Book Expo '07

Kirk Johnson

"Although there are FMD vaccines available, they are not currently used in this country because the United States has been free of the disease since 1929. There is no need to vaccinate against a disease that no animals have, especially when strict import restrictions are in place."

— Foot-and-Mouth Disease Vaccine Factsheet, US Department of Agriculture APHIS (*"Safeguarding American Agriculture"*)

"An unchecked FMD outbreak could cost billions of dollars. Because the last U.S. outbreak of FMD was in 1929, most producers and animal health workers are inexperienced with the disease."

— Report on FMD epidemiology, US Department of Agriculture APHIS

"For myself, I love to make people do what I want them to. I love to command. I love to rule people. That's why I'm a con artist."

— Unnamed confidence man, *Deceivers and Deceived*

CHAPTER 1

The men who keep Tike Lexington awake aren't in her bed; they're in her nightmares.

Not all of them are dead.

A cell phone buzzed somewhere in the darkened room. Tike cursed and fumbled for the nightstand lamp with one hand, knocking over a stack of books and a teacup. Half-full. Its icy liquid doused the back of her arm as the cup fell to the worn oak floor.

She dug the phone out of the bedcovers and read the glowing screen. A page, 515 area code. *Please Call.* She dialed and waited.

"Polk County Morgue."

"Tike Lexington here." She rubbed her eyes with a damp Earl Grey-scented pajama sleeve, not at her best in the illegal hours before dawn. "You called?"

"Lady, I don't know who called you," the man said with a snarl. "It wasn't me, and I'm the only one alive in this hallway."

"Sure," said Tike, and hung up before he could finish asking what she was wearing.

Sure, she said. Just a prank. She sank back into her pillows, hand on the phone, hearing the night whispers of the old farmhouse. Nickel sat in the doorway, twitching his kinked Siamese tail, staring back at Tike with her own unblinking, mismatched eyes, one blue, one green. One of his was scarred opaque in battle. Hers were set in a pale, lean face with a square chin, framed by a tangled mess of currently-blond hair.

Tike looked at the phone in her palm, tapped it with a blunt fingernail. It was the fifth call from a morgue this week, each from a different state. This one, from Des Moines, was the closest so far, a short three-hour drive.

She thought of the night calls she'd had over the years. Some from editors, some from sources, some from family and friends. Some from people who were definitely not friends.

These were her first from morgues.

Tike rubbed the fading scar on her thigh, the jagged line that started on her abdomen and curled, spiraling, between her legs. It was still raised enough to feel through her pajamas. That one had started as a phone call.

She paid more attention to phone calls now.

But these weren't calls, she thought, sitting up. *They were pages.* The caller could be anywhere, calling from any phone, entering morgue phone numbers on cue.

Tike scrolled back through the menus on her phone, looking for the originating number of the page.

Blocked.

"Damn." The number she had called at the Des Moines morgue wasn't blocked; it had popped right up on her screen. Someone had called it in from another location, another phone. A blocked phone. Tike's fingers raced, scrolling back through the earlier morgue calls; three were still listed in her phone.

Blocked.

Blocked.

Blocked.

Where was the caller? Her mouth was suddenly dry; her palms, wet. Not again.

Quietly Tike turned off her flickering lamp, then reached behind the low headboard and lifted up her shotgun. It was a 12-gauge pump, short and loaded with heavy buckshot; good for indoor work in the dark. She slid off the warm bed and into her cold slippers, flannel pajama pants making no sound as she moved.

Who hates me this time?

As she moved she popped open the breech and felt for shells, then snapped it shut. She put her cold grip in a ready position, barrel high, as she slunk down the stairs in the dark, stepping around the squeaky boards and prowling cats.

Room by room, she checked the doors and windows. She picked up the office phone, then the fax line: solid dial tones. The security bar on the cellar door—a two-by-six slipped through two rebar braces—was in place, her pencil marks in the right position.

Standing in the dark, she scanned the farmyard from behind living room curtains. The flat gravel yard was lit by 450 watts at the top of the utility pole next to her fuel tanks. The grove embracing the house was still and dark. There was fresh snow, no car, no human tracks to be seen. The white fields of corn stubble beyond the big barn were wide and empty. All seemed clear.

Tike went back upstairs. She put away the gun and sat on the edge of the bed, willing her heart rate to slow.

Tomorrow, she thought. *Everything's okay. Call it in tomorrow.* She knew the routine. Knew how meaningless it was, knew the blackness where the paper trail could lead, knew the resentment from the local law when she brought blackness onto their turf. They didn't like it. Or her.

"Shouldn't be out here," they said.

Shouldn't be so different, they meant. *We know about you. You're a failure.*

She reached behind the headboard with one hand and checked her shotgun once more, then slid under the quilt. "I'm safe here," she whispered to the dark room, pulling the blankets around her. "This is my world. Mine." The red flowers on the fabric looked black and gray and dead in the Iowa winter moonlight seeping through the clouds.

The quiet sky wouldn't last long. A storm was coming; she could feel it. She could hear it calling her name.

Tike grabbed Nickel as he tore across the bed. He bit her, slowly. They curled up together and dreamed of previous lives.

The man in sub-zero snow camo sat in a padded sling chair, suspended high in an eighty-year-old concolor fir. He'd been in the grove since before the afternoon snow started, reading and making notes in a small book, doing calculations, making diagrams. Now, in the moonlight, he occasionally took off his night vision goggles, adjusted a black watchcap over sun-bleached hair, and did slow stretches to ease his bad knee. His long legs moved through the branches, back and forth.

The movement didn't disturb the animals that passed below his nest. He smelled of them and made little noise; he was tolerated.

The man turned to a fresh page in his white canvas-bound notebook, then went back, flipping through several pages to retrieve a formula. Next to it was a sketch rendered with just a few strokes: A slope for the nose, a rounding for soft lips, a wisp for delicate eyelashes.

He reviewed the calculation, made a correction, then moved on to a fresh page and recorded a few notes, some in English, some not.

A deer appeared out of the depths of the grove, her sharp hooves stepping along the path below the man's nest. He moved his pen to the margin of the page and began a new sketch, using only a few lines to echo the animal's lean form, her grace and flow. He spent some time shading the musculature under the doe's coat. She paused and looked up, then behind her. A fawn crashed along the path, skidding on some ice, sliding between his mother's legs. The man made a few strokes with his pen, adding the movements to his sketch.

He set aside the pen and book as he slid a phone out of a camo pocket and checked for messages: Three, all text, from his brother. The man sighed. *Mister Jumpy, as usual.* He scrolled through the messages:

"P docs done"

"Update? Whr r u? Redy?"

"CBOT SN 725. Sell 40 CTKS?"

He wrote a quick response:

"Redy. Resting. Snd docs 2 Basl. Yes sell 40 CTKS SN @ 725."

He sent the message, then thought a moment and pulled up the Chicago Board of Trade commodity prices himself: July corn was up, as well. He wrote a second message:

"Sell 400 CTKS CN @ MKT."

The man checked his watch, put away the phone, and picked up his binoculars. He looked at his prey, watched, dreamed. The man thought of happy mornings. Biscuits. Newspapers. Teacups. He closed his pale green eyes, seeing. *Two teacups.* He put the binoculars back in their pocket on his chest, next to the silenced cell phone, then started another sketch next to the formulae: The woman, sleeping. A cat beside her.

He crossed out the cat with dark strokes, started over: The woman, sleeping.

Him beside her.

He looked at his watch again. It was almost time.

CHAPTER 2

The next morning Tike was up early, drinking her Darjeeling tea with skim milk and three cubes of sugar and reading the *Spencer Daily Reporter* at her kitchen table, circling errors in grammar and AP style with a red crayon she stole from the dentist's office. The first Christmas card of the season, from yesterday's mail, leaned against the sugar pot. The slick frost on the window panes melted and dripped into the dust and dead ladybugs on the frame. Tike wiped it up just before it spilled onto the still-shrink-wrapped issues of *Science* and the *Journal of Cell Biology*, to be read next with her toast, a chewy Swedish limpa bread from the Christmas bake sale at the fire station.

She sipped her tea and tried to relax, glancing up at the phone on the wall next to her, not thinking about morgues, waiting for the clock to hit 8:30. By that time, the sheriff would have had his first coffee, and the deputies would be out on the road.

"It's probably just a friend," he said after she made her report. "Playing a joke." He paused. "Maybe Nick. Where's he at these days, anyway?"

Tike's jaw clenched. "Gone."

"Huh."

She exhaled quietly and took a breath. "Anyway, I don't think it's just a friend. Or Nick. There's something very off about it."

"Off. Something off." He gave a deep sigh.

She paused. "It might be Zack."

"You gave me some paper on him. Expired no-contact order, Clay County?"

"Yeah. He used to call. Follow me. But it's been years." Four years. Four years, two months and twelve days since the last time. Tike fingered her throat. *The very last time.* "It doesn't seem like him."

They were both silent, scanning her messy life, arriving at the obvious next stop: the other guy, the one with the knife. Her scars. But neither of them mentioned him. He was dead, a tweaker. He cut his throat in her bedroom. Her knife.

Dead guy.

The sheriff sighed again. "We'll keep our eyes open. I'll pull your file. Meanwhile, why don't you make life easier on all of us and move to town? Then you'd be Carl's responsibility."

"Because you do a better job than your brother-in-law." She paused. "Because this is my home now."

He sighed.

"I'll stop by at lunchtime and fill out the paperwork," she said. *For all the good it'll do*, she didn't say.

On this bright winter morning, Tike sipped her tea and enjoyed her new size 8 red flannel lounge pants—eleven dollars at Farm Supply—which were making their debut as the new new thing in winter office wear, at least for the core group of independently employed writers in O'Brien County. All one of them. Nickel and his limping shadow, Pepper, slept by the warm stove, black limbs and tails intertwined, Nickel's paw on one of his brother's ragged ears. Tapes of interviews were stacked in her office, next to the kitchen, ready to be transformed into a story that would pay some bills.

Then she could get back to her real target: getting a book published. A money maker? Not likely. But it was something solid, real. She would be An Author. She wanted something, needed it, after so many failures: PhD? Failed. Biotech company? Failed. Marriage? Failed. *And, oh, by the way, your darling eccentric husband? Felon.* Brilliant as a biotech CEO, but absolute genius as embezzler, stock manipulator, and all-around con man. He was arrested and taken away in handcuffs in front of the staff. She had to fire them all by herself, deal with the investors and creditors herself, face the bankruptcy attorneys herself.

So add this to the list: Modest hard-earned fortune in the bank? Gone. Any chance of respect by her colleagues? Gone.

She started over, moved back to the sticks. The descent continued: New boyfriend? Abuser. Try again? Closet alcoholic. Worse decision? Join him at the bar.

That's where the crackhead—the one with the knife—got her phone number. He called to make sure she was home from the bar, smoked another foil, maybe two, maybe five, then let himself in. *It's a bad sign when they try to kill you and drop the knife. Worse: When you're too drunk to dial 911.*

It was a bitter track record after such a golden start: The golden girl, the young inventor, the gifted student. Awards. Patents. Invited speaker. *She's going to be Somebody, you can just tell!*

And then. And then and then. *Now I'm...what? What am I? Fucked up, for one thing.*

Tike shook her head and held out her hands. Not shaky. Things were getting better. She had gotten help, finally. Zack, the other crazies—they were just bad memories. Now Nick. Nick Capelli. Tall, dark, tough. Soft brown eyes, like a cat. He might be okay. But maybe not. He had spooked her, bad.

It didn't take much.

Tike glanced through the office door at the stack of files she was using in her latest book proposal. *They'll see. I'll be...Somebody.*

The phone rang. Tike leaned back and, halfway to the phone, her hand twitched. *Dead guy.* She gave her head a quick shake and picked up the receiver.

"Tike," said a basso profundo voice. "U.P. here. Come to Chicago. Something's happening."

"U.P., how nice to hear from you, too. And how is the lovely Madame Geneva?"

Ulysses Pritchard Alfonse Yatsis III, also known as U.P.—or more commonly "You Prick" or "You Greek Prick"—among his colleagues at the Chicago Board of Trade, was not the sociable sort. Not that U.P. gave a rat's ass what you thought. Unless you had information.

"Tike. You got to get on this right away. Gennie got you a ticket, usual deal."

Tike opened a can of Canadian blackcurrant jam and put some on her toast. "Sorry, U.P., can't do it. I'm in the middle of a big assignment. Four-page spread, magazine money, rush fees. This'll put a new roof on my barn."

"Whatever. You owe me."

"We're even-steven. Don't pull that on me, pal." Tike had met the U.P.-and-Geneva commodities trading team while researching a book proposal a few years earlier, right after she went freelance. U.P. and Geneva were both independent traders and full members of the Chicago Board of Trade, but they had a deal: U.P., who looked like the swarthy, stubby, ball-busting Greek sailor he was, operated in the testosterone of the trading pit, an alpha local in the chaos of open outcry. Meanwhile Geneva, his fair maiden—actually a flame-haired Amazon with tremendously-large feet and an IQ to match—traded electronically and did the intuitive deep research a hired analyst couldn't grasp. Geneva was U.P.'s well-known secret weapon.

"Tike, no kidding." He paused. "We need you."

This was not the You Prick that Tike knew and sometimes liked. She poured a new cup of tea and thought about her morgue calls: Denver, Atlanta, San Francisco, Newark, now Des Moines. Airport cities, mostly hubs. Nothing from Chicago.

So far.

"U.P., what's going on? Is Geneva okay?" She hesitated. "Are you getting calls?"

"Calls?" His voice was sharp. "What calls?"

"From a morgue. More than one morgue, actually. For about a week."

"A week? This week?"

"Yes. Why, U.P.? What's going on?"

"I don't want to talk about it over the phone."

"Just a hint?"

"No. Come and talk."

She took a sip of her tea, then sat back and stretched her legs under the kitchen table. One of the cats jumped on her lap. "Is it DeadSim?"

He was silent. *Bingo.*

DeadSim was their private goldmine—or would be, if FMD ever hit.

The book proposal that brought Tike to U.P. and Geneva was completed two years ago. She had forwarded it to her New York agent—now ex-agent—who sent it back by return post with a note: "No cow disaster stories. Who cares?"

Who cares? Bioterrorists and the U.S. economy, that's who—and commodities traders. U.P. and Geneva used her rejected book proposal and turned it into "DeadSim," a computer simulation that would let them trade their way to a fortune. DeadSim predicted the consequences of an outbreak of a silly-sounding livestock virus, FMD: foot-and-mouth disease. Like "mad cow," another silly-sounding livestock disease, FMD was tangled in the politics of international trade. However, unlike mad cow, FMD could spread as easily as a cold. Easier. The kicker: the only way to stop it was to immediately kill all the livestock for miles around each infected animal—a firewall of slaughter—and shut down state and national borders.

Sometimes it worked.

A single confirmed case in the U.S., one of the few countries still officially FMD-free, and the commodities markets would boil. Meat prices would plunge, then skyrocket. Grain prices—with fewer herds to feed—would also plunge, then skyrocket, since shipping was blocked. Trucking, fertilizer, diesel fuel, ethanol—everything related to food and fuel would be hit. It wouldn't take long for the price chaos to reach corner grocery stores.

The instant a single case of FMD was confirmed—just one animal with the painful foot-and-mouth blisters of FMD—U.P. and Geneva would crank up DeadSim and start executing the DeadSim trade recommendations. In fact, Geneva had just modified the software so the trades would be done automatically. They just had to pull the trigger. Every second they could move ahead of the pack was worth thousands of dollars, hundreds of thousands.

FMD would arrive someday, no question about it. It was going to happen, no matter what Tike did.

And now something was happening with DeadSim. Had U.P. heard something? Or Geneva, who seemed to know everybody? Did they get advance word of a confirmed case?

If so, U.P. and Geneva would be white hot. So would Tike's book. *Then they'll see.*

Tike closed her eyes and bit her lip. *And they'll cry. We'll all cry. People just don't get it.* An image of her neighbors' farm across the road flashed into her mind. A fat moon hanging over a wide grassy pasture, black-and-white cattle crowding together in a corner, warm and soft, leaning on each other, chewing sweet timothy, calves bucking around like fools. *A big yellow tractor digging a burial pit, veterinarians in white Tyvek coveralls loading captive bolt guns with .22 caliber rounds, a schoolbus coming up the gravel road with kids in the windows—there's Katelyn and Kirstie and Alex—crying. Bulldozers pushing piles of warm black-and-white bodies into pits...*

Tike released a deep breath and loosened her grip on the phone. That was what had driven her to write about FMD in the first place: People just didn't get it. Someone had to remind them. But editors wouldn't listen. Only U.P. and Geneva did. And now... Tike released a deep breath and loosened her grip on the phone. *Don't think about it. Don't don't don't think.* Her heart was thumping. "I'm on my way."

Pepper and Nickel stayed home and found new ways to shred reinforced computer wiring while Tike went to Chicago.

The small commuter plane was too noisy for sleeping, so en route she got through *Nature, Cell,* and the *Wall Street Journal.* In the cab from the airport she nodded off, dreaming about other places she had been, other cabs and carts she'd taken: Whining tuk-tuks in Karachi. Musky camel trains in the Sud. Gaudy enameled buses winding toward Simla.

Schoolbuses with kids. White Tyvek covered with blood and warm black-and-white scraps.

Then her phone buzzed. *Dead guy.* Her eyes snapped open, heart thudding.

It was U.P., checking on her ETA just as her taxi swerved to the curb of his building, where the regular doorman waved her in. The elevator stopped at PENT and she could see the only door in the short hallway was open. She went in.

"Hey there, Geneva," she said. "You guys married yet? Is that the surprise?"

Geneva La Croix blinked as she turned her face away from her computer monitor. "Tike," she said, blushing. Then she paused and blinked again. "Good to see you."

Tike paused too. "Everything okay, Gen?"

Gen turned back to her computer. "U.P.'s in the kitchen making lunch," she said, starting to type again. "Do you want anything?"

Tike stepped past her and threw her Hartmann overnighter on the long Italian couch facing the fireplace, yawning and flopping lengthwise next to the bag, ignoring the 180-degree view of the Chicago skyline, the financial district front and center.

"Did U.P. tell you I was coming?" said Tike. She grabbed a silky red pillow and stuffed it under her head to watch Geneva, who had a chewed-up pencil tucked behind one ear, her eyes scanning the screen before her. She didn't answer. Tike rubbed her eyes and stretched, listening to U.P. clattering in the kitchen, then took off her shoes. "I really need a quick nap. I pulled an all-nighter to get my story done."

"Tike, Geneva—omelet?" said U.P., calling from the kitchen doorway. He waved at her as he rolled up his sleeves.

She gave him a thumbs-up and turned back to Geneva. "What's going on?"

"I think U.P. wants to talk," she said, fidgeting. "With you. Something to drink?" Geneva redid the twist in her thick red hair, anchoring it with her gnawed pencil as she rolled her chair back from a workstation littered with empty Diet Dr. Pepper cans and Chee-tos bags.

The women walked into the kitchen and took up positions flanking the five 19-inch flat-screen monitors on the marble countertop, all muted.

On the left was Bloomberg, giving a market recap. In the middle were CNN and Reuters, and on the right was the Weather Channel. Stacked on top was DTN. Like Bloomberg, the DTN started out as a dedicated terminal. But while Bloomberg was general business and various stock, bond, and other markets, the DTN terminal displayed more specialized fare: the subculture of agribusiness and commodities markets, the lifeblood of U.P. and Geneva.

U.P. was deep in the Sub-Zero refrigerator, pulling out ingredients. All you could see were his charcoal gray suspenders and his broad backside, encased in the finest, most ill-fitting, synthetics new Chicago money could buy. He leaned back, his arms full. "Trip went fine?" he said, dumping yellow pear tomatoes and fresh basil and Vidalia onions and gruyere cheese on the counter, pulling a string of garlic from his pocket. "You want anything else? I'm starving."

"Great. I'm fine," said Tike. "How were the markets today?" It was 2:15; soft commodities had been closed for an hour.

U.P. spread the ingredients on the granite countertop next to the butcher block and half-smiled. His white teeth looked sharp. "Fucking whipsawed all morning," he said, pulling a cleaver from a block of teak. "Went short on the Brazilian weather report—new Bahia beans are toasting—rode it all the way up, then flipped with a big fill or kill and rode it all the way down. Bastard of a day. Kill would've saved me 500K." He twirled the cleaver handle and shrugged.

"Made up for it later," he said. "Just another day at the office. Eh, Gennie?" He pulled out some sprigs of basil and started rinsing them as Geneva got two cans of pop from the refrigerator. He gestured at her with a jerk of his chin. "Look at Geneva here. I keep trying to get her to buy a place downstairs, but she doesn't want to spend her money," he said. "Her crappy condo isn't safe. Piece of crap. Pay the nickel, Gennie. You Dutch, or what? It's a good investment." Geneva made a sound of disgust as she turned, pop cans in hand. Tike saw them exchange a look. Geneva elbowed him as she passed and handed Tike a cold drink. Tike sipped and waited. U.P. scanned the monitors as he blotted the basil dry, then chopped it. Tike flinched, expecting little bits of U.P. to end up in the basil.

He stopped chopping and laid down the knife, still staring at the screens. "It's DeadSim, Tike." He turned and looked her in the eye. "Someone is making perfect DeadSim trades. Someone got in, got our latest profiles, and is using them."

Tike's heart jolted as she was hit with a tumble of realizations:

We've been hacked.

Something big is going to happen.

The hacker knows what, and we don't.

Then a chill: *Dead guy.*

She looked at Geneva, then U.P. "Another trader? Someone jealous of you guys?"

Geneva shook her head. "Too sophisticated. This was a pro."

Was it her dead guy? Were the morgue calls about DeadSim, not her? Then it wasn't such a big deal. She closed her eyes and shook her head as she blew out a short breath. *With millions to be made? It's a big deal.*

She shivered. Then she looked at Geneva, who had built DeadSim from U.P.'s napkin sketches and her proposal, plus boxes of data Tike helped gather over a two-year period. Geneva was looking at the floor. Tike looked back at U.P. He was chopping basil again, his face a deep red.

"Well, don't look at me," said Tike. "For pete's sake. I snoop but I don't hack. Really now." She popped a sweet tiny yellow pear tomato into her mouth and sucked on it, shaking her head. "Sheesh."

U.P. looked at Geneva. She shrugged and shook her head at him. "I told you she couldn't have done it, U.P. It was a pro, someone who knows what they're doing."

Tike frowned. "Thanks, I think."

Geneva put her palms up. "I just want to know what's going on. If foot-and-mouth is here, we want to know. Now. We need to trade on it. We can worry about hackers later."

"Is DeadSim ready?" said U.P. "If Tike can confirm there's an outbreak, are we ready to roll?"

"Obviously," said Geneva, scowling. "Someone thinks so."

"Okay." He put down his knife. "There are only two reasons someone would be making those trades. One: They have better sources than us, and got an early tip of a confirmed case in the U.S., the start of an outbreak." He paused and licked his lips. "Or, Two: They're planning one," he said.

Tike raised her eyebrows and swallowed her tomato. "Oh man," she said. "We've talked about the possibility, but...a deliberate outbreak?" She rubbed her forehead with her fingertips. "They'd really have to plan ahead. But if they did, and it worked, they could clean up. With our software. Um..." She frowned and paused.

"Yes, um." U.P looked at her and nodded. "Exactly. They clean up, and we take the fall."

Tike blew out the breath she'd been holding. "This could get ugly."

U.P. took Tike back to O'Hare after lunch, letting her drive his new Ferrari once they got out on county roads. He gripped the dash and flinched as she practiced her rusty shuffle steering on 60-mph-corners, but he had the class to keep his mouth shut.

Once Tike got checked in for her flight back to Iowa, she hit the phones. Her first call was to her editor at the *Sioux City Journal*. She sold him a Sunday feature: *In The Shadow Of Death: Defending Iowa Against Global Livestock Plagues*. This was her cover; being a freelance reporter is a very handy excuse to snoop.

She was able to squeeze in a few calls before boarding. She started with the vets and clinics she knew, putting out feelers. Someone out there must know something. She spent the rest of the trip scrolling through her address book, planning her attack.

The next day, back at work in her farmhouse office, Tike kept one phone busy with outbound calls; the other was reserved for call-backs from sources.

She took breaks, thinking. She walked around the house, dangling a string for Nickel, looking out the windows and thinking about adding a line of lilac bushes behind the old feedlot, now planted with wildflowers. *Sweet white lilacs.* And another row of concolor firs in the grove.

As she passed the cellar door her eyes dropped to the security bar, pencil marks in place. *Just keep working*, she thought with a shiver. *Stay alert. That's all you can do.* She picked up Nickel and went upstairs. In her library, lit by tall south windows, she ran a finger along the books on her walnut shelves. They were overflowing; small stacks were scattered around the room, littering the floor. Time to add more shelves. *My books will be here someday. And I'll pay my debts. Someday.*

By 11 a.m. her time, offices on the West Coast were opening. Tike gritted her teeth and started with San Diego.

The first call went fine. The vets at the San Diego Zoo and Wild Animal Park hadn't heard any alerts, or even whispers, about an FMD outbreak.

The second call was to Isaac Mendez, the Chief Technical Officer of

Euvaxx, an ag biotech on Torrey Pines Mesa. The call started out fine. Tike liked talking to CTOs. They were, as a rule, no-bullshit guys. This one confirmed they had an anti-FMD vaccine in development, and said he'd be thrilled to hear if there was an outbreak on the way. "But I haven't heard squat," he said.

Then he paused.

Here it comes. Tike closed her eyes. She knew the other side of the CTO personality: Zero social skills, zero tact, beaucoup obsessive curiosity.

"Say, are you *that* Tike Lexington?" he said. "Didn't you have a biotech out here? Something about fraud, wasn't it? Your partner? Husband? Whatever happened to him, anyway?"

She pinched the bridge of her nose. "He's in prison."

"Oh, I bet that was a mess, wasn't it?"

"Yes." Tike put her head on the desk and looked over at the picture of Baby: Porsche 911 C4S, custom ordered. Midnight blue. Camel interior. 285 Pirellis and Novatti rims. Just enough room in the front boot for a jumping saddle. She touched the California license plate on her wall. They let her keep that.

"So what've you been doing since then?" he said.

"Not much." She rubbed her scars. "Getting by. Learning new things." She looked at her award from the Santa Barbara Writers Conference, reached up, touched it. *They knew me.*

"Too bad. You had a good technology. I hear Oasis has it now."

"Right. But their CTO is a moron."

He laughed. "I always heard you were sharp. Too bad you couldn't cut it."

Tike winced. "Well, thanks for your time, Isaac," she said. "I appreciate it." She hung up and took a deep breath, then picked up the phone and started dialing.

"Hi, Pete? Tike Lexington...Yeah, it's been a while. Of course I didn't forget you. How's the world-famous Russell lab doing?"

By early afternoon Tike was ready to call Plum Island. She'd checked around enough to know there wasn't an alert out at any level, and nothing posted on the alert page of the Plum Island website. But now she could lay a paper trail by telling the director, Dr. Roy McCall, that she'd heard word there was something happening. He could also direct her to someone upstream in Homeland Security.

It took a while to connect. He was a busy guy. *Your lucky day*, his assistant said. *He has ten minutes open at 2:35.* While Tike waited, she paced. She ate a peanut butter and jelly sandwich. She read the manual for her security system, installed and customized by Nick; password: NICK-L. Something was wrong with it. *I might have to call Nick and ask. Damn.*

She went online, leaving the phone clear, just in case. But snooping online was dry and dull. The best leaks and information spills came from wetware: the human brain. She was always amazed at what people blurt out, then say, "Now, you can't print that." Bless their hearts. People are so innocent.

Roy called as Tike sat at her desk, leafing through her old rotary Rolodex, each card covered with scribbled notes.

"Tike," he said. "Tike Lexington. Don't I know you?"

She reminded him of the Emerging Infectious Diseases conference where they met a while back. She left out the details of his trying to pick her up, an effort that hastily ended when he realized she was a reporter.

"Oh, of course. You're the reporter with those interesting eyes and the velvet pencil. How are you, Tike?"

Roy was smoother than ever. But so was Tike. "Well, Roy, I'm doing another story," she said. "And I hear rumors there's an outbreak of FMD being kept under wraps, maybe a deliberate outbreak." She didn't mention she heard the rumors before she started the story, but her wording was adequate CYA: their asses were now covered. She checked her voice recorder to be sure it was rolling.

"Sounds like a *National Enquirer* assignment, Tike." He assured her there was no cover-up, and reports of confirmed disease would go out as usual.

"But should I alert someone at Homeland Security, maybe a tip line?" she said, again leaning over to eye the spindles of the tape recorder.

He made a snorting sound. "We get so many reports of disease outbreaks, rumors of bioterrorists at large, nasty foreigners infecting the local feedlot. If we investigated every one, I'd need a hundred times the budget. It's the same at Homeland. But go to the tip line and tell them what you've heard. They've got a bigger budget than us."

He paused and she knew she had given him the opening he wanted. "Speaking of budgets," he said, and off he went: the vital nature of Plum Island, the struggle for funding, et cetera, et cetera. *Arrogant jerk*, she thought, but he was right. If Plum Island had to shut its doors, there would be problems. Big problems. Not only did the island house the national vaccine stockpile, ready for a crisis, but it was the only secure, offshore location in the U.S. able to test for the bad ones like FMD.

There was a reason Plum Island was an island.

The only back-up was the second national lab, "Plum Acres," in Ames, Iowa. But did anyone want to forward the Plum Island mail—thousands of suspicious samples every month—to the state with more chickens, hogs, and cattle than people? Not an option. Homeland testing for the bad ones would simply stop.

This was Roy's budget leverage: Without Plum Island monitoring U.S. livestock, the multi-trillion dollar status of the US as a safe international food source would plummet. To put it simply, they wouldn't be able to prove they weren't exporting FMD with every hamburger; prices would tank, and the ripple effect would be a bloodbath.

"Why don't you come visit us here sometime, Tike? Maybe we could work something out with our p.r. office, get you to do some contract work for us?"

She gave him her contact info, and made sure she was on the fax and e-mail list for press releases.

"And say hello to that charming fiancé of yours," he said. "What was his name?"

"He's not around anymore."

"Oh, sorry."

Yeah, I bet. She thought she could hear him licking his lips.

"All the more reason to come visit," he said. "Lots of single men out here. And me, of course."

She told him she'd think about it, and she did. Which reminded her she needed to clean the cats' litter boxes.

Done with her calls, the sun long-sunk, Tike burrowed into her warm bed with a nice glass of wine. Pepper and Nickel wrapped around her knees while she read a newly-discovered Elizabeth George, awash in crimes of the landed gentry. She felt almost good.

But then she looked up and couldn't help seeing them, next to the dusty jewelry box with the ring she didn't wear any more: the photos. Nick and Tike in Santa Barbara, having dinner with Mom and Aunt Doris. Nick and Tike at a journalism conference in Omaha, he speaking, she learning, both of them laughing, dreams intact. Nickel as a kitten on

Nick's lap, both of them asleep on the tattered recliner downstairs. Nick out by the old chicken barn, his hands rough and grimed from their own library, bigger than the one next to their bedroom. Her bedroom. A much-younger Nick at work in a big newsroom, the twin towers of the World Trade Center visible in the windows behind him.

She reached behind the pile of books on the nightstand and replayed Nick's message on the answering machine.

"Tike. You there? Tike? Please don't do this to me, sweetheart. To us. Please call. Let's talk it through. We have to let them know." She played it again, twice. She sipped her wine and stared at her photos. Nick. Her. Nickel. Nick.

January 1. She had until January 1 to decide. Nick had an offer for an international editorial slot at the *Post*. His base would be Washington, D.C., but there would be significant travel, staff in three cities, high rank, high pay. But if she moved to the Capitol, moved with him, Nick would take a domestic slot. Lower rank, less money, but more free time. Time to be together again. Time to work things out. She could still write and travel, make her calls—just like here. *It'll be worth it,* he said.

Would it? She sipped her wine. What about the sweet white lilacs? The bookshelves?

The dead guys.

She went to the dresser and laid the photos face down, then paused. She opened the bottom drawer and stuffed them inside, then got back in bed. She reached out to the answering machine, hesitated, then hit "play" one more time. When the machine finished, she stacked some books on it, topped off by her alarm clock.

She tried to read again, threw down her book, picked up the phone, dialed, hung up before the first ring. She buried the phone under a stack of magazines and sipped her wine. She thought about lilacs and dead guys; she read Elizabeth George and waited for someone to die. She didn't look up any more.

From the December 17 Spencer (Iowa) Daily Reporter:

Ag Security Office Cut Back

'Higher priorities' cited

DES MOINES, Ia. (AP) — The Iowa Department of Agriculture announced a reorganization of the Office of Ag Security.

"The Director of Ag Security has retired, and the position will not be refilled," said Department spokesperson Susanna Wander. She pointed out that the remaining staff—one full-time field agent and one part-time office assistant—was still more than most states.

"Farm and food security is still a high priority in this state," she said. "Clearly, we have done our job well and it's time to focus on more pressing issues."

In other news, the Department of Agriculture has commissioned a $270,000 study to determine the impact of odor emissions of swine operations on economic development in metropolitan areas.

CHAPTER 3

After three days of calls from her quiet office in O'Brien county, Tike had no results, not even a hint of a suspected hushed-up outbreak. On the fourth day she woke up to clear skies and decided to take a break. After breakfast with a stack of magazines, she went outside with the cats and watched them bound across the snowy yard to the barn. *Mice, beware.* It was a proven fact in their household: two out of two cats preferred a dead mouse to a slice of fried bacon. A live one started a cat fight.

While the cats hunted, Tike went around back to check the level of her 1;000-gallon propane tank; a cold snap was forecast. Halfway there, marching through snow to the top of her Ugg boots, she heard her phone ring. She dug it out of her coat. "Tike here."

"Hi, this is the Old Saybrook Medical Examiner, returning your page."

"Old Saybrook, Connecticut? Page?"

He recited her number.

"That's me, but I didn't page you."

"I thought the area code was odd, but not many people have this pager number. I always respond. Where are you, anyway?"

Tike told him about the prank pages from other morgues, and that she was a writer in Iowa. "At the moment, in fact, I'm working on a story about FMD," she said. "A livestock disease. Foot-and-mouth. Not something that'll cross your slab." As she spoke she saw the mailman driving up the icy gravel road; she turned back toward the driveway to meet him at the mailbox.

"Oh, I know FMD," the M.E. was saying. "I have friends who work at Plum Island. They stop by on their way to work and bring me a coffee."

"On the way? But it's an island. It's in New York."

"My morgue is a block from the ferry terminal, the ferry from the Connecticut side. I can see the island out my window."

By late afternoon, Tike had done everything she could. *At least I'll get a Sunday feature out of it*, she thought, looking over the notes piled in tidy stacks on her office desk. Good enough to pay a couple of bills.

She leaned back in her chair and scanned the rough draft of her story, then called her editor to confirm the column inches and space for art. He gave her the numbers and sighed. "That's it. No more farm stories. People don't care about this. I want people stories."

"But this *is* a people story," she said.

"No, it's a cow story. A pig story. No people get sick."

"But people will go broke. Farms will shut down."

"Maybe they shouldn't be raising pigs here anyway. Nobody wants them here. People are tired of smelly pig farms."

"Okay, bankers will go broke. Banks will shut down."

"I don't want stories about banks, either. People don't like banks. I want people. I want to see some people. Some Siouxland residents. People our readers can relate to, struggling people, winners, criminals, whatever.

"Bank robbers?"

"That would be fine. Not old dead ones, though. Contemporary bank robbers. What drove them to it. Prison interviews. How their families feel. What they did with the money."

"Cattle rustlers?"

"No," he said. "No, no, and no."

They argued for a while, and Tike could tell she'd have to get more creative if she wanted to write anything interesting. She told him she'd have the story in by 9 a.m.; she didn't want to give him time to change his mind and yank it altogether.

Next she called U.P. with an update. "Not a peep. No change," she said.

"We've got a change here," he said. "All of the DeadSim-type trading stopped."

"What?"

"Yeah. I don't understand. Maybe we were wrong."

"But the timing. My morgue calls. They didn't stop. I got another one, U.P."

"Well, I'm sorry about that, but the trading did stop. It was tapering, then dried up. Maybe there isn't an outbreak out there. You didn't hear anything, right? A fluke, that's all it was."

"Someone did hack into the system, right?"

"Yes, but that's happened before. Geneva thinks we're making a big deal out of nothing. If we don't see more trading again by tomorrow morning, we're going to shut the software down. Then Geneva says she can wipe the sector with the back door and rebuild. Whatever that means. I just know DeadSim would be out of order for a few days."

He said they'd keep her posted.

Tike slumped in her chair, looking at the list of book titles she'd been scribbling during interviews. Also some names of potential co-authors, marquee types who would help clinch a publisher. A few names of people to write jacket blurbs. She crumpled up the sheet of paper and threw it in the trash. It bounced out and hit Pepper, who woke up with a hiss. Tike jumped to her feet, scooped up the overflowing wastebasket, yanked her coat off the rack, and slammed open the door, headed for the burn barrel.

Good day to burn crap.

———————

CHAPTER 4

The man in padded coveralls and a black knit cap trotted from the old stone farmhouse to the low barn. Nothing else on the farm was moving except the wind from the Bering Sea, blowing in vain over the squat buildings, pulling across the heavy slate shingles encrusted with lichens.

He approached the side door of the barn. Next to the door, at eye level, was a small weathered plaque·engraved with an ancient Finnish family name. The letters were rendered in Saami script over a heraldic crest: a winged reindeer arcing over a wide river. He pressed his fingers against the side of the crest, just below the feet of the stag. The plaque slid down into a recess, revealing a panel of electronic controls and a round lens. The man centered one pale eye in front of the lens, looking straight through it without blinking until he heard the click of a latch. He gripped the worn wooden handle in the center of the door and pulled. Inside, he pushed a yellow button on the wall; the barn door hissed shut behind him.

The inside of the barn was nothing like the outside. More than four tons of glistening 218-gauge stainless steel lined the interior walls, and a glass partition separated the loading zone from the surrounding storage areas. The periphery of the ground floor, once used to shelter herd animals in winter, was now populated by cryotanks, also of 218 stainless, ready to use. Only a few of the tanks were empty.

The man made a circuit on foot, inspecting the tanks.

Some of the full tanks were dusty. Not dusty like an old haunted house in a Hollywood film, but dusty by the standards of a modern biotechnology lab. Not a big issue, but he wiped them down automatically, pocketing the used Steri-Wipes as he went. He checked the pipes entering each tank as he made his rounds. This plumbing didn't transport water; it carried ultra-cold liquid nitrogen. The tanks, dusty or not, were automatically monitored and topped off with fresh nitrogen as needed. Like other well-tended long-term investments, the precious samples remained ready for the future.

A tour of the sample labels, hand-inked in permanent black, would be a sweep through global history: *Botswana 1982 Bluetongue. Taiwan 1996 Hanta.* But the man didn't spend time looking at labels. He knew them; some of the handwriting was his father's, some was his brother's. Most, certainly over the last few years, was his own.

A set of stone stairs at the back of the barn led down to the granite cave carved out by the earliest residents of this site, long before the concept of "barn" or "cryotank." It also was lined with 218 stainless. Here were tanks with the older specimens of the collection: *Nigeria 1933 Swine Cholera. Ukraine 1914 Avian Plague.* Freezers in those days were inadequate, but someone had thoughtfully kept some of each sample preserved by other means—in dried manure, or live chickens, for example—until good freezing was possible.

Like any family treasure, most of these assets were left untouched for decades, gathering dust. Gathering value.

In a workshop in another building on the farm were cases of items including one set of bound laboratory notebooks, swollen with pasted-in documents and photos, each page autographed and dated, each notebook cover embossed with the Plum Island medallion. One box was labeled "VIROLOGY ARCHIVES." Eventually, the materials would be catalogued in the workshop, then filed in the cave.

Today was not for filing. He was just making rounds.

The man threw away his gloves, washed, and picked up a packet of digestive biscuits from a cabinet in the kitchen nook by the office. He perched on a wooden stool and peeled open the wrapper, popping one biscuit in his mouth and letting it slowly dissolve into a mash of flavor. He studied photos on the wall as he snacked. They were old photos, black and white with a silvery sheen: A stone house in the snow. A father with two sons, the father large, the sons small, all with dark hair and pale eyes. A mother, in the background, looking off camera.

Halfway through the packet, a muffled beeping in the man's pocket announced a call.

"*Hei hei,*" he said, sitting up straight as he licked his lips and swallowed biscuit mash.

"It's me."

The man settled back, smiling. "Excellent. We are okay? Everything set?"

"Yes. And our trading positions?"

"Ready."

"Good. Now, I need you to forward the JBC manuscript to our friend Roy. Check the electrophoresis figures first; Zoltan always gets the labels backward. Add a cover letter from the Institute: 'Honored collaborator, blah, blah, blah.' You know."

The man in the stone barn tipped his head to the side and squinted one eye. "Brother? You are behaving?"

A pause. "Behaving?"

A sigh. The man put down his packet of biscuits and rubbed his forehead. "*Saakeli*," he said under his breath. He gripped the phone. "Don't do this to me. To us. You remember last time."

"That was an accident."

"She? She was an accident?"

"Leave me alone."

"That's exactly what I want. You, alone. Forget the women, forget distractions, stick to our project. You can relax soon, when we're done. Okay?"

"I'm not doing a thing. It's not about fun, anyway."

The man sighed, picked up the biscuits, put one in his mouth and sucked. "Just focus. Okay? Stay focused."

As the man trotted back to the stone house, a wild caribou stag in the surrounding forest raised his head to watch, tail raised in alert. When the crunch of human footsteps faded, the animal lowered his tail and put his muzzle back into the frozen bed of forest violets, the sweet petals tangled in dried moss and fallen acorns.

A man in a crisp white labcoat, his pale green eyes calm, replaced the phone handset and leaned back in the cushioned office chair. He swung his long legs up and put his feet on the crowded desk, wedging them between a stack of death certificates and a leaning pile of autopsy case files. Next to the files was a computer monitor with a split screen in the middle of the desktop, commodity prices scrolling across the left panel, an e-mail inbox on the right. The man closed the e-mail screen and increased the size of the commodities ticker.

Behind the man, beyond the closed office door that read "DR. MARFAN," was a busy beehive of activity. Dozens of staff wearing labcoats like his swarmed the hallways, some with gloves and face masks, some with goggles shielding bloodshot eyes. Some carried trays of small plastic food tubs filled with chunks of cirrhotic liver or edematous lung or polycystic kidney swimming in formalin. Some pushed long rattling carts with quiet passengers.

Dr. Marfan was out there somewhere, too. Actually, Dr. Marfan, according to the night roster, was in autopsy suite seven, busy as a bee.

The man in Dr. Marfan's chair scanned the shelves next to the desk. A framed photo of, presumably, Mrs. Marfan and the juniors Marfan. Another photo with Dr. Marfan—rather chubby—receiving an award. *Ah, a chubby one. Good sign.* The man slid open the bottom right-hand desk drawer and—bingo—a box of cookies. He smiled, selecting a handful of oatmeal raisin cookies from the box, then looked back at the phone, his face turning serious.

No, brother, it's not about fun. I just...need to do it. I know it doesn't make sense. But I can't help it.

He knew he shouldn't. He sighed and ate the cookies, one by one, from largest to smallest, knowing he should just push it out of his head. It was a frustrating flaw. A weakness. *Forget her.*

It wasn't always this way. When Father was alive, when they all worked together, Father cracked the whip.

"Vuoi vuoi! What have you done now?" That was the worst. And it was no good to run and hide. Father had the patience of the old people; he could wait, without moving, without eating, without, it seemed, breathing. The boys learned from him.

Now Father was gone. The brothers had to crack their own whips. It didn't always work.

The man in Dr. Marfan's chair picked up the phone.

Just once more.

Geneva sat down at her workstation in the living room of U.P.'s condo in downtown Chicago, a cappuccino in one hand and a half-eaten bialy in the other. She looked at the clock next to the monitor. Almost 9 a.m., half an hour before the market opened.

Time's up.

The DeadSim trades hadn't started again. Geneva had spent the evening reviewing the projections with U.P. and it was clear: If these were DeadSim trades, there should have been a solid pattern of activity over the last 24 hours.

We're chasing a phantom. It was time to shut down the system and start clean-up. She put the last bit of bialy in her mouth and was setting her drink on a coaster when the doorbell rang. She checked the camera monitor by the door and saw the delivery man from the market, downstairs at the elevator, his cart full of groceries. She went to the control panel by the door, buzzed him into the lobby, left his tip in the private foyer, and locked the door.

After he went back down the elevator, she retrieved the groceries and carried them into the kitchen. She put the carton labeled "COLD" into the second refrigerator, grabbed two bags of Chee-tos from another carton, which she left sitting by the stack of TV monitors, volume at a low buzz, and headed back to her workstation as the phone on her desktop rang.

She sat back, tearing open a Chee-tos bag, watching the phone ring a second time. It didn't ring again. She raised her eyebrows, then popped a few Chee-tos in her mouth and walked to the door of the former guest room, wiping her fingertips on her slacks. She pulled a long flat key from her pocket and slid it into the lock of the door, releasing the bolt. She entered and shut the thick door behind her. The latch snicked shut, and the sounds of U.P.'s living room vanished.

Here, on a small barren desk, tight between four insulated walls lined with fireproof Steelcase file cabinets, was a rotary Rolodex and an old-fashioned phone, a landline with a heavy cable. This is where Geneva did the work that went behind the software, the *real* work: the wetware.

Human histories, relationships, flaws, mistakes, surprises, successes—the unpredictability, the human-ness of wetware could mess up any computer-driven simulation or any market analysis, no matter how deep. Geneva's data, gathered over the years on her key drivers—agency heads, senior economists, CEOs—anyone who could move her markets, was used to test and troubleshoot each new version of DeadSim.

The data also had other uses. It was a long-term investment.

Geneva sat on the wooden chair and rotated the card file, checking her watch, flipping through the names and reading the notes written in her hand. Notes on photos received, confidential memos and restricted documents delivered. Notes on payments given. Geneva checked her watch again just as the phone rang, on schedule.

"Geneva here." It was a short call, but a known and reliable voice on the other end of the line. Geneva, her hands shaking, made a note on one of the cards ("payment due") and left the room, locking it behind her, fumbling with the key. She went back to her workstation and pulled on her headset while hitting the speed dial, calling U.P.

There was work to do, but it wouldn't involve shutting down DeadSim. 9:20 a.m. Ten minutes to the market open. She knew U.P. was in his position in the corn pit, his own headset—a double, with one phone for the left ear and another for the right—strapped on, both microphones in ready position, his shoulders bumping his neighbors and marking his territory, ready for the bell. Geneva opened up the main screen of DeadSim and started feeding him instructions.

Clarissa Ivy was enjoying fresh melon and raspberries with the morning *Washington Post* at The Palm, her regular restaurant near Capitol Hill. Across from her sat a fat young aide to Senator Robertson (R-Ohio), one of her strongest supporters on the hill. He was eating pancakes and sausage, and there was grease on his chin. He once again tried to use his spare hand to feel her thigh under the table. This time she let him; sometimes it made him more talkative.

Laurence brought them two cappuccinos. He leaned over their table as he poured, his neat white jacket smelling of bleach. "Miss Ivy." He spoke softly.

The fat aide didn't even raise his eyes from his plate, where a particularly stubborn sausage might require him to extract his other hand from Clarissa's lap so he could use his knife. "Miss, a note," said Laurence, no more than a soft breath of air as he leaned to straighten the flowers on the table. Clarissa saw a small fold of paper trapped under her coffee cup.

"Thank you, Laurence," she said. "It looks perfect."

He nodded, already departing. Clarissa picked up her coffee and looked the aide in the eye while palming the note with her other hand. He had stuffed a whole link of sausage in his mouth, and was vigorously chewing.

"I'm sorry if this bothers you," he said, the chewed meat showing. "The meat and all."

Clarissa shrugged and smiled. "To each his own." She picked up her newspaper and opened it, watching his eyes go back to his plate. Behind the paper, she thumbed open the note and read the short message, then folded the newspaper and laid it back down, sliding the note into her pocket. She stood, pushing back from the table, the fat aide's hand sliding from her lap as he looked up, mouth agape, concern in his eyes. Sausage on his tongue.

"Sorry, Rupert. I've got to run."

"I'm sorry. Is it the meat?"

"Not at all. I just remembered an appointment. Next week?"

He swallowed and smiled. "That would be great. I'll get the eggs instead, I promise. Or are eggs a problem? Lox?" Rupert was using his now-free hand to pull her plate across the table.

Clarissa headed for the Metro, her mind already composing text, laughing out loud as she reached the steps and descended to her train. *It was too easy.* Normally, there was never any progress. First they tell her, "Yes, Clarissa, we're cutting that from the bill" or amendment or whatever, and then they swarm like mating rat snakes and make more deals and everything comes out different and she looks like a fool. Again.

Not this time. Today, dammit, they couldn't do anything to mess this up for her, even if they tried. Finally, MATA could make a statement about a true crisis. They brought this on themselves, and now they were going to bleed from every orifice. And MATA would be right there, saying "I told you so."

About time.

Clarissa Ivy, public information officer for MATA, the Mission for Approved Treatment of Animals, pushed her way into a seat on the train headed for her office and dug a bent notepad out of her coat pocket, whistling.

She had a press release to write.

———————

Mike Salt's BlackBerry buzzed as he hit Malibu, passing Gladstone's, doing just over the limit on the Pacific Coast Highway. It was a good morning for a pleasure drive down the coast to San Diego. He wiggled his tanned, toned ass in the bucket seat, enjoying the feel of his new Shantung silk slacks—Armani, of course, perfectly tailored.

Mike had a thermos of non-fat latte and a ten-stack of Grateful Dead CDs in the changer of the Blauplunkt X35 eight-speaker 75-watt system of his Mercedes CL-650—and the residual buzz after a good night of what Veronica, still sleeping in Montecito, did best. *That damn BlackBerry can wait,* he thought. He put on his phone earpiece, pushed the power button, and said, "Florist," starting a set of isotonic ab exercises.

The sound of the speed-dialer on all eight speakers was deafening. The camel-tan leather of the seats vibrated. The answering machine came on.

"Ciao, belli. This is deFazio House of Beauty and Greenery. We make flowers as beautiful as you. Please leave us your wishes."

"Ciao, bello. Er, sono Michelangelo. Please send three dozen white long-stems to Veronica. Say 'You're the best, babe. Love, Me.' Use a different vase this time, maybe something from that antique shop in the Plaza Del Mar. Bill me. Ciao."

Veronica loved that shop. Mike took her there every time she came down to stay at his place by the racetrack in Del Mar. Not that he encouraged her to visit very often. No, he liked her place in Montecito better. There was nothing like the feel of old money. Besides, it cramped his style having her in Del Mar.

No time for that. This was going to be a big year. It had to be. *Big plans*, Mike thought to himself as he sucked latte. *Big plans.* First, he would wrap up the due diligence and close the financing. "It *will* happen," he said out loud, running a hand through his sculpted brown hair. "I am a *great* and *admired* success in my life." Fucking affirmations. *Maybe I should make a tape and play them while I'm sleeping*, he thought, nodding his head, whacking the CD player to re-start the Grateful Dead, then cranking the rearview mirror sideways to check his hair. *Hmm. Another week on the highlights?*

Mike was a closer. The big-five accounting firm the investors called in was up to its elbows in his financials. The technical consultants were up to their prodigious buttholes in his laboratory notebooks. The intellectual property attorneys were up to their frontal lobes in his patent estate, he said out loud: "Patent estate." The term rolled off his tongue. "Patent estate. The Euvaxx I.P. estate." English was a beautiful language.

That would be the best part of his plan, harvesting the fruits of the patents of Euvaxx, Inc. All thanks to Cynthia, his best score in Del Mar. He had discovered her, turned her into a huge asset. Boobs too small, low self-esteem, zero social skills, but could she crank out the disclosures? Novel, non-obvious, and jam-packed with utility—her Roman cognomen would be *Patentus maximus*.

Cynthia built on the polio vaccine strategy. For inspiration, she would walk around the home of the polio vaccine, the futuristic Salk Institute across the street from Euvaxx. Mike had never heard of the four stupid diseases she tackled. Who cared about spinning cod in Nova Scotia, flabby clams in Wales, fainting hyraxes in New Guinea, or limping, drooling Cape Buffalo in Namibia?

Homeland Security, it turns out. Three of those four stupid diseases were each caused by not-so-stupid infectious agents that could bring the U.S. economy to its knees, if someone so desired. And someone always did.

Now, of course, Mike was An Expert, and told audience after audience about the proof-of-principle work they had done and the Global

Significance of This Powerful Toolbox of Biological Methods. They had two keystone methods patents awarded, four applications pending. A notice of allowance on one application just arrived last week. They had two strategic partnerships with Homeland Security doing pilot studies to really put some legs on the patents. One of the studies was just wrapping up and looked promising.

With Mike as her handler, Cynthia's patentable ideas over the last three years for new methods of making vaccines were the bait that snagged the $35.9 million venture round now on the table. This would let Euvaxx move up to the next level, one step away from an IPO. Where the big boys play. That was the plan. And just in time. Mike had pushed the accounting to the limit. Running Euvaxx was not cheap.

What he hadn't planned was peace and quiet. Too much of it. Homeland Security didn't have the clout—or anxiety—they used to. If they dropped the Euvaxx project, it was a deal breaker. *A back breaker.* The financing would vaporize, and Euvaxx would tank within two months.

Mike sighed. He moved the latte to his right hand and plucked the BlackBerry off his belt with his left while steering with his knee past the Santa Monica pier, the ferris wheel and carousel still asleep, the surging Pacific waves crashing unheeded on the beach.

The brain of Michelangelo A. Salt, MBA, PhD, CEO, IQ 214, lightning-fast and running at full speed after 3.4 pints of Kenyan latte, knew, the instant he saw the glowing little blue screen, that his life had just changed.

Well, call me a winner, thought Mike as he put the BlackBerry back on his belt, reached for the phone, sucked some latte, and crossed two lanes while turning up the stereo.

He couldn't have planned it better.

As the North American morning turned to afternoon, a large mass of cold air from the western edge of the Arctic Upper Winter System broke away and moved south. It slid over the top of the warm front blanketing central Canada, then dropped down to 15,000 feet over the Upper Plains. The air mass spread out, slipping into the trough of the Buffalo Ridge Wind Belt, capping off the airstream already flowing down through Saskatchewan, Minnesota and Iowa, south to Missouri, west to Nebraska, occasionally hitting a pocket of warmer or cooler air and coiling up or down.

As twilight turned to black, the flow of the wind belt accelerated, super-cooling the spinning blades of the wind turbines marking its path. The red lights on the tips of the turbine housings were echoed by colored lights strung along rooftops of infrequent farmhouses, large white stars on the tops of barns and occasional illuminated displays with sleighs and Santa, elves and reindeer.

The wind moved along, full of moisture, beginning to drop it, picking up replacement moisture where it could find it. The warm, damp exhalations from long barnsful of dairy cattle or sleeping hogs were crystallized and drawn aloft, to mingle and be dropped elsewhere.

Two men in blue nylon parkas stopped their truck at an intersection, their breath torn away by the wind before it became frost. One of the men stepped out of the truck and pulled a clipboard from the cab. The wind tore some papers loose from the clipboard and threw them across a cornfield. The man snatched for them and missed, then watched them go. He turned and, with his counterpart, lifted the first barricade from the truck.

Dr. Elizabeth Thomas, asleep in the middle of her wide bed in her empty house, thirty miles from the east-west interstate that divides Iowa like a stray equator, dreamed her phone was ringing. This was unfortunate, because it was the phone she had dropped in the icy muck that day, right between the feet of a cow she was checking for reproductive problems, her state vet bag safely to the side. Shoulder-deep in cow, she could only watch as the phone sank, the stubby antenna sticking out until the cow stamped her foot on it.

And now it was ringing and ringing. *Someone hold the cow*, she thought, thrashing in the bed, crawling through the slop in her dream, trying to find the phone, the cow complaining and stamping. Her hands gripped something solid. She hoped it was the phone. She put it, slimy and dripping, up to her ear.

"Elizabeth," said the phone. "Liz."

She sat up and rubbed her eyes. The slop was gone, and so was the cell phone. The landline, though, was in her hand. She tried to find the clock in the dark. Who was calling her at this hour? As a district vet for the State of Iowa, she never went out in the middle of the night for a horse with colic or a breech calf, like private vets. That was no accident. Liz liked her sleep.

"Liz," said the phone again. "This is Roy."

Roy. The tall blond one from the bar? Or the cowboy? Whichever.
"Oh," said Liz. "Right. Thanks for the drink."

"Roy McCall, from Plum Island."

Oh God. "Yes, Roy. How are you?" Roy McCall from Plum Island
wasn't calling for chitchat at 1:37 a.m.

"Yes. Liz. Listen."

She knew what was coming. She hadn't thought it would really happen. Not a chance. She was just doing her job, being cautious. She sent
some samples to Plum this week, but it wasn't the first time. Maybe
eight, ten times before. Always negative. The guys always gave her flak,
laughing behind her back—she heard them—but she slept better at night,
knowing she had done her duty.

But no one ever called like this. Roy never called. Her muscles tensed.
Plum Island has never called back. She could feel goosebumps rise on her
arms. She held her breath.

"Liz, we're sending out a team. They're on their way. I've got the DOT
closing off the area. You have to go secure the site where you collected
the samples. West Soo. You'll be the primary. It's here, Liz. FMD."

Liz retched as she hung up, and ran for the bathroom. Then she started to pack, grabbing her cell phone—the clunky old back-up—hitting the
speed-dial as she moved through her house.

She knew it could be weeks before she returned.

———————

From the December 18 Ottumwa (Iowa) Observer:

Disease Outbreak Freezes Exports

FMD Confirmed in Iowa

DES MOINES, Ia. (AP) — The Department of Commerce announced that all beef, dairy and pork exports had been halted while the U.S. trade status was being reviewed by the Paris-based livestock disease organization, O.I.E. Iowa's State Veterinarian Dr. Jonathan Childs announced a confirmed case of foot-and-mouth disease, a highly-contagious livestock infection, in northwest Iowa early this morning.

"The area around the site of the confirmed FMD case is now closed for traffic," said Childs. He verified that all livestock in the area are under quarantine and control measures have begun.

"Our team is assembling a fact sheet that will be released later this morning by our media office," he said.

He declined to provide further details.

FMD has not been confirmed in the U.S. since 1929. It is one of 16 livestock diseases in an international economic alert category called "List A."

"We will be providing updates to the O.I.E. as we learn more about the source and extent of the outbreak," said Childs.

CHAPTER 5

Tike was frying an early breakfast of bacon for the cats when the first news of the outbreak came on the radio. She scrambled to turn off the stove and ran for the phones, heart pounding, a surge of nausea reaching her throat.

While she waited for her editor to get on the line, Tike dialed U.P. on her cell phone, holding it to the other ear. The cats were agitated and started fighting on the floor behind her.

"Yeah, got the news," said U.P. She could hear the chaos of the trading floor behind him. "All hell broke loose."

"I can't believe it. Just can't believe it. It's really here," she said, wiping her forehead. *I'm sweating?* She shook her head. "DeadSim trading? Is it happening?"

"No. That's the interesting part. Call Gen. She's got a theory. The first surge in trades we saw were ones this guy could sit on, she says, all longer-term positions. But the trading like I'm doing now takes some babysitting. Call it Plan A and Plan B trades. She thinks he set his position in advance, that's Plan A, but now he's got something else going on and he's skipping the Plan B trades. She says we've got a surprise ahead, something big if he's skipping Plan B trading."

Tike raised her eyebrows. "Like this isn't a surprise?"

"Whatever. I can't think about it now. Got to go."

Just as she hung up the other phone clicked.

"We're running your package tonight," said her editor, shouting into the phone. She held it away from her ear. "I already added an intro. The *Des Moines Register* can kiss my ass," he hollered. "No one else'll be ready like this." It just came over the wire, he said: *State Vet Confirms FMD Outbreak.*

"The *Register*'ll just run interviews with thrilled activists, anyway," said Tike, pacing the kitchen. She sat down, then stood again. It didn't feel normal to be on the receiving end of good news. *Bad news. What about Kathy and Ron? And the Johnsons?* She wiped her forehead again, her eyes welling up. "Fricking *Register*. City boys."

"For sure, your package'll get picked up by AP," he said.

"Am I good?"

"You're adequate. Now..."

"I know," she said, leaning forward again, cutting in. "People. People stories. I'm working on it. Plenty of people to talk to now." She closed her eyes and shook her head, gave a full-body shiver. *Work to do. Got to help get the word out.* She looked out the window. A livestock trailer was driving by, gravel dust billowing up in its wake.

There were plenty of calls to make, but not most of the people she had already interviewed. Since the outbreak, they were off limits. They were either swamped or on information clamp-down. The public relations hacks were now in control. Even the big guys couldn't get through.

Meanwhile, she got on the story budget for daily reports—on the front, above the fold—and weekend recaps until the outbreak was over.

Tike spent the rest of the historic day digging, calling and digging, focusing on people and events that would: (a) give good quotes for the report by her now-daily 6 p.m. deadline, and (b) help her figure out what was really going on. U.P., Geneva, and she agreed there was only one way someone could have known about this outbreak so far in advance: if they started it. But the stalled DeadSim trading by the hacker—what did it mean? Why wasn't he doing Part B of the trades? Was something else happening? Keeping him busy?

The Department of Agriculture and Homeland Security were looking into the outbreak as well. *But they're not being framed.*

So Tike worked the phones. She called livestock trucking registries at state borders. Were animals moving as usual? Anything unusual? She called private, state, and federal vets. Who was on duty in the area, and when? She called feed and chemical dealers, Extension agents, crop consultants, and auction houses. She called some of her scientists again. Had they heard any rumors? Did they have any thoughts? Remember anything unusual before the outbreak?

The nice ones called back.

"Tike?" said one message. "Pete Russell...yeah, the world-famous Russell Lab. Sorry, I haven't heard anything. But hey, you've got ESP or something. How about that outbreak? Hello, funding, eh? If I hear anything I'll let you know. Hey, are you going to the Keystone Integrin conference again this year? Hope so. We had a good time there, you and I.

I've been thinking about you. See ya."

When Tike was taking a break at midday, she called U.P. again.

"It's hot, Tike. Can't talk." The trading floor behind him was near hysteria.

"DeadSim trades?"

"By us, yes, and the DeadSim stuff already in the can. The Plan A trades. That's it."

"I got one thing, U.P." Tike looked at her notepad. "The state vet who spotted the first cases, Liz Thomas—she's probably the only vet in western Iowa who could've made that call. I had called her last week for my story, but never did get through. Anyway, she's had special training, went to Plum Island, on her request, some kind of unusual circumstances."

"Handy. Coincidence?"

"I've interviewed her before, a series I did last year. She's tough."

"Think she did it? Planned the outbreak?"

"This will make her career. Local guys are ready to kill her for calling Plum Island, since they're locked into the hot zone now, but her chutzpah basically saved the rest of the U.S. farm economy."

"Is she broke? Or recently not broke anymore?"

"Don't know. I'll check, if you'll pay."

"I'll pay. And Tike, I still think we should give you a piece of this. We couldn't have done DeadSim without you. We're having a fantastic day. Let me set up a brokerage account for you."

Tike bit her lip. One day the previous summer U.P. had let slip his take for the day, a "decent" day: $300,000. And today was "fantastic." The next two weeks would be "fantastic."

She closed her eyes. "Can't do it, U.P. Let's stick with my hourly fees. Besides, you guys take the big risks, not me."

Tike hung up, then called her financial snoop and gave him an assignment. He said he'd call when he had the information. She didn't stop working. *Can't stop. Can't think.*

My neighbors.

Tike was wandering around her house, pruning plants and making calls, when her pink princess phone rang. She pulled the wireless headset to the side and tucked the old princess against her ear. The voice on the line was crisp and manly; her Aunt Doris would have been pleased.

"Hello, is this Tike Lexington? Dr. Thomas recommended we call you."

"Liz Thomas? Elizabeth Thomas?"

"Yes, that's affirmative."

Affirmative? This was definitely not an editor calling. "Who is this?" she said.

"Oh, pardon me, ma'am, Ms. Lexington. Things are a bit hectic here. This is Deputy Sergeant Richard Fosco. I'm the communications officer for E Ops here at Johnston."

Johnston? *Oh ho.* Johnston: the State of Iowa Disaster Command Center. Emergency Operations. Ground Zero.

"Ms. Lexington, Dr. Thomas received your messages and has recommended you as an embedded media contact to interact with our staff here at central ops. We request you appear here for a briefing, then join Dr. Thomas at West Soo Feedlot for the duration of the quarantine."

Hot damn. Hot hot hot damn.

"Okay, thank you, officer, er, Deputy Sergeant," she said, glancing at her notepad. He gave her the number for the media office so she could start working on details and paperwork immediately. She put the princess back in her soft pink basket on the shelf, her brain doing double time, her shears still in one hand. She hacked at a dead gardenia branch and snagged her sleeve.

She said "You Prick" into her wireless headset. A phone in Chicago started ringing as she put away the shears and reached into the closet, pulling out suitcases.

Tike called her editor at the *Journal* as she drove away from the acreage, suitcases and supplies strapped in the back, camera bags and miscellaneous electronics in the utility box. She was ready for a siege.

"No, I think I'll be the only outside writer," she told him. "Their media chief said they keep the group small to keep things streamlined."

"Nobody from the *Register*?"

"I don't think so."

"Screw them! Screw them!"

"I'd rather not."

"But how did you swing it? The *Register* must be steaming."

Tike shrugged. "I'm freelance, they're not. No loyalties. Plus I'm local. And Liz asked for me. Not to mention I'm willing to live at a quarantined feedlot full of frozen cowshit for an undetermined amount of time." She didn't mention that she had held out for one condition: she wanted her byline on at least some of the pieces she wrote. The national exposure was worth twenty times what they would pay her.

"Don't make a mess," he said. "I've had some calls from the Capitol. They don't want us to stir things up."

"Stir things up? Stir things up? Are they insane? How much more stirred up could I make things? What could go wrong?"

"Do you want a list?"

"Leave me alone. I get to send out a few independent pieces, and I'm sending some to you. Not that I owe you anything. So, do you want them or not?"

Tike blew out a deep breath as she hung up. *It had to happen. A fantasy world. To hell with the politicians. They were living in a fantasy world. Preparedness? My ass. Try learning some biology, assholes. And no one would listen. Now it doesn't matter. Nothing matters. Here comes a cluster fuck.* The phone rang again and her hand reached for it, then twitched.

Dead guy. She shook her head. *Stop it.*

Time to move on. Deal with it. Forget the politicians.

My neighbors need me.

CHAPTER 6

Tike hung up the phone at Deputy Sergeant Fosco's desk at E-Ops in Johnston, trying to keep from shouting and spiking her notebook. She had passed inspection: one-hundred and twenty-nine "yes, sirs" to the local commander was not too high a price for clearance to enter the quarantined area.

Security was surprisingly tight, she thought, zipping up her coat as she walked toward the exit with Fosco. *There's something they're not telling me.*

Fosco walked her back to the garage. His team was nearly through inspecting her gear, which they loaded into one of their trucks as they finished. She saw her phone recording gear, laptop, and Rolodex already on board. Her Domke J-25 camera bag with various MEDIA stickers on it was open on one table, a gloved woman in fatigues opening each lens case and carefully wrapped accessory. On another long bench were her five cardboard banker's boxes full of hanging files. A gloved man leafed through the files while a second man scanned the boxes with some kind of electronic monitor.

The boxes held Tike's personal treasure, a goldmine of information on FMD: Reports and old news clips on the nine previous US outbreaks between 1870 and 1929. The latest reports on FMD hot spots worldwide. Contact numbers and bios of the top twenty-seven FMD experts, each cultivated with care, each reassured she wasn't a fanatic trying to access their frozen zoo of virus.

She had contact info in the hot countries, stats on livestock movement, and regulations on import/export restrictions.

Then there was the box marked with a blood-red "X." It wasn't about pigs or cows. It was about people, the people who tended the animals— and killed and buried them when FMD arrived.

This box she avoided opening. She just put new stuff in as she pulled it off the wires, filed by country, by category: Lawsuits. Divorces. School closures. Suicides. Bankruptcies.

Another man in fatigues finished going through her suitcase of clothes and necessities. Her truck, now empty, was under a dust cover at the end of the warehouse. The fewer vehicles to decontaminate later, the better, they said. She could pick it up then. After.

When the inspections were done, Fosco wished her good luck and handed her paperwork to the driver. She strapped into the passenger seat, and they left for the hot zone.

Twenty miles from West Soo, Tike's phone rang. The number on the screen was Nick's. She held it in her hand, watching it ring. Watching it stop ringing. When the message light flashed, she hit retrieve.

"Tike, please call me, sweetheart. I heard about the outbreak. Will you be doing anything on it? I know you'll get in there somehow. I'm at the editors' conference in Chicago for a few days, so call my cell. It's going really well. Everyone's heard there's a new guy coming to the *Post*, but no one knows it's me. Tonight there's a group of us going out, but don't worry. I'm doing fine. Tike, I got some housing information for the D.C. area and maybe we..."

Tike pressed "erase."

As they approached the barricades around West Soo, Tike's driver slowed the truck and pulled a clipboard of papers from the seat between them. When they reached the sentry, he rolled down the window and handed over the papers.

"Thank you, Lieutenant," said the sentry. "Ma'am," he said, nodding toward Tike. She smiled.

He didn't smile. "Ma'am, something's come up. If you would step over to our vehicle here, the Captain has some questions." The driver's eyebrows raised, but he didn't turn toward Tike or say a word.

She got out of the truck and followed the sentry. He opened the door to a drab green military cargo van and she stepped in. The man inside rose and gestured her to a seat in front of a chipped metal desk, then seated himself across from her. He opened the fat file that lay before him.

"Ms. Lexington, some more information came up that wasn't retrieved in your initial background check," he said.

Her stomach tightened. *Here we go again.*

"Some information from the California federal courts," he said.

"Ah," she said. I'm calm, she thought. *One two three four five. I'm calm.*

He leaned back in his chair and looked at her. She was silent, her mind racing. She could smell the singed odor of electronics in the van. She let out a deep breath. "What would you like to know?"

"My job is to judge whether you should be allowed to work at this site. I report jointly to the Secretary of Agriculture and the Secretary of Homeland Security. Unless we determine otherwise, we are going forward with the assumption this outbreak was an act of bioterrorism."

He paused and leafed through the file on his desk. Tike could see her name in red letters on the tab. "I want to know one thing," he said, looking up. "Why should we let someone with felony charges of fraud represent our efforts on this sensitive incident?"

Tike nodded, her mouth dry. *Wondered when that tidbit would come up.* She swallowed, seeing herself shut out, on the sidelines, nothing to do but watch as the biggest crisis of a century unfolded. Nothing to do but sit at home and watch the veterinarians arrive at the neighbor' farm. *And the bulldozers.*

"I understand your concern," she said. "This is a real black mark on my record." She could feel sweat on her forehead and could tell by the heat of her cheeks that she had turned bright red. Her neck, she knew, would be covered with huge red blotches.

He didn't move or blink as he watched her.

"If you read the record thoroughly," she said, "as I'm sure you have, you can see the felony charges were dropped." She paused and took a deep breath as she wiped her upper lip. "My business partner was convicted and I was cleared."

"He was also your husband?"

"Yes. At the time."

He leaned forward. "Were you innocent?"

She paused. "I was stupid. If I had looked I could have seen it, stopped it. But I believed in him. In us." She could feel her eyes starting to tear up. *Damn it. When will this let go of me?* Under the table she dug her thumbnails into her fingertips.

He leaned back and looked at her. "And now you say you're a reporter."

"Yes."

"Are you good?"

"Yes."

"You've had some difficult incidents since California."

Under the desk, her hand jumped to the scar on her thigh. "Yes." *Hold still hold still hold still.*

"You don't choose your associates well, do you?"

"I encounter a wide range of people in my work," she said, then paused. "And some of them choose me."

He sat back and closed her file. "Is there anything else I should know?"

Tike thought about U.P. and Geneva. She thought about the dead guy, about the morgue calls. She thought about DeadSim. "I'd like to write a book about this outbreak. Later."

"Yes, the media office is aware of that."

She paused. "I consult for a commodities trader. Used to consult."

"We know of him. You won't do that while working here."

"I'm here to do a job, and I'll do a good job."

He sat still and silent. Tike swallowed, her throat tight. He closed the file. "I know Nick," he said, his voice quiet. "I understand he's moving."

Tike's eyebrows raised. *How did he know Nick? And know about the move?* "That's not public information, about him moving."

He nodded as he stood and put her file in a briefcase on the desk, then snapped the case shut and locked it, sliding it up against the wall. He went to the door and turned to face her, his hand on the door latch. "You can go. The driver will take you to Dr. Thomas."

She walked toward him, toward the door.

As he turned the latch, he paused and spoke softly. "I'll be watching you." He opened the door for her and she stepped out into the cold air.

Tike's driver took her through the barricades and down a gravel road to a grubby building surrounded by acres of cattle pens, sheds, and silos. The sign out front, "West Soo Feedlot," was half buried in a snow drift. As they approached they could hear gunshots.

Captive bolt guns. Gunpowder. Tike shivered. *Tyvek suits with blood and scraps of warm black-and-white flesh.*

They parked and walked through the front door to pandemonium.

"West Zoo, we should call this," said Liz Thomas as she got up from a desk to shake Tike's hand with a firm grip, her icy blue eyes looking into Tike's mismatched blue and green set. "Hmm," said Liz, then turned and nodded at the driver; he left.

Telephones rang somewhere on Liz's desk in a pile of battery chargers, calculators, FedEx envelopes, and manila folders. Phones on other desks rang, unanswered, as the few people inside the office building studied stacks of papers or computer screens. Coffee cups, food wrappers, and adding machine tapes were strewn across every surface. Tike could see cattle, men and equipment in motion outside the window behind Liz. Liz was tall in her stockinged feet, her boots a muddy pile by the door; she unzipped her insulated coveralls another few inches and pulled off a dirty cap, shaking out her long reddish-brown hair. She stuffed the cap in a pocket.

"Whew, I need to get back outside before I melt," said Liz. "I just came in to get fresh batteries. I've got the guys wrapping up the cull; then we've got to finish crunching numbers and there's a phone conference with the Governor and the A.G. at three. You can talk to our crew after that."

She wiped a stray wisp of hair out of her face with the back of her hand as she looked at Tike and smiled, her teeth white and straight, her face tapering to a delicate point. There was a rusty smear of dried blood on her smooth forehead.

I wish I was a veterinarian, thought Tike, at a loss for words. *In charge, like her.*

But not today. Not here.

Liz pointed Tike to a desk she could use, then got her batteries and headed for the door. Tike started to unpack her own tangle of battery chargers and manila folders, her coat draped over the back of her chair.

At the door Liz turned, hand on the grimy doorknob. "I'm glad you're here," she said. "There's way too much emotion flying around, even though everyone is acting tough. Let's keep this calm, super-professional. It will go okay."

Tike nodded and unpacked her laptop as Liz left, a cold bolt of air coming in to replace her. Tike rigged up her recorder to the house phone and dialed, recorder on, as she watched Liz cross the yard to the crew outside. Several of them stood as she approached.

How much of a coincidence was it that Liz spotted the outbreak first? Liz had the touch, the feel of intuitive power. But what did she really want? How far would she go to get it? Tike eyed Liz's desk from her base across the room. Her purse was probably there, with at least a checkbook, maybe other financial information she'd need during a long stay here. Account numbers.

Time for that later.

Tike finished unpacking as her first call out of the hot zone went through. As she spoke—questioning, laughing, sympathizing with her interviews—she scrolled through her notes and her Palm Pilot, choosing her next contacts, checking the pulse of the country. As she told the captain, she was doing her job. She would save her notes to write a book later, and, okay, she wasn't working for U.P. anymore. She could live with that.

She was, however, working for herself. She still wanted to know who had hacked DeadSim. She had to; she was on track to be blamed for it. Was it her dead guy? She needed to know if the morgue calls were involved. *Fluke? I don't think so.*

Somebody knew something, and it wasn't her.

Tike paused and stood by the window, listening to the gunshots, watching livestock trailers pull into the main feedlot, where the depopulation team was at work. They pulled in full and left empty. She could see bulldozers working in a nearby corn field. Some digging. Some filling pits. Scraps of black-and-white.

Addiction? I understand it, Tike thought later that day, sitting at her desk at West Soo, her finger poised over her phone keypad. The trick is learning how to make addiction work for you. *A better trick? Denial.*

She didn't want to call Nick. She shouldn't call Nick. It would not be good for her mental health to call Nick. She knew this, had learned this, had spent hours working through this. Therefore, her fingertip dropped to the keypad and punched out a number. Nick. "I'm at West Soo," she said.

"So I hear," said Nick. "You're going to be famous, Tike."

"That and a nickel."

The line was silent.

"Thank you for calling," he said, his voice soft.

"Well. So," she said, her voice too chipper and too fast. "I'm doing onsite p.r. for the disaster command center. But I can sell a few pieces, so I wanted to see if you, the *Register*, want to buy something exclusive. I could do an angle "from the inside," something like that. Like a diary. Short, a series of daily notes. Sioux City doesn't run pieces like that. But I can do that. If you want me to do that."

She clamped her mouth closed and shut up. She felt out of control. She was. Her face was hot. She hated herself, her weakness. She missed him so. Missed his laugh, his strong hands, his soft lips. Missed his arms around her at night, his peaceful face in dim morning light.

Didn't miss the pain.

"Sounds good," he said, quiet and calm. "I'd like that. Start tomorrow, 4 p.m. deadlines. Send it to my e-mail. I'll call the office and have them set up a topbox. We'll send people to the *Lifestyles* front."

"Yeah. Okay."

"It'll be great."

She could hear people talking in the background, people laughing.

"Tike? You okay? Can we talk?"

Her mouth opened and closed.

"When are we going to talk?" he said. "About us."

She bit her lip and closed her eyes. *Why did I call? Why do I keep doing that?* Just let him go. Move on.

"Tike? I have to go. The sessions are starting. I'm going to call you later, okay? I want to talk. I want us to talk. I miss you. And our little Nicky. And Pepper, that ugly bastard. Are they okay?"

"Everyone's fine." She hung up the phone and went to make a sandwich. Her skin was red hot.

Everyone was not fine.

———————

CHAPTER 7

Ulysses Pritchard Alphonse Yatsis the Third flopped into his chair near the trading floor at the Chicago Board of Trade and pulled his dual headset off. He replaced it with his Bose, flipping the switch for noise reduction. He pulled on silk British Airways eyeshades, swung his feet up on the desk, knocking a stack of used order cards to the floor, and leaned back for a quick nap.

Days like this, he thought, his eyes closing behind the eyeshades, *are the reason I am on this planet.* By this point in the trading day, a day unlike any other, U.P. was out of Tums. He was out of decongestant, out of tissues, out of lozenges, his pants were ripped and he was missing one shoe.

But he sure as hell wasn't out of money.

U.P. was a pro. Even when trade volume was down, he was digging, thinking, asking questions. Meanwhile his fellow brokers were boffing each others' wives and mistresses and sailing on that stupid lake. U.P thought back to his first call from Tike a couple years back. *What a pest*, he thought, smiling. He hung up on her more than once. She asked the stupidest questions, as if she could learn in a few phone calls what he had studied—lived—for years. Decades.

Then she had confessed. She was interested in one thing: FMD. If there was an outbreak, what would happen to canola futures? Natural gas contracts? Land prices? He had been patient with her pestering.

Before long, U.P. was the one asking questions.

And now, by God, here it is. Time for a little rest, then time to think, grab Geneva, review his strategy, and move his chessmen.

Their *chessmen.* *Geneva.*

U.P. gave a great sigh and slept like a baby for a full six minutes.

The noise of the growing crowd of media in the auditorium seeped through the wall. Bruce Ter Wee suspended a fat make-up brush in midair over the Governor's head and wiggled a finger on his other hand. "This way, sir, turn this way. Good. Now look up."

The door to the green room opened and a man in military fatigues poked his head through the doorway. "Live in seven," he said. "The pit is hooked in now."

The swarm of people in the control pit, just down the hall from the Iowa Disaster Command auditorium, would watch the press conference from their desks. It would be projected on screens facing the stacked rings of workstations, each covered with ringing phones, computer terminals, coffee cups, and notes scribbled over the last 12 hours. At the top of the pit—the back of the room—there was a clear Lucite box on a waist-high platform; it was locked. In it was a red phone.

Bruce finished powdering his boss's neck, then gave the thin, pale hair a last spritz with maximum-hold hair spray and yanked the tissues covering Governor Wilton's suit collar. "Okay. All clear."

"Numbers?" said the Governor, rotating on his tall stool as he opened his eyes and examined his tie for spots of powder, extending his other palm toward his assistant. Bruce grabbed a folder from the equipment cart beside them and slid it into the Governor's hand. "Here are the latest."

William Arthur Wilton, Governor of Iowa, took the folder and leafed through the pages. The noise from the auditorium was louder. "What say you, Bruce? Is the plan going along all right?"

Bruce Ter Wee, the Governor's senior assistant, paused. He didn't get his job by being honest. The plan, the official "State of Iowa FMD Emergency Response Plan," was impressive. It was elegantly written and packed with information, pages and pages of thoughtful responses to tricky state problems that would emerge if FMD erupted. For example: Who would be liable for shipping losses if I-80 was shut down? Could a hog producer use his neighbor's land for burial pits? And what were the chances of a human form of the disease developing? The plan was also available on-line in English, Spanish, and Japanese.

Very thoughtful.

Nonetheless, it sucked big air, and pretty soon people were going to find out why. Bruce sighed and plucked a scrap of tissue from his boss's shoulder as he handed him another folder. "Here are a few notes, sir. The plan is on schedule. The Tier One agencies and individuals have been contacted. Here's the full list."

South Dakota had already shut down I-90, their version of I-80, and every other road into their weenie ag state. They had even shut down their airspace. "This is war," their governor had said, pounding on his podium, at his press conference an hour—*only an hour*—after the news broke. *That was a leader,* thought Bruce. *Why didn't I take the job with the Governor of South Dakota? Or Minnesota?*

Governor Wilton took the folder and glanced through it, then leaned into a hand mirror and patted his hair. "All of that hard work is paying off. I need to be sure the planning committees get credit for this work."

"Great idea, sir," said Bruce. *Then you can blame them when the shit storm starts. Won't be long.* "Tier Two is still being contacted," said Bruce, ushering the Governor to the stage entrance. He could pick out familiar voices in the rising noise from the auditorium. *Judy Miller, from NBC in Omaha. Jerry, from the Register.*

"That list has all the producers in the affected and threatened area," he continued, his hand plucking some stray lint from the Governor's shoulder as they maneuvered around obstacles offstage. "Today was supposed to be a big auction day, so lots of producers were on the road. Most should be on their way back home now. Your TV broadcast—in, let's see, three minutes—will go on radio as well and should catch a lot of them. The Ops Center is coordinating all information flow in and out and provided these public information hotline numbers you can announce." Bruce handed over a final sheet of paper as he checked his watch.

"Thanks, Bruce. Good job."

"Yes, sir." Bruce stepped back as the Governor passed between the curtains and approached the podium. He could hear the media rumble as cameras started to roll.

"My fellow Iowans..." said the Governor, his hair perfect.

In the shadows offstage, Bruce Ter Wee dropped his head and pinched the bridge of his nose as he blew out a long breath. After a few moments he straightened up, then turned and went down the hall to the command room to prepare for the Governor's next performance.

Two miles from the capitol building in Pierre, South Dakota, four-term governor Jack Billings was in his slippers, seated at his burr oak desk in his media office at Peregrine House, the traditional governor's residence since 1884.

"We have the best convicts in the country!" said Jack, looking straight into the camera and giving a solemn thumbs-up. "You've seen the convict crews working on roadsides around the state. Once they've finished clearing snow from the emergency pits, I'll put them on standby."

Dang handy, those convicts, he thought. No hassles about quarantining them after handling—God forbid—infected carcasses, either. *Excellent arrangement.* Jack ran a hand through his silver stubble of hair and looked straight into the camera lens, his glasses slipping down the bridge of his nose.

"For now, we're off limits and off the roads," he said, his voice low and hard. "Don't leave your farm, don't let anyone—that's anyone—on your farm. Every county has trained Highway Patrol and National Guards on duty now. If you live in town, ask these men and women in uniform where you can and can't drive." Jack picked up a tidy white rectangle of cardboard with some handwriting in thick black magic marker and showed it to the camera.

"I gave you the number you can call with any questions whatsoever about this state of emergency here in South Dakota; here it is again: 1-800-333-FOOT. You can go to the website, too, and see a copy of the plan we're following. Here's the address: www.FootAndMouthDisease.info." He leaned the cardboard against his coffee mug and put his big hands back on the desk.

"Both the phone number and website will tell you the companies that are now closed and will stay closed as long as we have this quarantine. These include the packing plants, the stockyards, and all livestock auction houses. Other companies that rely on out-of-state shipments may or may not be closed, depending on what kind of inventory they have on hand. We'll update the lists whenever we get new information."

Governor Billings paused and a took a deep breath. He looked at the faded photos on his desktop, photos taken of his wife and son the day before the fire. The Fire. The fire in their house, the house he wasn't in because of yet-another committee meeting, the house he never went back to, the house he turned into a public garden after bulldozers removed the ashes and cinders and melted wires and charred bones and ruined dreams and blackened life.

Jack Billings was ready for this latest disaster, this damn livestock disease. The whole state—where black-hatted cattlemen were rarely seen in town, but didn't hesitate to march into Jack's office—was ready. But Jack hadn't thought it would really happen.

And the public. *God bless them; they have no idea what is about to hit.*

Jack had been to England after their outbreak in '01. He had seen the local people in town meetings during the clean-up, silent, tears running down their faces, just staring. At nothing. Not moving anymore. The foul scorched-hair smell of the smoke from the piles of burning carcasses oozed from every curtain, every home, as it would for months to come.

After that? It got worse. Some of the UK district governors kept in touch. Farm closures. Suicides, whole families at once, dogs and cats dead alongside. Later, Jack was in some of the African and Asian countries where FMD is endemic, always there, all the time, and they've given up trying to fight it. Their cattle and pigs were pathetic. *The Minnehaha Township Little Blueberries 4-H Club would beat the pants off them at the county fair.*

At Jack's slippered feet, Squidge, an old rat-terrier-plus-something-presumably-dog-like, stretched out and gave a lazy scratch at a shiny hairless scar, the shape of a burning curtain, a burning toy, a burning child's hand, on his left side. The dog's tail slapped the carpet. Then the dog sighed and rolled over, tangling his feet in some camera cables. *I'd like to roll over, too.* Almost done. Four terms, almost done.

Just a few more months and some young pup could take over. But this—this he would do for his people. That pussy in Iowa would roll over and let the packers and internationals push him around. It would destroy them. Not this state, not this man. The State of South Dakota would remain standing after all of Iowa was taken down, animal by animal, family by family.

Fire by fire.

Jack's eyes turned to the camera. His voice got softer. "All schools are closed until I tell you otherwise. Kids, be good and do what your parents say. Show your mom and dad how to use e-mail, and use it to send notes to your friends and cousins on the farm. Don't send regular mail if you can help it—not for now, that's tricky for us to clean up. Church for the next two weeks will be broadcast on your local radio stations. Sorry, but we just can't have anyone out on the roads until the coast is clear. This is war, folks. It's that serious."

Jack looked at his checklist. "Okay. You've already got your emergency supplies since it's winter. If you're in town, you can go to your local market. Outside of city limits, we have trained volunteers that will deliver groceries if you phone them in."

What else could he say now? Once the cattle pits in Iowa started filling up, once the bonfires started in the lowlands, and they saw the parade of blank, crying faces on KTIV-4/Sioux City, they'd understand. Then, they wouldn't *want* to leave their houses.

"God bless you, and may He have mercy on us all."

The cameraman gave the all-clear. Jack leaned back in his rolling chair and closed his eyes. He could hear staff members surging through both doors of his office at once. *Like pig manure through a slat floor.*

"Jake Brinsky from CitiBank Personnel to see you, sir."

"John Morrell's has a team from the packing plant unions here, sir."

"The CEO of Union-Pacific Railroad is on line three, sir."

Squidge ran under the couch.

Jack Billings stood up and stretched. "Tell them I'm busy. George, tidy up here, would you? Thanks. I'm going to grab a beer and take a nap in the Blue Room. It was a long night, and it's going to be a long day. Let's go, Squidge."

———————

CHAPTER 8

Tike reached into the toaster oven on one of the abandoned desks in the West Soo front office and poked a fork at their frozen mini pizzas.

Liz and she were taking a mid-morning break after a grueling session of calls at their desks. Liz handled the panicked vets and frantic livestock operators, Tike got the cynical editors and ignorant reporters. Now they were debating what might be in the pepperoni slices on their pizzas, taking into account their respective tours of packing plants over the years.

The barn manager stormed into the office. He tore off his cap and threw it onto Liz's desk. "Okay. The guys said you wanted to know about Roger's trailer. I'll tell you. But there's no way it's a problem. It's not."

The women froze in mid-debate as the man stomped around them, his hands swinging above his head and his face flushed.

"Roger only took the two calves," he said. "It was a joke. They were his boys' 4-H calves, hidden here. It was right before the District 3 show. Just a boy and his dad playing a joke, playing cattle rustler, sneaking the brother's pet calves away in the middle of the night." His voice broke. "Those two calves weren't here long enough to get infected. I'm sure of it. It's a waste of time—that's why he didn't bother...didn't say..."

Liz and Tike, sitting at their desks, looked away from him.

It was hard to watch a man crumble.

"I know they're fine. There's no way you could say that whole herd has to be put down. It's so clean at Roger's. Have you seen it? Roger's wife is in a wheelchair." He was winding down, his voice almost a whisper. "Did you know that?" He slumped in a chair. The toaster oven dinged.

"Clay County Fairgrounds? Last week?" said Liz.

"Yes," he said, head down. "Won best of class. Got home yesterday."

Tike looked out the window and saw Roger, Roger-the-fun-dad, driving the skid loader, cleaning pens, working hard. She had interviewed him that morning. He had worked at West Soo for eleven years, first part-time, now full-time, helping support a struggling livestock operation at his home farm. Helping cover health insurance. Buying braces. Buying wheelchair parts.

That's one home farm that won't struggle after today. It was over. She bit her lip and winced as an image flashed through her head: Roger, his wife, his boys, the calves, lined up on the floor next to mom's wheelchair, silent, cold. No more struggle.

"It's you," said the barn manager, turning and pointing a long finger at Liz. His voice started to rise. "Your fault. You've been there, to this disease island. No one else was there."

A couple of workers peeked around the corner, checking on their boss. Liz sat at her desk, staring at a pen suspended between her fingers. She dropped the pen and unrolled a large map on her desk, picking up a pencil, making some marks.

"You took the samples," he continued. "No one else did. You shipped them to the lab. Or what? You shipped something. What was it? Something you brought home? Something to make you famous? You bitch."

By now he was screaming. More workers gathered. Tike watched their faces. This, apparently, wasn't a new line of thinking. The workers didn't even blink as their boss went on, spitting and sweating, leaning farther and farther over Liz's desk, poking at her chest.

Liz sat with her pencil, rotating it in her fingers. Her lips were tight.

"I want you out of here," he said, his hands braced on her desk, leaning in and shouting so close to Liz's face her hair was moving as he yelled. "I'm not cooperating anymore. Let one of the other vets run this circus. Any vet. But not you." He stood, panting and sweaty, glaring at her.

Tike watched, holding her breath.

Liz put down her pencil and, looking the barn manager in the eye, picked up her cell phone and leaned back in her chair. Without breaking her gaze, she pressed one key and put the phone to her ear.

"Yeah, it's me. We've got a new hot zone. A primary. Roger Andreeson's place, about thirty miles due east, north central Plymouth County...yeah, that's right, just outside Le Mars: Ice Cream Capitol of the World. First set up the quarantine rings—do that right away—then pull together another team...From Des Moines? Do they have more people?...Yeah, sounds good."

Liz kept looking at the barn manager as she spoke. He dropped into the chair facing her desk, his eyes starting to tear up, his lips tight.

"No, the water table's too high there," said Liz, tapping the map. "Right, no burials. They'll have to burn. See what the local propane supply looks like. And tell the livestock manager of the Clay County fair board to call me right away...Yes, right away. Top priority." Liz snapped the phone shut and dropped it onto the pile of debris on her desktop. She finished her Pepsi and crumpled the can, tossing it into the trash basket.

She narrowed her eyes and looked straight at the barn manager as she stood up and came around the desk. "You dumb schmuck," she said, her voice hard and even. "We could've just shut down the one farm if you reported what you should have. But not after this much time. You just destroyed Plymouth County. Too soon to tell about Clay County and everyone else who was in the district show." She took a breath and leaned over him, an inch from his face. Her voice dropped. "Now get back to work."

Liz spun around and walked away as his head dropped into his hands. She passed through the silent workers and headed down the hall to the break room. Tike grabbed some aspirin and coins from her desk and followed, heart pounding.

Glad I'm not her, Tike thought. *Glad I'm not him.*

Liz got a cold carton of milk from a machine in the empty West Soo break room and slumped against the wall. Tike put in some coins and got a pop, opening it and downing her aspirin, watching Liz.

"It's the only way," said Liz. "If I let him get out of control, if I give up my authority, who'll track the missing cattle? Who'll order the depopulations? No one here wants to be the bad guy. And the feds aren't up to speed. But it's the only way to shut this outbreak down. Be the major bad guy." She held the icy box against her forehead and sighed. "What a job."

Tike thought about some of the brutal scenes she'd been a part of, usually on the receiving end, as she did her job. *It's not just a job. It never is.*

Liz, her face flat and expressionless, turned to face Tike. "Since my husband died, all I do is work. It's all I do. We used to have friends. Bowl. Go to potluck suppers. Now I just don't care." She took a long drink of her milk.

"I'm sorry," said Tike, quiet, unsure what to say. She had found a man's photo when she went through Liz's desk. The photo was face-down in a bottom drawer, under Liz's purse. Tike had wondered. The man was lean and fit, dark wavy hair, big eyes, warm smile. *A Roman face. Like Nick.*

Liz was wearing a wedding ring; she twisted it around as she spoke, saw Tike watching, smiled and shrugged.

"I should take this off. But why? I knew, statistically, I would outlive him. Women always do. But not like this."

"How long has it been?"

"Five years." She dug in her pocket, pulled out a slim wallet, opened it to a worn picture she handed to Tike. "We met in vet school, loved the same things. We both won slots in the Foreign Animal Disease training program at Plum Island." She paused, took a tiny sip of her drink, closed her eyes.

"Joseph had a heart attack while we were packing. Bad family heart history. Died in my arms. I couldn't save him."

"I'm so sorry." Tike bit her lower lip and handed back the picture. She thought of her cats, of Nick. Thought how pathetic she was, thinking of her cats. Imagined how she would feel with Nick dying in her arms.

"I've had some bad times," said Tike. "Not like this, but a different bad. Man things."

"This Nick you mentioned?"

"Before him. Violence. Various." She waved her hand, gave a tight smile. "And before that, a shyster. Absolute genius, and adorable, but still a shyster. I married that one. Still miss him sometimes, can you believe it? He's in for the next decade yet—no parole in the federal system, you know." She shook her head and smiled, her lips tight. "I know how to pick 'em." She pulled out her wallet, flipped it open to her own set of pictures. "This is what I come home to now."

Liz smiled as she looked. "Cats. The ultimate survivors."

Tike laughed, then they were both silent. Liz scuffed her heel against the wall, looking at the floor, then looked up at Tike as she handed back the wallet.

"After Joseph died, I finished packing. I went to Plum Island anyway. It was that or shoot myself. I had to go. They almost didn't let me in."

"I understand." Tike nodded her head. "You do what you have to."

"Yeah." She stayed slumped against the wall, silent, head down again. "This thing is wearing on me."

"You're doing great, really great."

Liz tilted her head and looked at Tike with half a smile. "You're just happy because you're scoring some great stories. Miss Hot-Shot Reporter."

Tike shrugged. "Doesn't hurt. You'll be getting some brownie points out of this, too." She paused, watching her. *Was that it? Her motive?*

"Maybe some serious advancing. This is State Secretary of Ag campaign material you're living."

Liz smiled and shook her head. "Not me, Tike. I've already got my resignation letter written."

"What?"

"My step-dad died. I'm going home to help mom with their—her—antiques shop when this is all over. Maybe get a few things sorted out."

"But you're a vet. You can't do that."

"Everything's different now, since Joseph died. Something's got to change. I don't know what else to do." Liz finished her milk and threw the carton in the bin as she got to her feet. "Maybe I'll come back in a few years and be a zoo vet. Nothing like a monkey with diarrhea to brighten up your day." She smiled as they headed down the hall. "Except maybe an elephant with diarrhea."

By the time the women got back to their desks, the barn manager was gone. So was Roger. Tike plopped down in her creaky wooden chair and stared at her phone, thinking about Liz's Joseph.

She pushed the tape recorder aside and called Nick. "Hi, Nick. Um. I just wanted to check. Do the first journal entries look okay? I sent a couple to start."

"You know they're good." His voice, so smooth and low, always made her breath catch.

"Okay. Just checking. You know."

He paused. "It sounds pretty tough there. You doing okay? I'm glad you called."

"I'm fine."

The line was silent for several fast heartbeats.

"I miss you, Tike. I miss you so much." He took a deep breath. "Have you decided? Are you going to move with me?"

She sighed. "I haven't decided. We've got bigger issues to work out."

"We can work them out if we have time together," he said.

She fiddled with a pencil, said nothing.

"Tike, things have changed." She heard his chair creak. "I've changed. I've been going to meetings, talking with someone. You know I started that right away, after...after that night. Damn it."

Tike didn't say anything. She heard him take a deep breath.

"I'm not like Zack, honey. You're not just going through the same bullshit dance again. Think about all the good times we had together, before.

I just snapped, just that once. If I hadn't thrown that damn thing."

"Your aim was pretty damn good."

"Yeah, and I wish it wasn't. Look, I was an idiot, okay? And yeah, I was drunk. But you know I'm not like Zack. Please believe in me." His voice got softer. "And I worry about you. Sweetheart. Especially now, with all this crap, and you in the middle of it. Please call me. Anytime."

"I'm fine."

"You're fine," he said, and sighed. "Okay, that's okay. Just think about it, Tike. About me. Please."

"I'll think about it." She hung up. Thinking about it.

By late afternoon Tike's desk at West Soo was covered with the debris of war: press releases, interview transcripts, and a half-empty package of cookies. She had put together four short pieces for Liz and the ag department lawyers to review. Most of it was fact blurbs she could scribble off the top of her head. She'd tag one or another onto the end of her reports in upcoming days, depending on the topic.

She dropped copies on Liz's desk and e-mailed the rest to the suits, then put her feet up for a few minutes to read the papers, see what everyone else was writing up. There were enough stories to go around: packing plant shut-downs; irate truckers and travelers stuck at closed borders; panicking legislators scrambling for funds.

She switched to an old Archie comic book she found in the desk. Just as Jughead was going to explain the missing car door to Betty and Veronica, her phone rang.

"Tike, your cats got out."

"What? Who is this?"

"It's Dewey. I'm in your house."

"Dewey? From the lumberyard? Why are you in my house?"

"Fire alarm."

"At the lumberyard? Couldn't you use the phone at the co-op? I'm not even nearby."

"Fire alarm at your place. I'm on the volunteer fire department, you know."

"Oh, no."

"It was a false alarm. We checked. But some cats got out. Two, maybe."

"The cats will be okay. They can get into the barn. And Maureen Kay is checking on them." She paused. "But I'm not wired into the fire department. I don't even have a fire alarm, Dewey. Why did you think there was a fire?"

"Someone called it in."

"Called it in?"

"Said they saw smoke."

"Was there smoke? I thought you said there wasn't a fire. Who called?"

"We didn't see any smoke, but we still had to come check. Don't know who it was. We don't have their name."

"But for all they know I was just burning trash." On a calm day, she could usually see smoke coming from half a dozen farms, scattered around the horizon, each burning one or two weeks' accumulation of trash.

"They were driving by, they said. Almost hit a deer, slowed down, happened to look over, and saw smoke. Coming from the upstairs bedroom."

"They said that?"

"Yeah."

"The bedroom?" Tike frowned. "How would they know which room was the bedroom?"

"All these old farmhouses, that's what you have upstairs. Bedrooms. Then the call got cut off. Cell phone. Number was blocked."

Blocked? *Dead guy.*

"Oh, and I put the package in the kitchen," said Dewey.

"Package? I'm not expecting anything. What's the return address?"

"Medical Examiner, Old Saybrook."

"Oh, right." He was sending her some literature from his Plum Island friends. "Thanks, Dewey."

"I'll leave the bill, there, too."

"Bill?"

"For the false alarm. New policy. It cuts down on false alarms."

"But I don't even have a fire alarm. You said someone called it in."

"Sorry. We have to do it. You know how our budget is."

Tike said she might be gone a while, but she'd call Rose Anne at the bank to send out a check—an uncontaminated one—if she was gone too long.

A false alarm? If some dead guy wanted her attention, he had it.

———————

As the sun got closer to the horizon outside the West Soo windows, Tike reviewed her slate of calls for the rest of the afternoon: vets from bordering states, livestock judges—now walking disease carriers—from the Clay County district show, companies affected by the border closures. Her p.r. duties for Liz were done, and it was time to do some scouting for her own stories. She and Liz had an official field trip to the local rendering plant in the morning, but there was still time to cram a few calls in.

As Tike jotted down a few names, her cell phone beeped. A page, 202 area code: Washington, D.C. She dialed while starting a new manila folder for her notes. The line picked up before the first ring finished.

"This is Robby."

"Hi Robby, this is Tike Lexington. You paged me?"

"You have the gorilla mort?"

"Excuse me?"

"Is this the keeper from the primate house?"

"No, this is Tike Lexington. I'm a reporter."

"How did you find out so fast?"

"Find out what?"

"About our big mort," he said. "The gorilla."

"A gorilla? Named Mort?"

"Is this a joke?"

"Who's Mort?"

"You mean *what* is mort," he said. "Mortality. This is the morgue at National Zoo in Washington. I'm the chief pathologist. I dissect the mortalities to see why they died. Why did you call?"

"I thought you called."

"No, I'm working on a zebra, and waiting for a gorilla. I'm up to my elbows in duodenum."

"Aren't we all?"

He laughed. Tike wished him happy holidays and signed off, then leaned back in her chair, frowning at her phone. She scrolled through the menus and found the number for the originating call, the phone that was used to send the Washington page. It was very close to the number she had called back, Robby's number, but the last two digits were different. She called Robby back.

"Sorry to bother you," she said.

"Got to be quick," said Robby. "The gorilla just arrived."

"Is this number in your facility?" She read him the number.

"That's the cooler."

"Pardon?"

"The cooler," he said. "Where we keep the bodies before necropsy."

"There's a phone in there?"

"I know. Who's a dead zebra going to call? Everyone makes jokes about it. It's an emergency line, in case someone gets locked in."

"Someone paged me from there."

"Well, no one's locked in," he said. "I was just there, checking the line-up for the rest of the afternoon. The gorilla gets priority. Maybe our media gal called you. But I'm surprised she would go into the cooler. Or give you her direct number. It's not for public use. No offense."

"No problem. So it's locked? The cooler?"

"Just a latch on the outside, not a real lock. Who wants a dead zebra? Look, I have to go. Sorry I can't help."

Tike sat at her desk, staring at the phone in her hand, now starting to shake. *He was there. Why?*

CHAPTER 9

Bud shifted gears in his Caterpillar 446D backhoe and slammed the steel-toothed bucket into the icy soil of the bare corn field, one mile east of West Soo Feedlot. "Sure, drag my sorry ass out here," he said to himself, muttering. "For nothing." A blue late-model sedan with the state seal on the door pulled off the road onto the edge of the field. It parked by the truck and trailer Bud had used to haul the big Cat from his machine shed 47 miles away, and the driver got out. The rest of Bud's crew was scattered across the field, surveying and spiking the black soil with pink nylon flags on long metal stems.

Bud pulled back the steel-toothed bucket, dropped out of gear, jumped out of the cab and hiked over to his truck. He took off his gloves and shoved them in the pocket of his worn Carhartt coveralls.

He poured himself some coffee from the dented thermos on the tailgate and cupped his hands around it, standing on the lee side of his observer, letting him block the wind.

"You want a hole?" Bud grumbled into the cup. "We don't have enough ice cutters in this state to do what you need. You'd better start stacking."

Lawrence Bothell, senior engineer for the state of Iowa, writing notes on a State of Iowa notepad, his shiny booted foot perched on the tailgate next to the thermos, blinked and adjusted his tie. "Stacking. Stacking?"

"Yes. Stacking. Digging won't get you squat-all. Ground's frozen, Mr. Engineer. You've got to build a hole above ground."

"Okay, so start. We can work with that."

"Not with this topsoil you don't," said Bud. "You'd have to scrape the whole square-mile section to get enough cubic yards to make a hole half the size you want."

"That's okay. We'll bring more equipment in to help you."

"No, sweet cheeks. You didn't hear me. I said stacking."

"Yes, stacking. You will have the men stack the dirt."

"Jesus H. Christianson," said Bud, snorting out a short breath. "It's not dirt. It's soil. Dirt is what you have under your fingernails, at least some of us do. Soil is what these fields are full of, and stuff grows in it. A lot of stuff, especially here in Iowa. You might as well napalm the state and shoot all the farmers if you're going to strip off the topsoil. And you don't stack dirt, or soil. When I said stack, I meant stack. Hay. Straw. Round bales. Square bales. Got it?"

"Bales. You want to stack bales on this field."

"You got it, city boy. You want a hole to bury deadstock, cattle and hog, number to-be-determined, fast, and soon. This is Iowa. It's January. We got no dirt, we got soil. Can't use soil. We do have lots of bales. I can get bales here, and my men can build you some big holes. In the spring, it's all got to move, or meanwhile you can burn it all. Got it?"

"Well. Okay. Bales. I'm in charge here, you know. So I can make this decision." Lawrence Bothell, senior engineer, took out his calculator. He straightened his tie. He pressed some numbers on the calculator and stared at the grill of his state car. He pressed in some more numbers, then looked up at Bud.

"Bud, go ahead. Start gathering bales and make a first, ah, hole of the size we discussed. I'll have my engineers work on some designs for different load requirements for the next ones." He shook Bud's hand, got into his state car, and left, icy gravel dust blooming behind him.

Bud put his gloves on as he hiked back to the Cat, got in the cab and shut the door. He picked up his phone. And someone planned this? he thought, dialing. *Pillow-butt bureaucrats.*

"Hi, Vid? This is Bud. How's that new hay barn looking?"

———————

Liz took a deep breath of cold feedlot air and relaxed her grip on the cell phone. "What do you mean, they don't have the pits ready?" she said into the phone.

She counted to five and looked around the empty West Soo feedlot as she took another deep breath, then exhaled slowly. "Deputy Sergeant Fosco. You're doing a great job. Thank you for that. But are you telling me the burial team does not, as the plan specified, have the Phase One Pits ready to go?"

"Yes sir, er, ma'am. The Governor's office was still in negotiations with the counties over jurisdiction and compensation, based on what the new soil survey was going to report, and—ma'am, no, the Phase One Pits for are not done. I *do* have some alternatives 25 miles south or 30 miles east. Ravines. We could fill them in. Would you like me to arrange shipping teams?"

Liz sighed and watched the cloud of her frosty breath dissipate. She watched some feedlot workers trying to clean frozen pens with skidloaders. Back and forth they went, scraping and dumping, scraping and dumping. *How will we ever decontaminate this place once everything is under control?*

"Fosco, have you ever driven from here over to Alta?"

"Yes ma'am, yes I have."

"And what is the most interesting part of that drive, Fosco?"

"Well, I would say the new wind farm is the most interesting, ma'am."

"That's right, Fosco, that's right. Do you know how many wind turbines are in that area, Fosco?"

"No, ma'am."

"Fosco, there are 254 wind turbines within a ten-by-ten mile area. At any time on your drive along Highway 59 or 71, you can see anywhere from ten to twenty-seven wind turbines at once. They are 237 feet tall, and the three, black, four-ton blades are each sixty-five feet long—they were shipped up here from Texas on special double-length tractor-trailers, following a special route with very few curves or turns."

Liz took a deep breath. "Guess why I'm telling you this, Fosco."

"That's the problem, ma'am, isn't it? The wind."

Liz looked up at the sky. It was cloudy and gray. The wind was picking up. *Snow's coming.*

"Yes, Fosco, that's it. We're smack in the middle of the Buffalo Ridge Wind Belt. We can't truck the carcasses west because the border is closed. We can't truck them north, south, or east because we'd have to cross the Wind Belt. We would send enough virus into the air to infect millions of cattle and hogs. The cold doesn't hurt it. We can't even do it with sealed trucks because we don't have enough of them, and we can't take the risk anyway. What if one leaked—just one?"

Liz thought it through as she talked to Fosco.

"The wind path curves into Nebraska and extends into Missouri. We could wipe out Omaha and Kansas City with one leaky truck. We're supposed to use our own pits here by the feedlot; that's what the plan was for, so this couldn't happen. The other parts of the state must—*must*—do the same. Shit."

The line was quiet again.

"Ma'am, they're working on building some above-ground storage bunkers using hay bales."

"Above-ground? Oh. Well. You see the problem there, don't you Fosco?"

"Yes, ma'am."

"You get that stopped, and if you need to, you have the state engineer call me. If they can't bury, they have to burn. Right now."

"Yes, ma'am, right away."

"Keep up the good work, Fosco."

"Yes, ma'am. Thank you."

Liz put the phone back in the warm pocket of her coveralls and headed back through the feedlot to the main office. Snow started to fall. It blew sideways. She could barely see the lights of the office building, or the cattle shed on the edge of the lot, somewhere there in the swirling gray air. She stopped for a moment, taking off her wool cap and turning toward the storm, eyes closed, the snow blowing straight into her face. She could hear the icy grains of snow as they hit her cold skin and bounced off. *Joseph loved cold weather. "Let's go light a fire,"* he'd whisper in her ear, slipping an icy hand under her coat, making her jump and laugh.

The feedlot, normally jammed with lowing cattle, was quiet. Quiet as a tomb. Liz stuffed her cap in her pocket and marched toward the yellow lights of the office, head down.

––––––––––

Roy handed the smooth goblet of cognac to his guest, one of the few ever invited to his unusual home: the Plum Island Rock House. It was one of only four homes on the island, and one of only two designated for full-time residence. As director of the Plum Island research and diagnostics facility, he got to be a full-timer. The second occupied home was smaller, but closer to the facility in case of emergency. It was for the head of maintenance and operations.

Roy hefted his own glass, enjoying the weight of the leaded crystal in his hand. It was one of a set he bought on a package tour of a crystal factory in Ireland the previous year. Roy poured a measure of liquor into the sparkling vessel. The Scotch was forty-seven years old. "I only drink Scotch as mature and cultured as me," he said to his guest. They both laughed. Then the men sipped in silence, listening to the storm raging outside.

"You're handling the scientists well, Roy," said his guest, inhaling deeply of his golden liquor. The fire crackled. The soft leather couches facing the hearth were warm.

"I hope so, Panko. They know I'm committed, as dedicated as they are. This island is my life, too. The country needs us. Times like this, even the public can see that." He sighed. "If we can just hang on. Our budgets are awful. I just try to roll with the punches, as we say here."

"To roll with your punches—I like that." Panko smiled, his small, stained teeth a dull yellow in the firelight. His eyes were only a few shades darker, a golden brown. Dr. Panko Roskovich, a visiting scientist at Plum Island, worked on Crimean respiratory viruses of Targassic sheep. His research was published in top journals, and his sabbatical at Plum Island was a real coup for Roy, part of Roy's long-term program to boost the island's reputation. The program also stretched the Plum Island budget, as visiting scientists paid their own way—and often brought rare samples for the Plum Island collection.

"I've been reading your new JBC manuscript," said Roy. He smiled. "*Our* manuscript." He leaned forward. "You're absolutely onto something, way beyond virus structure. God, if I could think like you." He sat back, shaking his head. "I'm proud to be listed as a co-author."

Panko gave a brief wave of his hand. "We are colleagues. Our discussions gave me great insight. And I appreciate the hospitality while my university is, is...reorganizing." He dropped his head and ran his hand through his hair.

"Oh, hell," said Roy. "I don't know how you can keep working with all the disruptions there."

Panko shrugged, then took a deep breath and smiled. "It helps to have friends."

"I'll drink to that," said Roy, toasting his guest. "Anyway. You're settling in well here?"

Panko nodded. "I have a quaint flat on the mainland." He frowned. "Temporary. A sub-let? But *tres cher*, my friend. I could buy a dacha for this, back home."

Roy laughed. "But you *will* stay at the guesthouse if you need? We know housing expenses can be extraordinary for our guests."

"For the late nights. It is helpful when I have much work, and the ferry captain will not wait for me." Panko smiled. "I tried."

Roy laughed and took a sip of his drink. "You would. And on a night like this, it's better not to travel."

"Agreed, friend. And the laboratories? They can survive this storming?"

"No problem," said Roy. "We've got our own power generators, back-up systems, everything. We're like a little country." He toasted his guest. "And I am my little country's servant." Roy laughed. "Enough about Plum and me. What's your adventure next week? I hear you're leaving us again."

Panko tipped his head to one side. "We should talk. I'm going to meet with another colleague. In biotechnology, an investor. Venture capitalist, you would call him?" He took a sip of his drink.

"Fascinating. I follow some of the biotech news myself. 'VCs,' they call them."

"Fantastic. VC. Well, my friend the VC is looking at a company that makes vaccines against animal viruses; I'm sure you know them, Roy: Euvaxx?"

"Oh, yes. Great technology. Very innovative. A possible FMD vaccine, very important. But how do you know the VC?"

"Family connections," said Panko. "A long story, you know? This year he had me talk to the CEO, do some...inspecting."

"Due diligence?"

"Exactly."

"So, the CEO, too?" Roy shook his head. "You've really got some great connections. I never have time for this."

Panko looked at his watch. "You have time now?"

"What?"

"I have to call him now, the CEO. Mike Salt. One more question from my VC friend. It's just suppertime in La Jolla. Let's call him together, Roy."

"Really?"

Panko picked up Roy's phone and dialed.

On a wooden table in the corner of the small locked and soundproof room, twenty-six stories above Chicago's financial district, Geneva La Croix's old fax machine squeaked as wheels turned and three pages scrolled between the rollers. It stopped printing just as the lock clicked and the door opened. Geneva put the long key in her pocket as she entered. Behind her, the wall-to-wall view of the twilight Chicago skyline was silent, with Ceres at center, powerful and ever-fruitful, topping the art deco facade of the Chicago Board of Trade. U.P. drowsed in an Italian leather recliner by the fireplace, his worn leather shoes—Hush Puppies—on the floor, a half-emptied snifter of cognac on the glass table beside him, a stack of charts on his lap, the top chart labeled "November Corn Daily."

Geneva brought a cognac with her into the small, windowless room and closed the door. The dull beige walls and ceiling, covered with egg-carton-puckered padding, absorbed the click as she set the glass on a coaster on one of the file cabinets. She pulled the stack of pages off the fax machine and sorted through them; most went into the shredder. Two pages she stapled and carried to a fireproof file cabinet along the far wall, where she opened the drawer labeled "G-H-I."

Geneva's fingers flitted through the files, then pulled out a thick one: "IVY, Clarissa." She added the pages to the file. Clipped to the inside cover was an 8 x 10 black-and-white of Ms. Ivy, photographed speaking to a crowd on the steps of the Washington, D.C., headquarters of the National Cattleman's Beef Association. Next to Ms. Ivy were individuals dressed as carrots.

A glassine sleeve overlaying the photo held some negatives of Ms. Ivy engaged in other activities. Grainy prints of these images had the faint green tinge of a night vision lens. Ms. Ivy's skin, however, and that of the senator beneath her, looked like creamy china. Duplicates of the negatives and prints were also in his file, along with press releases from the U.S. Senate Agriculture Committee, of which the senator was the chair, and photos of his wife.

Geneva filed IVY and locked the cabinet, then locked the door to the little room and went back out into the larger room. She glanced at one of the three monitors on her computer workstation. The massive Chinese commodities exchange, Dalian, was in full swing. Geneva watched the Dalian trades for a minute, made a few notes on a chart with a silver pen, then shut down the screen.

She set the snifter on the glass table, then tucked U.P.'s blanket around his feet—one sock had a large hole in the heel, the other was darned—as he snored and muttered. She eased onto the armrest of his recliner without a sound, reached over, and caressed his hair, the light crown that remained. His muttering softened to a murmur, then silence, as his head leaned into her hand.

Geneva looked at her watch and withdrew her hand from the man's warmth. She walked in silence to the front door, picked up her coat and keys, and left, closing the door with a quiet click behind her. She punched the elevator button as she put on her coat, then dug out her phone.

———————

Clarissa Ivy leaned back on the worn couch in her Washington, D.C., apartment and snugged the cotton chenille blanket around her. She had pink terry slippers on her feet and a cordless phone in hand. A china plate with a fork and remnants of a piece of cherry pie sat next to a mug on the coffee table before her.

"You're welcome," said Clarissa into the phone, suppressing a yawn. "Anytime." She disconnected and sighed, dropping the phone onto the couch beside her. One more interview, done. One more calm voice in the wilderness, fighting for the defenseless and mute. Done.

Clarissa leaned her head back onto the couch cushions and closed her eyes, fatigued from the long day of calls and TV cameras. She thought her new hairstyle had looked very professional on the CNN interview.

The phone rang again. She had forwarded the MATA line to her home office, so it was likely to be a MATA call. She picked it up, eyes still closed. "MATA headquarters. This is Clarissa."

As Clarissa listened to the caller she opened her eyes and sat up. The blanket fell to her lap. She kept listening. She stood up. The blanket fell to the floor. The call ended. She hadn't said a word after "This is Clarissa." She turned off the phone and set it on the coffee table next to the couch.

Clarissa went to the door and opened it. There, in the middle of the "Animals Love MATA" doormat, in the carpeted hallway of her apartment complex, was a package. She looked up and down the hall, saw no one, picked up the package, and went quickly inside, shutting the door and locking it.

She sat on the couch and set the package on the chipped veneer of the coffee table. She carefully peeled the tape back and removed the wrapping paper, green with red reindeer, to reveal a shoebox. She lifted the lid a narrow few inches and leaned close to peek.

Inside the box was a plastic zipper bag wedged between two ice packs. She pulled open the lid and gripped the top two corners of the bag in her fingertips, lifting it out of the box, holding it up against the light. The contents of the zipper bag were just as the caller had described on the phone.

Clarissa put the bag back in the box, tucked it in carefully, shut the lid, and threw away the wrapping paper. She set it by the door and, opening her closet, pulled out a suitcase.

It was time to pack. Clarissa had a mission.

CHAPTER 10

At dawn on Tike's third day at West Soo, the sun filtered through the gray sky into the feedlot offices. Tike and Liz huddled over their morning tea and planned their day. It turned out Tike would have a bit more time to make calls before the women went to inspect the rendering plant at Quimby.

Not that Tike was in a big hurry to get there. Last time she went to Quimby she had to burn her clothes afterward to get rid of the smell.

After Liz left the office to check on the crews outside, Tike got her preparations done so she could settle in and make calls up until the last minute. She changed into some old chore clothes, and borrowed an insulated jacket from the rack of extras in the West Soo office. She piled the jacket by the door with her camera, which she had put in a paper sack, and tucked an extra memory card in the pocket of her jeans. Tike's Domke camera bag, full of gear, wasn't going near Quimby; it was bad enough that she'd have to wipe down the camera with cotton swabs when she got back.

Ready to roll, she swung her feet up on her desk and started on her phone list. "Tike Lexington from the Iowa Department of Agriculture media group calling for Governor Billings." She reached over and picked up a box of animal crackers. *The Rendering Plant Diet*, she thought, biting the head off a hippo.

"One moment, please."

Tike wondered if he'd get on the line. She'd been to his ranch for the big Fourth of July barbecue, but didn't know him well. He probably wouldn't remember her, and she'd have to talk to some slippery assistant.

"Tike Lexington, how the hell have you been?"

Hot dog. Tike dropped her feet to the floor and sat up straight, animal crackers dropping into her lap. "Governor, I've been fine, thank you."

They spent the next few minutes going through the drill. Tike got an update on the South Dakota disease response plan from the horse's mouth. Governor Billings told her a flight from Northwest Iowa had tried to land at the Sioux Falls airport, even though he had shut down airspace to flights from Iowa, Minnesota, and Nebraska.

"Bastards thought I wouldn't shoot them down. And you can quote me on that—if that sissy editor of yours lets you." He laughed. "Took one through the wing before they took me serious."

He asked if she was still freelance, said he remembered she "had a lot of sass."

"I do my best," she told him.

"So do I," he said. "So do I."

Next Tike called the Iowa Governor's office. She didn't even try to get the Governor. It wouldn't be good for her blood pressure today. She went straight for his senior aide, Bruce Ter Wee.

"Hi Tike, how are you?" he said. Bruce, a smart guy, was painfully aware he worked for a moron. He and Tike had discussed his pain over multiple adult beverages at and after various public and state events.

"An update?" he said. "Sure, try this, Tike: Look at section 9.2 of the emergency response plan. Did you notice that section has no funding? Look at sub-section 32-g."

She flipped through the dog-eared copy on her desk and found the section. "Dang, Bruce. Are you serious? I can't believe I would've missed that."

"I can. At first, it was funded, thanks to the last big outbreak in the UK. Lots of burning piles of livestock on TV, that helps. But then we had that budget crunch last year, and some budgets got reviewed, we dip into the rainy day fund, et cetera, et cetera."

"So who's going to pay for this circus?" said Tike. "Not insurance, we know that. Yeah, the Department of Ag will pay for some—some—of the herd value. But...burial crews? Fuel for burn piles? Clean-up and decontamination? Who pays?"

"Excellent question, Ms. Lexington. Perhaps that would be an excellent question during our excellent press conference at 4:30 p.m. this afternoon."

"Bruce, I owe you. You're excellent."

"Ah, Tike, remember me when you find someone in need of a good chief-of-staff."

"I will."

Liz, out in the West Soo feedlot with her crew, banged on Tike's window. When Tike turned to look Liz opened her hand, palm out, fingers spread: Five minutes. *Enough time to make one more call.* Tike called her Sioux City editor.

"Hi, Tike," he said. "Please don't tell me you're in the lobby."

She reassured him she was still at ground zero, and wasn't dropping by to contaminate the newsroom. She gave him an update on the scene at West Soo.

"I've been talking with the publisher," he said. "We're thinking about adding a roving ag editor position. Maybe when this is over you can come in and talk about it. We can have lunch."

Tike blinked and raised her eyebrows. What? The publisher, who was his boss, was an immense woman who dreamed of moving away and having a personal shopper at Nordstrom's. She had always thought the ag section was a waste of time and ink.

"Seriously?" Tike heard Liz coming in the door behind her, and put her feet back on the floor as she checked her watch. She saw Liz stop by the fax machine and sort through the new faxes.

"Yes," he said, his voice warmer than she had heard for a long time. "You're doing a great job with the people stories. We're starting to see some value here."

They agreed to talk later, after the outbreak was under control. As she hung up, reaching for the last animal crackers and getting up from her chair, Liz stomped over to her desk.

"Deal with it, Tike," Liz said, stuffing a crumpled piece of paper in her tea mug. "Spike the bitch." She kicked a chair out of her way and yanked open the door, then turned as she yanked on her gloves. "Five more minutes. Meet you at the car." Tike pulled the dripping paper out of her mug and laid it on the table, smoothing it down with her hand. It was a fax.

re: MATA applauds Iowa outbreak

Dear Dr. Liz Thomas,

Your husband would have been disappointed.

While we are proud that you, a fine American, have devoted your life to protecting helpless animals, we are disappointed that you have taken the side of the corporate mega-hog and anti-family-farm behemoths.

We would like to take credit for starting this outbreak of disease in Iowa. While a tragic loss for the animal kingdom, the deaths of these captive animals will show the world the cruelty of their artificial lives.

I say "we would like" to take credit, because we applaud this situation, but we did not initiate it. You see, we are not alone. There are many others who feel—or felt—the way we do.

Perhaps you will rethink your life choices, Dr. Thomas. I am waiting to hear from you.

Best regards,
Clarissa Ivy
Vice-President, Communications
Mission for Approved Treatment of Animals
Washington, D.C.
1-800-452-MATA

Tike thought for a few moments as she put on her boots and borrowed jacket. She had never met Clarissa Ivy, but had certainly been irritated enough by her. Tike had previously stumbled onto a few tidbits about Clarissa; it was time to use them. Tike picked up the phone; Clarissa answered on the first ring.

"Clarissa, just to clarify, did MATA have anything to do with the outbreak?"

"No, we did not," she said. "But the system was doomed to fail, even without our help."

"Okay, thank you. Now. You've really done a great job turning MATA into an international force since you started working for them six years ago. Could the England branch of MATA, or some of your affiliates there, have anything to do with the current outbreak in the U.S.?"

"They wouldn't need to. As long as animals are imprisoned for abuse by humans, the system is in a dangerous state of imbalance. It's our duty to help these innocent creatures. Our mission."

"Okay, thank you. Now. Clarissa, you have cousins in England. They raise champion dairy cattle. How do they feel about this?"

She could hear her breathing on the phone. "My cousins? In England?"

"Yes. The Suffolk Ivies. Such a nice family. How is Aunt Beatrice's hip, by the way? All healed up?"

"Her hip? But...but..."

"How do they feel about your work? Didn't you spend summers there as a kid? Little American girl in the country?"

"As a kid? Summers?"

"Did something happen at the farm? Something traumatic?" Tike waited. "Clarissa?"

"I don't know where you get this absurd information," she said, stuttering. "Absurd."

"I bet it involved sex. Am I right? And animals?"

"You're bonkers."

"That's the word I was looking for: bonking. Isn't that what they call it over there? At least that's what I have in my photos."

"Photos? Impossible."

"I know, that's what I thought."

"You're lying," said Clarissa.

"Lying?"

"Leave my family out of this."

"Oh, Liz is here. Would you like to talk her now?" said Tike. "She's sitting right next to me." Tike stood and looked out the window; Liz was in her dented state car, parked by the door, talking on the phone. She saw Tike and honked the horn, gesturing at her to hurry up. "The photos are hers, by the way," said Tike. "Gosh, they sure look like you. They came in the mail. From England. Should I send them back? Or maybe to your colleagues at MATA in London?"

Clarissa hung up.

Tike laughed and dropped the handset back in its cradle. *The secret to successful lying,* she thought, smiling as she zipped up her coat, *is using the right ratio of fact to fiction.* She trotted out to the car. Liz, still on the phone, popped the sedan into gear before Tike had the door shut. They still had to stop at the barricades to decontaminate and swap cars before they could drive to Saandval Rendering.

As Tike strapped on her seatbelt and listened to Liz argue with someone about the stability of FMD virus while frozen—a month in frozen mud—she wondered if Clarissa Ivy, animal lover, had read Part 6, Section 5A, Rule 3.3.2 of the Iowa response plan. Rule 3.3.2 aimed at preventing one of the worst possible complications of the current outbreak, a complication that would mean they could never get rid of FMD in the U.S., a complication that would mean the ruin of US agriculture.

Rule 3.3.2 said they had to kill the deer. All of them. Every fawn, doe, and buck for a hundred square miles around each hot zone. Then they had to bury them.

Deer could get FMD, easily. And wild deer populations were at an all-time high. If FMD got into the wild deer population, which freely roamed feedlots and ranches nationwide, it was here to stay.

Rule 3.3.2 would be activated in about 48 hours, even with little or no funding left in the budget. It didn't cost much to issue no-limit deer hunting permits for a bonus season. Night hunting, helicopter hunting— everything was going to be opened up. *Might* make *money. The hunters'll stampede into the state when the announcement goes out, quarantine or no.* At latest count, there were 525,000 wild white-tail deer in Iowa.

Not for long.

Tike picked up an old newspaper from the floor of the car and flipped through the entertainment section to find the comics. Liz finished her call and dropped her phone on her lap with a sigh.

"That was pretty low, her mentioning your husband in the fax," Tike said, turning to the movie section. "Clarissa plays hardball."

Liz nodded. "Joseph met with them a few times, tried to reason with them. They laughed at him. Then they tried to claim him as a supporter...later. They issued a statement saying he was lucky he died, because he wouldn't have to go to the Plum Island training."

Tike dropped the paper to her lap and gave a low whistle. "Cheap shot."

"Now they won't leave me alone."

"I think I zinged her," said Tike, picking up the paper again. "Maybe she'll back off."

"Thanks."

"If she calls again, just mention the photos."

Liz raised her eyebrows. "Photos?"

"Don't ask."

They could see the barricades up ahead. The decontamination station was on the right; Liz slowed and turned toward it as she patted her pockets to be sure she had everything she needed. Liz spoke, her voice soft. "She still doesn't get it, does she?"

"No," said Tike, leaning back as they pulled to a stop alongside a small team of uniformed men and women wearing Tyvek suits and rubber boots. They would decontaminate them and walk them out to a clean car outside the barricade. "Not yet," she said. "Not yet. Soon."

It was a quiet ride to Quimby.

Five miles from Quimby, Liz shut off the heater of her battered state car and closed the vents. This would be the last good air they'd have for a while. They were warm enough to get by; the Tyvek suits they'd donned at the decontamination station were thin, but impermeable.

Even with the car sealed, it wasn't long before the smells started seeping in. Fresh dog biscuit. Hot, steaming, fresh dog biscuit. And the dead things ground up to make the biscuit dough. It wasn't the smell of livestock. You didn't find livestock here, no trailers full of robust lowing cattle or squealing pigs, pink with health. The only trucks here had silent cargo, the animals dead, from illness or injury, before their assigned time.

The deadstock.

Tike and Liz parked at the front office, near a battered metal sign: Saandval Rendering, est. 1901. There was a short line of trucks at the scale. Some were full, some had already unloaded across the gravel yard at the building that held the first station, the peeling room.

Tike looked at Liz. "Ready?"

Liz nodded, and they swung open their doors. The smells and sounds were nearly overwhelming. They hopped out and slammed the car doors quickly.

"Oh my God," said Tike, shouting. "It's worse than I remembered." Liz cupped her hand behind her ear and shook her head. "Never mind," said Tike, louder, then snapped her mouth shut, trying not to make a face and resisting the urge to spit. There was a terrible rank taste in her mouth. Wet dog biscuit. Hot wet dog biscuit. They scuttled into the office by the scale, slamming the door shut behind them.

"Dr. Thomas?" A tall middle-aged man in jeans and a dress shirt, a pair of orange industrial earplugs dangling from a cord around his neck, gestured to them. "I'm Al Saandval. Third generation here."

Liz extended her hand. "Sorry to meet this way." She nodded in Tike's direction. "My assistant."

He gave Tike a nod and waved them down the hall into his office. As he shut the door behind them, the noise level dropped enough that they could hear their Tyvek suits rustle. They sat in chairs facing his desk as he pulled some notebooks from the file cabinets along the wall. Tike sat still in her chair, observing; this wasn't going to be her conversation.

"I've got some of the paperwork here for you," he said, pushing the materials across the desk to Liz as he flopped into his chair. He leaned back and crossed his arms. "But we don't document everything you wanted. That's just the way the industry is. We're the end of the food chain. The bottom end."

Liz nodded as she leaned forward and opened one of the binders. "I'm sure everything is in order. I just need to confirm you're not receiving animals from our hot zones, and that you're checking for FMD lesions.

Blisters and raw skin, on the feet, mouth, tongue..."

He frowned. "The drivers know which routes are shut down. But being a vet isn't our problem."

Liz sighed and spread her hands wide. "Well, it is now. We're trying, but so far I don't have any vets to spare. We can't put one here to help out. You've got to do it."

He laughed. "You know how things look when they arrive here. We're not going to see blisters, or sores. How's that going to look different than rat damage anyway? Plus you know the kind of guys I've got in the peeling room. You want to tell them this song and dance? Or their parole officers?" He shook his head. "Not going to work."

"We need you to at least watch," she said. "If you see any signs, you have to tell us the route, and we'll send someone to check."

"So now we're going to be the bad guy?"

"It doesn't have to be that way," said Liz.

He blew out a deep breath as he shook his head.

"Instead, I could shut you down now," she said. "Those are our options."

"And maybe I'll choose that option. We're losing money anyway." He tipped back his chair and tented his fingers together on his chest. "Then you can see what happens when carcasses start piling up around the state. A million pounds a week. It adds up." He smiled. "Won't that be an interesting spring thaw."

Liz got up and moved to the front of his desk, her back to Tike. She leafed through the notebooks, head down, tracking the pages as they turned. She spoke without looking up, her voice low. "Work with me, Al. This'll be over soon." She flipped through a few more pages. "I know you're having trouble with the water reg guys; maybe I can do something there."

Saandval cursed under his breath. After a few moments he leaned forward, slapping the desk with his hands and getting to his feet. "Let's go talk with my son, Davy. He's in the peeling shed."

———

Liz and Tike followed Al Saandval across the icy gravel yard to the nearest building. They stepped around the trucks lined up to unload just inside the industrial doors of what Tike remembered was the teeth-rattling din of the peeling shed. She fumbled, desperate, with the packet of disposable earplugs Saandval had given her. By the time she got them in, they were across the lot. The earplugs took the noise down a few decibels. Not enough. As her eyes adjusted to the dim of the warehouse-sized peeling room, the noise level suddenly plunged to near-tolerable. The smell did not. This was the room where fly-infested roadkill and bloated livestock carcasses were peeled and chopped before going into the heated extruder, on the other side of the wall. At the far end of the building they came out as dog biscuit paste. Her eyes watered.

"That was the chopper," said Al, in the relative silence. "Must be Davy." Tike silently prayed the chopper would stay off until they left, but even before she finished her prayer the deafening noise started again. She resisted covering her ears with her gloved hands as they followed Saandval across the room. He picked a path between mounds of carcass-es, piled by species: cattle, hogs, goats, deer, miscellaneous. Tike saw a flat skunk. Couldn't even smell it. She stepped carefully. The entire floor was slick with rotted blood and fluids, and occasional scraps of fatty skin were icy greased boobytraps. She forced herself to breathe through her nose, not wanting to let anything in the air in this room land in her open mouth, thankful her Tyvek jumpsuit would keep splatters off her skin. Thankful it was too cold for flies; noticing it wasn't too cold for maggots.

They passed a tall man with a long stringy ponytail at work on a pile of steaming hog carcasses. He snagged the skin of one hog with a rusty hook dangling from the ceiling, then used a few slashes of a long blade to free the carcass from the skin as the hook slowly rose, taking the skin with it to a hole in the wall. Tike knew a salted tank was just beyond; the tank of skins would reincarnate as men's shoes and ladies' handbags. Meanwhile the peeled carcass slapped to the floor, and he used a blunt shovel to push it over to a long, two-foot-wide slot in the floor. Tike knew what was in there: the screw. One of the hog's flayed limbs slid into the slot and caught, jerking and yanking, as the three-ton screw turned, inch by inch. The rolling metal didn't even hesitate as it pulled in the swollen, 400-pound mass of muscle and bone.

It's better we don't hear that.

As they walked parallel to the screw, passing the disappearing carcass, Tike glanced back at the man wielding the knife. He was standing with the dangling hook in one hand, his long wet blade in the other, his eyes narrow and mouth twitching as he watched Liz. He rubbed the rusty hook on his crotch.

She does look pretty hot in a Tyvek garbage sack, thought Tike, rolling her eyes. She shivered and snapped her focus back to watch her step. There was no safety rail around the screw, nor around the big hole they were approaching at the end of the screw. The hole, the destination of the crushed material inching along the screw, was the epicenter of the crashing noise. Several men in muck boots stood looking down at the gnashing metal inside it.

The chopper.

Tike covered her ears with her fists, staying a few feet back, and watched as the men moved their lips and gestured. One of the men, who looked like a younger version of Al, had a wrench so large it looked like an inflatable gag gift. He stepped to the very edge of the pit, three feet above a pair of intermeshing, toothed rollers, several tons of American steel each, which crashed together as they turned only slightly faster than the screw. The man turned around as he stood at the rim and gestured. The man behind him, standing before a giant pair of on-off switches, flipped both switches to "off" and the crashing noise stopped, leaving her ears ringing. Both the chopper and the screw rolled to a stop. The man hopped into the pit with the wrench and for the first time she could hear his voice.

"There's only one place you can do the adjustment, and it's directly under the blades. Watch."

She heard a sharp squealing of metal on metal as the men up top leaned in to look. One hopped down into the pit. Liz and Tike approached with their host as the younger Al re-emerged, without his wrench.

"Everything in order, Davy?" said Al to the younger man.

"I think we'll be fine," said Davy, wiping greasy material onto a rag. "We'll get another year on those blades."

"Good," said Al. "Got a minute?"

"Hold on." He turned to his crew. "Every month. Got that?" The second man climbed out of the pit and handed the wrench to his colleagues, tattoos on his knuckles smeared with brown grease. "Lewallen, got that?" The man nodded. "Okay. Good." He gestured for them to start up the engines and turned to Al. "Office?"

Al nodded. As the chopper and screw started to turn, they marched single file back through the peeling room. Tike kept her hands over her ears the whole way and only slipped once.

When Liz and Tike got back to West Soo from Saandval Rendering, they each took a long shower and tied their clothes in garbage bags. They dumped the bags outside in the snow.

Tike's pile of clothes was especially messy. Liz had taken the opportunity at the rendering plant to teach her how to use the captive bolt gun, which was basically a single-shot, hand-held, gunpowder-powered hammer. Fired into even the most massive skull, it killed instantly. If more hot zones came up, Liz said, Tike might need to help the depopulation teams. So Liz made her practice using it to punch holes in swollen, hissing hog carcasses at Saandval's.

"Work on his head again," she had said. If you don't hit the right spot, she told Tike, the animal doesn't die—and might run off with the gun sticking out of his head. "Here—use mine," said Liz. "I'll clean yours again."

Tike was so glad to be back at West Soo. So glad.

By the time she reached her desk, Liz was already on the phone, getting ready for the 4:30 p.m. press conference. Since they shouldn't leave quarantine more than possible, they would be linked in by phone.

Tike went back to the break room and made them some hot cocoa, then settled in at her station, cocoa at her elbow. She was sorting through the papers on her desk, making her own plan for the press conference and the remainder of the afternoon, when the phone rang.

"Tike? This is Bob Gasparowicz at the SEC."

She sighed. *Now what? Haven't I talked to him enough? Isn't this over already?*

"We understand you're working for Ulysses Yatsis with respect to the FMD outbreak," he said.

She blinked. Yatsis? What? Who? *Oh: U.P.* "Why?" She bit her lip, consciously trying to keep her mouth shut. She knew she wasn't obliged to say anything.

"With your history," he said, "are you sure you want to do that?"

She paused. "Is there something I need to know?" She turned and looked around the room. Other than Liz and her, it was empty.

"I'm liasing a case with the CFTC," he said.

Uh-oh. The SEC was the stocks-and-bonds police, but the CFTC—the Commodity Futures Trading Commission—hit closer to home: the CFTC could shut down U.P. and Geneva in a hot second.

"Is there something you want to tell us?," he said. "About the outbreak?" His voice didn't change. Cold and level.

"Should there be? You think I'm working for U.P. For Yatsis. What would that matter, since he had nothing to do with the outbreak?"

"That's not what I hear."

"From who?"

"You sound pretty cold about this, Tike." He paused. "Pretty cold. I know the situation in California was tough on you." He cleared his throat. "On both of you." He was silent. She was silent. He broke first. "Why don't you come in and talk with me, Tike. Just the two of us, you and me."

It was never "just the two of us" when the SEC was involved. It was the two of us, their lawyers, her lawyers, the court reporter, the microphones, the duplicate tape recorders, the video cameras, the paperwork and signatures and clock ticking and phones ringing beyond the closed doors while all the lawyers stared at you and waited for an answer to their triple-layered questions.

She declined and he hung up.

When U.P. called ten minutes later she didn't mention Bob Gasparowicz. She was going with her gut on this one, and her gut chose U.P. over the SEC and CFTC. Gasparowicz was history, her past. Not her future.

———————

CHAPTER 11

Mike Salt looked around the Euvaxx conference table, littered with half-eaten pastries and sandwiches and dotted with empty coffee cups. At the far end, a large posterboard with the Euvaxx logo leaned against the wall. Along the side of the room, a window with half-open blinds obscured the view of palm trees, gnarled Torrey pines, and groomed lawn in the plaza of the biotech complex, shadows growing as the sun dipped closer to the nearby ocean. On the long veneered table, binders with copies of the proposed Department of Agriculture vaccine contract sat in front of each member of Mike's Board of Directors, seated around the table in varying poses of fatigue.

Mike made eye contact with each man and woman. "Do we have a vote?" A transcriber sat in the corner near Mike, watching the group, hands poised over her laptop computer.

The motion was made and seconded and entered into the minutes: Euvaxx, Inc., would accept the emergency contract for 2.4 million doses of the new Euvaxx vaccine against FMD, and would receive a fast-tracked permit for U.S. sales and distribution.

Mike watched through the lobby curtains until the last board member got into his Mercedes and left the parking lot, then whooped and threw a copy of the contract into the air and laughed as the pages floated down around him. He ran over to the receptionist's desk and leaned into the P.A. system. "Champagne for everyone in five minutes in the lunchroom."

He winked at Gina, the receptionist, and leaned into the microphone again. "Meanwhile, call home and tell your families you'll be working overtime for the next month." Mike ran to the refrigerator in his office and started pulling out bottles of dry Veuve Cliquot.

He'd known this day would come.

———————

The man with pale green eyes drove his rental car north from the Chicago airport to the lakeshore marina where a 27-foot sailboat was in drydock. He used a keycard to drive through the gate nearest his slip, unlocked the boathouse, went in, and locked the door behind him. Stepping carefully over heavy-duty extension cords strung from the boathouse up over the foredeck, he climbed onboard and crawled down into the galley.

A bright red "-80° C" glowed from a panel on a small stainless-steel freezer. He filled a lunch cooler with ice packs from the regular freezer, then removed three tubes from the -80 and put them on the ice. He pulled a package of empty aerosol sprayers from a cabinet under the sink. He put these, along with three packs of baby wipes, in an empty tote bag. He took his supplies off the boat, locked up, and got into his car, securing his supplies into the front seat beside him.

He settled into the leather driver's seat as the car rolled out of the marina and toward the interstate. At the last stoplight before the on-ramp, he reviewed his atlas one last time, but it wasn't necessary. He knew where he was going: I-80 westbound, 197 miles, turn right. He was careful not to speed too much as he headed west-southwest from Chicago. Traffic was light; not much other than long-haul truckers manned the highways at this hour.

The drive went well.

At mile 195, he peeked into the ice chest on the seat beside him. The muddy liquid in the tubes was nearly thawed, the debris settling at the bottom of the tubes. He had never had the liquids tested, of course, but he had extrapolated the number of live virus particles—"PFU," in lab lingo—that should be floating there: 100 million from the saliva he had scraped from some drooling buffalo in Namibia. One hundred and eighty million from muck in a pig pen in Brazil. Other countries, other sources; about two billion PFU altogether, between the wet, muddy souvenirs and wet, muddy hiking boots he so carefully bagged and packed in his luggage.

Two billion PFU, he thought, glancing at the cooler. Enough, he had calculated, to infect approximately 131,000 hogs or 225,000 cattle. *More than enough for tonight.*

The man exited the interstate, pulling into the last rest area before his destination, seventeen miles down the road. He rolled to a careful stop in the dark slot between two sleeping truckers and turned off his engine. The stereo went silent. He worked in the dark, assembling his materials, moving slowly so he wouldn't spill.

He pulled a jar of Vick's mentholatum from the small duffel bag on the bucket seat beside him and slathered a dollop on his upper lip. He zipped up his coat, pulled his cap down over his ears, and reached up to deactivate the interior dome light, then tested it by opening and closing the door. He slid his hand over to rest on the three aerosol sprayers, now full, in the ice chest where the tubes had been, and got back onto the highway.

When he reached the final stretch of road before his destination, he turned off his headlights. Only the moonlight and the contrast between the snow and the dark gravel kept him on the road. There were no streetlights, and the facility was at least a mile from any farmstead. His previous visit, on a similar night, had confirmed this. The lot was surrounded by a chain-link fence, but the security gate, designed to restrict vehicular traffic, was a simple bar.   There were no signs other than "No Trespassing." The motion-detecting lights had the sensitivity set low to tolerate the deer which jumped the fence to eat spilled feed. At this hour, the offices were locked, but the back doors of the main buildings—where the hogs were now sleeping—were not. Good intentions always gave way to real world practicalities, such as keys lost once too often.

The man rolled his car to a stop in the shadow of the dead box on the edge of the road. By the time the rendering truck made the rounds and emptied the box of deadstock in the morning, he and his car would be long gone. The man closed his car door with a quiet click, stepped around the security bar, and walked on the gravel toward the back of the first hog building.

He opened the door a slit and slipped inside, closing it behind him. Even with the aromatic grease under his nose, he could still smell the powerful ammonia stench of the hogs. His eyes watered as he patted the sprayers in his coat pockets, then pulled out his mini Maglite and switched it on. As he scanned the room to get his bearings, his beam lit a notice posted by the door: "Worker's Compensation Notice—Glory Swine, LLC." It was also in Spanish. As his eyes adjusted to the dark, a large pair of doors took shape before him. Moving closer to the doors, he could hear the hogs snoring with slow wheezes.

The man had come this far before, on rehearsal night, but there was one final check he had to do before moving forward. He pulled out a headset with embedded industrial hearing protectors and slipped it over his ears. It was rated to 110 decibels, the noise level of a typical jackhammer. He reached for one of the door handles and started to turn it.

As the door swung open he froze, gasping.

The noise as the hogs were awakened, startled, was an astounding cacophony, a piercing chorus of 115-decibel squeals, painful even through his headset. Gritting his teeth, he scanned the huge room with his flashlight and got the visual confirmation he needed: a swollen tube of thin, clear, plastic hung along the central rafter the length of the barn. The fat tube, rippling from an air current that was keeping it inflated, had holes every foot or so on the sides facing the pens of pigs. At the far end of the barn, the tube flapped and wiggled and was tied to a post. At the near end, up on the wall over the door he had just opened, the tube came straight out of the wall, taut and firm.

The man quickly stepped back into the small ante-room, closed the insulated door, and slumped against it, exhaling with relief. He pointed his flashlight up. "There you are, my beauty," he said. Above him, big and round, shiny, silently spinning, was a fan.

It was an inlet fan, blowing air through the wall into the fat, long tube, so the air would pour into the room and flow over the animals, day and night, helping them cool their steaming bodies and stay cozy. He pulled out a slim cigar, a Cuban Cohiba, and lit it. He pulled a crate in front of the door, under the fan, and stepped up onto it. He took a long draw on the cigar, and puffed the smoke into the swirling blade, then hopped down, jerked open the door, and shone his flashlight on the fat tube. The smoke swirled there, and streams of the sweet cloud flowed out the holes over the first pens. That was all he needed to see.

The man scooted out again, shut the door on the deafening pigs, put his headset back in his coat pocket, put the crate back in place, and grabbed his aerosol sprayer.

Time to work.

He was done with all four hog buildings and back on the road within fifteen minutes, cigar in hand. He plugged an air ionizer into the cigarette lighter and ran it at full blast, stopping at another dark rest area to change clothes and wipe himself down with the baby wipes. He discarded the hog-scented clothes, dividing them between several trash barrels at the rest stop.

De-scented and relaxed, the man smoked another Cohiba and settled into his butter-soft seat as the car entered the interstate and aimed for the airport.

CHAPTER 12

Tike had a splitting headache the morning after she visited the rendering plant with Liz. By mid-morning, she had taken a double dose of every analgesic on the premises and still ached, slumped over her desk at West Soo. She massaged her temples as she watched Liz flip through the day's newspapers, eating donuts, the phones still for a moment. Tike shut her eyes and flopped back in her chair.

"Oh, no," said Liz.

Tike could hear a newspaper rustling, but kept her eyelids shut, working very hard at being relaxed, doing deep breathing as she worked various pressure points. "What?" said Tike, mumbling.

"There's that picture again," said Liz. "Oh, great."

Tike stretched one hand toward her, fingers extended, while the other continued to work on her forehead. Liz slapped the paper into her palm.

"Who dug those up, anyway?" said Liz, pushing back her chair and jumping up, then sweeping the other papers off her desktop and cramming them into the trashcan.

Tike gave up on relaxation and opened her eyes, scanning the crumpled page in her hand. In the top right corner was a story on the press conference held yesterday by Liz and Governor Wilton. Next to the story was a photo of the Governor at the media room in Johnston, Bruce Ter Wee at his side. Just below this was a sidebar with a two-column black-and-white of Liz. In a bikini.

Under the photo was the sidebar title: *Former Model Fights Farm Plague.* Tike gave a low whistle. "Special uniform for female plague fighters?"

"That was years ago," said Liz, yanking on her boots and tugging at the laces, "while I was working my way through vet school."

Tike waggled her eyebrows. "Working?"

"As a model," said Liz, frowning at her. "A swimsuit model. Before I met Joseph."

"Well, you look better than the Governor."

"He's a moron."

"You made that very clear," said Tike. "The reporters had good questions, present company included. And I swear I had nothing to do with that excellent question about the lack of funding of subsection 32-g."

Liz looked sideways at Tike and frowned, then shook her head and plopped into her chair, taking another bite of donut. "His administration's a loser," she said, mouth full. "They never did take this seriously. Bunch of sissies. Homeland Security preparedness, my ass."

"Where do you buy swimsuits like that? Are they legal in Iowa?"

"Shut up."

"Is that, like, Plum Island beachwear?"

"Shut up." Liz crumpled up her napkin and threw it at Tike.

"What *do* you wear under those plastic coveralls, anyway, Dr. Thomas?"

"Shut up."

One of the few remaining office assistants came in and handed Liz a note, which she read and passed to Tike.

Tike raised her eyebrows as she read. "David Letterman's office called?"

Liz shrugged, her mouth full of donut. She leaned back, swinging her booted feet onto her desk with a thud. Mud and debris of undesirable origins showered onto her papers. She changed the channel of the TV on her desk to CNN. Liz's photo flashed on screen with the caption, *Former Model In Hot Zone.*

"I know just the thing for you to wear on the show," said Tike, snatching a donut.

"Shut up."

———

By late afternoon, headache dimmed by modern chemistry and a therapeutic dose of glazed pastry, Tike tapped into the West Soo Internet connection and sent out her feed: the daily briefings for the Department of Agriculture media suits, the daily journal entry for Nick's paper, and a short story on residents of Quimby—*poor bastards*—for her editor at the *Sioux City Journal.* The workload was dreadful, but it was an investment; the stacks of interview tapes and notes piling up on her desk were going to be a book before this was all over. Not that it mattered anymore. *Who's going to want to read it?* But maybe, she thought, it would help prevent the next time, the next disease, the next crisis.

At least it was better than thinking about bulldozers. About school-buses.

Tike called Sioux City to check in and confirm they received her story. "When'll this be wrapped up?" said her editor.

"Wrapped up? It's not like we have control over everything."

"Well, it's got to end sometime," he said. "And it's almost Christmas. We need some good news. This can't go on forever."

"In theory it could."

"What?"

"Look, we're just about done tracking all the animals that went through West Soo," said Tike. "If no new outbreaks pop, then we start clean-up and get through the probation period. Then we're back to normal."

"So we're almost done with the highlights."

"Yes," she said, rolling her eyes. "Could be." As she was hanging up, she got a call on her cell phone. Nick. She didn't pick up. She watched until the message light flashed, then dialed in.

"Tike, please call," said Nick's message. "I need to see you. We have to talk. About us. I need to give my decision ten days from now. *We* need to. I know you're busy, but we're always busy, aren't we? Let's talk about it, sweetheart." His voice paused. Tike rubbed the bridge of her nose. Her headache was coming back.

"We have one more day of sessions here," his voice said. "I have to stay because I'm a speaker, then I fly back. I'm coming out to see you. I don't care about the quarantine. My boss's a jerk anyway. Let him run the ag desk for a while. Tike. Please call. We could have Christmas together." Tike sat back in her chair and hit "erase."

If only.

Too many promises, too many lies, too many apologies.

Too many scars.

He wouldn't show; she was sure of it. Her headache was now at full throb. Her eyes were going to explode. She left the phone on her desk and put on her jacket and boots to go see what everyone was doing. Maybe Liz could dart her with some horse tranquilizers.

———————

At 6:05 p.m., back at her desk with a calming cup of chamomile, supplemented by a double dose of butalbital, Tike got a call from "New York State Coro," according to the caller ID on the West Soo house phone. Liz was outside in the feedlot working with the crews.

"Tike Lexington?" said the caller, a woman.

"Who's calling?"

"This is the coroner's office for the State of New York. We have some personal information for Tike Lexington. Are you Tike Lexington?"

She frowned. Coroner? *These morgue calls are getting pretty elaborate.* She let out a long sigh, slumped in her chair, and started digging mud out of her boot treads with a pen. "Yeah," she said. "*Now* what?"

The caller hesitated. "Now what? Well, I'm sorry to have to tell you this, but we have you listed as the next of kin for a body in our Manhattan facility."

Tike sat up straight. "What?"

"I'm calling to inform you we have a body here for which you are listed as next-of-kin. I'm sorry, dear," she said, her voice soft and gentle, "but we need you to provide identification of this individual."

Tike fell back in her chair, her mouth hanging open. New York. *Mom. My mother...dead?* Mom and Grandma were flying into La Guardia this week after their Russia trip. *Heart attack. I always told her to take her Lipitor.* "Oh, no," said Tike. *Now it's just me and my cats.* She burst into tears, her heart pounding.

"I'm sorry," said the woman on the phone. "This is always difficult. But I need to ask you for some information. Can you manage?"

"Yes, okay." Tike gasped with pain and slumped over the desk, nearly retching.

"We don't have a photo identification of the body ready, but perhaps you could tell us..."

"Blue eyes," said Tike, interrupting her. "She has bright blue eyes."

"Excuse me?"

"Or maybe you haven't looked at her eyes. Or maybe you...can't? Oh..." She started sobbing again. *Oh mom. Were you crushed beyond recognition in a fiery crash? Or were your blue eyes dulled to milky white by a lethal fever? Or...*

"Miss Lexington, I think there's been a..."

"Crooked finger. She has a crooked finger on her right hand. She smashed it in a hot kiln once. She's an artist, you know. Was. Oh."

"Calm down, dear..."

"How can I calm down? This is my mother we're talking about. I only have one. Had...oh..." Tike let the phone slide from her grip. It dropped to the desk and lay by her outstretched hand.

"Miss Lexington, it's not your mother. It's a man."

Tike stopped, mid-sigh, and snatched up the phone. "Man?" She wiped her chin on her sleeve.

"Yes. The John Doe in our facility is five foot two, 110 pounds, seventy to seventy-five years of age, Asian, black hair, brown eyes. Your name and phone number were in his pocket, with the phrase 'She is my only dear family.' I'm sorry, but we need you to identify him for us, please."

Tike narrowed her eyes as she sat up. She asked the woman to describe the note. Hand-written, on a scrap of paper, she said.

"Scrap?" Tike leaned back in her chair.

"Yes. A scrap of wrapping paper. Blue with white reindeer."

"Reindeer?" Tike's eyes closed and she shook her head. She asked for the note to be faxed, both sides, said she'd check with her family, and hung up the phone.

Reindeer, my ass. It's my dead guy. And this time he really is dead.

Tike leaned toward the windows of the West Soo office, peering through the frosted glass, watching Liz outside in the feedlot. She was standing under the arc of one of the yard lights, pointing at something on a clipboard, showing it to one of the workers. A light snow was falling.

What now? Tike used her fingertip to melt a stick reindeer in the frost. She sat back down at her desk and flipped through her Rolodex until she found the number for the sheriff back home. "It's me again," she said.

"Now what," he said, sighing.

She told him about the latest call, and he sighed again.

"I'll add it to your file," he said. "Anything else we can do for you today? Something in the state of Iowa, for example? Something involving an actual criminal activity, so I can actually do something?" He sighed.

Tike wished him a Merry Christmas, then called Manhattan. The Manhattan coroner's office gave her the name of the detective in charge of her dead guy.

"This guy wasn't making your calls," said the detective when she finally got through. "We just got an I.D. from his prints. Ray Chen, one of our frequent fliers. He got out of County yesterday. Thirty days on assault. No phones for inmates there."

"What was he doing in Manhattan?"

He yawned. "Who knows? Something criminal, perchance?"

"How did he die?"

"We don't have all the details yet, but it might've had something to do with the train that squashed him."

"A *train*?"

"Jumped, fell, or shoved from the platform, impossible to tell. Rush hour, really pissed people off when they stopped the line, waiting for my guys with the crime scene tape." He yawned again. "As if anyone was going to wait around to tell us they saw it happen."

She thanked him and hung up. She went back to the window. Liz was crossing the yard, making a beeline back to the office.

She called the detective again. "Which train?" she said.

"Which?" He sighed. She heard papers rustling. "He got nailed by the 5:15 Lex, northbound. That's 5:15 in the p.m."

"Lex?"

"Yeah, the Lexington Ave. Line."

Tike hung up as Liz came in, waving at her as she dumped her coat and boots and headed for the shower.

Lexington?

Tike spent a few minutes with her feet up on her desk, jotting a few notes on a notepad: The calls and pages. The morgues. The false fire alarm. The dead guy. Multiple states, multiple phone lines. The call from the Manhattan coroner came in on the West Soo line. No actual threats had been made. Might or might not be related to hacking DeadSim. *What do I really have to report? Why let this get to me? Who can I report it to, anyway?* She sat for a while, tapping her pen on her notepad, then pulled her Rolodex across the desk and flipped through the "M" section. She dialed. Halfway across the country, a phone rang.

"Magnus." Loud street noises and sirens filled the background.

"Agent Magnus? Tike Lexington."

"Tike, good to hear from you." He said he'd get back to her in ten minutes, after he finished walking a crime scene.

When he called, she told him about the morgue calls.

"Is it Zack?" he said.

"I don't know." Tike had met Special Agent Ed Magnus a lifetime ago, when he was still Officer Magnus. It was the year she thought things were going so much better with her then-fiance, Zack.

Until Zack tried to strangle her.

"It was just a little strangle," she had said to Magnus's desktop in the police station, her forehead on the cool Formica. She remembered hearing Magnus chewing his gum. He kept chewing. Something minty. He slid the box of tissues across his desk and left the room. A tall and beautiful woman—from the shelter, she said—came and pulled up a chair next to Tike, shaking the snow from her long hair. They went through the list of red flags, the list of dangerous behaviors compiled by the death committees, the panels that reviewed the domestic homicides. A score of six out of sixteen red flags was bad. A score of eight required police action.

Zack got a twelve.

It was a bad year and got worse. Tike got to know Ed Magnus well. But it was never over with someone like Zack. Was he making the morgue calls?

"I don't know," Tike said again. "He's left me alone the last couple of years. I don't even have a no-contact order anymore. But the calls are so...Zack. Checking in. Letting me know he's there, that he knows where I am. A threat without being a threat."

"My thoughts, too. Mind games."

"Any suggestions?"

"Well, what's new?" he said. "There's not a lot you can do. Keep taping your calls. Keep a log. But if there are no actual threats of violence, not to mention you don't have an ID—well, you're stuck."

"I know, I know."

"Remember Stacy?" he said. Stacy was in Tike's group sessions at the shelter; her ex-husband had stalked and harassed her for three years after she left him. He didn't stop until he got hit by a bus.

"You're suggesting I get a bus?" said Tike.

He laughed. "Not quite. But let's just hope he didn't fixate on you again for some reason."

"Yeah, I know."

"I'll make a few calls, okay? Check on how he's been behaving. But Tike—be alert." He snapped his gum.

"I will." After she hung up she went through her camera bag and dug out a dusty little can of pepper spray. She shoved it in her pocket and went down to their make-shift sleeping quarters to see Liz. It was time to tell her about the dead guy. And the live guy, Zack.

After talking to Liz, Tike went back to the dark West Soo offices to make one more call. She picked up her cell phone and hit speed-dial #4. Nick.

"It's me," she said, slumped in her chair, exhausted, the faxed scrap of reindeer paper in her hand.

"Tike? Tike? Thank God," said Nick. "Where are you?" In the background there were people laughing, yelling. Glasses clattering. "Tike?

Talk to me, honey."

Tike heard a brassy female voice: "Nick honey! Your round! More olives this time!"

She lowered the phone to her lap for a moment, then hit "END." She picked up the phone again and erased speed-dial #4, just as the phone rang.

"Yeah," she said, rubbing her eyes. "Tike here."

"Tike? Um, hi. It's Pete. Pete Russell. The world famous?"

Tike gave a half smile and leaned back. "Hey, hi Pete."

"You don't sound so good."

"You know, one of those days."

"Want to talk about it? I've got time to listen—I'm waiting for a gel to run."

Tike let out a deep breath and laughed, picturing the blond surfer-dude-scientist who wooed her at the Keystone conference, before Nick. "You're not normal, mister. For a guy, anyway. What did you do, a post-doc with Dr. Phil?"

"Is he the integrin guy at UCLA?"

Tike laughed. "Seriously, I appreciate it. I don't have that many people to talk to these days."

"I bet you feel like you're the dog in the dog-and-pony show."

"You know about dog-and-pony shows?"

"Yeah. Why? You think I just hang out with PhDs?"

"Well, you know. The tarnish of industry, and all that."

He snorted. "Give me a break. My biotech consulting helps pay for my research. If it wasn't for my VC friends, I'd have two less postdocs in my lab."

Tike whistled. "Well done."

"Hey, when they let you out of that zoo, I'll hook you up. You've got the perfect background. And you've been on the inside of a live biotech."

"Yeah, I've seen the blood."

"It makes a difference, I'm telling you."

An hour later, Tike put away her phone and scuffed down the hall to her sleeping bag.

CHAPTER 13

The motors on the heavy, automatic, roll-up curtains on the south side of four Glory Swine finishing barns started their slow grinding, rolling the curtains down from the top to open just a few inches, just as they had ten minutes before. And ten minutes before that, and ten minutes before that. A gush of warm, smelly air flowed out each time, pouring down the side of the barn, getting caught by the icy Iowa wind as the wind tore over the apex of the roof and whipped through the farmyard. All the particles of dust, and oils, and scent, and everything that was in the little controlled world of the hogs, got carried away on whatever wind came through.

Just ask the neighbors.

Or just look. A mile north, some of the grumpier neighbors posted signs in their ditches: KEEP GLORY SWINE OUT. JUST SAY NO TO MEGAHOG. IOWA: FIELD OF SMELLS.

The day had been pretty warm for late December in Iowa. The hogs inside the barn were cozy. As they should be: They were walking, crapping, grunting furnaces, throwing off heat as they ate—like pigs—and slept and grew. A hog barn doesn't need to be heated, not even in the middle of an Iowa winter. Today, the wind helped the thermostats and the automatic rolling curtain keep the hog barn temperature just right.

The wind leaving the farm had little resistance before dropping down and cooling the neighbors' hog barns, then it crossed a flat field with corn stubble poking up through the snow. After a mile of this, the wind picked up a little dust from a gravel road and hopped the ditch to a mile of soybean stubble. Finally, one more set of barns, cattle warm and sleepy inside, and the air curled up into the next strata of the atmosphere. It cooled above 150 feet, and started moving faster.

This was wind turbine height.

"Now," the wind would say, if the wind could say anything, "Now for the fun part."

The massive, black, elegant blades of the 257 wind turbines on the Alta wind farm spun at a steady speed, mixing the air, shifting to face it head-on. South if the wind was going north; north if the wind was going south. It rarely blew east or west, here.

The air from the Glory Swine barns raced between the blades, twirling, and finally straightening out again just in time to race through another set of blades half a mile away. Down below, corn and soybean stubble stretched on, as far as the eye could see, dotted with a few house-tops, and several-fold more barn-tops, and shed-tops, and calving barns,   · and cattle feedlots, and gravel roads and, rarely, a paved highway running east and west.

Deer, leaning against the wind, walked single file from an old grove toward a quiet farmyard with corn scattered around feed troughs.

A man in insulated coveralls, grabbing his seed cap as the wind yanked it from his head, walked through the lit center of a tidy farmyard toward his barn.

But up at wind turbine height, the air moved on and on, flowing along the Buffalo Ridge Wind Belt, south to Missouri, west to Nebraska, occasionally hitting a pocket of warmer or cooler air and coiling up or down, away from wind turbine height.

Occasionally dropping down to barn height.

———————

Mike Salt shoved another stuffed mushroom into his mouth as he looked out the restaurant window at the sun setting over the pounding La Jolla surf. The steaming mushrooms were filled with Maytag blue cheese and dry black Turkish olives and baked in Armagnac—exquisite, a Le Papillon house specialty. He ordered them every time he brought a business colleague here for dinner. On his Euvaxx executive expense account, of course.

"Good terms on the vaccine sale, Mike," said Parker Roos, managing partner of the White Oak Fund, and potential lifeline for Euvaxx. "I think you're really going to do it."

Mike shrugged and waved his hand at the venture capitalist facing him across the small linen-clad table. "Stuff sold itself. What else could they do?" He forked another mushroom and spun it around in the buttery liqueur in the gold-rimmed dish between them before leaning over the table and popping it in his mouth.

"We should have gotten in earlier." Roos chose a mushroom and used his spoon and knife to transfer it to his bread plate, where he cut the mushroom into exact quarters.

Roos, Mike noticed, was wearing a better suit than his. But Mike had better cufflinks. They were miniature crystal replicas of the *Wall Street Journal* tombstone from his last IPO. Mike hitched up his jacket sleeves slightly, so the cufflinks could pick up the candlelight. "Not too late," said Mike. "Not yet." He winked.

Roos used his knife and fork to put the mushroom segments in a row, then ate one. "You need to do some fast scale-up, Mike. The faster the better."

Mike nodded and snapped another mushroom into his mouth, then took a drink of his wine, an outstanding Australian shiraz. His lips left a buttery print on the glass.

"White Oak can go the distance," said Roos. "We just exited two portfolio companies this year, and we're sitting on cash. The other partners want to move."

"Our valuation is up," said Mike. He wiped his mouth with the linen napkin. "The vaccine deal gave us a good bump."

"I know, I know," said Roos with a shrug, smiling. "And don't think my partners let me forget it." His smile dropped. "But we think you're a meal ticket, Mike. You've got the touch," said Roos. "We want on your ride."

Mike stared at the last mushroom. *This could do it.* The investment Roos had proposed would take Euvaxx beyond the end of product development and into the black, since this outbreak started greasing the skids. No more fucking dog-and-pony shows. No more penny-pinching when the venture money got short, like now. It was a big risk to commit to just one venture fund for this size of deal, but the FMD outbreak had been a gift from heaven: it would be smooth sailing from now on. Nothing could take them off the golden path. Roos was a strange bird, but weren't all VCs? He was a foreigner, with a shitload of money. Family money, people said. Perfect combination for strange-birdness. And White Oak was tough, very tough to crack. They didn't make many deals. Mike hadn't met anyone who had met Roos in person, in fact; it was always the other partners who worked the few deals they did. But Roos was apparently the money behind the scenes, and now, sure as shit, here was Roos, sitting right in front of him. *And he wants on my ride.*

Mike pushed the mushroom platter over to Roos. "That one's yours."

"Thanks. Say, beautiful cufflinks. Were those custom-made?"

Mike, his lips shiny with butter, leaned back in his soft chair and smiled.

———————

Neither Liz nor Tike could sleep, so they were perched in their chairs in the West Soo office, stockinged feet and popcorn strewn across their desks, watching an old movie on the TV they otherwise monitored continuously for news.

During a commercial, with the TV muted, Tike made them each a fresh cup of instant cocoa; she set Liz's beside her. Liz shook her head and let out a deep breath, popcorn residue on her chin, eyes unfocused. "This is a disaster, Tike."

The room was quiet. All the calls had been diverted to Disaster Command at Johnston. Liz's ears were still red from being on the phone—sometimes two phones at once—non-stop as she went in and out of the offices and pens of the feedlot. She had a rack of batteries constantly recharging. They steamed as they charged and dried.

The movie came back on, but neither of them moved to turn on the sound. Liz got up, walked over and shut off the set, the remote long-gone, then sat down again and closed her eyes.

Good, thought Tike. She needs some peace.

Liz's desk phone rang. Tike raised her eyebrows. "I thought Fosco was handling calls now." She got up to fetch more popcorn.

Liz shrugged as she reached for the handset. "Dr. Thomas here...That's okay, Fosco. What is it?" As she listened she frowned and leaned forward. She snapped her fingers toward Tike as Tike crossed the room toward the popcorn. "Channel three," she said. "He says we need to watch. Right away." Tike reached over and snapped on the set, finding the right channel and turning up the sound. Liz hung up the phone as the voice of Governor Wilton, in the press room at Disaster Command in Johnston, boomed through the TV speakers into the West Soo office.

"Next question," the Governor was saying, pointing at a reporter at the front of the pack. "Yes. Bob."

"Governor, if this is true, what will happen to farmers whose livestock have already been killed? Will they still get reimbursed by the state?"

"If this is true?" said Liz, dropping her feet to the floor. "If this is true? What happened? Nobody called me."

Tike was frozen in her chair, her mind racing through possibilities. *Now what?*

"Yes," said Wilton, shaking his head. "That's an excellent question. I'm reviewing that with the attorney general now." He dipped his head toward the A.G., standing to his left, near the podium. Wilton pointed at a hand waving in the back of the room. "Yes. You."

"What about the vet? The one who sent in the first samples. Will she be disciplined?"

"Disciplined? What?" said Liz, jumping up and kicking one of the chairs over. "To hell with them."

The lights went on outside and the empty, silent feedlot became bright as day. Snow was falling.

"Another good question," said Wilton, nodding and frowning. "We need to get more information, review the steps she took, find out where the problem began. We're not blaming her yet, but we'll have to review the facts. I can't say more now." The Governor pointed at another hand. The reporter, a tall woman with a ponytail, stood.

"What about the media contact, Lexington." She looked at her notebook. "She had earlier links with the vet, and has some history with fraud."

"We're looking at all angles," said the Governor.

Oh fuck.

Tike could hear heavy boots running in the hall, coming toward them. Liz's phone rang.

On screen, Bruce Ter Wee whispered in the Governor's ear. "Last question," said the Governor. "You, in the blue parka."

"Governor, since it was just a false alarm, will the quarantines be lifted?"

"Yes, it's already been done. Business can now proceed as usual in the great state of Iowa."

Liz crossed the room and switched off the TV with a slap, then gripped the monitor with both hands. Her phone kept ringing.

Tike whistled, a low exhale. "Oh wow. A false alarm." Liz was still, staring into the blank TV, face to face with the cold glass screen. "Now what?" said Tike. Her mouth watered; a surge of nausea made her stand and glance toward the restroom.

Liz turned and faced her. "Now what?" she said. "What else?" She walked past Tike to her desk and lowered herself into the chair, leaning back, raising her arms to the ceiling and closing her eyes. "Now they're going to crucify me."

Another phone on Liz's desk rang, then another, as the heavy boots reached the door.

From the December 22 Sacramento (California) Bee:

FMD Disease Outbreak Declared False Alarm

PLUM ISLAND, N.Y. (CNN.com, 11:45 p.m. EST) — Officials at the US Department of Agriculture have confirmed the recent reported Iowa outbreak of foot-and-mouth disease, a livestock infection, was a false alarm.

"It's a Christmas gift," said Iowa Governor William Wilton. "We have some clean-up to do, but things can go back to normal now."

The state will also investigate the events leading up to the false alarm, said the Governor. "We're looking at all angles," he said.

Roy McCall, director of Homeland Security's Plum Island lab-oratory where testing was done, said tight budgets were partly to blame.

"By law, we're the only lab in the nation authorized to handle FMD samples," he said. "Our scientists do a great job protecting national security with the limited budget we have, but we don't have the resources to deal with samples that may have been deliberately manipulated."

McCall declined to clarify.

The Chicago Board of Trade has announced a two-hour delay for the opening of commodities trading tomorrow morning.

CHAPTER 14

Liz turned her back to the people swarming into the West Soo office and punched a number into her cell phone. "Come on...come on..." She took a quick look back over her shoulder as the phone pressed against her ear continued to ring far away, unanswered. "Come on..."

"Roy here."

"Roy. What the hell?" Liz stood and gripped the phone with both hands, her back to the room.

"Liz. I'm glad you called. I've been trying to reach you."

Trying to reach me? Eyebrows raised, Liz pulled the phone away from her ear and looked at it. A little Nokia 3420 with a blue faceplate. Her other phone was the same model but pearly green. She talked to those phones more than she talked to any human being on earth. She yanked the pearly green phone from the charger stand and looked at the glowing panel: no messages. Same as the blue one.

She put the blue phone back to her ear. "Roy. You tried to call me. That's interesting. Didn't catch the call." Liz stood up straighter, rigid as a steel rod, one eye squinted, teeth clamped together, her back to a growing crowd in the West Soo office. Someone tapped her shoulder and asked a question; Liz batted the hand away without looking.

"Yes, Liz," said Roy, "we re-did the tests on the samples you sent. We're short-handed here, you know, budget cuts and what-not."

"Yes, I understand. It's a problem, isn't it? So, what did you find?"

"Well. So. It's actually very interesting. The original tests were definitely positive. No doubt. All the controls checked out. But the repeats were negative."

"Negative," said Liz. "Right."

"And the PCR. Well, you know how that is. We've had so much activity here, so many samples to look at, there just isn't the budget to have a dedicated PCR clean room like we used to. Obviously, there was some contamination. We sent some viral DNA to Plum Acres there in Iowa and they confirmed it."

Liz stood still, silent.

"We're looking into how the first set of tests came out positive," Roy said. He cleared his throat. "I have some theories on that, and a visiting scientist here—an expert on Crimean viruses, who has extensive, extensive experience in this area—is investigating this with me. But that's not the problem."

He paused. *A nice little drama for The Man.* The little prick. She waited.

"We're wondering what else might have gotten into the first samples," he said. "You've done some traveling, seen FMD in the wild. You've even been here, worked with our FMD research animals." He paused. "You know how easy it would be for a sample to get...ah...mixed."

"Mixed? Get mixed? You don't think I did something? On purpose?"

"Liz, Liz. Calm down. Nobody has said such a thing. I was just conferencing with Fred—the director of Homeland Security, you know—we work closely together, of course, closely—and he's already called your supervisor. I understand you've had some disciplinary action out there. Several cases where you ordered testing, rather reckless. Scaring people."

"But the symptoms were there. I *had* to check."

"Bluetongue and HHK are not going to pop up in Iowa, Liz. And they were negative, right? You see what I'm saying. This doesn't look so good." He paused. "Ah. Well. Perhaps you need some personal time? To deal with your, ah, recent loss?"

Liz's arm dropped as she signed off, blue phone dangling from her fingertips, her jaw muscles working. A hand poked at her shoulder again. "Phone for you," said the barn manager. "Your boss. Seems like you were too busy for him, so I've been telling him about our experiences here with you. About your little attitude and so on." He smiled.

Liz put her cell phone in her pocket and reached for the landline phone on her desk. All four lines were blinking. The green phone started ringing, then the blue phone in her pocket.

"He asked me to put everything in writing," said the barn manager. He turned and started walking off. "Line four," he yelled back over his shoulder. "By the way, he'll be here in thirty minutes. With the Governor."

The Pacific sun had set and the moon was rising over the ocean outside the windows of Le Papillon. Mike Salt and his guest were enjoying their cigars and after-dinner drinks, and well they should: The terms for the White Oak financing of Euvaxx were inked on the Le Papillon linen napkin resting between them. Everything was there but signatures. The lawyers would paper the deal in the morning.

Mike's phone rang, and he glanced at the number. *What the hell?* He took a puff on his cigar and leaned toward Parker Roos. "Mind if I take this? One of my scientists, excited about some new breakthrough, no doubt."

"Go ahead," said the investor, pulling out his own phone. "I'll just check the markets. Commodities—a bad habit." He smiled.

Mike grinned and leaned back, away from Roos, and held the phone close to his ear. "Mike," said the caller. "Sorry to bother you."

"No problemo, Steve. We're just about done here." Mike raised his drink to his soon-to-be-investor, Parker Roos, and gave him a wink. Roos tipped his head and raised his snifter of cognac in salute, then went back to the data scrolling across his small screen.

"Ah, Mike," said the caller. "Our Plum Island guy called with bad news. It'll be announced any minute now."

"Oh, really?" Mike kept smiling and leaned back, draping his elbow over the back of the chair.

"It was a false alarm. The Iowa outbreak. It's over."

Mike kept smiling but he felt his testicles shrink and, at the same time, nausea. He pulled the phone tighter to his head. Roos was cupping his glass in his palm, swirling and warming the liquor, looking around the room, his phone back in his pocket.

"That's interesting. And?"

"I know, I know. You're sitting right there with him. I don't know how we'll handle this. What about the financing?"

Mike saw the value of his company dropping like a stone tumbling from the Torrey Pines Park cliff. His mind spun frantically. He made himself loosen his grip on the phone. He took, discreetly, a deep breath. Faintly, vaguely, he could see the sketch of an answer.

"Mike, Mike," said the voice on the phone. "What should I do? Should I call the..."

"Thanks, Steve-o. That's fantastic news. Keep me posted." Mike snapped the phone shut and put it back on the table. "Well," he said, taking a drink of his wine and smacking his lips, then rubbing his hands together. "Today's your lucky day, Roos."

"Oh?" The venture capitalist smiled and sipped his drink, leaning back in the soft leather chair.

"I just had some excellent news, and I want you to know I'm still going to stick with our deal." Mike leaned forward and patted the marked-up napkin with the flat of his hand.

"So? What's the news?"

"The outbreak: It was a false alarm."

Roos looked puzzled. "That's good?"

"Think about it, Roos. False or not, the outbreak put the fear of God into the government here. They're converts; they're ready to vaccinate. One problem: You can't very well sell vaccine if all the livestock are dead, can you?" Mike laughed and slapped his palm on the table. "Now we'll sell ten times as much!" *Damn, I'm good.* A trickle of sweat rolled down his back as he laughed.

The men toasted their good fortune and added a few more details to the napkin.

Later, back at home, Mike lowered himself into his steaming hot-tub. "Jaynie?" he yelled. "What's taking you? Get that bare ass out here. Your Big Daddy had a great day today."

CHAPTER 15

Tike tapped the return key on her laptop, her West Soo desk strewn with more than the usual assemblage of notes and marked-up interview transcripts. There: *Plik,* her story was sent. She let out a deep breath as she closed the lid of her laptop, then leaned back. She started tidying up while calling her editor to alert him. The latest story, in time for the late edition, was a composite of the briefings she had sent to the state media office on costs of the false alarm, and an outline—just a taste—of complications on the horizon.

The outbreak was over, but the fall-out was just beginning.

It had been a long night and morning in the West Soo offices, people going in and out, employees packing up and leaving for their homes, phones ringing, TV news on, reporters calling and driving in. Liz was at her desk nearby, making official calls confirming the false alarm. Tike closed her eyes and laid her head on the desk as she waited for her editor to pick up the phone.

She sat up when he answered. "I'm leaving here tonight," she said. "They want to get this place running again. I'll stop by Johnston, then be working from my office at the farm."

He paused. "We'll be in touch."

In touch? "I'll have more time for follow-up stories once I leave." She paused. "Effects on local people. The human side."

He sighed. "Let's just let it be. I can put some staff people on those stories."

Tike sat back in her chair. "Staff? But I was *here.*" She looked at the stack of interview tapes, ready to be transcribed. "I've been talking to *people,*" she said. "I know what's going on."

"Do you?"

"What? What do you mean?"

"I'm going to have Susan re-work the story you just filed. There's some concern about using your byline."

"What? Why?"

"You shouldn't have been put on-site there. You were in over your head." He spoke to someone on his end of the phone, then came back on the line. "Look, that's what happens when you're not properly trained as a journalist. We'll be in touch."

After he hung up Tike sat staring at the phone in her hand. Someone turned up the volume on the TV; a news headline behind a broadcaster read "$450 MILLION MISTAKE." Liz got up from her desk as a Department of Agriculture official commented on the tally of costs of the false alarm, the damage to consumer confidence and expected increases in insurance rates.

"Liz?" said Tike as the veterinarian marched past, silent. "How's it going? Liz, I had to do it. I'm not the only one who wrote up the cost side. It's my job." Liz left the room without a word or glance in Tike's direction. Tike watched her through the window, then slumped in her chair. Someone walking by bumped her desk, sending a stack of tapes sliding onto a pile of notes. She could hear trucks leaving, heading for the front gates. She sighed and leaned forward, reaching for a tape, then another. She started sorting them by topic. By book chapter topic. *Let's work on the book. There's got to be some angle here that I can use. That I can salvage. There we go. Think positive.*

The door slammed open and two men in suits came in, stomping their feet to get the snow off their shoes. They scanned the room, then one of them pointed at her and they came her way, taking off their gloves. A third man followed, carrying a nested stack of empty plastic cartons in his arms. The first two men stopped in front of her desk as she continued her sorting. "Tike Lexington?"

She nodded, now recognizing them. The attorney general. The state media chief.

"We're picking up our materials," said the media chief, gesturing to the assistant with the cartons, who put one carton on her desk and started putting her tapes and notes into it.

"*Your* materials?" Tike stood up. Her chair slammed back and hit the desk behind her. "We had an agreement."

The attorney general stepped forward. "It's void. The presumed outbreak was not legitimate, thus conditional exceptions to our standard agreements were rendered void. You have no further rights to access this material."

The assistant reached up and unsnapped the media pass from Tike's jacket and dropped it into his carton, then started to fill a second carton. He hit the eject button on her tape recorder and removed the tape.

"Wait a minute," she said. Liz had come into the room and stood with the few remaining West Soo staff, watching. The assistant reached for Tike's laptop computer. "Hold on," she said, blocking his hands. "You can't take that."

"Does it have a removable hard drive?" he said.

"No," she said.

He shrugged, then unplugged the laptop and pushed past her hands, gripping the computer. "We'll return it after it's been purged." He put the computer in the carton, then bent down to unplug the charger.

She reached past him for her laptop. The attorney general stepped forward. "No," he said. "You don't want to do that."

Tike's hands stopped, her fingertips on the warm lid of her laptop. She looked at Liz. Liz turned and walked out of the room. The others remained, watching. A light flashed as a visiting reporter took a photo. The assistant dumped the charger into the carton, bouncing it off her suspended hands, then leaned over and started opening the drawers on her desk.

Tike withdrew her hands and stepped back. She sat in her chair. She watched as the assistant finished, picked up the cartons, and carried them out the door.

The media chief leaned over her desk. "We'll be in touch. We've got some things to discuss. But later. You're not a high priority right now." He gestured to the A.G., and they headed down the hall where Liz had gone.

One by one, Tike closed her desk drawers. She picked up the empty cups and stale popcorn and crumpled napkins remaining on the desktop, then wiped it clean. The party was definitely over. It was time to go home.

It didn't take long for Tike to pack what little remained in her desk. As she packed, trying to recall how she was supposed to get her car back from storage in Johnston up to West Soo, she watched the visitors escort Liz to her desk. They let her pick up some notebooks, then moved en masse to the conference room; the door closed behind them. The chief state vet arrived a few minutes later and joined them. She caught a glance of Liz as he opened the door. She was sitting at the long conference table, her forehead leaning on one palm.

Tike's phone rang as she sealed up her last cardboard box. She hesitated when she saw U.P.'s number on the caller ID. *Screw the SEC,* she thought, and picked up.

"Tike," he said. "What's going on?"

She ran her hands over the empty desktop before her. "Not much, now. You got my message?" She winced. "Did you get hit bad?"

"Not too bad." He paused. "So what's with the lady vet? I heard clips of your Governor."

Tike blew out a short breath. "Pretty bad, wasn't it."

"And?" He waited. "Well? Did she set this whole thing up? She could've banked some serious coin from the right people."

Tike paused and looked over at the door of the conference room. She could hear muffled shouting. "I don't think so," she said. "It just doesn't fit."

"No?"

"No. She just doesn't have a motive, U.P. And the DeadSim trading stopped anyway, didn't it? I think we were all just wound up." She watched as the A.G. came out and got a cup of coffee, black, then went back in. His face was flushed and shiny.

"So what's your plan?" said U.P.

Tike sighed. "I don't know. Take a break. Go home." She leaned back in her chair to pluck an incoming fax off the machine beside her. She had her mouth open to ask U.P. another question when she froze. "Here we go, U.P. Here's tonight's top headline." She read from the press release in her hand:

CARELESS VET SLAUGHTERS THOUSANDS
"OOPS," SAYS LADY KILLER

It was from MATA. "So much for defense of the innocent," she said, reading through the text, yawning and rubbing her eyes.

"Tike," said U.P. "You there?"   ·

"Yep." She crumpled up the fax and threw it in the trash. *Not my problem anymore.*

"I'm going to go wrap things up here," he said. "Keep in touch, okay?"

After she hung up she sat for a minute, watching the conference room door. She got up, walked down to the break room and made two cups of tea. She came back and set one on her desk, then carried the other to the conference room and knocked on the door. The door opened and she stepped in past the media chief, his mouth open and face red, and put the tea on the table by Liz. Liz looked up, blinking, notebooks and papers spread over the tabletop, a tissue crushed in one tight fist, red blotches on her cheeks. Tike winked at her. "Thank you," mouthed Liz.

"What are you doing here?" said the A.G.

"Liz forgot her tea," said Tike, then smiled, shrugged her shoulders, and left, flipping him off as the door closed behind her. Tike carted her bags and boxes to her truck, which, it turned out, had been trailered up from Johnston, where everything had started. *Was it only a week ago?* She drank her tea between trips to her truck, loading up her bags and boxes, locking them into the utility cases bolted to the pick-up bed. The tea didn't make a dent in her fatigue, however. She was exhausted; neither Liz nor she had slept since the false alarm was reported the night before. Liz was still cloistered in the conference room when Tike came back in, her truck loaded and ready. The rest of the office area was nearly empty. Abandoned.

Tike found a dark office and laid down on the floor for a quick nap, using her coat as a pillow. *When I get up, I'll leave,* she told herself.

———————

Something pushed Tike's shoulder, waking her from her dreamless sleep on the West Soo floor, heavy duty carpet inches from her face. "Tike, wake up." It was Liz, holding out a phone. "Nick's on the phone. On my phone."

Tike pushed up onto her elbows and looked at Liz, then shook her head. She couldn't keep her eyes open. "Sorry. Tell him I'm busy," she said.

"He said he wants you to go to New York with him," said Liz, holding out the phone.

Tike laid her head back down on her coat. "Sorry to drag you into this," she said, talking into her coat-pillow. "Just tell him I can't talk. Won't."

Liz spoke into the line and disappeared as Tike fell back into the abyss. *Another half hour and I'll go.*

———————

CHAPTER 16

Clarissa Ivy's phone rang as she entered the downtown MATA office with her arms full of manila files, one gloved hand wrapped around a tall cappuccino from Capitol Hill o' Beans. She put down the drink and, from habit, glanced at the caller ID as she picked up the phone: blocked. She waved at a co-worker who walked past her door as she snugged the phone against her shoulder. "MATA headquarters."

"Hello, Clarissa. It's me."

She dropped into her chair, files still piled in her arms, her face starting to flush.

"I must apologize," said the caller. "I haven't been honest."

Clarissa's eyes narrowed. She shifted in her chair and let her armload of files slide onto her desk, then leaned back.

"I phoned your office and pretended I was an editor," he said, "and then I asked your secretary for the photo mentioned on your press release." The voice became warm and soft. "You're a very beautiful woman."

Clarissa blushed and smoothed her hair.

"Is that okay? I'm sorry," he said.

"Well...really. My photo?"

"Yes, it was lovely. You're so...elegant. Will you forgive me?"

"I never liked that picture," she said, shifting the pile of folders on her lap.

"I just wanted to see how you looked, since we've talked these few times. I didn't know you'd be so beautiful."

"Well...thank you."

"I've got another package for you. And, well, this time I have to rush, but maybe next time, we could meet?"

Clarissa bit at a fingernail. "I don't know. Maybe."

"Promise me."

"Well..."

He laughed. "That's good enough." He gave her some more information and, after the call, she put away her files and went home to start packing.

Three hours later, a courier delivered a package to her apartment. Clarissa put the contents in her bag and went down the hall to the elevator, which she rode to the parking garage.

Time for a little road trip.

———————

CHAPTER 17

When Tike finally woke, groggy and disoriented in the dark after a too-long nap, she staggered back down the quiet hall of West Soo to the main office area. It was early evening, but few lights were on. The office was deserted. She uncurled her coat, creased during her nap, and pulled it on as she walked. She dug out her phone as she walked and checked messages: Nick, again. Geoffrey-the-suit, from legal, from the paper. A lawyer from the state Attorney General's office. Pete Russell, hoping she was okay, asking her to call when she could. She sighed, put the phone away and went through the dark to her desk. Former desk. She could see the moon outside the office windows, shining over the empty feedlot.

As she crossed the room she saw Liz. She was asleep at her desk, head down on her notebook, phones off the hook. "Liz." Tike nudged her shoulder. "Liz."

Liz sat up, eyes still closed, hair standing up. "What? I'm here. Go ahead."

"Liz, I'm going."

Liz was silent, swaying slightly. Tike paused, then looked at Liz's empty tea mug. Tike spoke softly. "Would you like a cup of tea before I go?"

Eyes still closed, Liz nodded.

"Just lay your head down. I'll bring it over in a minute." As Liz laid back down on her desk Tike reached over and picked up the mug. She paused, then with her free hand stroked Liz's hair smooth. "Everything's going to be okay. We're survivors, remember? Nine lives. Meow."

Liz mumbled something; Tike couldn't tell what. She went to make tea.

———

Liz and Tike sipped their tea in the silent West Soo offices and talked. Liz needed to get away. Had to, in fact: she had been suspended. But she couldn't—wouldn't—resign now, not like this. She wouldn't let them push her out. Tike agreed. She also needed to step back. Her editors, other than Nick, were more than willing to comply. And Nick she wasn't going to think about. Ever again.

They sat at Liz's desk, feet up on open drawers, slumped in silence.

"I'm sorry about that last article," said Tike. "The statistics."

Liz sighed. "That's okay. You were doing your job."

"At least I was straight with the numbers. I didn't bias it against you, like someone else could've."

"I appreciate that." Liz gave a half-smile. "And you didn't include that cheesy photo."

"I'm all class."

Liz dug some crackers out of her desk and gave a handful to Tike. "You're on my side, aren't you." She spoke softly.

"Yes."

They listened to a lone truck going by on the highway. They watched the moon and sipped their tea, sitting in the headquarters of a feedlot with no cattle left to feed.

"Christmas is the day after tomorrow," said Liz.

Tike nodded. "I got a message from my mom and grandma today. They're staying longer, won't be back for two weeks. Now I don't have any Christmas plans. I thought I'd be here, anyway."

"Me too."

Tike sipped her tea. "Let's do something. Go somewhere."

Liz tilted her head and looked at her. "Go?"

"Sure, why not? Geographic therapy."

Liz leaned back and stretched her arms, yawning. "Away from here. Anywhere away from here."

Tike snapped her fingers. "Letterman. You had that note from the David Letterman Show guys."

"And another note today: Thanks anyway. Legal conflicts. Have a nice day." Liz shook her head. "Face it. We're dirt again."

Tike frowned. "Speak for yourself."

"Sorry. Bad hair day."

Tike laughed and flicked a broken cracker at her. "Well, let's go anyway. We can act like stupid tourists, look at the Christmas decorations, and go to the show, even if we're not on it."

"Serious?"

Tike nodded. "I can't get any work done for the next week anyway. No one answers their phones."

"We could catch a redeye from Sioux Falls," said Liz, looking at her watch. "Tonight."

"*If* we can get seats. Or a hotel."

"If we can, will you do it?"

Tike sat back in her chair, then shrugged. "Why not? We need to do something."

Liz worked the keyboard at her desk, checking on flights, while Tike worked at her own station, empty now except for a phone and old computer, looking for a Manhattan hotel room. Liz got them on standby for a flight they could catch if they left within an hour. Tike got them on a waiting list for cancellations at three hotels.

The women looked at each other and nodded. "I'll start the truck," said Tike, getting up and pulling her coat back on.

"All I have left is my desktop," said Liz, stuffing papers and files into a box. "Can you...?" She pointed at a small stack of duffel bags by the door.

"No problemo." Tike grabbed her luggage and headed for the door. "If we hustle, we can squeeze in a drink before our flight." Liz gave her a thumbs up as she worked.

Liz slept most of the two-hour drive to the airport. Tike stopped by her farm on the way and picked up mail, stealing a minute to check on the cats. They were snug in the barn. Nickel was off somewhere, probably hunting mice. The sky was clear and still as they approached Joe Foss Field in Sioux Falls and headed for long-term parking.

From the December 23
Royal (Iowa) Gazette:

Extra Auction Tomorrow A.M.

By Sue Behrenstorm
Gazette Staff

An extra Auction will be held tomorrow morning at 7 to 10 o'clock at the Royal Sale Barn to accommodate local demand.

Buyers and Sellers are asked to please follow the same Procedure as for the regular Tuesday Auctions. The regular Tuesday auction schedule will resume the Tuesday after Christmas.

CHAPTER 18

Clarissa Ivy stood stock-still under the Texas moon. Not forty feet away, some rough-edged shadows made their way from the scrub toward the feedlot where she stood, flashlight in one hand and two now-empty tubes in the other. Some of the shadows were easier to see. As they got closer, she saw they had tusks, and pointy ridges of stiff hair running down the backs of their necks.

Wild hogs. Razorbacks.

The hogs aggressively pushed through the cattle to the feed bunker, putting their forelegs right in the trough and grunting as they ate their fill. Clarissa held her breath as one stopped eating, sniffed the air and turned his head and small eyes toward her.

Just then a farm dog came tearing around the corner, barking and snarling. The razorbacks grabbed another mouthful of feed and trotted off, unworried.

They'll be back.

The dog took a quick look and snarl at Clarissa, then went after the wild intruders. Sounds of more dogs approached. Clarissa went straight to her car and slammed the door as she started the engine. As she drove out of the feedlot she put the two empty tubes behind the passenger seat in a sack with four other tubes, also empty. Then she checked the cooler on the floor: six full tubes, on ice, remained.

She closed the cooler and studied the map taped to its lid, her route and stops highlighted in yellow and red. *Such an organized man.* Clarissa gave a half smile and started to hum. She found her location, turned off the dome light, and pulled back onto the road, heading north.

———

Panko stood at his laboratory bench, lighting a bunsen burner in his quiet lab on Plum Island. He started sorting and marking a stack of petri dishes spiked with some microbe that would blossom into colorful polka dot patterns overnight in the incubator down the hall.

Roy stuck his head in the door. The hall behind him was empty and quiet, no one left but the cleaning man making his evening rounds. Roy stepped inside and let the door swing shut behind him as he pulled up a seat, rolling one of the tall stools to Panko's lab bench. He picked up a pencil from the benchtop and turned it between his fingers.

"Long day for you, Panko," said Roy. "I thought I was the only one left tonight."

"I spent my morning in the airports; now it is good to work. Besides, it is only breakfast time now at my mother's table in St. Petersburg."

"Perhaps she can send us some supper?"

Panko smiled as he finished one stack and moved to the next. Roy sat beside Panko and watched him work.

A man in gray cotton pants and shirt opened the door and wheeled in a trash barrel, nodding at Roy. He reached under the lab benches and pulled out bulging trash bags stuffed with used pipettes, gloves, tubes, and Kim-wipes. His hands, in tight stained latex gloves, tied each bag with a deft knot and threw it in the barrel, then put fresh bags under the lab benches. The man moved on to the next room down the deserted hall, leaving the door ajar behind him.

Panko sighed. "You are on your own, are you not, Roy? The scientists complain, the veterinarians sending samples complain. And the government complains, of course."

Roy squeezed the pencil, digging his fingernails into the wood. He used his thumbnail to make a series of deep indentations circling the pencil. A *noose*, he thought, making the gouges deeper.

"Yes, it's stupid," said Roy. "What do they think I am, a magician? How can I get the tests done and the salaries paid if I don't get the budgets I want? It's absurd." He stared at the dented pencil, then snapped it in half. He put the pieces in his pocket and picked up a fresh pencil. "At least in a private company you can raise more money. Work with your investors. They understand that it takes money to get results."

"You are too kind to your government, Roy," said Panko. "Do they realize how much they need you? They should support you."

Roy worked his way around the new pencil. "I can't allow another strike here on the island, Panko. It would be the end of me. I'd be canned in a heartbeat. And scientists just don't strike. They don't even join unions. The support staff, yes. Plumbers and janitors are the same every-where. But scientists? That would be like priests going on strike."

Panko shrugged. "So you do not support it. But imagine, if it hap-pened anyway, with your protest, during a critical time. Like during the so-called outbreak—but of course, a real one."

Roy's hands stilled. He stared at his pencil, his lips pursed, his eyes blinking. He shook his head. "That would be very interesting. But no way could I even whisper the thought to the research staff. It would end up killing me." He sighed and went back to torturing his pencil. "Some of the senior staff would like that, I'm sure."

Panko held a petri dish up to the lamp over his bench, looking at the colonies of microbes dotting its moist surface, translucent against the light. "Perhaps you'll be moving on anyway, Roy. Moving up." He turned and looked Roy in the eye. "I had another discussion with our friend Mike Salt today. He's very busy. He needs good colleagues, on his side. People who understand the importance of this work."

Roy was silent.

Panko picked up another dish. "People like you, Roy." The room was silent for a full minute. "It could perhaps be another scientist who spoke with the staff here," said Panko. "A visiting scientist, like me, perhaps. A strike that increased your budget would be the best thing you could do for this great research center. It could be your parting gift."

CHAPTER 19

The tiny crystal reindeer sparkled when Tike held it up against the dim light of the blue neon beer sign. She and Liz were perched on squeaky bar stools in a crowded haven on the west end of the Sioux Falls airport terminal. Liz reached for the figurine and set down her drink. "Hey, that's nice," she said. "A Christmas present?" She took a sip of her gin and tonic.

"It was in my mail, from the farm. It's from Nick."

"No kidding? I'm impressed."

It was Swarovski crystal—Tike's favorite. She had at least two dozen other Swarovski miniatures at home, most of them from Nick. She handed the figurine to Liz and picked up the padded envelope it came in. "No return address. A Manhattan postmark."

"Didn't you say he was just at a conference?"

"Yeah. But in Chicago. And it's not his signature." Tike showed Liz the little card.

"So some shop in Chicago was sold out, and they had their Manhattan branch ship it out."

Tike stared at the tiny card and shrugged. "I don't know." She sipped at her beer, then picked up the figurine and held it up to the light. "No, he wouldn't send this. He already gave me this one, three years ago."

"So he's being sentimental."

Tike put the tiny reindeer back on the table and took a deep breath. "He'd send any Swarovski but this. This is the one he threw at me six months ago. He was drunk. I had him arrested and threw him out." She pulled back her hair and showed Liz the thin scar, still red, high on her forehead. "From the reindeer. Five stitches."

"Ah."

"I just can't believe he would do this to me." Tike's eyes filled. She shut them, turning to the window to face the full moon pouring its pathetic reflection of sunlight over the snow-filled runway. "We should go to our gate," she said.

Fifteen minutes later, Liz and Tike were back at the same table in the Sioux Falls airport bar, sitting on the same stools, ordering the same drinks.

Chicago was iced in, flights were delayed across the board. Other stranded holiday travelers milled up and down the terminal. Liz and Tike finished their drinks and a small pizza before the announcement: the flight was canceled.

An hour later the women were checked into the Airport Holiday Inn and were starting over in the hotel bar. Tike was using a cocktail straw to drain the last drops of an oversized Kahlua on ice when the lean backside of a tall black-hatted cowboy walked by the table.

"Hey there, cowboy," said Tike, making little kissing sounds. "Where's your horse?"

Liz kicked her under the table as the cowboy paused and turned toward the women. "Shit," said Liz, under her breath, sitting up straight, then hopping to her feet. She kicked Tike again as the cowboy approached their table. "Good evening, sir."

"My horse?" said the man, garment bag in one hand and *Wall Street Journal* in the other, black Stetson on his head. It was Jack Billings, Governor of South Dakota. "He sure ain't flying tonight, ladies. Neither is my Cessna CJ3."

He greeted Tike, then looked closer at Liz. "Dr. Thomas," he said, his voice softer. Liz flinched. He shoved his newspaper under his other arm and gripped her shoulder. "It's been a while. Too long, Lizzie."

Tike looked from one to the other. *Lizzie?*

Liz's face was tight. "Since the funeral," she said.

Oh hell. Tike waved away the approaching waitress.

"I miss Joseph," he said, hunching over to put his face closer to hers. "That was one no-bullshit man." He turned to Tike, still holding Liz's shoulder. "Joe's daddy was right across the river from me. Used to steal my cattle, dye 'em pink, and put them in my front yard in the dead of night. Said he was teaching me about politics. Crazy as a loon."

He turned back to Liz. "But Joseph turned out fine. Sure could use his help now." He cocked his head and looked at her. "Couldn't we?"

Liz was silent as she dropped back into her chair. Tike gestured at the chair next to Liz, waving the Governor to be seated. He dropped his bag on the floor and set his black hat on an empty chair nearby.

"Saw you on the TV, Lizzie. You're a tough lady," he said, turning his chair to face hers. "Wilton needs his ass kicked like that more often."

Tike sat back and sipped her drink, trying to not make any noise.

Billings flagged the bartender. "Bourbon, Deke. Thanks."

He reached over and cupped Liz's chin in his calloused hand, turning it toward him. "Look at me, girl. Tell me what the hell went on," he said. "This crap is coming for real some day. You and I both know that. Tell me everything. Let's get something out of this."

Liz gave a half-smile. "Hell, Jack. I just did my duty. My sworn duty. Just trying to do my best." She bit her lip and took a deep breath, then let it out. "Wilton is an idiot, isn't he?"

Jack leaned back and smiled at her. "Yes he is, he surely is."

Liz talked and Jack listened. Tike threw in a few tidbits as well, but mostly she sat and watched. After another Kahlua Tike left to finish going through her mail and repack before their 7:36 a.m. flight. Liz and Jack stayed at the bar. As Tike walked away she glanced back and watched them: talking, scribbling on napkins, laughing. Watching each other.

Airport? What airport? Tike punched the button for the elevator, smiling a moment for them, staring a moment at herself in the mirrored border of the elevator frame. Behind her, next to a black hat in the dim bar of Deke's Run-a-Way Holiday Lounge on the bitter winter plains of South Dakota, a new world emerged and an alien sun began to shine. But it wasn't her world.

––––––––––

When Tike got back to her room she smoothed out the bedcovers, dumped the crate of mail in the center, and did her sort. She made tidy piles around the periphery of the bed: pay-me, toss-me, handle-now, file-me, read-me. When everything was done, she started working through the handle-now pile.

She started with the thin envelope with a return address starting with "SEC." *Bob. Bobby G, Bobby Gotcha,* she thought, humming, slicing the envelope open with a knife from the mini-bar. *Right: Bob Gasparowicz.* SEC, Fraud Division, Investigator. "What's a nice looking man like you doing working for the SEC," she had said into his microphone during one deposition.

"...hope you appreciated the significance of my call on behalf of the SEC and CFTC, Ms. Lexington," read his letter. His sense of humor was still missing. "You seem unaffected by current..."

Tike crumpled up the letter and threw it at the tiny hotel trash can, already overflowing with toss-me. *Yes, Bob, do call and mess with my head again.*

She moved on to the runner-up. This one was from "#1005-12991, FCF, Lompoc, Calif., 93436-2705." She got the envelope half-opened, then hesitated, feeling something sag inside her. Lompoc Federal. The Federal Correctional Facility in scenic Lompoc. *This can wait. I'll read this last.*

Tike went through the rest of the mail, wrote a few checks to pay some bills, and set aside the read-me stack for the plane ride, including the package with Plum Island literature sent by the Old Saybrook M.E. When everything was as done as she could get it, she bundled up each surviving stack, stashing them either in her luggage or in a pile she would lock in her truck to take home later. She turned out most of the lights, leaving the dim hall light on for Liz, and a small lamp by the bed for reading, then crawled under the cold sheets with her letter from Lompoc.

My Dear Tike, she read. *How are you, my dear? Thank you so much for your last letter. It helped.*

She could already feel the cracks forming, the walls crumbling.

I have a new cellmate. He's also a Berkeley grad. We know some of the same people.

Tike let the letter drop to her lap and pressed her fingertips against her eyelids, letting the tears come. *If Bob Gasparowicz could see us now. Bastard.*

In the dark of the morning, Liz and Tike were back in their seats at Gate 4, ready to blast off from Sioux Falls at 7:36 a.m. Liz fell asleep in her chair while Tike tried to read the newspaper.

She was interrupted by a call, and recognized the number. It was her new friend, the medical examiner of Old Saybrook.

"Tike here."

"Hi Tike, Old Saybrook M.E. again." He said he figured it was a prank when he recognized her number on his pager, but thought he should check anyway. "Never know who's got an interesting corpse for me. By the way, I read about you in the paper," he said. "'Reporter at Outbreak Ground Zero'—saw your picture, too. Sorry how it turned out. My friends want your autograph anyway."

"Those would be some current patients, I assume," she said.

He invited her to stop in for a tour of the morgue if she was in the city sometime. "Can't smell worse than cow pies," he said. "And it's more fun than a singles bar."

She told him thanks and said, in fact, she hoped to be there very soon. As she spoke she walked over and checked their flight status on the departure board. "Not that soon, I guess," she said. The flight was delayed an hour. "We might be there today. Or tomorrow. We might be spending Christmas Eve in an airport."

He said he'd be around, and she said she'd call before they stopped by. "Oh, thanks for the package," she said. "Hello? Hello?" *Dead battery.* Tike shut off her phone and went to dig her charger out of her luggage. It was going to be a long day.

———

CHAPTER 20

The scissors snipped and small sheaves of Geneva's red hair fell to a glossy drop-cloth labeled "Mr. David and Friends" on the kitchen floor of U.P.'s condo. Geneva was perched on a kitchen stool centered on the drop-cloth, eyes shut, hands clenched as Mr. David clipped and tugged. U.P. was at the kitchen table reading the *Wall Street Journal*.

"Ouch!" said Geneva. "Take it easy."

"Oh, sorry, madame," said Mr. David. "But please hold still."

"U.P.—this is stupid."

"Geneva," said U.P., turning a page of the paper. "This is no time to neglect good grooming. Panic is emotion. We have no emotions, not now. Life goes on. We are in control of our destinies. So hold still." He groaned. "Oh, yes, right there."

A masseuse stood behind U.P.'s breakfast table chair, working on his left shoulder. He looked over his reading glasses at Geneva.

"Looks good, Geneva," he said. "I'm telling you, this suits you. Might catch you a man yet. Don't you think so, Mr. David?"

"Absolutely, Mr. U.P. She has fabulous cheekbones. And delicious color. Who does your color, darling? To die for."

"We're kicking ass, Gennie," said U.P. "You got us turned around just in time."

Her head was pinned between Mr. David's elegant hands as he turned her left and right to study her profile. Between turns she winked at U.P. in the mirror.

U.P.'s heart accelerated. He fingered the worn box in his pocket. Nine carats, blue fancy, flawless. Faded Christmas wrapping. *It could never be enough.*

Maybe this year he would finally give it to her.

Nick dropped into a chair by his departure gate in the Des Moines airport and played the cell phone message again, setting his coffee and pastry on the chair beside him.

"I don't know if this was a joke, but I got the Swarovski reindeer in the mail, and I don't think that's very nice." It was Tike's voice. He could hear her take a deep breath, heard airport sounds behind her. "Especially now. You know things are tough for me now. And there's other stuff going on. I think that was really a mean trick. I'd like you to leave me alone. It's just too much."

She was silent a few seconds, which he knew meant she was crying, then went on, rushing. "You know I don't have the no-contact order anymore. I didn't renew it after I thought you were really trying, and my counselor thought so too, but I'm going to document this and if there's one more incident I'm going to the county attorney and file for another one."

And she hung up.

Nick dropped the phone in his lap and buried his face in his hands. *Dear Lord. The wounds we leave behind.* He eyed the face and hands of each person approaching the gate beside him. Each handed their boarding passes to the attendant, hefted their bags, and disappeared down the jetway.

After a few moments Nick took a deep breath and dialed her number. He got voicemail, wondered if she was holding the phone in her hand, watching his number be sent to purgatory.

"Tike, sweetheart, I didn't send it," he said into his small phone. "I wouldn't. I couldn't. I still have nightmares about that night. About the look in your eyes. The blood." Nick closed his eyes. "That's the last thing I want you thinking about now. I want us to move away, start over." He paused as a loudspeaker boomed over his head: *Flight 372 to New York, last call to board at Gate 13.*

"Tike, please call me," he said, picking up his bags and moving toward the gate. "I'm going to New York. Liz told me you're going with her. Please let me see you. And Tike, there's something I need to tell you about." He hesitated. "It's about the crystal deer. There's something going on now. I need to talk to you about it."

Nick handed his boarding pass and ID to the attendant and put away his phone as he walked down the jetway; the attendant closed and locked the door behind him.

The wires, as they said in the old days, were humming.

One hundred thousand shares of Marson Chicken, sold, long. After a brief pause, another transaction: 20,000 shares of Hespel Swine LLC, sold, short. Another pause. Ten thousand shares of Lonnerman Trucking, sold.

Fifty thousand shares of Minnesota Beef Packers, Inc., sold.

Ten thousand contracts, March corn, short.

Five thousand contracts, January boxed beef, long.

Pause. Pause. Pause.

Sold. Sold. Sold.

CHAPTER 21

Tike and Liz finally got to New York by early afternoon. They checked into their hotel, worn and crabby, but thankful to have a room. They headed out on foot to be consumed by the city, shoving their way through mobs of shoppers and regular New York crazy people. They went from window to window, looking at the Christmas displays without comment. People with fur-lined coats and armloads of wrapped packages pushed past them.

Tike was nearly ready to turn her friend around and go back, overwhelmed by the noise and signs of excess flowing around them, when she spotted a familiar door. Her stomach clenched. A limo had just pulled up and two couples, the women in ankle-length furs, were stepping out onto the carpet under the awning leading to the door. She pointed them out to Liz.

"I went in there."

"You did? When?" she said, looking at Tike sideways.

"Some meetings," she said. "A while back. Before."

"What kind of meeting?"

"Business. Investors." She paused, then turned her face away from Liz. "I stayed at the Waldorf on that trip."

Liz looked at her closely, then smiled and tucked her arm in Tike's. "Let's get coffee, over there." She pointed. "And you can tell me about the Waldorf. Do they really put chocolate-dipped strawberries in your room at night? What kind of chocolate? Is it good?"

Liz dragged Tike back into the world. They dragged each other.

As the women stood with the crowd in the lobby of the Ed Sullivan theater, waiting to get to their seats for the 5 p.m. taping of the David

Letterman Show, Tike's phone rang. She looked at the small screen: U.P. She gestured to Liz and answered the call.

"I've been talking with Geneva," he said, with no other introduction. "We don't think it's over."

"Pardon?"

"We think something's still going on. The DeadSim trading started again."

"What? No."

"Yeah. It started two days ago. *Before* the false alarm report, not after. We just noticed now. Geneva's going over the trading history now. And something else."

She waited.

"The Plan B trades," he said. "They started. They spiked this morning when the markets finally opened."

"Plan B? The hands-on trades?"

"Yeah. He, she—whatever—he's trading like he's expecting some action. And Gen looked again at the Plan A trades. We wondered why it wasn't all of the possible trades from our DeadSim package. She figured out it was the ones that would really ramp up after a false alarm."

Tike looked around at the crowd. It was starting to move. "Son of a gun," she said. "So the false alarm is part of the plan."

"Looks like it. Tike, we want you to keep snooping. We're going to keep trading in parallel with this guy, but something's cooking."

"It's not like I won't have time now." She hesitated, then turned her back to Liz and spoke, cupping the phone with her hand. "I'm still getting those morgue calls, U.P."

"Have you talked to the police?"

"Like that helps. Nothing they can do."

"And?"

"And nothing. There's nothing to go on, anyway." Tike made a scoffing sound. "Whatever. I get calls once in a while from people who read my stuff. My contact info is all over the place. I don't know why I even told you." Liz tugged at her shoulder. Tike turned and followed her. There was a sign on the doorway ahead of them: *All Cell Phones OFF.*

"So you think it's like, a reader?" said U.P. "Just someone you pissed off with a story?"

"No. Maybe. But it's weird. And if the DeadSim activity is going on again, I'm paying more attention to the calls. Look, U.P., I'll check around, keep you posted."

"Okay, good. Money?"

"More would be good."

"I'll make a deposit," he said.

After she hung up, she shut down the phone and poked Liz in the ribs as they entered the theater. They could see David Letterman's empty desk on the stage down below. The band was warming up.

Was someone behind the outbreak—the false alarm—after all? Tike handed her ticket stub to an usher as they reached their row. *Am I still being set up?*

For what?

————————

During a break in the show Tike went to a quiet corner of the lobby and made a phone call.

"I want to schedule a phone appointment with inmate 1005-12991, please," she said, her back to people walking by. "Tike Lexington. I'm on the green list." She waited while they looked up the records, then worked out the details.

When they were done she went back to her seat, just as David Letterman was greeting the last guest.

————————

After the show, Tike and Liz walked around looking at Fifth Avenue window displays, now all lit up, while they waited for their dinner reservation. Tike's phone rang. Area code 805: *Lompoc Federal*. She signaled to Liz and tucked in against a wall to answer while Liz got them some coffees from a cart.

"I know you weren't calling to wish me a Merry Christmas," said a voice on the line.

"Well, happy Hanukkah, anyway," she said, then paused. "How's the dialysis going?"

"Not good. But I got on the transplant list."

"I'm so sorry."

"Not as sorry as I am every day."

Neither of them spoke for a long moment. He cleared his throat. "My mom visited last month. Her first time."

"Dear God. After all these years, she comes? I just can't see Leah there..."

"Yeah. She won't be back," he said.

"Five more years still?"

"It was too much for her. She shouldn't have come."

Silence again.

"Whatever," he said, clearing his throat. "I've got time on my hands. Got something for me to do? I figured that's why you called."

"Yes, I need your help. Something's happening." She gave him a quick recap: The morgues, the cities, the crystal deer, the Manhattan John Doe with the reindeer wrapping paper note, the false alarm, now DeadSim again. Too much strangeness. Too too much.

"I'll ask around," he said. "In my own humble way."

Tike laughed. "Humble my ass. You're more plugged in now than you ever were, you bastard."

"Thank you, my dear. I love you too."

As she put the phone back in her pocket she reached for the coffee from Liz. Tike's hands were shaking. Liz pulled the coffee out of her reach and looked at her friend, eyebrows raised.

"Okay," Tike said, sighing. "Got time for a story?"

Tike and Liz had a traditional Manhattan Christmas Eve dinner of benghan bhartha and garlic naan. By the time they got to the gulub jamun and fennel, Liz had listened to Tike's stories about former loves, about betrayals and despair. An old love in Lompoc, less-old love for Nick, scars, morgue calls—it was all tangled and confusing.

By the time their cab deposited them at the hotel, the tangle had loosened. *Okay, I can manage,* thought Tike. *It's not so bad.* As they entered the hotel lobby and headed for the elevators, a man stood up from a couch near the doors and approached.

"Tiburnia Lexington? Elizabeth Thomas?"

Tike was laughing at a joke Liz was telling. "Yes," said Tike, turning to him as she untied the scarf at her throat. Liz had bought it for her as a Christmas present, a soft red cashmere.

The man thrust a packet of papers in Tike's hands, then Liz's. "These are for you. Happy holidays." He turned around and walked off.

"Damn," said Tike. "Shit." She stamped her foot and shook her head, clenching her teeth. "Got me."

"What is it?" said Liz, trying to unfold her bundle.

"I wondered if this would happen," said Tike, scanning the top page of her packet. "Yep." She turned to Liz. "We've been sued. Class action against you, me, and the State of Iowa. The cattlemen want our heads. Pork producers do, too."

"But...but...," said Liz, reading through the cover pages. "But I was working for the state. I was doing my job."

"Not if the state says you weren't. They'll sure try, anyway. Liability could shift to you. To us. Let's guess who told the cattlemen to add our names to the suit—our friend the Attorney General? Here comes a shit storm." She stuffed the papers in her coat pocket. "Liz, no offense, but did you tell someone where we were staying?"

Liz looked at her with a start. "Well, I had to leave word with my office. A condition of my suspension." She winced. "Sorry."

"That's okay. Just checking." Tike unzipped her jacket as Liz bent over the legal papers, her forehead furrowed. "Hey, come on. Let's go order room service ice cream," said Tike. "I'll tell you what I know about this kind of thing."

Liz looked at her and shook her head. "I'm being sued? *Sued!*" She folded the papers in half and twisted them in her hands as they started to walk again.

"We'll manage," said Tike as they stepped into the elevator. "We'll manage."

CHAPTER 22

Nick sat low in his seat, cap on, collar up. He was seventeen rows behind Tike and Liz, near the back of the Ed Sullivan theater.

Near the end of the show, Nick's phone vibrated. He checked the incoming number on the small screen, then stepped out to the lobby. "Nick Capelli here." He pulled a small notebook from his pocket and started making notes. "Weapons?...Uh-huh...History of that?...Okay. No, I don't think so. Any dead?"

A stagehand walking past paused and raised an eyebrow at Nick. Nick put his hand over the phone. "Reporter," he whispered, then went back to his call and watched as the young man entered the studio.

After a few more questions Nick closed his notebook and put it back in his pocket. "A few more days," he said into the phone. "She hasn't spotted me."

He went back into the studio just as Letterman came back from a commercial break, bringing in a new guest, a nervous-looking blond man with tortoise-shell glasses. Nick looked at Tike's seat: empty. *Wait—there she comes.* After she returned to her seat he went back to the lobby and out on the street. He checked his watch.

No need to hurry. The ladies had a dinner reservation down the street at the Star of India in an hour. Nick went across the street to a pizzeria and ordered a deep-dish pie with the works.

———·———

An average-looking man in an average suit sat in the center of the back row of the Ed Sullivan Theater. To his left he could see Nick, slouched down in his seat. Ahead and to his right, he could see Tike and Liz. The man watched Nick go to the lobby, phone in hand, then return. He watched Tike go to the lobby, then return. Liz stayed in her seat.

The man left twenty minutes before the show ended and went to a bar nearby, one with windows overlooking the street. He gave the maitre d' enough to get a table by the window, then ordered a club soda and paid in cash. He gave the waitress an average tip.

The man checked his watch. Three a.m. Not in New York; his Tag-Heuer was still set on Helsinki time. He never changed it, no matter where he was. It was simpler that way. By now it was a reflex to convert to local time zones. Currencies, too.

He slid a small notebook from his breast pocket and sketched the street before him, his pen warm and light in his hand, stretching his stiff knee as he sketched. He watched Nick come out the front door, alone, and go to an Italian restaurant across the street. Later, a crowd came out of the theater, all of the doors opening at once. Tike and Liz emerged and walked up the street, the crowd flowing past, around them. As the women approached he sketched them. Tike speaking. Liz leaning close, listening. They went by, arm in arm, not two feet away from his window perch.

He closed his book, slipped it into his jacket, finished his club soda, visited the restroom, and left. There was enough time to do some shopping before dinner.

He had reservations just down the street, at the Star of India.

———————

CHAPTER 23

Clarissa licked the few remaining crumbs of tea cake from her fingertips and set the empty plate on her coffee table. Christmas music played softly on the stereo, and the muted TV was tuned to the Christmas service at Capitol City Lutheran, just down the street. She tucked her chenille blanket around her legs, her pink terry slippers peeping out; a stack of MATA documents, including the draft of a new press release, sat on the couch beside her.

"I can't thank you enough," she said into the cell phone in her free hand. "I've been nibbling on it all day." She glanced over at the kitchen counter, where the half-empty cake tin sat open, next to a colorful gift basket still strewn with fruits and ribbons. "I'm going to a party later, but you really made it feel like Christmas this morning."

"I made it myself," said the caller. "My mother's secret recipe. It's organic rhubarb I stole from the neighbors this summer." He laughed. "It freezes well. But I'm sure you know that. I bet you're a great cook."

Clarissa blushed. "I do alright," she said. "But this was so moist."

"Tender," he said, his voice soft. "Like you."

Clarissa shivered and smiled. "Oh, you. You..."

His voice got softer. "My mother would have liked you. She died last year."

"Oh, I'm so sorry."

"She made this cake every year. She taught me how to make it when I was little, and we'd make a big batch together every Christmas when I was home from boarding school."

She heard him sniff. "I'm so sorry," she said softly.

"Well. Enough about me," he said, blowing out his breath. "I'm glad to hear you're going to a party."

Clarissa carried the phone to the kitchen and cut another square of cake. "You must be from the South," Clarissa said, trying to imagine his face.

"Oh, you're too kind. I've tried and tried, but I can't get that fine Northern accent like you have. It sounds so much more educated, more...intelligent. I wish I had been raised in the North, like you."

"You don't think I have an accent?" Clarissa settled back on the couch, putting her new plate of cake on the coffee table.

"Your diction is perfect. Like a national news anchor."

Clarissa laughed. "You don't know how close you are," she said. "I spent years working on my voice once I moved here, to D.C. Even back home—in Gunnyville, Arkansas, by the way—I sat for hours in front of the TV news, repeating everything they said. My family thought I was crazy."

"Arkansas? You're kidding. I'd have never guessed. And you're not going to believe it: I have family in Heberton, just across the state line."

"No kidding." She paused. "And your family? Children?"

"No, I'm not married, unfortunately," he said.

They were both silent for a moment.

"Anyway," said Clarissa, "you were asking about groups like MATA around the world. Yes, they're definitely out there. I've visited a few of them."

"Oh—do you like to travel?"

"Love it."

"I travel a lot for my work. I suppose it could be nice. But not traveling alone all the time like I do."

Clarissa described some of the groups she knew, and told stories about some of the friends she had made there. In a quiet voice he asked if they might be interested in meeting him.

"Perhaps," said Clarissa.

Then perhaps, he said, they could go together. They could travel to visit her friends.

"That could be nice," she said.

"I'll be on the road for a few days yet," he said, "but when I get back can we talk again? Perhaps dine?"

"That would be lovely," she said, in her softest Southern voice.

Heather Turnbull was sitting at her sterile work hood in the third floor diagnostics lab at Plum Island, gloved up, face against a glass panel that kept contaminating germs out of the samples before her, and other germs in. The microbes she handled, today and every day, were the reason for Plum Island's existence.

"He told me he's got kids," said Heather.

"And what did you say?" Yolanda Weathers, next to her, was sitting in the same position, facing the glass, hands working inside the sterile area before her. She was using a hand-held dispenser to pour a small dose of sangria-colored liquid into each flask, then tightening the cap and laying the flask on its side. The liquid spread out, just covering the flask wall, where the test cells would live or die, depending on the test.

"Well, I said okay. But they live with his ex, back home, he said. He's really sweet, Yolanda. We get along great. We go into Manhattan and just walk, or get a cappuccino, and look at people. And such eyes. Oh." She shook her head.

"So tell me his name," said Yolanda.

"Can't do it."

"Come on."

Heather smiled. "Maybe later. You'll understand."

In addition to gloves, Yolanda and Heather were wearing Tyvek coveralls, shoes covered with blue paper booties, surgical masks, and hairnets. In full BSL-3 gear, they were indistinguishable.

Yolanda and Heather were the only people on the floor this soon after Christmas. Their high rank let them claim the coveted holiday slot: Triple overtime. They were skilled technicians; they had to be. *You had to be the best to work On The Island*, the joke ran. *Everyone else disappeared.*

The women finished setting up the tests and took them out of the sterile work stations. They carried stacks of the small plastic flasks into the next room, where they put them into one of the numbered cabinets lining the next room. The cabinets were incubators that would keep the flasks warm and moist overnight. Any viruses in the flasks would grow like weeds and annihilate the cells Yolanda and Heather had put into the flasks as bait.

Yolanda and Heather kept chatting about Heather's new boyfriend as they cleaned up, recording their work carefully in notebooks, in pen, along with the incubator numbers, current temperatures, time, flask numbers, sample number and sample origin. That was their back-up when something like the Iowa false alarm occurred. They did their job, and had the notebooks to prove it. It wasn't their fault when someone else screwed up and sent them sloppy samples.

There were so many tests to run this week, more than usual. This happened every time there was a disease scare. All would be negative, almost always. But still, people checked. That's what kept the Plum Island lab busy.

Paranoia paid the bills.

Finally, the last notes recorded on the day's work, Yolanda and Heather signed their notebooks, entered some of the data on their computers, where it would be registered in the Plum Island spur of the Homeland Security network, and logged out. They went through the first air lock, yanked off their booties, stripped off their Tyvek suits and threw them in the bin to be autoclaved, threw their underclothes in other bins to be sanitized, and stepped into the first of two showers they would take. With fresh clothes, they would be decontaminated enough to leave the building. The women talked the whole time.

Plum Island was silent as the last ferry cast off at the end of the day, Heather and Yolanda on board. The staff was always glad to leave, to see normal people, normal animals, normal life again.

This night, one person stayed behind. No one noticed; he could have been on either of the last ferries, after all.

Early the next morning, several hours before the first ferry was due to arrive, a pair of gloved hands flipped through the previous day's entries upstairs in Yolanda's notebook. A gloved finger ran down a column of sample numbers, and over to the column showing the corresponding incubator number. The notebook was closed, then opened again, a small figure penciled in the margin before closing it again and carefully putting it back on Yolanda's shelf.

Bootie-covered feet went next door to the room with the heated cabinets. One was opened and a stack of flasks carried to a nearby microscope. One by one, the flasks were slipped onto the microscope stage, and quickly scanned. A pair of unblinking eyes, framed by a surgical mask and a paper cap, gazed expertly at each flask, one after the other. Nothing. Nothing. Nothing.

Then: Zing. The eyes blinked.

The flasks were stacked and returned to the warm cabinet, just as they were. The incubator door was closed.

Well, almost. Perhaps it was left open just a crack.

The eyes watched the digital readout at the top of the cabinet, again without blinking. The temperature dropped, oh so slightly, and dropped again. The CO_2 levels, indicating the proper oxygen-to-carbon-dioxide ratio needed to keep the experiments percolating properly, also dropped as the heavy CO_2 poured out invisibly onto the floor. Oh so slightly it dropped. And again. The man reached behind the incubator and popped out a fuse embedded in the CO_2 sensor. He watched as the CO_2 levels dropped lower. The sensor alarm did not sound.

The bootie-covered feet turned and went out the door, to the airlock, to the showers, through the next airlock, through the next showers, and out, in street clothes once again, and to the old staircase leading to the sub-basement.

There were a few more chores to do. It was time to check on the emergency power system.

———————

CHAPTER 24

Yolanda hummed under her breath as she turned on the lamp over her desk, the Atlantic sun not yet bright through the Plum Island windows. She pulled her laboratory notebook from the shelf and flipped through it. She found the list of assays set up the day before, and pulled out the forms she would use to record the results of each. When she was ready, she went down the hall to the tissue culture room, heading for the incubators she had filled sixteen hours before.

She reached for the thick insulated door of the incubator, then her hand stopped, an inch away. The door was ajar. She tilted her head, then swung the door open. The thin glass door inside, normally sealed tight, was unlatched and swung loose.

Yolanda looked around the room as she reached for the door. "Heather? Heather? Come here." She opened the glass door and looked inside. "Shit."

Heather entered the room, her notebook in her hand. "What?" She walked over and stood beside Yolanda, looking at the stacks of flasks inside. "Shit."

The liquid in the stacks of flasks, which should have been blood red, like sangria, was instead neon pink.

"We're in trouble."

"Damn. We're going to have to do them all over."

"Have you been in already, Heather?"

"Me? No, I just came up. I stopped in the library before I showered in. Why?"

"The incubator door was open."

"The door was open?"

"The door. It was open."

"Shit. Everything'll be dead."

"Yes, shit."

Yolanda and Heather stood side by side, staring at the door. Heather grasped the door handle and opened and closed it, checking the latch. "I know I closed it last night," she said, then paused. "Why didn't the alarm go?" They both stood, staring at the panel of numbers on top of the unit.

"Are you going to tell the big man?" said Yolanda.

"Why, don't you want to?"

"We have to. We don't have enough of some of the samples to repeat the test. We'll have to request more."

"Shit," said Heather.

"Yes."

"Okay, let's do it together. If we do it soon, we can get the dupe samples in the air today, and have them tomorrow."

"Okay. Let's go. You first."

"No, you first."

They walked to the director's office to confess their sins.

———

Geneva was working at her old wooden desk in the small locked room at U.P.'s condo, insulated from the sounds of downtown Chicago, when her phone rang.

"I've got something for you," said a voice. It was one of the persons Geneva called upon occasionally for services. She had never met him in person, but he had a talent for finding things. Things and people. Geneva closed the file she had been reading and checked to be sure the in-line tape recorder was rolling.

"It's about land," he said. "I was checking the list of names you sent and found some interesting transactions: land sales, a whole series of them." Land ripe for development—if only the smelly farms upwind would go away. He explained the details he had tracked down so far and said he'd be sending her copies.

In the notes she wrote as he spoke, she circled the name "Serval Corp." with red ink. At the end of the call, Geneva said thanks and made another note, this time in her Rolodex. She'd mail his check in the morning.

Geneva pushed back from the desk and left the small room, locking it behind her as she went into the living room overlooking the financial district. U.P. was sitting in front of the fireplace reading newspapers, taking them from a stack on his left and throwing each section into the fire when he finished it. Geneva sat on the ottoman, next to his stockinged feet.

"U.P.? There are some things I want to tell you about." He put down his paper and looked at her. "I'd like your opinion," she said.

———

CHAPTER 25

Two days after the incident with the open incubator door, seven replacement samples arrived in the FedEx pouch on the second ferry to Plum Island. Yolanda and Heather, who could look out their office window and see the ferry as it chugged its way from Long Island, were waiting at the door to their lab when the package finally made its way through the airlocks. The other samples were almost ready to go.

Yolanda and Heather split up the new arrivals and sat at their desks to record them. Yolanda flipped back to the earlier entries to confirm the numbers of the replacement samples. She ran her finger down the column, then paused and smiled.

"Why, you rascal," she said, lifting her head. "Such an artist... Heather?" Yolanda raised herself enough to see over the partition and see that Heather's chair was empty. She shrugged and finished entering the information, then called the shipping department to check on an order of antibiotics that was supposed to be on the same ferry. While she waited, on hold, she outlined the little animal sketched in the margin, a reindeer, and drew some Christmas trees around it. Heather was already down there, they told her, picking up the antibiotics.

By the time Heather came back, antibiotics in hand, Yolanda was busy processing their samples. Within minutes, they finished centrifuging and filtering the samples before making serial dilutions, then squirted the diluted samples into the labeled flasks and carried them to the incubators. Again. This time, they checked the incubator doors. Twice. Each.

Time to shower out.

Clarissa sat on the couch of her apartment in Washington, D.C., slippers on, weeping and dabbing her eyes.

"Here's looking at you, kid," said the familiar voice from the TV. Clarissa sobbed as Humphrey Bogart turned his back and walked away from the plane, over the tarmac, away from the woman he should be with, stay with. *He should turn around and run to her,* she thought, giving a deep sigh and reaching for the remote control. As she muted the set for the commercials, she checked the TV guide and smiled: *The African Queen* was on in fifteen minutes.

Just enough time for a treat, she thought, getting up and walking to the kitchen, dabbing her eyes. She pulled the remains of her foil-covered Christmas tea cake from the freezer and carved a frozen piece out onto a plate. While it warmed in the microwave, she dug a can of whipped cream from the back of the refrigerator and shook it.

Plopping back on the couch, she licked crumbs from her fingers and picked up the draft of her talk for the New Year's Day/New World rally while she waited for the film to start. She sighed. *It's good for the group. Get out there after the talk and shake some hands. Good one-on-one face time.*

She smiled and took a bite of cake. *Who knows, maybe* he *will be there.*

CHAPTER 26

Five days into their New York week, Tike and Liz were about done in. The city was a good diversion, but it was time for some quiet.

In the afternoon, while Tike read and Liz napped before their dinner out, Tike got a call from area code 805. Lompoc. *12991. My dear.* Tike took the phone into the bathroom and shut the door quietly behind her.

"What day of Hanukkah is it?" she said softly into the phone, stretching out in the empty tub.

"Oh, it's all over, alas," he said. "Thank you for the presents."

"It's hard to know what to give the guy who can't have anything."

"Hey, books are great."

"Signed, too. And not just by me."

"Saw that," he said. "Thanks."

They were silent for a moment.

"I've got some information for you," he said. "Not good stuff."

She closed her eyes. "Shoot."

"It's your reindeer guy," he said.

"Reindeer guy?"

"Whoever sent the Swarovski reindeer," he said. "Who might be your morgue guy. Pretty odd coincidence if it's not the same guy."

"Yeah. I was thinking that."

"I'll send the crystal one back to you by the way. Nothing's safe here. Have you gotten anything else with reindeer? Letters, photos? Other than the one on the wrapping paper."

"No," she said. "But that's just a Christmas thing, right?"

"Could be. But it could be something else. For one thing, you can't get that crystal reindeer from Swarovski anymore. That was a limited edition, thirty-two years ago. If he just wanted a Christmas thing, he could've gotten something from more recent collections. Trees, bells, angels, stuff like that."

"So he likes deer."

"Reindeer. And the wrapping paper, with the note? It's Italian, a very expensive gift paper. Old. Did you notice the reindeer on it have wings?"

"I didn't." Tike shifted, adjusting the towels underneath her in the bathtub, swinging her feet up over the edge.

"I have this friend from South America. I was talking to him and mentioned your reindeer, the reindeer guy." He paused again. "He didn't respond well, Tike. He crossed himself."

"What?"

"Yeah, turns out he's had his own reindeer guy before, down there. It wasn't good. His reindeer guy was invisible, totally untraceable. A ghost, he said. From a family of ghosts. And my friend said there was money involved. Major money. He wouldn't say more than that. He's pretty much avoiding me now."

"But what's with the reindeer?" said Tike. "They're not exactly scary animals. I mean, Rudolph, for pete's sake. Not like it's snarling wolves or tigers or something."

"That's because we think of Santa's reindeer, right? Rudolph. Donder and Blitzen. Forget that for a while. Rudolph, the whole Rudolph myth? That was an ad gimmick started in 1939."

"No."

"Yeah, sorry to ruin your childhood. But reindeer, the real ones, have been around a long time. Caribou, reindeer—same thing. The old northern tribes herd them like cattle, call them reindeer."

"Didn't know that."

"Okay," he said. "The key was the wings, the winged reindeer from the wrapping paper you sent. The paper was pre-1939, meaning those flying reindeer are from the old days, the old reindeer mythology. Some ancient cultures depended on reindeer for survival, still do, to a point. Like the Saami, from northern Scandinavia. Arctic nomads. Finland, Sweden, Norway, Russia; all across their northern territories. Some interesting alliances during the World Wars."

"I think I've seen pictures. Roundups with snowmobiles, people who dress like Eskimos? Fur tents?"

"And old mythology. For the Saami, the reindeer are an ancient symbol. They have a reindeer god, Meandash. He's got wings and talks to the dead. They believe Meandash mated with a woman, a human, and had a child. The child was the beginning of the Saami reindeer herds."

Tike was silent. *A reindeer god? Who talks to the dead?*

To dead guys.

He paused. "Who knows what this reindeer guy really believes? Doesn't matter. These are some major symbols—power, sex, death—a deep part of the Saami culture, wherever they ended up. A lot of them scattered when the government tried to make them live in cities. And there's more. Do you want to know?"

"I'd better."

"Okay. The word 'Meandash' has another meaning for the Saami. It's not just the name for the reindeer god; it's also the name of a river in the land of the gods, a river you cross to get to the bone house, to your future. Not a good river."

"What could be so bad about a river?" said Tike.

"It's a river of blood."

"Oh man."

"Yeah. I don't care for your reindeer guy, Tike. I'm worried for you."

River of blood? Did some guy out there think he was the next Meandash? *What does he want from me?*

CHAPTER 27

Nick woke late in his Manhattan hotel room. The sun was pouring between the heavy hotel curtains, not well enough closed. As he dressed and made instant coffee at the minibar, he heard a muffled buzzing sound coming from his coat: his phone, still set on vibrate.

He looked at the glowing screen. There was a message, several hours old. Nick played the message as he poured his coffee.

"Nick, it's me." It was Tike. She said she was ready to talk. He checked his watch and called.

"You got my message," said Tike.

"Yes," he said. "I'm here. In New York. Please let me see you."

"Not this afternoon. We're going to Ellis Island."

"Okay. How about this morning? Right now," he said. He looked at his watch. "I'm ready."

"We're on our way to Rockefeller Center."

"I can be there in thirty minutes."

"Okay, but just for a minute. We'll just talk for a minute," she said. "Then...we'll see."

"Okay." He paused. "Be careful, okay?"

"Why?"

"Just please do." Nick dumped out his coffee as he put away the phone and pulled open the curtains. Fifteen floors below, the pearly white skating rink of Rockefeller Plaza was already crowded with skaters. He pulled on his coat and walked out the door.

———

Liz sat on a bench beside the skating rink, the sounds of classical music and blades on ice battling with the sounds of cabs and buses. She watched a tall woman in blue satin tights float by. Liz's eyes went back to Tike and Nick, several benches away.

She saw Nick reach over and pick up Tike's hand, then grip it between his own. Tike kept her other hand in her pocket, her head still, her gaze locked on the skaters.

Liz saw Nick speaking, dipping his head and trying to meet Tike's eyes. He stroked Tike's jaw with one finger, caressing her cheek. He wasn't speaking; Liz couldn't see if Tike was. Liz looked away.

A well-dressed businessman holding a small bouquet of flowers stopped next to her bench. "Miss?" He held the bouquet out toward her. "I know it looks crazy, but would you like these? I made it my goal for this Christmas season to give someone flowers every day. Would you be willing to accept these? Otherwise I can give them to someone else. But you looked like you could use some flowers."

Liz looked at him, her eyebrows raised. "Are you nuts?"

"Well, my late wife thought so." He bit his lip, his voice falling to a whisper. "I'm trying to make up for all the flowers I should have given her." He turned his head away, shook it briefly, then turned back with a small smile.

Liz looked closer at the flowers. Her stomach lurched. *Violets. Joseph. My wedding bouquet.* She swallowed and looked around the man at Tike and Nick. "I'm here with my friends." The man nodded at her. "Just set the flowers down," she said. "I'll share them with my friends." He gave a brief sad smile, then laid the violets on the bench. He walked off with a small wave of his fingers.

Liz reached over to touch the thin petals, shivering in the icy breeze.

She jerked her hand back as a group of children fell on the ice at her feet, chattering and squealing as they slipped and slid. When they finally got to their feet and skated on, Nick and Tike were approaching.

"Nice flowers," said Nick. "Who was that?" Tike stood next to him, frowning.

Liz shrugged. "Some guy. It's a project he's doing." She picked up the flowers. *Oh Joseph.*

"Nick and I are going to meet later for dinner," said Tike, glancing at Nick as she spoke to Liz. "If that's okay with you. After we get back from Ellis Island. Will you be okay on your own?"

"Yeah, I think I'll be okay," said Liz. She stroked the violets. "I'll be okay."

Nick turned to Tike. "And we can talk then?"

"Yes. We can talk," she said. "I'll be ready to talk. And listen."

"Thank you," he said. He gave her a short kiss on the lips, then paused and whispered in her ear. "Thank you."

CHAPTER 28

Gerald Jannssen closed the door to his machine shed and walked out across his central Nebraska farmyard. His worn work boots crunched on the iced gravel. He had seen the old vet's truck pull up by the cattle barn. Three farm cats were curling up on the still-warm hood of the truck in the weak mid-day sun. Jerry walked into the dark of the barn and stopped abruptly in the doorway of his barn office. The flickering fluorescent lights were on, and two small veterinary sample jars sat empty on the old linoleum countertop along the far wall.

"Doc?"

Doc Olson stood next to a jumble of liniment tubes, antibiotic pastes, ear tags, and ropes, his back turned. The pile of cattleman debris was on the same countertop as the empty sample jars, the countertop of the cabinet Jerry built from wood scraps when he was ten years old with perhaps a bit of help from his dad. But not much.

Jerry had thought he heard the Doc on the phone as he walked in. The test results—the second, final, results—should be in. The old man was digging through his bag. Then he turned around, unscrewing the cap of a pint whisky bottle. Doc slowly filled each of the sample jars halfway. He handed one to Jerry. Doc raised his jar and looked Jerry in the eyes.

Jerry looked back at the man who had been a part of his life as long as he could remember. He saw himself: tired, fearful, creased, reflected in Doc's watery eyes. Doc held his look, as if to hold the man, then spoke.

"God save us, my friend."

They sipped slowly, tears running down their cheeks, as they heard trucks pulling up outside the barn.

———————

After a long afternoon at Ellis Island on their sixth day of New York immersion therapy, Tike and Liz shoved their way into a cab like natives and headed back to the hotel. Even after nearly a week, it was still a pleasure to watch the strange universe of New York pass by their windows. *Another world*, thought Tike, then smiled. *Thank goodness.*

As they pushed through congested Manhattan, the cab stopped in traffic next to the giant Bloomberg news ticker on Lexington Ave. Liz was trying to talk to the cab driver, who couldn't understand a word she said, and Tike was looking out her window.

Oh no.

Tike saw the headline. She knew what it meant, knew what would happen, knew she was out of the picture.

I missed it.

Or did I? She kept staring. The cab started moving. Tike started yelling, she didn't know what, but it worked. The cab slammed to a stop. The cab behind them started honking and swearing in some language that only the cabbies understood. He started yelling back, at Tike and Liz, not at the other cab. Tike grabbed Liz's arm.

"Look," she said, pointing at the news ticker. "Look."

...FMD IN NEBRASKA...

"Oh boy," said Liz. "Oh wow."

"Oh fuck is more like it," said Tike. "Liz, we've got to go."

Liz nodded. "If they're smart, they'll want us there anyway. No one else here has been through this crap like us."

"No kidding," said Tike. She was already digging for her phone. "Let's make it happen."

From the December 29 Osceola Butte (Nebraska) Clarion:

Second FMD Outbreak Reported By USDA

LINCOLN, Neb. (AP) — The second report this month of a U.S. outbreak of FMD (foot and mouth disease), a highly infectious livestock disease, was reported today by Department of Agriculture officials. "We got the word today," said Dr. Martin Rasmussen, Nebraska Chief State Veterinarian. The disease was detected at the Gerald Jannssen livestock operation near Jasperville, in northeast Nebraska. "[The USDA] did extra confirmations of the tests for the Jannssen's, just to be sure. Quarantines and response teams have been activated."

Dr. Roy McCall of the Plum Island diagnostic center said the testing was thorough.

"Disease outbreaks like this illustrate the importance of a strong national diagnostic facility like Plum Island," said McCall. "Because of our experience with the recent false alarm, we've been able to add crucial new procedures."

The impact on trading has been mixed.

"We're in a wait-and-see mode," said Josh Bruce, independent trader at the Chicago Board of Trade. "The international sanctions are in place, but there's concern about getting caught by a false alarm again."

The previous reported outbreak of FMD, announced Dec. 18, was revealed on Dec. 22 to be a false alarm. The resulting industry losses were estimated to exceed $650 million; liability is still being determined. The last confirmed outbreak of FMD in the U.S. was in 1929.

FMD Vaccine Officials Meet

WASHINGTON, D.C. (AP) — Advisors to the US Department of Agriculture were called in today for an emergency meeting to determine whether vaccination against FMD will be allowed in the US.

"It may be time to bite the bullet," said Dr. Kurvin Gustadt, head of the Department of Agriculture vaccine division. "It'll lock us out of the top export markets, but we can't afford to risk the health and productivity of our national herds."

He anticipates a decision "within days," but notes that vaccination would take over a month to be effective.

"At most, we would only vaccinate strategic herds," he said. "Like a firebreak."

CHAPTER 29

Tike and Liz each had one hand on a phone and one gripping a hand-hold in the taxi as they sped to their hotel, midtown style: five miles an hour, lurching through Manhattan traffic. Liz was working on flights, and Tike was working on access. They couldn't just walk into the hot zone; they had to have some kind of authorization. The smoke-damaged voice on the other end of Tike's phone was not helping.

"Well, thanks, Tike, but I've got Marsha on the story," said her editor at the *Journal*.

"Marsha? She's sports. What does she know about FMD?"

"She's learning. And *she* checks her sources."

Ah, the knife. Tike tightened, trying not to slam the phone on the glass partition behind the driver, or throw it out the window into traffic. "Sources? Sources? Like, the Director of Plum Island, if she could even figure out how to talk to him?"

"She's already hooked up, got an exclusive with him three hours ago."

The bitch. Roy is mine.

"He had a few things to say about you, but we sat on most of them," he said.

"Roy? Me? What?"

"I've got to go. We'll be in touch. Geoffery has some papers for you to sign."

Geoffery? Geoffery-the-suit, in legal? "What does he want?"

"He'll let you know. There were some...questions. About the false alarms. Now this. It's better we don't talk."

Tike punched the "end" button. She shook her head, glaring at a pedestrian who tried to run in front of the cab, then hit the redial button.

"It's me again. Go ahead. Let Marsha deal with that asshole." She hung up again and was thrown back into the seat as the taxi accelerated.

Liz was arguing with someone. The taxi was nearly at the hotel, and the program didn't look good.

Tike thought about calling Nick. She got as far as reciting his number in her head, then pulled back. *Just say no. Let go. Not worth it.* She stared out the window. *Who? Which editor can get me in?*

Then, on top of that: *Those bastards.* She shook her head and loosened her grip on her phone. *After last time? After they dumped me? They can go screw themselves.* They could just find someone else to go camp out in a dead zone full of cow shit.

As she nudged Liz to ask how she was doing getting flights, her phone rang. Tike looked at the number: her former-favorite editor at *Progressive Farming.* The editor who deleted all of her stories from their website three days ago. Tike let it go to voicemail, then erased the message.

Screw them. She and Liz would find another way in.

Liz was still on the phone when their taxi jerked to a stop in front of the hotel. The doorman came over to investigate. As Tike opened her door she turned to Liz.

"Any luck?" she said.

"Got us a ride," said Liz, nodding her head. "You?"

"No," said Tike, shaking her head. "I need ideas."

"Got one. Let's pack and go. I'll tell you on the way."

Tike hopped out and told the taxi driver to wait. That and a twenty got her message across. Liz told the doorman to let the taxi wait where it was; this was a medical emergency. She flashed her state vet badge. He was not impressed. He wiggled his fingertips in a come-hither movement. She stared, puzzled. Tike elbowed her out of the way and slapped a twenty in his palm. He snapped it shut and waved the cab to the curb in the same movement.

Tike was already at the front desk, telling them to expedite check-out and pull up the bill. Liz, back on the phone, held the elevator for her and they went up to pack and head for their red-eye flight from Newark.

Dinner with Nick would have to wait. A hot zone was out there, waiting.

Tike plopped into the back seat of their waiting taxi, next to Liz, and gave a big sigh. The taxi took off, plunging back into the metal river of Manhattan, as Liz put away her phone, rubbing her ear.

"Wow. Serious phone ear."

"Phone brain," Tike said, nodding.

Liz poked her as the cab lurched around a stalled sedan. "So here's the scoop," she said, shifting in the seat to face Tike. "We're going to work for Jack."

"What?"

"Forget Iowa. They're so busy pointing fingers it's like they haven't noticed their next-door neighbor has a real outbreak."

Tike muttered some profanities under her breath.

"I concur," said Liz. "But Jack's the boss in South Dakota, which has a lot more border with Nebraska anyway. He's shutting down the state again, and he wants his own team to keep an eye on Nebraska. *In* Nebraska, on-site. That's us. We're going to be his eyes in the sky."

"Sky?" Tike raised her eyebrows.

Liz smiled and gave two thumbs-up. "Woo hoo. We've got a helicopter. "

"What?"

"Nice to have friends in high corporate places. Sounds like Jack's got some aviation pals. They're giving him—us—a pilot, too."

"Good looking, I hope," said Tike, bracing herself as they turned a sharp corner.

"Aren't they all?"

Tike laughed, then thought for a moment. "But once we go in, we can't come out. Why would we need a helicopter? We can just drive in."

Liz gave a pained look. "That's the bad news. Things are going to get ugly."

"What? Why?"

"The infected cattle had only been at the farm a couple of days. They just came from an auction." She paused, watching Tike.

Tike tilted her head, looking at Liz. "A couple days? Oh shit."

"Yeah."

"So the other livestock at the auction were probably exposed." Tike winced, thinking of the size of some of the sale barns in Nebraska. "I don't even want to know. Which auction?"

"Omaha Western."

"Holy moley."

"Uh huh. And it gets worse."

"Don't tell me."

"Yep. The sale barn can't find them all. Big storm last week, computers fried, records scrambled. Now they're trying to sort out forty pounds of sale receipts stuffed in cardboard boxes.

"But no one..." Tike looked at Liz, shaking her head. "Oh man."

"Exactly. No one else has reported any cases of FMD, in Nebraska or anywhere else those cattle probably ended up."

"And they should have by now."

"They should've. There should be other cases now at the originating farm, the farm the infected animals came from. Plus there should be more at other farms that bought infected animals, and another round of cases in animals that picked it up at Omaha Western."

"They're sure this one isn't a false alarm."

"Yeah. I can't get through to Plum anymore—thank you very much—but Jack talked to the Nebraska people, and they have the word. This is the real thing."

Tike sat and looked out the window, her throat tight. "People are afraid to report it. Cattlemen. Vets."

"Yeah," said Liz, her voice soft.

"Because of us." Tike bit her lip and blinked her eyes, swallowed hard. "They saw what happened in Iowa. To farms there. To us." She turned to Liz. "So now they're afraid to report, and this time it's real."

"Yes." Her voice was soft.

"So we may be visiting a lot of hot zones."

"Yes." Liz cleared her throat. "The helicopter will let us hop between sites—of course they're all rural—without dealing with roadblocks or airport security. Jack made a deal: Nebraska gets us, Jack gets information and a tight border. I'll talk to the vet teams, you talk to everyone else and report all our notes to South Dakota and Nebraska. They're going to work us like dogs. Homeland Security is in the loop, too. No one thinks this is just a big fat coincidence."

It started to snow. Tike stared out the window and thought about flying. Planes. Helicopters. Reindeer with wings.

Is my reindeer guy, my morgue guy, involved in this? Had to be. DeadSim. Dead guys. The false alarm. Meandash and the river of blood.

There was a river of blood coming, all right. Tike was silent the rest of the way to Newark.

————

Once the women got to their departure gate at Newark, Liz went scouting for food while Tike guarded their bags. She sat for a while, letting her brain uncoil, then dug out her phone and called U.P.

"U.P., I have to ask you something," said Tike. "It's been bugging me. You might not like it."

"Like that ever stopped you." He laughed. "What's going on?"

"Are you having some problems with the SEC? Or what's-their-name, the CFTC?"

He was silent.

"U.P.?"

"Tike," he said, then paused. "Tike, we all have some history. I won't deny I've been communicating with the CFTC lately. But this won't affect you. Believe in me, Tike."

She shook her head and sighed. *That's all I need.*

The line was silent for a long minute. Then U.P. spoke. "Geneva is helping them out. She gives them some information. Here and there."

"Geneva?"

"That's all I can say. Only two people there know about our arrangement. It's complicated."

After Tike hung up she sat for a while and stared at her shoes. Liz came back with pizza, soft pretzels, and frozen yogurt; they ate in silence. Tike pulled out her folder of bills and paid them, pasting on stamps and reminding herself to mail them in South Dakota, before they got into the hot zone. Correction: Zones.

———————

CHAPTER 30

The Manhattan taxi driver eyed Nick in his rear-view mirror and stepped on the gas a little harder.

"I'm on my way," said Nick, shouting into the phone jammed against his shoulder while he scrabbled through the briefcase on his lap. "Don't give me any more crap, Charlie, or you can just find another editor to underpay."

The argument continued at high volume. The taxi driver made good time to La Guardia, the faster to get rid of his fare.

"Discussion over. I'll talk to you when I get back to Des Moines," said Nick. "Now put Jason on the line."

After a minute Nick spoke again, but with a quiet voice. The driver had to strain to hear. "No, the next drawer down. Got it? Yes. Sealed with red tape? Okay. I've told Charlie I'm sending you. But the envelope is just between you and me. Got it? Okay. Lock my office on your way out."

Nick gave the young reporter the name of the person who should receive the envelope, and two cell phone numbers. "You call me if there are any problems," Nick told the reporter.

CHAPTER 31

Liz and the Governor—Jack—were huddled in the library of the Governor's residence in the South Dakota capitol, Pierre. They were studying a map of the South Dakota-Nebraska border, coffee and empty breakfast plates on the table beside them. *Sitting a tad closer than necessary*, thought Tike as she entered the room, luggage in each hand. "Ready to roll?"

Liz sat back in her chair and looked at her watch. "Should be any time now."

As she spoke they heard the thwacking of the helicopter making its approach. The Governor folded up the map they had been studying and handed it to Liz. "Be careful," he said to her, his voice soft. Liz nodded. Their fingertips touched as she took the map; Tike looked away.

Liz pulled on her coat and picked up her bags from the end of the couch, and the women went outside to catch their ride.

"I've never been in one of these," Liz said, shouting, as they crouched down and scooted toward the open door of the helicopter. They scrambled to their seats, strapped in, and put on headsets while the pilot secured the bags behind their seats.

Tike didn't like the thought of what the helicopter blades would stir up wherever they landed, but it was the only way. There weren't many airports where they were going, either at the one destination they knew, or at the other destinations that were likely. There were also too many blocked roads to argue their way through. But there was one thing available in excess: wide open space. The helicopter taxi could take them as close as they wanted to get. Closer.

"Everybody settled back there?" The voice in Tike's headset was loud and clear. She and Liz each gave the pilot a thumbs-up. "I'll put you on channel B so you can talk to each other," he said. "If you want to talk to me flip the switch on the mouthpiece."

During their two-hour flight Liz unfolded the map and showed Tike what she had learned about the Nebraska response plan. When they reached the infected ranch, the pilot brought them down on a field behind a big barn. They unhitched their harnesses as the rotor wound to a halt, then marched across the field toward the farmyard.

Liz found the local vet, Olson, and they started vet-speak. Tike left them and saw a sad-looking man who seemed to know his way around, so she collared him. He was Gerald Jannssen, the owner. She shook his hand, gripping it tightly.

"Dr. Thomas and I are here to do what we can to help," she said, flinching at the sound of a gunshot. *A captive bolt gun. I know about those.* "I know this is a nightmare for you," she said.

His eyes began to blink rapidly and he turned away. "Follow me." They passed a team of people unloading a trailer piled high with tarps and 50-gallon barrels of bleach. Another trailer, empty, was parked on the edge of a field of corn stubble; an ice cutter nearby was making slow progress carving through the frozen soil. A steaming pile of cattle carcasses—deadstock—was next to the field. A tractor pulling a full flatbed of carcasses was approaching it from the far side.

Tike heard another gunshot as she followed Jannssen. She looked toward the sound and saw a depopulation team working on a small pen of animals. *Looks like they're almost done,* she thought, watching the crew move another animal into position in the chute. One of the men pressed the barrel of the captive bolt gun against the steer's warm forehead, the animal's eyes white and rolling. Tike saw the shooter whisper something, then close his eyes in pain:

Bang.

Jannssen led Tike to an office inside the big barn. The barn was empty. And silent. As they walked through the main door, Tike winced at the wide, dark streaks on the concrete floor under her feet. There were dark puddles and splatters on the rest of the floor. She looked back and saw an empty tractor-trailer pulling up to the barn they were in, next to a skid-loader and a tractor with a very messy-looking bucket on it.

Jannssen saw her looking. "We've been working all night." His voice cracked as he said it. He cleared his throat and didn't say any more until they got to the office, their footsteps echoing behind them. "Here's what I've got."

They went through the paperwork. Tike made some calls from Jannssen's quiet barn office, but it wasn't encouraging. There was still no information about where his infected cattle came from before arriving at the Omaha auction.

Somewhere out there was at least one more hot zone, and no one knew where it was.

At least, no one would admit it.

Tike and Liz spent the rest of the day talking to teams already on-site at the Nebraska hot zone, and making calls from Jannssen's barn office. Tike did learn one interesting thing from U.P. He said one of Geneva's contacts reported something was fishy about the tests on the Nebraska cattle.

"Geneva has a friend at Plum Island?" said Tike.

"Tike, you don't even want to know where all she has friends," said U.P.

Tike agreed. They dropped the subject immediately.

Geneva's friend, said U.P., pointed out that the tests took too long. While talking to Jannssen, Tike had noticed the time gap between his vet's first visit and the final test results, but hadn't thought much more about it. Until now. First, Geneva's friend had said, there had been a screw-up—something about a door being left open—then an extra day was spent doing confirmation tests, which was not normal, but not too surprising, considering what they just went through with Iowa. It wasn't much, but it bothered Tike. She filed it away.

Near the end of their first day at the Nebraska hot zone, Tike was sitting outside, leaning against the barn, perched on a bale of hay in the farmyard twilight. She watched the Department of Agriculture team set up a second truck decontamination station just outside the farm gate. The first had frozen solid. Now they were setting one up with a heater. The cell phone in her pocket rang; it was her old friend, Bob Gasparowicz of the SEC.

"There's nothing happening," she said, getting up and walking into the empty barn as she spoke. "I'm doing my job, I don't know anything that isn't public information anyway. Frankly, I just wouldn't be very useful to anyone you would want to catch, certainly not U.P. I don't see why you keep calling me. Or why you keep focusing on him."

"There are things going on you aren't aware of," he said. "Or you know but you're not telling me." Tike could hear a door slam in the background. "One word of caution: Maybe you should get to know your friend better. Maybe he's not who you think."

Tike sighed. "You're wasting your time."

"I'll decide that." He paused. "You're walking on thin ice here."

"But I'm not doing anything. I'm a nobody now."

"You'd better open your eyes."

She sighed again. "Anything else?"

He hung up. She stared at the phone. Did they know something about her reindeer guy? Was he behind the DeadSim trades? Is that what was stirring up Gasparowicz? She shook her head. She just couldn't see it. *Why would it lead him to U.P.? And to me?*

Tike stepped back outside. Liz was slouched on her bale of hay, her collar up, scarf tight, eyes closed, and legs stretched out, her heels perched on a pile of icy manure that had been pushed out of the barn.

"Tell me this is just a bad dream," she said, stretching out one leather-mittened hand toward Tike. "Tell me we're in Bermuda and you're bringing me a daiquiri."

Tike flopped down beside her. "Yeah. I've got a whole tray of them just on the other side of that decon station. All we have to do is strip buck naked and walk through."

Liz gave a full-body shudder and opened her eyes, turning to Tike with a scowl. "You're no fun."

She shrugged. "Yeah. Sorry."

Tike was brushing her teeth and leaning over the miniature sink in their loaner RV parked next to Jannssen's barn, more than ready to hit the sack, when her phone rang. She looked at the screen to see who couldn't live without her at this hour of the night.

Blocked.

She leaned back to look around the RV. Liz wasn't in yet. She sighed, spat her toothpaste into the sink, and hit "Answer."

"Now what?" she said into the phone, her fist gripping her toothbrush handle.

"*Bonjour*, I have had the message to call most urgently a *Docteur Le Cerveau*," said a man's voice, tinny and with a strong echo. "He is there?"

Tike relaxed. "You must have a wrong number." She put the toothbrush into a tin cup bolted to the wall over the sink, then wiped the sink with a paper towel. *"Il n'est pas içi,"* she said. *"Um...ce n'est pas son numéro...numeral de téléphone."* She turned around, reaching over the tiny kitchen table to unfold her bed.

"Mais non," said the caller. *"Mais,* this must be Madame Tike? *Quelle nom...*unusual, *non?* Perhaps it is more petite than...Tiburnia?"

Tike stood up straight, banging her head on a kitchen cupboard. "Who the hell is this?"

"Oh, Tike, we must watch the temper. *Que masculin, non?"*

"I'm tracing this." Tike heard the door latch rattle, saw the door open a few inches, snow blowing in.

"Oh, la la," said the tinny voice. "But do I care? *Bonne nûit, ma cherie."* He hung up. The door swung open. Tike stepped back, hitting the back of her head on the kitchen cupboard. Liz stumbled in, her arms full.

"Oh, hi, Tike" she said, her cheeks and nose red with cold. "Look what the Jannssens sent over." She shoved the door shut behind her with one booted foot, then dropped her armload—two oversized holiday gift bags—on the kitchen table. "Care packages. That family is just so nice."

Liz stood back and started extracting herself from her insulated cover-alls, grunting as she tried to untangle the zipper, which had snagged on her scarf.

Tike stayed back against the kitchen cupboard, staring at the glossy gift bags, a plate of Christmas cookies perched on top of one bag, a bottle of purple bubble bath sticking up out of the other. The bag handles were secured with duct tape. One of the bags had a giant Rudolph on it; duct tape reinforcement covered his eyes.

"Tike?" Liz looked up at her, pausing in her wrestle with the zipper. "Are you okay?"

Tike's hand went to the back of her head; she could feel the bumps from hitting the cabinets. Her cheeks burned red hot as her mind raced, replaying the call. *Docteur le Cerveau. Cerveau*—French for deer.

Rudolph looked blindly back at her, his nose blood-red.

Meandash.

CHAPTER 32

Joe Anderson, driver for Glory Swine's Iowa operation, downshifted as he approached the west end of Alta, Iowa. The truck was riding low with a full load of hogs making their final road trip. Destination: America's frying pans. *Might be the last delivery to the pack for a while. Who knew if Iowa would shut down? Or when?*

Joe rolled down his window and rested his arm on the sun-warmed door frame, tapping his fingers in time to a song on the radio. He slowed for the stoplight, the only one in downtown Alta. He rolled past an SUV with the driver's side windows open. As he passed, he saw a little arm holding a doll. The doll was doing a puppet show, dancing on the window frame.

He could hear the pigs squealing in the back as he tapped the brakes. Three. Two. One. Bingo: They would now be alongside the SUV.

"Mommy, pee-ew! Mommy, pigs!" The doll and arm disappeared, and the SUV windows rolled up quickly.

Joe grinned. Right on the nose; he still had the touch. As the light changed and the SUV started to accelerate, he watched in the side-view mirror. Yes! Gotcha, he thought, as a squirt of brown liquid manure jetted out from between the aluminum slats of the livestock trailer. *Good thing Mommy closed the windows, eh?* He could hear more squeals and they weren't from his pigs.

Now. Time for lunch. He could see the sign for a cafe from the road, with a backdrop of at least twenty of the famous giant wind turbines on the horizon:

The Alta Wind Farm Tavern
Maid-rites, $1. Tap, $1
Go Buccaneers!
Just 5 Miles East Of Town

Well, all righty then. After a quick lunch, it was a short hop to the packing plant to drop this load of porkers. He would be unloaded by mid-afternoon, and on his way home.

———————

An hour and a half later, Joe was still parked on a stool at the Alta Wind Farm Tavern, just east of town. His trailer of hogs was still in the parking lot, the animals grunting and snoring in the afternoon sun and breeze. Inside the tavern, Joe was perched next to some old friends. They had been passing through in the opposite direction, coincidentally stopping in Alta at the same time.

"We really better hustle, I suppose," said Tex, sliding off his stool. "Never know when y'all are going to shut down the border. And wouldn't that be the shits."

Joe nodded. "Crazy world these days." They paid their bills and went out to the parking lot, where it turned out they were parked side by side.

"Fine looking heifers," said Joe, peeking through the slats of Tex's trailer.

"Yep," said Tex. "Good prices up here this week. Couldn't resist. Foot-and-mouth be damned, these animals are in fine condition. They'll be out on the range along the Rio Grande by tomorrow night."

Joe climbed back up into his cab, waving at his friends as he pulled onto the Alta blacktop, the dotted yellow line nice and fresh. *Nice road.* He could feel the sideways drag of the wind. Always windy as hell in this part of the state, and you never knew which way it would go, north or south. Today it was going south.

A strong gust hit, and Joe corrected, pulling the truck back to the center line of the two-lane blacktop.

Another gust hit, bigger. He corrected again. He glanced at the sideview mirror. *Hell, stirred up a little gravel dust from the shoulder.* He glanced at the mirror again.

Shouldn't have done that.

———————

In the westbound lane of the Alta blacktop, heading due west toward the Alta Wind Farm Tavern, was a mid-sized sedan. Not too big, not too small, but just right for Mrs. Karl Houtsma, now that Mr. Houtsma was gone and she had to drive herself. Most days she did fine.

Today she did not. When that last gust of wind blew, she over-corrected. Her right-hand tires went off the pavement and onto the flat gravel shoulder. Not normally a problem.

But it was for Mrs. Houtsma. She panicked, because she saw, barreling down the highway at her, another one of those huge trucks that leaves a 65-mile-per-hour wave of suction behind them, yanking her to the center line as they pass no matter how hard she grips the wheel. She hated that.

So she panicked. She turned the wheel to the left, trying to get the wheels off the gravel and back onto blacktop before the oncoming truck would pass her and suck her into its wake. But today, just this once, her first time in all of her seventy-nine years, at least sixty-eight of them driving, ever since Daddy taught her how to drive the Model T around the farmyard, both Daddy and his little girl laughing and screaming, Mrs. Houtsma turned the wheel too far. And unfortunately, at precisely that same time, just as the oncoming truck was getting close enough that she could see the face of its driver, and he could see hers, there was another gust of wind. A hard one.

Mrs. Houtsma had one brief thought: *Oh, Karl*.

And that was all.

It was not a normal day for the hogs on Joe's truck, which was now twisted across the Alta blacktop like a large bloody tinkertoy, red and metallic against the white Iowa snow and frozen black asphalt.

First they had heard the horrible noise of squealing metal as the aluminum-slat truck body toppled and skidded; then pain. Then more noise, as the hogs roared, and fell, somehow, in the air, sideways, upside down, rolling, one on top of each other. Then it was all black. And red.

One hog, weighing 275 pounds and now missing one ear, woke and found there was a foot in his mouth. It was not his. Nothing attached to it. He bit into it. He ate it. He tried to squeeze free of the live and still carcasses jammed around him. He was hungry, and thirsty. Another pig bit him when he stepped on it, trying to squeeze out through the gate, which was not the same shape as when they were loaded on the truck early that morning.

The one-eared hog pushed the gate with his snout. The gate, which was already twisted from its hinges, fell. The hog, and two dozen others, poured out through the open space and fell, flopping and squealing (the ones that were alive) onto the highway twelve feet below.

The highway surface should have been concrete, but hogs had already fallen and jumped out from the other gates on the three-level truck.

The one-eared hog landed on his brethren, and the two dozen hogs from his level landed on and around him, nearly smothering him. He bit and clawed his way through the mass, all slick and wet with the manure and urine that had poured out of the truck with the animals.

Once he surfaced, the smell of blood hit like a wave of heat. He couldn't smell the hogs—or what was left of them—on the road to the west, along lines curving back and forth across the road. Some were moving, although in strange, crawling, jerking movements. But next to the truck, sheltered from the wind, the smell was strong.

The hog nosed some soft, meaty material on the ground between his feet. He ate it. He found another lump of something soft and ate that. It was warm.

Another truck, large with flashing lights, came screaming along the road toward the one-eared hog. It had to slow, to make its way through the animals and debris on the road behind the truck.

The hog abandoned his food and ran into the ditch. He looked back. The flashing truck was getting closer, and the sirens louder. He turned, nosed his way under the fencing, scrambled to his feet, and ran into the field. Other hogs did the same.

There was a large section of fence missing to his left. It had wrapped around something in the ditch that was like a truck and not like a truck, but also smelled of blood.

The 250-pound animals pounded across the field. Many limped, some dragged themselves. The smell of blood diminished as they moved away from the road. Eventually the one-eared hog slowed and looked around. There, to one side, was a long tangled grove of trees. He turned and entered the grove, then walked a short distance, shivering. He collapsed in the dark shelter of low branches and closed his eyes; he listened as other hogs collapsed around him.

———————

The doe shivered, shaking the light snow off her thick winter coat, and stood up, her long legs unfolding from her bed in the sheltered grove. Her fawn snapped his eyes open and watched her rise. But the doe stood calmly, scanning the group and smelling the cold Iowa twilight air.

Another five does sat nearby, legs folded, most of them shoulder to shoulder, with at least a dozen fawns and yearlings squeezed in between. The few bucks, two junior and one senior, were toward the outside. The long grove where they were gathered was good shelter from the wind roaring out of the north today, but it was chilly nonetheless.

The standing doe still smelled the hogs. Since mid-afternoon, the odor had been strong. There was blood, too. She knew that metallic smell. There had been many noises, too. Very unusual. The whole group had been on alert, there in the grove.

The group often smelled hogs, blood sometimes, too, as the deer roamed the fields at night, going from grove to grove, farm to farm, scouting for easy food. Some of the farms put out corn, or had corn spilled in the fields after harvest, or were sloppy with their feed wagons. Those farms, they visited more often.

There were also two feedlots within the foraging domain of this group. The cattle made room when the deer hopped the fences and joined them at the feed troughs. That was a nice visit for the deer on a cold night, since the cattle steamed from their own heat. But tonight— where would they go? Perhaps to the field just west. There were some fresh round bales of hay put out for the cattle today; she had heard the pick-up truck bouncing across the field. That field always had a salt lick, too; the farmer put out fresh blocks when the cattle—and deer—had licked the old one down to a nubbin.

The group rose on their long legs, one animal at a time. Each stretched or nipped at some small itch before moving to the trail behind the doe. She was moving south, away from their now-cooling beds in the leaves under the pin oaks and buckthorn of the grove.

The smell of hogs got stronger.

The group continued to follow their trail, wending westward to the end of the deep grove, then turning south, down the mile-long north-south windbreak forming the other border of this field.

The lead doe stopped in mid-stride, on full alert, her white tail up, a flag in the shadows. Ahead of the group, downwind, there was a rustling sound. And...something. Snorting? Grunting?

It was a hog, two of them, three. All were bloody. They were trying to stand, listing from their resting positions in the leaves under the scrubby trees of the wind-break.

The one in front, leaves stuck on the blood along his side, was missing one ear and had one eye swollen shut. But he stood, solid and legs spread wide. He outweighed any of the deer, except, perhaps, the old buck. Behind him, one of the other hogs, his drooling mouth a mass of fresh blisters, collapsed back to the ground with a grunt and a sigh.

———

CHAPTER 33

Geneva put down her cold diet Dr. Pepper, an AOL CD serving as a coaster on her old wooden desk, and leaned back in her chair. The Chicago condo beyond her locked and soundproofed door was quiet. U.P. had gone downtown to the trading floor.

The envelope had been on the doormat this morning. On the phone, U.P. had said it wasn't there when he left for the floor at 4:30 a.m.

Now the contents were spread out in a neat matrix on the desk: Grainy photos. Receipts. Bank statements. Deposit slips, some in French.

Geneva already knew about Tike's history, between what Tike had disclosed after they first met, and the additional homework Geneva had done as a matter of course. But she hadn't seen most of this. *Why not? Who wanted me to see it now? Certainly not Tike. And why?*

Nick closed the door to his office at the *Des Moines Register*, locking the chaotic din of the newsroom outside, and used a key to open a lower drawer of his desk. He kept the phone wedged against his shoulder and maneuvered the drawer open as he spoke into the receiver.

"Things are getting out of hand," said Nick. "You got the package?...Good. I'm at my office...Des Moines, yeah. You need to...Okay. Good. I'll be in touch."

He hung up the phone and got down on the floor, ducking his head to scoot into the knee space. He reached into one corner, behind the end of the open drawer, and peeled away a thin veneer. He gripped the handle of a dusty black case the width of the drawers—about the size of a Chicago phone book—and pulled it out of its slot.

The weight of the familiar hard plastic case was solid in his hands. He set it on his desk and used another key to open the lock.

The rest didn't take long. He plucked his Sig Sauer P226 from the case, took it apart, and cleaned it, then repeated the process with the matching silencer. He did the same with the Walther from his briefcase, then loaded both.

When he was done, he put everything in his briefcase, relocked the door behind himself, and went back on the editorial floor.

He had a story to finish.

———————

CHAPTER 34

Liz stood outside talking with the Department of Agriculture team leader, a vet she knew from school, at the Nebraska hot zone farm. The afternoon sun was weak on their tired faces. Tike huddled in the heated barn office, looking out the window at the empty farmyard and feedlot— empty except for veterinarians and decontamination teams—as she made calls to fill in blanks in the story of two outbreaks, one real, one false. Related or not by origin, it was becoming more and more clear they were inextricably entwined: No one acted without thinking of the false alarm.

Tike twiddled her pen and leaned over to be sure the spindles of her tape recorder were rotating as she prodded her interviewee into spilling her guts.

"I still shouldn't talk to you," said Yolanda, an employee at the testing lab on Plum Island. She had returned Tike's call from her parents' home in Brooklyn. "I'm on probation. They won't let me on the island for two weeks, and I'm not supposed to talk to anyone."

"I don't have to use your name," said Tike. "And I'm not a reporter here. I'm working for the State of Nebraska and its neighbors, part of a special team. We just want to be sure we know what happened so it doesn't happen again. I'll be talking to your boss, too, but he won't get to know who I talked to or what they said. Roy—is that him?"

"Yes." Yolanda sighed.

Tike lowered her voice. "You know, I've met him. At a conference. He hit on me."

Yolanda laughed. "Yeah, that's him."

Tike waited.

"I love my job, okay?" Yolanda blew her nose. "I love the Island. I've been there eleven years. But since Roy got there—Roy, he's not...a good boss."

Tike made sympathetic girltalk noises.

"We're just tools. Tools for Roy and his big plans," said Yolanda. "His precious Island. All he cares about is his holy mission for the Island. Which is really just 'Part One' of his holy mission for himself. But what about me?" And so she talked. The door left open, the repeated tests, the humiliation at the staff meeting, the finger-pointing at Yolanda and her friend, the gossip about his affairs.

"You're doing great, getting through this," said Tike. "Don't let it break you."

"I just want a peaceful life, you know?" Yolanda blew her nose again. "Maybe it's time for me to leave the Island. I want to live on a ranch someday, you know? Have a dog, maybe a horse. Just like on TV. Can't do that here."

Tike paused. "Can I send your number to someone?" Governor Jack, she knew, was pushing to start an alternate Plum Island: "Plum Cave," deep in the old gold mines of South Dakota, about as close as you could get to being offshore. Better. "I know someone you should talk to," she said.

Yolanda said, sure, send it. What did she have to lose?

It was a dim late Nebraska afternoon, and a frigid New Year's Eve, before Tike had a chance to not think about dead animals. She slouched in her grimy padded chair in the barn office headquarters and used the remote to switch on a dusty TV sitting on a file cabinet along the wall. Tike flipped through the channels, settling on a news feature describing preparations for the night in Times Square. They showed footage of the crews setting up barricades around the square; she spotted the shoe shop where Liz and she had spent a happy afternoon. *Was that just three days ago?* She muted the program when it went to commercial and picked up her phone, staring at the keypad, then reached out a finger and punched in Nick's number.

He was quiet when he answered. Hesitant. "I'm glad you called," he said. He was quiet for a long moment. "I'm getting packed. We're short handed, two reporters out sick. I have to go do some man-on-the-scenes, armed barricades at state borders, things like that." He dropped his voice to a whisper. "And it'll get me out of this nest of back-stabbers. I swear I'm going to kill someone."

She tried to laugh. "No problem."

"I heard about your task force. Good job."

"Thanks. Same old scene here. Lots of blood." She could hear people talking in the background, phones ringing. "Sounds busy there."

"Tike, we need to decide. Tomorrow is the deadline." He took a deep breath. "I know you're in the thick of it there. But you have to tell me what you want to do. Will you come with me?"

Tike played with the remote control, flipping the channels. There were only three. "I haven't decided," she said. She turned the TV on and off, on and off. "Did I mention I've been sued?"

"What? Sued?"

"Yeah. If I sell my acreage, I might have enough to pay the lawyers. The only way I could keep it is to go bankrupt, then I could keep it. If I live there."

He was silent.

"We still have some big issues," she said. "You and me."

"Nothing's going to change if you're not with me," he said. "We wouldn't have time. We won't make any progress."

Tike heard the phones ringing again behind him. She took a deep breath. "I'm not the only one who has a choice here." She picked up the remote and pulled out the batteries. Double A. She reversed them and put them back in the remote.

"I didn't know you're being sued," he said, his voice softer.

She stood up and pushed in her chair. "So what else is new. I've got to go. Liz needs my help."

"You didn't tell me any more about those calls," he said, his voice rushing. "The morgue calls. Are they still coming? I worry about those."

"No," she said, zipping up her coat. "I'm fine."

"Tike, we need to talk."

"We just did. I told you. I'm not making a decision. Not now. You do what you have to do. I've got to go, Nick." She pulled on her boots. "You're a nice guy. Sorry I don't fit in your tidy life." She hung up.

Tike went outside. No one was around. It was windy, an icy wind that froze even the salty tears on her face as she stood looking at the setting sun, gray and dim. Alone again.

———————

CHAPTER 35

Nick pulled his phone away from his ear and stared at the heavy handset, oblivious to the newsroom din pouring through his office door.

"Sorry I don't fit in your tidy life," the voice had said, followed by a click and silence, then a dial tone. The phone was old, black, some kind of obsolete ceramic. It had a better feel than the fluffy multi-line devices they wanted him to use. *She hung up. Is that it? The end?*

Nick shut his door and locked it. He rocked back in his chair, his eyes closed, and touched his fingertips to his face. *If only I could tell her the truth.* After a few minutes he got up and stepped over to his file cabinets, opening one drawer, then another, pulling out a handful of files. Some were old and tattered. He peered into each file briefly, then dumped the contents into a new accordion folder. Each file yielded one or two or three envelopes, each envelope a quarter-inch thick, crumpled and molded into the shape of a stack of $100 bills. Or $500 bills. Rainy day funds.

Nick shoved the accordion folder into his computer bag, next to his laptop, then put his cell phone in his pocket. He unplugged the phone charging stand and stuffed it into his computer bag as well, then took his office door key off his key ring and put it in the middle desk drawer. He closed the drawer as he stood, scanning the office.

Nothing else.

He left the room. He didn't shut the door. No one noticed him leave.

From the January 1 Claringham (North Carolina) Daily Bugle:

Santa's Whitetails in Putney Woods?

Ralston Gebley, barn manager at Claringham Pork, reports that he and his sons saw some of Santa's reindeer in Putney Woods this week.

"We were out scouting for gobblers when we scared up a mess of whitetail," stated Gebley. "A couple of them were all polka dot colored, all pink and blue and red. Like some kinda weird Easter eggs."

Gebley said he's never seen anything like it. He said it looks like someone used the deer for paintball gun practice.

"We're pretty sure it was paintballs," he insisted, "because me and my boys saw a beer cooler with some busted paintballs floating in it, where we parked by the path into the woods."

He said they didn't think much of it till they saw the deer, then the cooler was gone when they got back to their truck.

"Must have been Santa came back and cleaned up," he chuckled.

CHAPTER 36

On New Year's Day Tike woke up with confetti and hay in her hair. She and Liz had joined the Jannssens's for a small party in their farm house the evening before, but the visit was strained. The Jannssen Century Farm was no more. Mrs. Jannssen spent the evening paging through photo albums, not saying a word. Avoiding her husband.

Tike rolled out of her small bed in their RV, the morning sun reflecting off the quiet feedlot and in through their small windows. Liz was still asleep; one hand hung from her bunk, twitching.

Tike stood at the window and looked outside through the miniature curtains, morning Nebraska before her. *Not much more to do here.* They had learned what they could, but no other hot zones had been identified. Was this the end of it, after all?

Tike watched the Jannssens, husband and wife, walk out of the now-empty barn. They were holding hands, walking slowly. Mrs. Jannssen stopped and put her hands over her face. Mr. Jannssen turned to her, bending his knees to look into her eyes, moving her hands aside, stroking her hair, adjusting her wool cap. Tike could see his lips moving as he spoke. He stood up straight and put his arms around his wife's shoulders, pulling her into him. He put one hand on the back of her head; his eyes closed, face tipped up to the sky. They stood like this, he slowly rocking her back and forth, the wind whipping up some snow from the empty farmyard, throwing it against their legs.

Tike sat back on her bed, thinking of Nick. Surely there was a way to work something out. Some kind of compromise. Nick always thought in black and white, never gray. She dug her phone out of her jacket and walked to the back of the RV, stepping softly past Liz, shutting herself into the tiny lavatory.

She pressed the buttons on her phone, thinking about the Jannssens.

Just standing there. When the rough voice answered she realized she had dialed Nick's office instead of his mobile phone.

"Oh. Robert?" she said.

"Yeah."

"It's Tike. Sorry. I was trying to reach Nick."

"Our Mr. Capelli? Out sick, the loser. Bronchitis. Hell of a time to do it to me. God, am I hung over."

"Bronchitis?"

"Me? Oh, Nick. Yeah. He sounded like shit. I better not get it. Asshole."

"He's not on the road, covering state boundaries, whatever?"

"Nick? Yeah, right. That's the kind of story he dumps on the little people. No offense," he said. "No, he was supposed to run the editorial confab today. As if we're actually going to get anything done anyway. Instead, he calls in yesterday and here I am, stuck taking his calls. Try him at home. I'll let him know you called, if he checks in."

"Thanks," she said. He was already gone.

She stared at her phone and folded it shut. "Bastard," she whispered. "Liar."

CHAPTER 37

Clarissa, sitting on the couch at her small but well-located condo just outside Washington, D.C., took another sip of chamomile tea and turned a page in her new book of poetry. She was taking a personal day. She had spent the morning, and far too much money, inside the beltway at an exclusive salon she had passed on the way to the MATA office every day for years, always thinking: maybe someday.

Well, someday was today. Didn't she possibly have a date coming up? Best to be ready.

She stroked her sleek hair, feeling the weight of it, but not disrupting it too much. She didn't want to ruin the styling. She spread out her fingers to look at her immaculate nails. MAC polish, of course; no animal testing. She had the same shade of red—"Carnal"—on her toes. Clarissa picked up her teacup and took a delicate sip. *If only I still had some of that teacake*, she thought. But that was long gone.

Halfway through a poem on lotus blossoms, the doorbell rang.

Clarissa stepped into her new slippers (open-toed maroon velvet mules with a two-inch heel and pearl medallions) and walked carefully to the door, practicing her walk. She saw the neighborhood FedEx carrier on the step and opened the door.

"Ma'am. Sign here please."

Clarissa looked at the addresses on the two packages—Jacindo's Exotic Greenhouse, and Becky's Antiques—and then signed for receipt. As she handed back the signature pad and stylus, she smiled at the courier and wondered if he liked the smell of her new perfume.

After she closed and locked the door, she was torn, trying to decide which box to open first. She had guessed something might be arriving; her Southern gentleman friend, as she described him to her mother, had suggested as much on the phone the evening before.

Something special, he said. More exactly, he said, "Something special, and something for the cause."

Clarissa started with the package from the antiques shop. After a few layers of tape and insulated material, she pulled out two bundles, one rectangular and one disc-shaped. The first—the rectangle—spilled its contents onto her lap as she cut away the paper wrapper: a stack of crisp fresh twenties. "Something for the cause," she said, smiling. She set them aside to count later.

Next, the large disc. It was heavy. She cut away the layers of bubble wrap and gasped. It was a beautiful pair of Majolica serving platters, one with lilacs and roses, the other with oak leaves and acorns. "Definitely, something special," she said. She set them carefully on the coffee table, stroking the smooth glaze of the sculpted patterns.

Clarissa went back to the living room, where the box from Jacindo's Exotic Greenhouse lay on the floor. She bit her lower lip and smiled as she knelt by the box, slicing it open with care. It was cool to the touch.

When she pulled off the lid, she saw the box had two sections. At the foot of the box, a lumpy package was insulated and secured with strapping tape. It was cold, and sweating with condensation. She cut away the tape, and held the package in her lap. She cut through the insulation, just enough to see the contents: a tube, identical to tubes she had already received. She got up and took the package to the kitchen, where she put it in the freezer.

Then she went back to the remaining package. She knelt over it, carefully slicing the rustling paper packaging from top to bottom.

Inside was an arrangement of waxy blood-red orchids, with a hand-written note from the nursery describing the history and care of this variety. As Clarissa read the note, she sat back on her heels and put her hand to her chest, blushing. The orchids, apparently, were a new variety named "Carnal." She slid her hand along the stems of the orchid sprays and spread her fingers again, displaying her nails next to the blossoms.

An exact match. *I can't wait to tell him.*

Jacques Delons ran his fingertip around the ragged border of the note on his desk. The envelope, postmarked Helsinki-Toukola, had arrived in the morning bag from Paris. Jacques, senior night technician at Du Barry Vaccine, 47 kilometers north of Marseille, sipped his espresso as he studied the thin note, handwritten in French—by a woman's hand? *Mais bien sûr*. It was an apology, begging forgiveness for causing him extra work, and promising, if he would be patient, recompense. Perhaps in person, it read. The margins of the note held sketches of sensuous forms, women smooth and round and curled in repose, like cats. He held the scrap of paper under the lamp, examining one sketch at a time. Seventeen women. Some of them together...but not in repose. He reviewed them again.

Jacques turned over the note, studying the colorful printed side. Holiday paper. *"Buone Natale,"* reindeer. No women.

He turned the paper back to the handwritten side and studied it, sipping his coffee. What to think? The memo from the chief lay next to the note. The memo, with no sketches, gave the details: "Special request for replacement batch, vaccine 335-MR2, Client 37. Off-schedule." Contaminated or spoiled by a sloppy technician, to be sure; that stockpile shouldn't have needed replacing for at least three years. *Imbeciles.* Jacques shook his head. *Jacques'* laboratory made no such mistakes. Now Client 37 must beg, wait in line. The giant tanks were booked solid, five years out. This Jacques knew; he set the schedules.

Besides, the Americans—arrogant fools, thought they were stronger than a virus—they were already starting to hint to Jacques: "We *may* need more vaccine. We *deserve* it." Hah. *Get in line, Yankee.*

Jacques fingered the note, then tucked it in the pocket of his labcoat and walked down the quiet hall. The walls were covered with posters of the great ones—Maradona, Pele, Beckham—and charts showing the inoculation schedules for his charges: anthrax, bluetongue, cryptosporidium—the infectious alphabet. He passed the airlock that led to the laboratory, then reached the library.

Jacques opened a file drawer and pulled out the protocol for 335-MR2, reviewing it as he walked back to his desk, calculating the number of tanks he would need to inoculate. *Est-ce possible?* He thought of the curled shapes on the note, the charming promise. *Who is this Client 37?*

He sat at his desk and picked up the envelope. Was Client 37 not of Brazil? Why postmarked in Helsinki, that cruel place? Jacques shivered, then upended the envelope and slid the sleeve of currency onto the desk. He picked up a small thermos, poured the last drop of espresso into his small cup, then sipped it slowly. He pulled out the scrap of holiday paper and studied the sketches. *Bien*, he thought, reaching across the desk to turn off the lamp. He put the cash and note in the pocket of his labcoat as he stood, then headed for the airlock. Perhaps he could find a tank or two for Client 37. But no more. The house would be full, and it would be several weeks before the next tanks would open.

The Yankees would just have to wait. Maybe this time they would learn to plan ahead.

———————

CHAPTER 38

Tike spent the afternoon of New Year's Day holed up in the RV at the Nebraska hot zone, cranky and tidying up her assorted debris. Liz had said she should do it while she could.

"Something's going to pop," said Liz. "It has to. I've been thinking about it all day. It's only a matter of time before the next case shows up. Keep your bags packed."

Tike was halfway through the stack of mail she had gotten forwarded from home, her little stacks sorted and organized and arranged around the tiny kitchen table. She tore open the envelope from her bank, her recent statement. She dug her checkbook out of her shoulder bag and sat down to reconcile the two. As she settled in at the kitchen table, her eyes picked up a bolded line: "Current balance: $41,939.62."

Ah. Not quite. *I should be so lucky*, she thought, squinting at the large figure on the bank statement.

She read through the statement from top to bottom. There were three large deposits, large and unexpected: Two deposits of $10,000, and one for $20,000. She called the bank and got the automated account menu.

Your current balance is $41,939.62, said the recording. *Do you wish to perform any additional inquiries or transactions?* Tike hung up.

She went through the other entries, marking off each on both the statement and in her checkbook. The largest deposits she expected, from U.P., and none larger than $3,000, were on the dates she had noted in her day book. Everything else was copacetic—except for the extra $40,000. She studied the entries for the big deposits to see if there was any more information. Were they made in person? By drop box? But no details. She'd have to wait for the bank to open. She opened her monthly calendar. *Did Mom make a deposit for me?* An early inheritance? She sat back in her chair, wishing it were so. A bonus from U.P.? *Three in one month?*

Tike's eyes wandered over the calendar and the statement. It had been a big month. Lots happening. She leaned over the table again and re-read the entries for the big deposits. One after the other, she used her pen to mark the dates of the deposits on the calendar.

She sat back, then leaned forward again and double-checked the dates. She jumped up from her chair and started to pace. "Shit," she said. "No." She came back to the table and moved her finger between three dates on the calendar:

The day after the West Soo outbreak was announced. Deposit: $10,000.

The day after the false alarm was announced. Deposit: $10,000.

The day after the Nebraska outbreak was reported. Deposit: $20,000.

Tike went to the window and looked out. She could see Liz talking with Jannssen by his office. She tapped her fingertips on the aluminum window sill. She went back to the papers spread out on the table and checked the dates again. She pulled out her daily calendar to see what she was doing before and after those days. Where she was. Who she was with. She had talked to Mom, overnighting in Kiev, between the first and second deposits. Mom hadn't said anything about a gift; she would have.

It wasn't U.P. His deposits were listed; smaller amounts, different days, matching the days she had talked to him on the phone and he had said he would make a deposit.

Who else could it be? Had she missed something?

She picked up her phone, then laid it down on her lap. She needed more information before she ran up the flag.

And anyway, who could she call? Nick? Pete? U.P.? Geneva? No, it was too messy, too...tangled. She put the phone away.

———

While Tike was pacing the RV, stumped over what to do about the unexplained deposits, she called her neighbor to get a report on her cats.

"I was just going to call," he said. "I stopped by to check on your farm. The LP tank was empty, your furnace was off, and the pipes are frozen."

Shit. The LP tank. *I never did get back to check it.* "Oh no. Please tell me you're teasing."

"No, I'm not. Tike, you really shouldn't have a farm if you can't take care of it. It's a lot of responsibility, you know."

Tike bit her lip. *How could I have let that slip? How? Oh, this is going to cost me.* "I'm trying."

She thanked him, then started making calls: the LP company, to get the LP tank filled and the furnace re-started; a plumber to start repairs; and the bank, to transfer money to pay for it all. She didn't plan to spend the anonymous $40,000 just yet, tempting though it was. She'd have to dip— deep—into her savings.

Tike went to the window again. The helicopter pilot was walking across the farmyard toward the Jannssens's house. He spent his afternoons there, playing Monopoly and doing puzzles with the Jannssen kids. Everyone was stuck on the farm, waiting out the quarantine.

The morgue calls, the John Doe, now money shuffling. *I'm someone's target. Why?* There was no way she could prove she hadn't gotten those deposits as payment for something. She could hear the reporters' questions already:

Tike, Tike—did you do it? Don't you live just a short drive from West Soo? And not much farther from the Jannssens? Couldn't you drive there and back in one evening?

Tike, Tike—isn't FMD your specialty? Don't some people call it your obsession? Do you own a piece of DeadSim? How much will you make off the outbreak?

Tike shivered. Who had her in their cross-hairs? Why?

The situation was getting out of her league. She took a deep breath and dialed a number she knew by heart, waited while it rang, heard the metallic voice answer.

"I'd like to schedule a call," she said, gripping the phone. "Inmate #1005-12991. I'm on the green list."

———————

CHAPTER 39

The heavy crates with French shipping labels barely shifted in the back of the delivery truck. The truck, a rusty Volvo with Finnish plates, maneuvered the rutted path to the old stone barn. The winds from the Bering Sea were strong, but broken by the ancient cypress grove around the farmstead. This remote place was tended by human hands even before it was a farm; older stone structures were buried below the cold soil of the empty paddocks.

When the truck reached the end of the path, the driver hopped out and approached the side door of the barn. Next to the door, at eye level, was the farm family's crest.

The driver pressed his fingers against the side of the gold plaque and triggered the latch. He got back into the driver's seat of the truck as the large barn door slid to the side. He drove into the barn and stopped the truck, then hopped out onto the concrete floor and closed the barn door behind him.

He heaved open the back gate of the battered truck, then put on latex gloves and unloaded the small load secured in the center of the truckbed. One by one, he went through the packing crates, slid out styrofoam coolers, and dug into piles of dry ice pellets to reveal pale yellow cryoboxes. He covered the labels on the small cryoboxes ("Client 37") with some fresh hand-inked labels as he stacked them on pre-chilled racks, then lowered each into a tank of liquid nitrogen.

He left space in the tanks for the matching virus—a fresh batch, the raw material used to make the vaccine—now brewing at DuBarry Vaccine, 47 kilometers north of Marseille. It would be added to the collection soon.

An investment in the future.

The man threw away his gloves, washed, and took a package of digestive biscuits from the kitchen nook by the office as he left, trotting back to the stone farmhouse to make a phone call.

---

*From the January 2 Atlanta
(Georgia) Post-Tribune:*

U.S. Poultry Leaders Meet on FMD

ATLANTA, Ga. — Leaders of the U.S. Poultry Association met in special session in Atlanta today to discuss the current outbreak of Foot-and-Mouth Disease.

"As fellow commodities producers, we hope this disease crisis for our colleagues in the pork and beef industry passes quickly," said Randall Crayton, board member of USPA and CEO of Tyndall Foods. "They have our best wishes on controlling this horrific plague."

The Poultry Association also released a report confirming U.S. poultry products—including chicken, turkey, and eggs—are not affected by the FMD virus, and remain some of the safest and most nutritious foods on the market.

FMD Source Traced to Iowa

WASHINGTON, D.C. (AP) — Officials at the US Department of Agriculture report that Nebraska livestock infected with FMD virus are believed to have been purchased from Ida Angus in Ida City, Iowa.

A team from the USDA has gone to the site to investigate.

Four other sites, including an alpaca farm in Ohio and a dairy in California, are quarantined pending FMD test confirmation.

CHAPTER 40

When word broke about the Ida Angus hot zone in Iowa, Tike and Liz scrambled to pack. The helicopter pilot abandoned his Monopoly game with the quarantined Nebraska kids, cranked up the rotor of his Bell 35J7, and took his passengers aloft.

Somehow, Tike was able to fall asleep in the helicopter, strapped into her seat with her headset on. She and Liz had been up early to listen in on a media call with the International Epizootics office in Paris, the O.I.E.; topic: U.S. trading status. Now here they sat, strapped in, heading east-northeast at 167 miles per hour.

Told you so, Liz had said. *It had to be out there, somewhere.*

Tike woke when Liz shook her shoulder. "Tike. Tike. We're going to land now."

Tike looked at her watch, yawning. "Already? I thought it would be another hour."

"Change of plans." The sound of the rotors shifted, getting deeper as they descended. "We're going to do a full decontamination and go to another site."

"Oh man, another hot zone already?" Tike paused. "So why a decon? They're more contaminated than us."

"Not this place," Liz said, then looked out the window. Tike looked too; they were approaching an open field, a bare, flat swath of clipped alfalfa, drifting with snow, surrounding a pair of small airport runways. There was a ring of vehicles on the concrete and the now-familiar tanks of bleach. Tike turned and looked at Liz. "Oh no, not here?" She groaned. "Please?"

Liz shrugged. "Sorry."

"I'm freezing just looking at it. Why didn't they tell us earlier? At least we had a heated decon tent in Nebraska."

"New assignment. We..."

The pilot cut in. "Mikes off, ladies. I'm going to talk to the locals. On the ground in four minutes."

The rotors slowed overhead as Tike and Liz ducked out of the helicopter and walked toward the cluster of vehicles. In their way, however, was the decon station, ready and waiting.

It was colder than it looked.

After the decontamination on the icy runway, which turned out to be on the outskirts of Sioux Center, Iowa, Tike toweled off her hair, hoping it would dry before it froze. She and Liz were approached by a Marlboro model in a tall pair of cigarette-leg jeans with worn boots and a black cowboy hat. Tike could have appreciated him more if she wasn't shivering uncontrollably.

He stopped in front of Liz. "Dr. Thomas?"

Liz nodded as she pulled on a clean coat, a loaner from the crew on the tarmac. "You must be Quint," she said, her teeth chattering. He nodded, handing them each some wool gloves and a cap.

"Well," said Liz, looking over at Tike, "we're ready. Let's go."

Tike handed her towel to one of the decon monitors and pulled on her cap and gloves as she followed Liz and Quint to a maroon king-cab pickup with South Dakota government plates.

"The boss said he'll call when he gets out of meetings," said Quint, opening the passenger door for Liz, who nodded and climbed in. Tike crawled into the back seat as Quint got behind the wheel, telling them there was hot coffee in the back. As he put the truck in drive his phone started ringing. "Yes, boss?" Quint's hat bobbed a couple of times as he listened, then handed the phone to Liz.

"I understand," she said. "We'll call when we get there...Me too." Her face flushed; she handed the phone back to Quint as they left the decon station behind.

"Coffee?" Tike handed Liz a cup, looking at her closely and waggling her eyebrows. "Everything okay?"

"Yeah," said Liz, and cleared her throat. "Now. Tell me what you know about EmbroGen. I haven't been there in ages. Jack says you have some recent history there."

Tike looked at her, eyebrows raised. "EmbroGen? The cattle embryo company? Those veterinarian guys?"

"Yeah," she said. "That EmbroGen. That's where we're going. The Department of Ag wants to take over their stockpile of frozen cattle embryos, and the EmbroGen CEO said 'Screw you.' I'm supposed to mediate."

Tike frowned. "With Barry Van Den Hoeve? The CEO? Why you?"

"For starters, I'm a vet, and I don't take any crap," she said, then shrugged. "Plus, Barry is my brother."

Tike leaned into the sheepskin seat covers in the back seat of Quint's truck and fished some aspirin and Tums out of one of the overnight bags. She downed the aspirin and chewed the chalk as she sipped her coffee, letting the steam float up over her face.

"Wow," said Tike. "You're a Van Den Hoeve. And here I thought you were Norwegian."

Liz shrugged. "When we were kids, Barry and I pretended we were vets, putting splints on the dog, taking care of baby birds. We had a little wagon we kept filled with vet supplies. Pulled it behind our bikes. We had our own zoo, too."

"So why ask me about EmbroGen? Doesn't Barry keep you filled in?"

Liz turned to the window. "We haven't talked much lately. Since Joseph died. They were close."

"Ah," said Tike. "Okay." She leaned back into her seat. "Awkward."

"They've moved into bigger facilities since then, I hear," said Liz, turning back and looking at Tike while gesturing for another cup of coffee. Tike poured carefully from the Thermos. "Tell me what you know," said Liz. "What you saw."

Tike handed her the coffee, then leaned back into her seat. "I have this thing for liquid nitrogen," she said. "Have since graduate school. Fun stuff. Freeze the lab chief's jelly donut while he's not looking, whatever. But you don't see LN_2 much out here. Mainly at vets, big breeders. And EmbroGen."

EmbroGen, she told Liz and Quint, wasn't so widely known back when she first stumbled across them, doing an unrelated story she couldn't even recall. But they were a great story: Founded by smart vets— Barry and a pal—pros at doing *in vitro* fertilization of cows, even better at freezing the embryos, which were much easier to ship and sell around the world than the bawling 200-pound calves they would turn into. Plus they had the biggest collection of LN_2 storage tanks—called cryotanks—

she had ever seen. Some of the tanks were big enough to freeze a whole carcass, beef or human. The remodeled hog building used for storage, called "the tank farm," didn't quite fit the corn-and-pigs neighborhood; it was ringed with security cameras and keycard locks.

"As it should be," said Tike. "The place is a gold mine."

Liz nodded. "What's the inventory up to by now?"

"As of four months ago, about $187 million worth of frozen cattle embryos stockpiled, ready to implant in host cows. Monthly turnover of 2,000 new embryos."

"Prices?"

"About $50 for a vial with a standard embryo, $5,000 for a high-value bloodline. Lots of vials in those big tanks." Tike stopped to watch out the window for a while. There was nothing in sight but frozen fields of corn and soybean stubble. They could be anywhere in the upper Midwest.

"Driving by, the new facility looks like a regular farm," said Tike. "But the big silos. Corn? There's no corn in them. They're full of liquid nitrogen. Thousands of gallons. And the big red barn? A cloning lab, just expanded this summer." She finished her coffee and poured another, just for the heat.

Quint and Liz were quiet. Quint was turning a bullet end-over-end with his right hand, passing it finger to finger. Liz was looking out the window. Tike could hear the heater blowing. She leaned forward between the front seats. "What's going on?" she said. "I get the feeling there's something you haven't told me."

Liz kept looking out the window as she spoke. "It's quiet now, but it's going to get ugly soon," she said. "Someone has barricaded the whole property, a square mile. Presumably Barry. They're supposed to be making contact in six hours."

"And we're going there?" said Tike. "We're not going in, are we? We went through decon, but still..."

"No," said Liz. "We're just going to talk. There's a teleconferencing suite at a library a few miles away from the company. We'll talk from there."

Tike leaned back. Quint flipped on the blinker and they turned onto a small county road. Tike leaned forward again. "No offense, Quint," she said, then turned to Liz, "but why is Quint here? Why is Jack involved?"

Liz spoke without turning away from the window. "Because of me."

Tike sat back and blew on her coffee. She thought about how long the tanks could stay frozen with that much LN_2. She thought about the future herds stored in the tanks, probably enough to jump-start the entire US cattle industry. *A national asset. The Fed was finally smart enough to realize it. But Barry was a step ahead.*

Liz turned and watched Quint's bullet, moving slowly between his fingers. "One of the silos you saw, Tike—Jack told me it doesn't hold liquid nitrogen any more. Apparently Barry made some changes after September 11. Preparations. Stuff he never told me about."

Tike held her coffee cup against her forehead, eyes closed, willing away the headache she could feel blooming inside. "So what's in it, fuel for the generators?"

"No," said Liz. "Weapons. For self defense. Just in case."

Quint pulled over at the first Iowa state squad car they saw, discreetly parked in the middle of the blacktop. He got out and approached the sedan; a trooper met him halfway. They stood with their backs to the truck, hats bobbing as they spoke.

The trooper got on his radio for a while, wrote a few notes on his pad, tore off the page and passed it to Quint. The trooper walked to the back of his car and popped the trunk. He reached inside briefly, then stood back. Quint looked into the trunk, puckered his lips, and shook his head. Both men stood back, looking into the trunk, nodding. Then they shook hands and Quint got back in the truck.

"They're ready for us," he said, putting the truck into gear. Tike and Liz looked at each other, eyebrows raised, as he drove on the shoulder around the trooper's car and immediately turned right on a gravel road.

They headed for a large black panel truck with a satellite dish on top. The cars clustered around it were a rainbow coalition from multiple states and multiple agencies: highway patrol, county sheriff, and at least one state fire marshal. Several other cars weren't labeled, but had lots of antennae.

Quint pulled up next to an unlabeled car and put the truck in park, leaving the engine running. He turned to the women. "I'll be right back," he said. "Wait here." He got out, locking the doors with a beep.

Tike and Liz watched him go to the door of the black truck. The door opened as he approached, and closed behind him slowly. Tike turned to Liz.

"Well? What's going on?"

Liz shrugged. "You know as much as I do," she said, and looked around at the cars.

Tike pressed her fingers against her temples, working on her approaching headache. "Somehow I doubt that."

Liz dug through a bag on the floor and found a package of cookies. She handed one to Tike and took some for herself. They sat and ate the cookies, looking at the panel truck, speculating on the gadgets it hid.

Ten minutes later, Liz got a call on her cell phone. "Hi...The trip went fine, no problem." She listened for a while. "Okay. I'll check with her, but that should be fine...Okay, I will. You too."

Liz put the phone in her pocket and turned in her seat to face Tike. "That was Jack. He's been talking with Quint and the guys in there." She swung her thumb over at the black truck, then took a deep breath and let it out before going on.

"I've been traded," she said, then smiled. "Apparently, since that dumb-ass Governor of Iowa still has me suspended, and hasn't got one nano-clue how to deal with FMD in his state, much less torqued Iowa-Dutch businessmen with a silo full of weapons and $200 million of frozen, disease-free cattle embryos, which will quadruple in value by the time this ten-clown circus is cleaned up, the feds want me on the team. Officially." She unbuckled her seatbelt and started to get out of the truck. "Time to go."

The door of the black panel truck opened a crack.

"But what about me?" said Tike. It came out as a whine. *She has all the fun.*

"Finish your cookies, Tike. And wipe your shirt off. You spilled something." Liz unlatched the door and got out. "Come on, dummy. You're my assistant. Bring your tape recorder and laptop."

Tike's seatbelt jammed. She shimmied out of it, catching her coat, tearing it.

"Let's go make a deal," said Liz, already heading for the van.

Tike grabbed her gear and hopped out of the truck. "So then, who's Quint?" she asked. She stumbled and bumped into Liz. "Who was that trooper? They're obviously pals. What were they looking at in the trunk?"

"Probably his working rig," said Liz, dropping her voice. The door to the black truck was silently gliding open as they approached. "Jack told me Quint and the trooper are sharpshooters, Tike. It's because of the damn weapons. If I don't get my brother out, they will."

An hour later, Liz shooed Tike from the crowded conference table in the black panel truck. "Get some sleep," she said. "I need to talk shop with the USDA vets. I'll catch up with you." She leaned over and whispered, "You look like crap."

Tike shrugged, gathered up her notes, and lurched out the door, wincing in the bright afternoon sun. She slowed to pull her sunglasses from her coat pocket, then came to a full stop when she heard Quint's voice around the corner:

"Sure, Nick...No, they're still inside, meeting with the team. Tonight, I think...Right. Okay, I'll do that...No, I don't think she knows."

Tike leaned back against the wall next to the door, playing with her sunglasses, pretending to clean them.

"Yeah, got the envelope," said the voice. "The photos were fine. Spotted them right away at the airport. Cute cat, by the way. What do you sweethearts call him, Nick Junior?...Oh, that's precious...Yeah, screw you too, wise guy."

Tike jammed her sunglasses onto her nose and started walking as quietly as she could back to the pick-up.

When Tike got back to Quint's pick-up, minus Quint, she crawled into the back seat with a blanket, thoughts spinning in her head: How in the world were Nick and Quint connected? *Why was Nick talking to Quint, not me?* She shook her head. Her phone beeped; she dug it out of her coat pocket.

"Hey, Tike," said U.P. "How's it going?"

"A little weird, U.P.," she said, still thinking about the possibilities of a Quint/Nick connection. "Not quite sure about some of this." She told him about EmbroGen. "I realize they're not public, but have you and Geneva been tracking them?"

"Don't need to," said U.P. "Geneva owns a piece of the company. She went to B-school—Wharton—with one of the founders. A vet. Kip somebody?"

"Yeah. Kip Sietsma. If I see him I'll say hi," she said.

CHAPTER 41

Geneva put the handset back in the cradle of the old-fashioned phone on her oak desktop. She leaned back in her chair and took a sip of Diet Dr. Pepper. The small locked room was silent, the soundproofed walls absorbing every movement, the sounds of Chicago twenty-six stories below, non-existent.

She picked up the 9- by 12-inch envelope and studied its face. As with the first one, there was no return address, but it bore the frank of the post office at La Guardia, four days ago. The stamps were common holiday kitsch: a cartoonish Santa, his team pulling a sleigh.

Geneva went to the file cabinet labeled "L" and pulled out another envelope, laying it beside the first. The envelopes looked almost the same. Same writing, same stamps, but the postmark on the earlier one was a Manhattan station, Dec. 24.

She set the envelopes to the side and spread out the new documents: account statements from Morgan, Sanford, Brown Investments, and from Oppenheimer Fidelity Trading Partners, each several pages thick. Good trades, and lots of them. A savvy investor. Buying low, selling high, holding, ramping, dumping. Tick, tock—solid decisions, like a loud clock. No emotions there. Riding the wave along with DeadSim. Not precisely the same, but catching the wave anyway. A good planner.

An investor Geneva would like to meet, to interview. That might not be too hard. The name on the accounts was Tiburnia Isola Kendall Lexington.

Tike.

Geneva took another sip of her drink.

"Damn it," she said. She leaned over her desk, opened the account statements, and started reading again.

———

CHAPTER 42

Tike was just about ready to lay her head down for a nap in the warm backseat of Quint's truck when she was fool enough to call her plumber for an update.

"A god-awful mess," he said. She cringed. "Too bad about your floor. But you don't want that old wood anyway. Not practical."

She closed her eyes and blew out a breath. "But you got it taken care of? No more leaks?"

"Oh, sure," he said. "All done. Say, I have a brother-in-law who's looking to buy an acreage. Yours isn't too run down. Why don't you just sell before it gets worse? You could move to town where things like this wouldn't happen. Neighbors to check on you, you know."

She thanked him and said she'd think about it. After putting away her phone she laid down and closed her eyes, but they wouldn't stay shut. Her phone gave a quiet beep, so she reached into her coat and dug it out, looking at the number calling. *Lompoc Federal.*

Tike sat up. *He's not scheduled to call. Now what?* She hit "Answer" and put the phone to her ear.

"Zack's dead," he said without preamble, prison sounds behind him. "I got a special pass so I could call you. Thought you ought to know."

"What? *My* Zack?" Her stomach clenched. How many times had she wished Zack dead back then? "Last I heard he was pushing around someone new, her kids, too."

"Yeah, a real hero."

"So what happened?" Scenes in violent color flashed through her mind, so easy to imagine. Too easy. Her: splayed, broken, silent. Him, weapon in hand, in control to the end, sprawled over her. Murder-suicide. *There but for the grace of God,* thought Tike, closing her eyes. She swallowed hard. "What about the woman? Is she okay?"

"Not involved."

"What?"

"I got a look at the police report," he said.

Tike gave a tight smile, leaned back and picked up the Thermos. "I won't ask how."

"Anyway," he said, "it wasn't what you'd think. A fight, yeah, but not with her. And it got nasty. Rape. He was on the receiving end."

"Zack? Oh man." Tike's forehead chilled with sweat; her mouth went dry and she put down the thermos. *Did he deserve it? Yeah. Taste of his own medicine.* "Oh man."

"I'm sorry to dump it on you like this," he said, then paused. She could hear metallic noises behind him. Doors slamming. *Locking?* "Look, I've got to go. This call cost me some favors." He sneezed. "Excuse me."

"Gesundheit," she murmured.

"Anyway," he said, "I didn't know if the police would contact you. Can't say I'm sorry about him. Tike, I messed up our marriage, messed up your life, but not like him. At least I wasn't like him."

Tike didn't respond, opened and shut her mouth.

"There's supposed to be more information," he said, "but I haven't got my hands on it yet. Something unusual. Grapevine's a bit slow around the holidays. Got to go. But I wanted you to know. You be careful, Tike. Strange things are happening."

"You be careful too," she said, but the line was dead. She looked out the window. Twilight was starting. The door to the black van opened a crack. Strange things were happening, all right.

———————

An hour later, Tike plopped down on the floor outside the bathroom of their latest motel room, a mile from the black van. She was toweling her hair again but this time she was warm and didn't stink of bleach. Liz was taking her turn in the shower, trying to use up the rest of the motel's hot water, though Tike hadn't left much.

"What about that display panel by the phone guy? The guy wearing camo. What do you think that was?" Tike had to yell over the noise from the shower.

"I don't know, Tike," Liz yelled back. "Maybe a switchboard?" She shut off the water. "Hand me a towel, will you?"

As Liz toweled off, Tike combed her damp hair, trying to picture Liz's session with the Department of Ag guys, who were chomping at the bit over EmbroGen.

"Jack was right," said Liz, dropping her towel on the motel floor and pulling some clean clothes out of her bag—one of their care packages, sent by Jack. "They were seeing the EmbroGen situation as a threat, not an opportunity. Cripes, what a testosterone fest." Liz put on a dash of makeup and closed her travel kit with a snap.

Tike moved to a chair by the door, making a few notes in her notebook as she remembered more bits and pieces of the meeting. Liz grabbed her bag and stood in front of Tike.

"Now, the hard part," she said. "Let's go see what the EmbroGen guys think. Ready?"

———————

Barry Van Den Hoeve, DVM, MBA, CEO of EmbroGen and a Director of the Iowa Biotechnology Association, would have looked positively elegant in other circumstances. Now, on screen in the teleconference room, he looked like a news anchor for RFD TV, with wavy reddish-blond hair and Liz's light blue eyes, seated at his desk and staring into the camera without blinking. His veterinary coveralls were partly unzipped, showing a clean white dress shirt underneath, his tie loosened. His long legs, chore boots and all, were stretched across his desk at EmbroGen, four miles away from Tike and Liz.

The women sat at the Sioux Center Public Library conference table with their own set of microphones and camera. They all just sat, Barry and Liz and Tike, staring at the cameras perched on top of the screens showing the opposition.

The Department of Ag, represented by Liz, was playing hardball. EmbroGen's treasure trove of embryos was 127 miles from a new foot-and-mouth hot zone—an unprecedented situation. Liz had told her brother that if the Department couldn't take possession and secure the site, they'd expand the hot zone and make EmbroGen incinerate everything in their cryotanks.

EmbroGen's silo full of weapons made the discussions a bit more serious, though neither Barry nor Liz mentioned them.

Tike looked back and forth between the sibling veterinarians. Tike was off to the side; it wasn't her discussion. Liz had the mike. Tike wondered if they had contests like this when they were kids: *Who'll blink first?*

It was Barry. He swung his booted feet to the floor, leaned forward and depressed the button on his mike. "They can kiss my ass," he said, his activated camera zooming in on him. "You can't do that to us. We've got everything under control here. And that so-called market value? According to who?" He let go of his mike and leaned back in his chair again.

Tike wrote a note and passed it to Liz: "Lying. Blinking too much."

Liz smiled at Tike, nodding slowly, and pinched her under the table.

Barry narrowed his eyes and leaned over his mike. "Now what?"

"We were just considering the option of petitioning the O.I.E. to define this region as a FMD-free special territory," said Liz. "We were just on the phone with Paris this morning. Did you think about that, Barry? You never were good at reading the fine print."

Barry raised his eyebrows and sat back, pulling the cord of the mike so he could hold it on his lap. "The O.I.E. would work with us?"

"It's never been tried, Barry. Talk to Kip about it."

He nodded, frowning. *What was that about?* thought Tike, glancing at Liz. Kip Sietsma, Barry's long-time business partner and co-founder of EmbroGen, was the more detail-oriented of the pair. *Where is Kip, anyway? He should be in on this meeting.* Tike looked at Liz again, who shrugged.

Barry looked at his watch. "I'm waiting for him to call," he said. "He's on the road."

Liz sat back, waiting.

"We're clean," he said. "And we act on it. Look at the suite you're in. We set that up from day one. You know that, Liz."

Liz nodded. EmbroGen sponsored the expensive high-tech annex so they could tap into the statewide network of conference rooms. From day one, the company had been very tight on biosecurity. Visitors were kept off the premises. Seeing them on-screen was usually enough, and meetings with other EmbroGen sites around the state were also more convenient (and cost-effective) this way. It was also a secure, closed system: fiber optic cables were tough to hack from dorm rooms. Even their pals in the black panel truck had to run a cable out the front door of the library so they could park out front and watch the show.

Liz pressed the button on her microphone again and the camera in the library conference room zoomed in on her.

"We would need to apply as a partnership, Barry. You, the state, and the federal government. It would be complicated, but it's your only chance right now. You're going to be in the middle of a hot zone, maybe within hours. I'm authorized to come in and purge your tanks and destroy your stock, both frozen and on the hoof. Regardless of..."

Liz picked up her coffee and took a sip. She leaned forward and pressed the button on the mike again, her voice softer.

"Work with me, Babar," she said. Her brother gave a quick smile. *Babar*? Tike bit her lip, trying not to laugh. Liz looked serious. "You know I'll take care of you here," she said. "It's your only chance. I'll probably need to put down your stock outdoors, if you haven't done that already."

He shook his head.

"But you could keep your frozen stock," said Liz. "I know your set-up. I know you're clean." She laughed. "You always were the tidy one. You could start to export again within the year. Legally, that is. And I know you want to do things right."

He nodded slowly as he rocked back in his chair. Tike could see part of his office around him. No ego wall or yachting trophies on the credenza for this guy. Just shelf after shelf of textbooks, diagnostic manuals, lab protocols, and bound reports. She couldn't read the titles from here, but she had taken a good snoop when she interviewed him the previous autumn.

"All it's going to cost you is a chunk of your inventory, which the Department of Ag would distribute as part of the national disaster recovery plan," said Liz. "You've got a hell of a resource here, Barry. Shame to start over."

He nodded again, still silent.

After a couple of minutes his camera zoomed back out to the default position, showing more of the room, including the door. The hallway outside looked empty.

He leaned forward and reactivated his mike, looking straight at Liz as the camera zoomed in on him again. "We can't let you in, of course," he said. "And no one here is coming out. A few of us agreed to stay in lock-down here until things get under control out there. I couldn't risk not being able to get back in and take care of the tanks, or risk contaminating them."

Tike watched him glance at the photos of his family on the desk. He looked back at the camera. "Choose two of your decision-makers and bring them to the library room you're in now. We can e-mail and fax documents back and forth—there's a dedicated terminal and fax in the corner behind you there—and we'll hammer something out."

Another voice came through the speakers, indistinct. Barry looked to his right, toward the door, now off camera.

"What?" he said, looking to his right, still gripping his mike. "Kip's here? I thought he was in Chicago." His eyebrows drew together and he started to rise from his seat. "He said what?"

The quiet voice spoke again, then Barry, low, angry, not clear.

He leaned back to face the camera as he set the mike back on the table. "I'll be right back," he said, and moved off-camera.

After a few minutes the camera deactivated and zoomed out to the default position. As it moved back the door came into view, and the hallway beyond. This time there was something in the hallway. A chore boot, lying on the floor. A chore boot like Barry's.

Liz jumped out of her chair and grabbed her mike.

"Barry!" she said. "Barry! What's going on?"

There was no answer. The view on-screen didn't change.

"Babar?" Liz let go of the mike and moved toward the screen, touching it. "Babar!" she shrieked. Tike stood up.

Liz, hands on the screen, turned and stared at Tike. "What happened? What?"

Tike looked out the window at the black panel truck. She knew the crowd inside it would be scrambling, zooming in on the image of the chore boot, pulling up image analysis software, picking up phones and yelling orders.

"Tike?" shouted Liz. "What the hell?"

Tike made an effort to move slowly. She sat down and reached out a hand to Liz. "Come sit. Sit with me. It's going to be okay." *Liar liar pants on fire. I don't have a good feeling about this. At all.*

But what else could anyone, even the panel truck guys, do? The EmbroGen compound was private property, still barricaded. And armed. If someone behind the lines didn't ask for help, and the outsiders didn't see something obviously criminal going on, they and the black truck had to just sit tight.

"Here, let's have another coffee," said Tike, refilling Liz's cup, watching the screen, praying, for Liz's sake, for Babar to reappear in his stockinged feet, scowling, boots thrown in frustration, his hands full of paperwork, or a cell phone, or zipping up his pants and coveralls, or whatever else took him away from their meeting. Liz got on the phone with the black truck, occasionally shouting into her microphone for Barry. She called Barry's cell phone, and office phone, and the main number at the EmbroGen front desk, probably not twenty feet from Barry's desk.

No answer. The clock ticked. No Barry. Then the screen flickered.

It went black.

Tike and Liz drank coffee and made calls from their chairs in the library conference room while they waited for something to happen. Other vehicles pulled up out front, surrounding the black panel truck. Men and women in heavy coats and various uniforms moved back and forth between them. The screen didn't come back. Neither did Barry, or anyone else.

"I'm sure we'll be going in, Tike," said Liz, coming back from one session in the black truck, plopping into her chair in the library conference room. "They want that stockpile. Uncontaminated." She laid her head on the table. "They think Barry's jerking us around, trying to get me to cave."

Tike sat back, watching the screen, silent. The women waited, made some calls, short, quiet.

Quint came in and shut the door as Tike was hanging up her phone. He sat on the leather chair between the women as Liz ended her call.

"They've found Kip," he said. "In Chicago."

"Thank God," said Tike.

"Chicago?" said Liz. "Can he call Barry? Maybe he has some other numbers, a direct line?"

"Doubt it," said Quint. He picked up their bags while Tike and Liz packed up their phones and notes. "Kip's dead," he said. "He's been dead for a week."

———

CHAPTER 43

Clarissa used the lit vanity mirror of her car visor to freshen her lip-stick, then smoothed the low collar of her dress under her black wool coat, watching the evening traffic flow by on Connecticut Avenue, four miles from the White House. She pressed a tissue carefully against her forehead and the crest of her cheeks, dabbing at perspiration. *Nerves? How silly of me.*

She was wearing her favorite dress: deep blue, to complement her eyes, and elegant but slightly bold—the better to please her date.

She took a deep breath and got out of her car, locking it carefully before crossing the dark parking lot to the Northern Italian restaurant.

It's not really a date, she told herself as the maitre d' seated her at a small table. *He's bringing a package, and we'll just happen to have a drink, maybe a small hors d'oeuvre, maybe dinner. Maybe...?*

Clarissa, it turned out, had those things: drink, hors d'oeuvre, dinner. But she had them alone, trying not to let the waiter or other diners see her check her watch, trying not to look up every time someone walked in, try-ing to look like she planned to eat alone. She found a small volume of short stories in her purse and read it, casually, as if she had planned to do so. She stopped in the ladies' room as she left the restaurant and took some aspirin, again damping her forehead and cheeks, which were warm and flushed.

When Clarissa got back to her car, she saw there was a brown paper grocery sack with a large red bow on the driver's seat. *Didn't I lock the doors?* She opened the unlocked door with one hand. *I thought I did.* Leaning in, she carefully peered into the sack; inside were two packages wrapped with the same holiday paper he had used before. She smiled and caressed the red bow.

That rascal.

She slipped into the driver's seat, smiling and sliding the sack over to the passenger side. A card fell from the bow onto the floor. She retrieved it, clicking on the dome light.

"My dear friend," read the spidery writing. "Forgive me. I could not bring myself to enter the restaurant. It was perhaps too much to bear, to begin to hope after so long. But you look beautiful in your dark blue dress—like a duchess. And please, may we try again sometime? Please be patient with me. I am just a man."

Clarissa made herself wait until she got home, then she opened the packages. The smaller one held cash; she set it aside. The larger package was a bottle, a very fine cabernet from a vinyard she only knew from reading *Wine Spectator*. A small note tied to the neck read "Drink me." *And so I will*, she thought with a smile, a shiver running through her. A glass of cabernet and a hot steamy bath were just the thing tonight.

Half an hour later Clarissa eased into her steaming tub with a crystal glass of cabernet and notes for her speech at the next day's rally. She was expecting a good crowd.

Before she went to bed she took more aspirin, a double dose.

After Clarissa's failed date, as she pulled out of the Washington restaurant parking lot, thinking about the red bow and the packages and her friend and *please be patient with me I am just a man*, Clarissa didn't notice the additional weight burdening her car.

First, there were the four empty paperboard cartons, folded, wedged under the spare tire. Originally the cartons held 42 pounds of C4; in other terms, the cartons had held enough C4 to destroy, for example, a laboratory complex. Now, the emptied and flattened cartons weighed only 17 ounces, only a trace of which was C4 residue.

Second, there were 23 ounces of disposables stuffed under the passenger seat. Specifically, this included 50-milliliter orange-cap Falcon tubes and 1.5-milliliter Eppendorf tubes, each with a wet, now frozen, meniscus. Upon closer examination, anyone inspecting the tubes would find the wet residue contained about 2.3×10^7 infectious units of FMD virus per milliliter, an excellent viral concentration for aerosol delivery to respiratory systems, and the same concentration as the tube now waiting in her home freezer.

Third, inconveniently deep in the sticky glove compartment, next to some packets of organic honey-mustard salad dressing, there were 31 ounces of Walther PPK, loaded with four ounces of Talon cartridges, most of them not yet used. The two that had been used were most unfortunately part of a recent Class C felony that had yet to come to light.

Altogether, the additions totaled about 75 ounces, less than five pounds, not enough that a driver, especially one with a rising fever and unrequited hopes for romance, would notice.

———————

A heavy disk of cold air rotated above Plum Island, the center pushed up by warm air from the generators and vents, the periphery depressed by seasonal currents blowing along the coastline, over the sands and rock.

Little snow was on the ground, and few people moved between the dark buildings. Three small clusters of people moved down the gravel paths toward the ferry landing. The ferry horn blew; the noise of the heavy diesel engines rose a notch. The people on the gravel paths moved faster.

Lights were bright in many windows on the research floors of the main building. The animal rooms in all divisions were dim.

The filtered exhaust from the fourth floor vents, faint with the scent of sheep and swine and horses, was torn from the embrace of the building and pulled into a spiral that moved outward. As the trail of the spiral reached over the ferry, the heat from the surging engines rose as a block, bumping the spiral up, into the path of the seasonal coastal currents.

The slow coastal wind absorbed the spiral, blending the scents of wool and hide with those of clams and salt and surf.

———————

CHAPTER 44

While Liz and Quint and the rest met into the night in the black panel truck, laying out plans for going into EmbroGen, Tike grabbed some quiet time. She scavenged some blankets and cushions and set herself up on the bed of Quint's pickup truck. It was time to sip Sambuca and count stars.

Tike added more ice from the cooler to her glass of Sambuca, using a scoop so she could leave her mittens on, then settled back on her cushions, pulling the blankets closer and leaning back. The cooler perched on the tailgate had enough ice and snacks to keep her entertained for a while.

Tike had already finished her calls for the evening, looking for information about Kip, Chicago, Barry, or EmbroGen. She had called U.P., and the MATA flack. A friend at the *Chicago Trib*. U.P. again. Others.

Now she had her hand on her phone, ready to call Pete for another round of "Dr. Phil" Russell, when Liz stepped out of the black truck, her own phone at her ear. "Yes," Tike heard her say as she approached. "Yes, we'll be here." Liz signed off, put her phone in her coat pocket and zipped up, hunkering down in her own soft igloo of blankets and cushions in the glow of the cargo light. She took the beer Tike handed her and held it next to her ear. "Mom's home remedy for phone ear," she said. She toasted Tike with her glass.

"I think we've got a plan," said Liz, breaking the silence of the dark night. "Just give me a minute to unwind. Tell me what you did. Any word on Chicago? I'll listen." Liz leaned back, eyes closed.

Tike leaned back too, but looked up, scanning for the Big Dipper. *Boring.* She pulled the night vision goggles she snagged from the black panel truck out of her pocket and turned off the cargo light.

"Chicago don't know nothing from nothing," said Tike. She put on the goggles. "They got Kip ID'd by accident, a pure fluke. Lucky, too, because someone tried hard to keep him anonymous."

She looked at Liz through the goggles. Liz's eyes were still closed but Tike could see her face clearly. Green, but clear.

"His fingers and thumbs were gone," said Tike, "and most of his teeth. Not a very tidy scene, they said. But one of the county coroners actually recognized him. They had gone to the same conference last year, on West Nile Virus."

Tike leaned back and tried to imagine what she would do to dispose of ten finger fragments. The teeth would be more difficult, she supposed. Perhaps they could be crushed and put on a gravel driveway. The fingertips, on the other hand, as it were, could go into...

BANG!

"Shit!" Tike jumped a foot and slid off her cushions, her drink soaking quickly into her coat. She yanked off the goggles and looked over at Liz. "What the hell?" she said.

Liz was already jumping over the side of the pickup, heading around the black van toward the sound. Tike followed, grabbing her flashlight.

They didn't need the flashlight, however. There was a moving semi-circle of spotlights on the cornfield facing the truck. The spotlights converged on something lying in the bare field. The spotlights went off and Tike pulled her night goggles back on.

Quint, she could see, was one of the three bodies holding spotlights. They were each also holding rifles. Very tricked-out rifles.

The fourth body was on the ground. She could see steam rising from it.

"It's a deer, Liz."

Liz was already heading for the black truck. "I'll get my bag," she said over her shoulder. "You bring the little cooler. Pack it with ice. We'll ship samples out in the morning."

"It's a reindeer," said Tike, but only to herself, as she reached for the cooler.

———

By morning, the shooters had bagged five deer from the secured zone outside the EmbroGen perimeter. No humans, however. Nor had there been any contact from EmbroGen.

Liz took samples from the deer carcasses to check for FMD. Quint had a runner take the cooler to the nearest courier pick-up; the samples would be in the Plum Island lab by afternoon. If the deer were negative, it helped Liz and Barry's odds of getting O.I.E. clearance from Paris for the EmbroGen facility.

Meanwhile, the group from the black van was setting up another perimeter, outside the EmbroGen boundary. The cattle in the region had already been depopulated, and deer scouting continued. The new perimeter marked more than a no-man's zone.

It was a zone of no living things.

Tike and Liz spent the day talking to the team from the black van, studying maps of the area around EmbroGen, and talking on the phone, looking for information. Waiting.

Late in the evening, Liz walked slowly back from a session in the black truck to their perch on Quint's pick-up, scrubbing her hands through her hair.

"Tough session?" said Tike.

Liz just growled and gritted her teeth, lips parted, as she hopped onto the tailgate and crawled onto her pile of cushions. A few minutes later she spoke to the sky. "We set the schedule. There's been no word; we can't be sure the cryotanks are being refilled with liquid nitrogen to maintain freezing. No more info available on Kip's story. We don't know who's left in the EmbroGen compound or why, but we can't risk losing the assets. We're going in at oh-two-hundred."

Tike heard Liz's teeth grind, her breath catch.

"And Barry?"

Liz was silent a moment longer, then cleared her throat. "No word."

"I'm sorry." Tike shivered. "Pop?"

Liz reached out a hand in the dark. Tike put an opened Pepsi securely in her palm. The night vision goggles helped.

At 2:49 a.m. Tike was awakened by Liz's summons on her loaner walkie-talkie.

"Tike. Tike. Over."

"Tike here. Uh, roger, Liz. Hi. Over."

"Tike, you can come in now. Bring your gear. Finish suiting up, like I showed you. I'll be waiting for you. The back door, the one marked on the map."

"On my way," said Tike. By 2:51 a.m. she had crawled fully-clothed out of her arctic sleeping bag at the EmbroGen perimeter and was reaching for an attractive Tyvek jumpsuit hanging on a tree by the fence. A camera bag was sitting at the foot of the tree, already sanitized and bagged. Tike was going to document the inspection of the site.

She wiped down the walkie-talkie with sanitizing tissues from the packets Liz had given her, then wrapped it in a clean baggie and tossed it over the fence onto her camera gear. She stripped and wiped herself down with more of the tissues, then put on new longjohns and the jumpsuit. Tall booties in the pockets went over her Ugg boots, and a bonnet went over her hair and the strap of her night goggles, which had been previously sanitized. They'd spritz her again when she got to the facility doors, but her pre-cleaning helped.

No way did she want to be the one to contaminate the stockpile in the cryotanks.

Tike started her march across the corn stubble. She kept her flashlight pouched to keep it clean. The goggles were enough. The clouds made the night dark; there was only a sliver of moon. She kept her eyes focused on the rough ground—she couldn't risk a fall tearing her suit.

She didn't see the shadow coming up quietly behind her until it was too late.

After that, she didn't see anything for a while.

CHAPTER 45

Tike woke up to darkness, foul smells, and pain. She was folded over and crammed into a space the size of a half-full trash barrel; her leg and back muscles were cramped, and her head was throbbing. The dominant smell was of something spoiled, decaying.

Her knees, wedged into a tangled pile of something metallic-sounding, seemed to be tied together. Her hands certainly were, plus they were behind her back.

She wiggled her fingers until she could grip one of the metallic things, then walked it through her fingers, feeling small cylinders attached to its length. *Are these...cryovials?* She could feel the small ridged caps on the vials, each the size of her pinkie finger. She felt along more of the metal stems. *These canes are all full. And all the samples are thawed.*

I'm sitting in a cryotank.

An EmbroGen cryotank?

If it was a cryotank, the opening was on top. Tike tried pushing up with her head, but nothing moved, neither could she maneuver to her knees to try to stand.

She sagged back down. Her mind felt dull, slow. She leaned on her side, trying to avoid poking her eye out on the tangled pile of aluminum canes, and trying not to breathe through her nose. The smell. She knew what it was now.

It's the smell of rotting embryos.

After a while, her sense of smell went flat and her attention shifted to the liquid seeping through rips in her Tyvek suit. The foul increasing taste of sulfur in her mouth confirmed these were—had been—samples of living material prepared for ultra-low freezing with the penetrating preservative DMSO, dimethyl sulfoxide. She wondered what else the preservative was carrying through her skin and straight into her blood.

She moved around as best she could, inspecting her suit. There were no pockets, nor were there pockets on her long underwear, underneath. But she checked, just in case anything—a welding torch, perhaps—had fallen down her front or up her sleeves. No luck. She probed the pitch black tank for anything other than canes. Nothing again. Not even a seam in the 218-gauge stainless steel floor or walls.

Her cap was gone, her goggles, and one of her booties. The uncovered boot was sticky and wet, and her suit had a score of tears. She didn't feel any major cuts in her skin, just some bruising. Her thinking was odd, dopey.

She shook herself with a start, realizing she'd lost track of time. *There must be something else in with the preservative after all.* This would not do.

"Ah, hello?" Tike's voice was rough and echoed in the cryotank. She could feel the aluminum canes resonate. She cleared her throat. "Hello? Is anyone out there?"

No reply.

"Fuck." She forced herself to concentrate. She noticed one of her eyes, the right one, the blue one, was leaking tears. She could feel the moisture on her cheek. She bent her head down to her knees and carefully used her fingertips to feel around the eye. The entire socket was badly swollen, and numb. It felt like she was touching someone else. The eye was nearly shut. She couldn't tell if she could see or not; it was, of course, pitch black in the tank.

Well, I assume it is.

She thought she heard a sound outside, maybe someone moving another tank. She had no idea what to do. She wished she had the walkie-talkie. She touched the rest of her face and her ears, looking for numb spots. The top of her right ear was numb, too, and swollen, and part of her scalp on that side. The noise outside the tank continued. Something was happening.

Then the noise stopped.

Something had to change. Bad things were happening to her flesh in here. Whoever was out there wasn't going to be on her side, but she had to get out of the tank somehow.

She spoke to her knee, pretending it was her cell phone, pretending she was calling in the cavalry, hoping someone outside her black lockbox believed her sham.

"Liz. Can you hear me now?" She cleared her throat. There was a great deal of mucus in it, a surprising amount. It tasted of blood. She spat in the dark. She spoke louder. "Is this better? Great."

She heard a noise outside the tank, closer now. *Come and get me, you bastards.* The bait was working.

"Got the GPS coordinates yet? Yeah, new battery." She paused, thinking wildly. *I have to keep talking. They have to think I'm calling, bringing cops. FBI. Anyone.* "How about Quint? Doesn't he smell good?"

Eyes open. Stay awake. Hold on.

"Yes, I'm in one of those tanks. The big ones. Right." She spat again. The mucus tasted bitter this time. She heard more movement outside the tank. Something scraped the tank. "You'll be here in ten minutes? Great."

The tank moved.

"Oh, I don't know." She was babbling. *Here they come. Keep talking.* "Hamburgers, I guess. Do you have any more of that pickle relish?"

The canes around her started to rattle. The floor rocked. A splash hit her good eye. She wiped it desperately on her shoulder, but her shoulder was already soaked. A cane sliced wetly across her forehead.

"That's great, Liz. And what does Jack think? Will he send helicopters? I like helicopters."

The tank stopped moving. It was silent.

"Uh-huh. With guns. Big ones. Yep. Okay."

The lid of the tank snapped open and light poured in. Tike's eyes were on fire. She screamed from the pain.

Everything went dark.

When Tike woke she was naked; however, she was dry. Her right eye was heavily bandaged. She could feel adhesive on her skin. Her left eye was weepy but functional. She didn't want to know any more about the right one. Her hands and feet were not bound, but it didn't matter: she was paralyzed.

At least she knew where she was. She was sitting in Barry Van Den Hoeve's chair, behind Barry's desk, in Barry's office on the main floor of EmbroGen. She had sat facing this very chair when she visited and interviewed Barry two years ago. Now she sat on Barry's side of the desk, just as Barry had done when they watched him on screen from the library conference room. Behind her, she knew, although she couldn't move her head or her eyes to look, were Barry's shelves with his manuals and protocols and books.

She could see, with her one good eye, a slightly blurry camera pointing at her. She could also see herself, on the monitor to the right of the camera. On the monitor, she could see that the IV drip hooked up to her arm looked pretty tidy and professional.

Ketamine. The date rape drug.

Every vet has it. As long as it dripped, she was paralyzed. She wouldn't even blink. Her eye was blurry because someone had been kind enough to put lubricating drops in it. Otherwise her one exposed eyeball would dry up and crack within an hour.

She could see the doorway on the monitor. The leg with the chore boot was still there. There was an arm, now, too. The hand on it had deep red nail polish. Blood red.

On screen, she saw someone walk by the doorway, step over the leg and the arm. She heard voices. No one came in the room. Business, some kind of business, went on. She could hear, she could still taste sulfur, plus something worse, and bloody mucus. She could feel pain, and she could feel hunger. Her bare skin was cool on Barry's leather chair. The stench of bad things was in the air. Rotting things. She couldn't speak.

Meanwhile, she watched herself. She looked dead. Not a pretty dead, either. A red light on the camera was blinking. *Who else is watching?*

Her mind wandered, still dopey and slow, and she lost track of time. She sensed movement and voices, but couldn't focus or react. Eventually everything went silent. She watched the red light. Then it went out. At some point she noticed there were donuts and coffee on the desk in front of her. One of the donuts had a bite missing.

Tike looked down at the donuts and slowly reached out and touched one. Her stomach growled. She wasn't tied up, other than some duct tape across her ribcage, binding her to the chair, holding her up. She pawed through the desk for a scissors and struggled to cut through the duct tape on each side of her chest. She tried to peel it off her skin but gave up. She couldn't lift her arms high enough.

She turned to the IV stand beside her, an empty bag reading "0.05% Ketamine in Ringers ISP" hanging from the rack, pulled the IV needle from her arm and dropped it; the line dangled from the IV stand.

She ate one donut, then another, barely strong enough to get them to her mouth. They tasted bitter, but better than the sulfur of dimethyl sulfoxide. *Yeah, my palate's going to be messed up for a while.* She stared at the desktop. She picked up the coffee and took a sip. It was cold.

She leaned back in Barry's leather chair and closed her eyes. She let out a deep breath, opened her eyes, and looked at the video monitor. The red light was on again. She didn't want to look; she had to. The leg with the chore boot and the arm were still in the doorway. No one was walking by. There were no noises outside her room.

She watched the video monitor, watched herself stand up, one inch at a time. She was still naked, and peppered with bruises and red welts. She had a cut on her forehead and her eye was still bandaged. Her right ear was red and swollen. The duct tape dangled from her side, drawing a neat rectangle across her torso.

She gripped the duct tape and tried again to peel it off, watching herself on the monitor. She stood, looking down at the desktop. Her shoulders started to turn toward the open doorway—and what lay there—but turned back to the desk. She reached for the phone, steadying herself. She was starting to feel woozy. As her hand touched the receiver, it rang. She picked it up but couldn't speak.

"Tike. Tike. Can you hear me?"

She sank back into the chair. "Quint? Barry?" The voice was so familiar. "Nick?" It hurt to speak.

"It's Jack, hon. There's a blue switch on the second video monitor. Flip that switch and you'll be able to see me."

She pushed herself back to her feet, glancing out the door as she braced herself on the desk. From this angle, she could see more than the camera had captured. *Barry's boots.* A man in coveralls lay face-down in the hall, a woman's arm—the one with red nail polish—flung across his legs. A dark puddle lay beneath them.

Tike pushed away from the desk and staggered across the room to the camera cabinet, found the blue switch, and turned the monitor on.

She collapsed back into Barry's chair and saw Jack on-screen. He was in an office that looked a lot like Barry's, but with the state seal of South Dakota behind him—he was in the Governor's office in Pierre. Jack started to say something else but she dropped the phone, overwhelmed by a wave of nausea, her hand weak and useless. She could feel her heart rushing in an irregular beat, and sweat on her cold forehead.

It took a while but she carefully lowered herself to the floor and picked up the phone receiver. "Jack," she said. She could see him on the monitor, talking to someone at his side.

His head turned to the camera as he snatched up the phone receiver. She must have been on the speakerphone. "Tike. Thank God."

"Yeah." She eyed the remaining donuts. "I think it was something I ate." She spat into the garbage can. She tasted blood again, and something bitter. She threw the donuts in the trash. *Who put them there? Nasty trick. Where is everybody I heard earlier?*

"Tike. How are you? Oh boy. Are you okay?"

It occurred to Tike that Jack was wearing a lot more clothes than she was. "Um, just a minute." She slid sideways out of the chair and went to Barry's closet. She dug out a clean set of coveralls and a white T-shirt and pulled them on, zipping up the coveralls with her slow left hand. The right was too stiff. She put on some loose tube socks and a pair of new chore boots sitting behind a nice pair of street shoes. *Barry's.* He had his old chore boots on already. *In the hall. It is Barry, isn't it? Where's Liz? Is Liz out there? Liz wasn't wearing red nail polish. Was she?*

She sat back in Barry's chair. "Jack, what's happening?" She was whispering, unable to look in the hall again. *Not yet.* But she had to. She pulled herself to her feet again. "Back in a minute," she said, setting down the phone. She staggered to the doorway, bracing herself against the frame, then dropped to her knees by the body in coveralls. She strained to roll him over, finally getting him onto his back. *Barry.* Barry Van Den Hoeve, a hole between his eyes, bloody brown material dripping to the floor under his head. *Babar. Gray matter. Sulci. Dura mater.* Tike closed her eyes. *Just keep going.* The woman was on her stomach, her face turned to one side. Also dead. But not Liz. *Red nail polish. Red red red.* No other bodies. *Not Liz.* Tike peered up and down the empty hall, then crawled back to Barry's desk and picked up the phone.

"Barry's dead. And some woman. Not Liz. No one else in sight."

"Can you hear anyone? Any noises at all?"

"No."

Jack ran his hand through his hair and rubbed the back of his neck. "Tike, I need you to do something."

She took a deep breath. "Jack. Where's Liz? And Quint? She called me. She was here. Is she out there?" *Please say yes.*

Jack took off his glasses and pinched the bridge of his nose, between his eyes. "Some EmbroGen staff came out yesterday. They said they'd been held against their will, weren't involved, didn't know anything about you; we're debriefing them now..."

"Wait—yesterday? What day is it now?"

"Thursday, Tike. You've been in there more than two days."

That explained her hunger. "Why am I still here? Where is everybody?"

Jack put his glasses back on. "I'm here, in Pierre, but my guys are still there outside Embrogen. By the time you showed up on camera, we—the guys—couldn't get in anymore. And we thought you were dead."

She looked at herself in the monitor and closed her eyes. "You could see me."

"Yes. For about an hour, last night. After the staff came out."

She looked at the desktop, wondering who the people were in the photos on Barry's desk. "I wasn't blinking."

He nodded. "But you were bandaged. We only knew it was a live feed because we could watch the clock behind you. It didn't make sense. But then the camera went black. And we couldn't call until today when we got the lines back up. They just got the cell tower repaired, too."

As he spoke she started to open the drawers of Barry's desk, looking for useful things. She needed to *do* something, anything. And to stop thinking: *Barry. Red nail polish. Kip. Quint/Nick. Liz. Who is down the hall? Alive? Not? Why? Oh Nick.* Thinking was getting too dangerous. Her hands were shaking.

Jack went silent.

"And now? Why couldn't you come in, Jack? You said you couldn't get in anymore." She didn't look at him as she asked the question. There was something else. There had to be.

"Right. And you can't come out. Not yet."

She didn't want to hear the rest. Her hands scrambled for diversion. She found Barry's wallet in the right-hand drawer, pulled out his driver's license. *Lousy photo.* She found a faded picture of him with Liz, each young, in coveralls, squinting into a cold sun, holding a squalling black and white calf. *Liz. Liz. Where are you? Don't be dead.*

Jack was pulling his hair straight up. "While we were tracing the break in the phone line we found some more wiring, a kind of military wiring."

She started sorting Barry's cash by denomination, her shaking hands trying to make tidy stacks of ones, fives, tens and twenties. $457. *Not bad for pocket money.*

She looked up at the screen, at Jack. "Supplies."

He shrugged. "Help yourself. Never can tell what you'll need."

She dumped the coins in the drawer and put the wallet in one of the pockets of the coveralls. They were Barry's coveralls, after all.

"Bottom line, Jack?"

Coveralls. Chore boots. Dead dead dead. The middle drawer was locked. She tried the small key she found in Barry's wallet and the drawer opened. There was nothing in it but two small notebooks, one red and one black. She put each in one of her hip pockets, red on the left and black on the right.

"Hell," said Jack. "Okay, Tike, the whole place is wired. We can't enter the compound—and you can't go out—or we may hit a trigger. We've got some of it figured out but we haven't located the control box."

"Ah." She pulled the middle drawer out onto her lap and inspected it. *No nail polish. Red red nail polish.* The bottom of the drawer looked lumpy. She used Barry's silver pen knife to peel up the corners of the lining. Underneath was a 12-inch square of red shiny fabric, like a tiny padded picnic tablecloth. *Blood red.* She stuffed it in her back pocket. Barry's pocket.

Jack cleared his throat. "We think it's inside the main building, where you are." He paused. "You have to help us find it."

Tike's hands stopped moving. She looked up at Jack. He looked back, silent.

"Is anyone else here?" she said.

Jack didn't say anything.

Tike sat back in the chair and closed her eyes. She folded up the pen knife and gripped it with both hands. "Jack. Anyone? What about Liz? Why are you out there talking to me, not her?" *Answer me. Answer answer. Say she's fine. Say, oh here's Liz. Say oh here's Nick.* She wanted to see Liz walk around the corner. "I got us some coffee," she'd say. "Lousy coffee."

"You have to find the control box," he said. "And deactivate it. We're tapped in to the wiring so we can monitor every power shift. We can walk you through it."

She took a deep breath, her eyes still closed. "Jack. *What* do you know?"

She heard him breathe. And again. "We don't know if anyone else is inside. There's been some confusion out here." He paused. "We found Liz's walkie-talkie at the perimeter, on the side of the road," he said. "And her cell phone." He rubbed his hand across his face, and pushed it back through his hair. "There was blood on it. Human blood."

Tike laid her head down on the desk; her arms dangled between her knees. The knife slid from her fingers to the floor.

"I didn't want to have to tell you now, Tike. It's too much. It might not be Liz's blood; we're still checking the DNA match." He cleared his throat. "But we don't know where she is."

Tike could hear the low humming of a small digital clock near her face. She opened her eyes. Five minutes past eight p.m. Six minutes past. Seven. Oh, she wanted Liz to be okay. She couldn't take much more. She *needed* Liz to be okay.

Nine minutes past eight. "Tike," said Jack. "Come back."

She dragged herself up, leaning back in the chair again. "Jack, what are you doing in this anyway? I thought the EmbroGen deal was with Iowa."

"You've been out of it, Tike. It's chaos out here now. The outbreak is beyond control, borders are a mess. The politicians are scrambling. EmbroGen got put on a back burner. No one else stepped up once Liz and Quint went off the radar screen. I had to do something."

"Quint, too? What happened to him?"

"Can't find him. His truck's gone. The guys at the perimeter said he drove out hours ago. No word since."

Tike stood up and stretched, her back stiff and sore. Her eye was starting to throb and she was horribly thirsty. She dug some aspirin out of the desk. "Give me your number," she said. "I've got to get a couple of things and I'll call you back." *And I'll look around, shall I? But no one else'll be there. No one no one no one. Just coffee. Lousy coffee.* "We'll make a plan."

She used a pen to write Jack's number on a notepad, then on her shaking hand.

Jack turned to the side for a moment, then came back. "The guys here said you should try to avoid opening doors. They might be wired, some kind of mechanical trigger." He shrugged and gave a small wave, unsmiling, and hung up.

Tike set the receiver in the cradle and touched her ear with her fingertips as she headed for the leg in the doorway. Before letting herself think about anything else, she had to check Barry's pockets.

She needed his phone.

———

CHAPTER 46

Tike pulled off the last pair of latex gloves and dropped them on the benchtop in the EmbroGen research lab. She had done all she could to clean the blood off the phone and the other useful items she found in Barry's pockets before putting them in her own. The woman with the red nail polish didn't have any pockets.

Tike also took the spare phone battery and charger she found on Barry's credenza, then went down the hall to the break room, looking into each open office and storeroom along the way. While investigating one office she stopped short when she caught sight of herself in a mirror behind the door. She stared at the red of her eyes, the bruising, the stitches. There was blood in her hair, and in her ear. Tears started coming down between the red welts on her cheeks.

Stop thinking. Stop. She had a job to do, or she might never find Liz. At least she hadn't found any other bodies so far, live or dead.

She continued down the hall to the lunch room. She bought some food and two cans of pop, snapped a can open, and collapsed onto a small sofa, then dug out the cell phone. Jack answered on the first ring. "Yes...yes," he said. "What?"

"I'm ready," she said. "No Liz yet." By the time she finished the first can of pop, a stale packaged sandwich, and a Hostess fruit pie, Jack's technical guy had given her the outlines of what they knew: the wiring in the building, likely sites for inserting devices, floor plans, and escape routes. She made notes in the back of Barry's black notebook with Barry's pen from the local Kiwanis club.

Jack's guy also told her what they didn't know: the kind of switch. The location of the presumed explosives. The size of the expected explosion.

Thanks for that.

She finished a second can of pop, stuffed the rest of her food and drink into the pockets of the coveralls and headed back to the lab. She had found a storeroom there with equipment that sounded useful now. Jack's guy helped her choose a few items she would need from the jumble on the shelves. Twice she went back to Barry's office to hold devices in front of the camera for him to see.

She also found a big leather tool belt in the storeroom and buckled it on. Her coveralls were starting to sag from all her acquisitions. She made a last stop in the restroom; she avoided looking in the mirrors.

Then she headed for the basement, making a final stop in Barry's office on the way. She rooted around in his closet for one last item that would give her some comfort.

She slid Barry's captive bolt gun through a loop on the leather belt as she waved at the camera and headed out the door.

———————

The EmbroGen basement was not as quiet as the labs and offices upstairs. Down below, utility pumps and blowers went off and on. Tike sat on a work stool in the middle of the room and ate her cupcakes as she slowly turned in circles, studying the room.

When she finished, she walked to one of the walls and started pacing counter-clockwise, running her right hand along the wall as she went. The room was packed with equipment and cables. She moved slowly, scanning from floor to ceiling, moving around machines and under ducts, looking for the box she had sketched in her black notebook. She completed the circuit of the main room and went back to sit on her stool. She called Jack.

"Any luck?" he said.

"It's not going to be here." Tike sat, looking, turning around on her stool, pushing with one foot as she leaned back and watched the walls go by. She opened a Gatorade and drank as she thought. "Tell me about the wiring again," she said. "What color? How big? Could it be different than you told me?"

Jack's guy came on and said, yes, it could be bundled in anything. She could hear Jack swearing in the background.

Tike got off the stool and walked around the room again, studying the ceiling along the outer walls, phone between her ear and shoulder. She shoved her black notebook in its pocket and kept the pen in her fingers, pointing at wires as she went along.

Blue, green, light blue. Gray, red. White. There was a light blue one again. Each wire was a different girth, but some looked distinctly less dusty. She went back to the two light blue wires, neither one dusty, and scanned them with her meter from the storeroom. Both were live. Each came from opposite sides of the room and went out through the same hole in the ceiling. She shone the tiny flashlight from Barry's keychain onto the floor directly underneath the exit hole. Wood shavings and fine spirals of green linoleum.

She snapped off the light and headed for the stairs. She went down the carpeted hall and made the U-turn into the empty receptionist's cubby. Green linoleum. She got on her hands and knees and moved a trash basket and a shredder aside.

Got you.

The box was larger than she expected, but she could see the light blue wires going down through the floor. She ran a finger across the top of the box. No dust. She sat in the receptionist's chair, pulled out her phone and dialed Jack. "Okay. I'm ready."

The technician got on the line and she started to pull tools out of her pockets. On the counter, next to the computer, sat a bottle of red nail polish.

Tike's last can of pop sat empty on the EmbroGen reception counter. She was sitting cross-legged on the floor below, staring into the guts of the control box, its cover opened wide. She had a wire gripped in one hand and a wire clipper in the other. "You're sure," she said into the cell phone clenched against her shoulder. "You're absolutely sure it's the black and white striped wire."

The voice assured her again. *Yes, that's the wire. The wire you should cut. It surely is. Then we'll see a power drop and it'll be over.* She put down her clipper, set aside the phone, stood and stretched. She tried to get one last sip out of the pop can, then lowered herself to the floor again. The black and white wire stared at her. She picked up the phone. "Jack. I'm going to get you for this."

She cut the wire.

She laid down on the floor, just for a moment. The green linoleum was nice and cool. And not covered with scraps of her body. *That's nice.* She heard a little tiny voice next to her ear. "Go ahead and cut it. Cut the wire. It'll be okay."

She closed her eyes really hard. If she squinted hard enough maybe she could have not heard that.

"Tike? Go ahead. I swear it's the right one."

Tike reached over and picked up the phone from where it lay, next to the garbage can. "I did."

That stopped the little voice, all right. She could hear Jack in the background. "What did she say? What's happening?"

"Crap."

"Tike? Did you say you cut it? The black and white one we were talking about?"

"Yes."

"Hell." That was the technician.

"Damn." That was Jack.

Tike lifted the ends of the black and white wire out of the box, one end at a time. Yes, they were cut. They were black, and they were white. There were no other black and white wires in the box. It was clear to her that all was not clear. She could hear the technician mumbling to himself, then silence.

"Um, Tike? We'll get right back to you." He hung up. She threw her pop can at the wastebasket but missed. She watched as the can rolled down the hall.

Ten minutes later, the phone rang. Tike was on page 27 of Barry's red notebook. "Tike here."

"Sorry," said Jack. "We had to check something."

Tike went on to page 28. It was in French.

"There's been a development," he said.

Is oublier "to forget," or "to bury?"

"The, uh, black and white wire?" he said. "It was a fake. That means there is no black and white wire, which means there's a timer."

Well, hell. It must mean "to bury."

"And there's no way for us to find the timer," he said. "It may be wireless."

She looked at her watch. She bet they all looked at their watches. It was 11:15 p.m. Thursday.

"We don't know when it's set to go off, Tike."

She wasn't looking at her watch, really. It was Barry's. It was a waterproof sports watch. It had been on the desk, next to the bitter donuts. *Nasty trick.*

"We're going to talk you out, through the basement," said Jack. "There's a tunnel on the floor plan. It goes under the tank farm." He started describing a door, and some tubes.

Tike laid down the phone. Jack kept talking.

She looked at her watch. Barry's watch.

Someone's watch.

The lighted panel on the top half of the watch face read 11:16 p.m. The lighted panel on the lower half read "Thurs." Next to "Thurs" was a small flashing alarm clock. One button on the right was labeled "Al Set." Another read "Al Displ." Tike pushed the button reading "Al Displ" and held it.

The upper panel read 3:15 a.m.

The lower panel read "Fri."

Tike picked up the phone.

In some ways, it was a relief for Tike to know the room she was in would explode in four hours. She had always been deadline-driven.

She dumped all the extra junk from her pockets in the EmbroGen hallway. She replaced it with a sledgehammer, a screwdriver, and a cordless hammer drill with a three-eighths-inch bit. *Just in case.* She tucked Barry's little red and black notebooks into the zippered pocket with the 12-inch square of thick red fabric she liberated from Barry's locked desk drawer. She made one last scan of the rooms, including the lab. Nothing—and no one—was left to take out.

She stopped by Barry's office one last time on the way to the basement. She waved at Jack on-screen as she left. He didn't look too good.

In the basement, she studied her sketch of the floor plan Jack had faxed in to the receptionist's desk. The tunnel to the tank farm—left over from when it was a hog barn—was the old manure pit underneath. The pump-out pipes used to empty it in the spring and fall were on the long side of the pit, now the west wall of the basement.

She should just fit.

Getting out of the pit—somehow—would come later. First she needed to get up into the tank farm. She needed to see who else might be in a tank. She didn't want to, but she needed to, even if Jack hadn't asked her to.

Liz was still missing.

At ten minutes past midnight, her back wedged against the insulated jacket of the blowing furnace in the EmbroGen basement, Tike broke the seal on a pump-out pipe. She used the sledge and screwdriver to peel the rusty steel cap away from the pipe. The edge came away in shreds until the cap hit the floor with a clang.

Cold, musky air flowed out of the pipe. She pointed the flashlight inside and switched it on but it didn't do any good. All she saw was black.

She bent down between the pipe and the furnace, sticking her face right up next to the pipe outlet. The back of her hair rubbed the hot furnace; she could smell it scorch.

It took a moment to figure out what she was seeing. There was a grid—a metal filter—blocking the pipe, five feet from her face. It was welded to the pipe walls, and clogged with debris. She stared another moment, trying to think. *Can I ram it with something? Are the other pipes like this?*

She pulled her head out and looked at her watch. 12:35 a.m.

She stared into the black pit again. The stench of the air flowing out was getting stronger. Not that it would matter much longer.

Then she heard it.

A tapping. Twice, then again. Then silence. She pulled her head back out of the pipe, listened, then stuck her head back in the pipe again.

The tapping was coming from the tank farm.

Sledgehammers are so handy, thought Tike, standing back to catch her breath. She had found another pump-out pipe behind a washer and dryer in the basement under the EmbroGen tank farm. With the appliances out of the way, she used the sledge to break through the grid. The pipe was coated with dried manure, but she wrapped herself in some lab coats that were in the dryer and shimmied through.

The floor under the tank farm was spongy and crunchy. She tried not to look at it. It didn't take long to pull out a ventilation duct and hammer her way through a grate in the floor above.

She scooted up into the tank farm. The light hurt her eyes. She peeled off the fouled lab coats, dropped them through the hole behind her, and checked her watch.

1:57 a.m.

To her right, the first tank was open. The lid was on the floor several feet away. She leaned over and looked inside. One of her Ugg boots, soaked in pink liquid, lay in a tangle of bent aluminum canes.

Her bandaged eye started to itch.

The other large tanks were closed. She went to the nearest and had the lid, which was already loose, nearly off before she noticed the temperature gauge on the side: 320 degrees below zero. As she pushed the lid back into place, she heard a snapping sound, and a small splash. She closed her eyes and shuddered.

That wasn't an aluminum cane.

She pulled the lid back up and leaned in, looking down into the swirling fog. The top of the thick, frigid liquid nitrogen lay somewhere underneath.

"Please, no," she whispered. She blew into the fog; it roiled over the edge of the tank, spilling onto the floor below, briefly revealing the surface of the liquid in the tank. A glance was enough.

"Thank you, God," she whispered. It wasn't Liz's hand whose three remaining fingertips were pointing up at her just above the surface of the super-freezing liquid. It was a man's.

She grabbed a cryoclaw leaning up against the tank and plunged it into the liquid nitrogen, gripping the arm. She pulled, trying to see more, and winced when she heard a cracking sound as it came free, sleeve and all. Six inches of arm rose easily out of the frozen fog, enough to see a familiar watch and shirtsleeve.

Quint.

She paused. *So who drove out in his truck?* Tike lowered Quint's arm back into the tank and replaced the lid. She moved on, checking the other tanks. No bodies. No Liz. She called out as she went. No response. No tapping.

2:14 a.m.

She tried to call Jack on Barry's cell phone. No signal.

2:15 a.m.

She would still have to go down to the manure pit and hammer through the other wall to get out. She had seen a vent she could probably get through, but she wasn't sure how long that would take. She scanned the room to see if she had missed any tanks.

Where is Liz?

2:16 a.m.

She couldn't risk going through the door to the building. Jack said they thought it was probably a trigger. *Should I leave now? Without Liz?* Tike looked at the clock on the west wall, the small red numbers of the digital display flashing.

The digital display...swipe keys...high-security storage. She had seen it on her tour. There was another room. She stumbled toward the clock, tripping over a tank lid. Tucked away behind a partition, next to the digital display of the clock, she could see the swipe key of the high-security storeroom door.

It was open.

She rushed over to the storeroom. Liz lay on the floor in a puddle of pinkish fluid, an aluminum cane of cryovials by her side. *Dimethyl sulfoxide. Thawed embryos.* The hair on the back of her head was wet and stuck to her skull. Her arms were covered with red welts, one hand on a wrench, next to a vent. *The tapping.*

Tike didn't want to see Liz's face. She knew what the pink puddle would have done to it.

The fluid she lay in was the end of a wet trail coming around the partition, from the tanks; Tike must have stepped right over the smears. Tike rolled her friend over and gripped her wrists, averting her eyes. Liz's hands were warm, wet.

Sulfur. The taste flooded Tike's mouth as her skin contacted Liz. Tike dragged her to the hole in the floor. She flipped Liz over, shoving her limp legs through the hole, where they dangled and swung over the old manure pit.

Tike slid down past her, then gathered the lab coats at her feet. She gripped Liz's feet and pulled her down through the hole, trying to catch her as she slid through, limp; both of them landed on the coats.

Tike lay for a moment on the lab coats, Liz's motionless body sprawled across her, the taste of sulfur building again. Tike could feel Liz's heartbeat; Liz was shivering. Tike bit her lip to keep from crying. "Not now," she said out loud. "No time."

2:39 a.m.

Struggling to her feet in the light from the hole above, she piled some of the coats on Liz, then found her sledge and went to work on the vent to the outside. One by one, rusted steel vent pieces broke loose and fell to the floor.

3:05 a.m.

Tike broke through the other side of the vent, holding the head of the sledge with her hands since breaking the handle on the cap of the tube. She shimmied backward out the tube to clear it, then went back to get Liz.

Liz was gone. A pile of empty lab coats lay in the light of the tank farm above. Tike gaped, tears starting, at last, to form.

"Tike." A warm hand touched her raw elbow. She wheeled and caught Liz as she stumbled.

"Oh," said Liz. "Tike? I can't see. I can't see anything."

Tike helped her to the tube and pushed her through.

————————————

An hour later, from the helicopter, on their way to the hospital, they saw the explosion. It wasn't 3:15 a.m. after all, but who were they to complain?

The explosion guaranteed the EmbroGen tanks weren't going to be any help getting the U.S. cattle industry restarted.

It didn't matter, anyway.

They had all been empty. Other than Quint, there were no bodies, and no frozen embryos. The tanks had all been emptied, nothing left but diminishing pools of liquid nitrogen and a litter of empty aluminum canes and canisters.

As they flew southeast across the night countryside, heading for the helipad at Des Moines Mercy, Tike sat motionless, staring out the window at the countryside below. *It's war. This is how a war looks, when it's over.*

At one farm after another, county after county, bright spotlights were aimed into crude pits piled with steaming carcasses. Red tractors tipped their buckets and dumped more steaming deadstock onto the piles. Yellow construction equipment dug more trenches. Blue skid loaders carried piles of carcasses out of long buildings with roll-up windows.

·Outdoors, small bodies in coveralls stepped up to lines of bellowing animals, who then jerked and dropped to the ground, one by one.

Other small figures—people: fathers, mothers, children—stood still. Watching. Watching the end of forever. Occasionally one of the smaller bodies would break away and run to the animals, to a particular one, to one named "Big Red" or "Allie," who liked carrots and won first place at the Clay County Calf Scramble. Another figure would take chase, pulling the smaller one away, holding him tight, then carrying him back into a small house.

Deer lurched back and forth across vacant fields of frozen soil and corn stubble, disturbed by the night noise and the smell of blood and fear and pain and the end of all things as they were, as they had been, in God's Country. Barricades stood, unmanned, at intersections and town boundaries; cars and trucks drove around them, drove too slow, drove too fast, it really didn't matter anymore. Nothing was sure anymore, nothing was clear, some farms would never come back, some would, but the bleeding wasn't over. The blood would run from the farms into the towns: banks would close, and stores would close, and schools would close, and people would leave and nothing would ever be the same.

It *was* a war, thought Tike, watching a police car move slowly through a small town with one stop sign.

We lost.

CHAPTER 47

The next morning Tike sat in a vacant corner of the cafeteria at Des Moines Mercy. She leaned forward over the empty table, resting her unbandaged cheek on the cool formica as she waited for Special Agent Ed Magnus. The smells of scorched coffee and frying sausage were briefly replaced by the antiseptic smell of the table.

Liz was upstairs under observation—by a salvage crew, said Jack. So far: a liver specialist, a neurologist, a plastic surgeon. And then there were her eyes. The eye surgeon.

Blind? No. It wouldn't happen. It couldn't.

Tike straightened up as footsteps approached. Magnus set two coffees on the table, then slid into the chair across from her, snapping his gum. He adjusted his tie, pinned with a small American flag, before pulling a fat envelope from his pocket and sliding it over to Tike. She cupped her coffee with her bandaged hands and leaned in to take a small sip, wincing at the heat. She slid the cup aside and picked up the envelope.

"Photos," he said, tearing open a sugar packet. "Mugshots." Men he wanted her to identify.

Dead men.

"Got one of Zack?" said Tike, rubbing her hands across the exposed part of her tired face.

"You heard, eh? Bang bang."

She shrugged and went through the photos again, but the only men she could identify were Barry, Quint, and one of the barn guys she knew from her previous visit. The barn hand, Magnus told her, had been in a pile out back of the building, by the silos.

He stuffed the photos back in the envelope and stuck it in his pocket as he stood. He said they'd drop her truck in the hospital lot, and send up her purse, found outside EmbroGen. "Let me know if anything is missing," he said, unwrapping a fresh stick of gum. "Keep in touch."

As he walked away she laid her forehead back on the cool formica and listened to the sounds of frying sausage.

The next morning Tike woke up on a cot next to Liz's hospital bed. In the dim light, Jack was huddled over the other side of Liz's bed, whispering, the news a quiet background on the overhead television. Tike opened her good eye and watched as Jack brushed Liz's hair, what little there was sticking out between bandages, his big rough hands holding the child's brush like it was a baby bird fallen out of a nest. His black cowboy hat was on the bedside table.

Tike slunk back down on her cot and pretended to sleep. It worked well. When she woke again, Jack was gone and Liz was weeping, her face turned to the curtained window.

"Liz," said Tike.

"Ah," said Liz, her voice a rasp. She turned from the window, her eyes covered with stained gauze. She reached out a hand and Tike touched their bandaged fingertips together. "Babar," said Liz. Tike closed her eyes. "I tried to find him," said Liz. "They wouldn't let me. They were emptying the tanks, we saw them loading up coolers. Quint told me to wait, he'd come back. He tried to stop them." Tike saw Barry's wallet in Liz's lap, cupped in her other hand. Babar's wallet.

Tike lowered herself into the chair next to the bed and the women spoke, then sat in silence, bandaged hands touching, eyes closed. When Tike looked again, Liz was asleep, Babar's wallet tucked against her cheek on the pillow. Tike got up, showered, put on fresh clothes from Liz's suitcase and went downstairs.

Halfway through a tuna salad sandwich in the hospital cafeteria, Tike decided to call Nick. She would call his office. Maybe he would be there; maybe there would be some perfectly reasonable explanation for why he lied. Again.

His extension didn't ring through. The phone system transferred her back to the receptionist. "Tike? Oh, we've been worrying about you."

"Thanks, Marcella," said Tike, mangling her sandwich with her taped hands. "Yeah, I've had better assignments."

Marcella gave a short laugh. "I bet the school board is looking like a pretty good beat right now."

Tike started to smile, felt the bandage pull at her cheek. "So, is Nick around?"

"Nick?"

"Yeah," said Tike. "Or is he still sick?"

Marcella was quiet.

"Marcella? What's going on?"

"Don't you know?"

"Know what?"

"Nick's gone," she said.

Tike's taped hand clenched, and she gasped from the burst of pain. "Dead? Gone, like dead gone? Marcella?"

"No, no," she said. "Sorry, I didn't mean that. But he's left the paper. Left his key and we haven't heard from him. I was hoping you'd know something. He's not returning messages."

Gone? "What about...What about a forwarding address?" *Did he go to Washington already? Without me. No more waiting.*

"No," said Marcella. "Nothing."

Tike put the phone in her bag. She threw away the second half of her sandwich and left the cafeteria.

Nick opened the passenger door of the black sedan before it slid to a stop behind Tike's truck in the hospital parking lot. A sharp wind blew debris from the sidewalk in gusts, slapping it against the icy cars and barren hedge.

Nick jumped out and slipped, lunging for the truck's door handle with one hand; it wouldn't open.

"Move it, Capelli. Time to roll," said a voice from the black car.

"Minute." Nick struggled, fumbling a notepad and pen with his gloved hands. He tore off a small page and tucked it under the truck's icy windshield wiper, then hopped back into the black car.

The door slammed behind him. The car fishtailed in the slush as it left the hospital parking lot.

A crumpled food wrapper rose up from the salty concrete pad by the employee entrance and flew to the parking lot; the corners of the note under the windshield wiper rattled against the safety glass.

Tike walked slowly from the hospital cafeteria back upstairs, stopping twice to rest before she reached Liz's room. Jack was sitting in the hall, leaning his chair against the wall. He stood as she approached. "They're changing dressings," he said, clearing off a chair for Tike.

One of Jack's crew, now in uniform, came up the hall with a tray of coffees. "Ma'am?"

Tike took a cup, her hands clumsy, and sat back. The officer sat at his post on the other side of Liz's door. They all watched the staff answering calls and pushing carts from room to room.

A doctor came out of Liz's room and spoke to Jack, who was already on his feet. "You can go in now."

Jack turned back to Tike, touched her shoulder. "I'll be right back." As the door closed behind him, a man in a dark wool coat stepped off the elevator and approached, raising his eyebrows and picking up his pace when he saw Tike.

"What are you doing here, Lexington?"

"Pardon? Who are you?"

"You think you're going in there? I should have you arrested."

"I'm just here to see Liz." She studied his face. "I'm sorry, do I know you?"

"I really don't care. But do you know Geneva LaCroix? That name ring a bell? Wait," he said, holding out his hands. "Don't answer. We're still figuring out jurisdiction on this. Let's just say we're really curious about your brokerage accounts and some interesting deposits you've received."

"Brokerage accounts?" Tike set her coffee on the floor, nearly tipping it over. "What?"

He shook his head. "LaCroix sent us copies. You really know how to get mixed up in shit. And what's with the cell phone bills?"

The door behind him opened, a voice murmured. Jack stepped out into the hall, his hand rubbing his forehead.

"Charlie?"

"Yeah, hey Jack."

Jack looked from Charlie to Tike.

"What's going on?"

Tike got up from her chair. "Look, guys, let me explain the situation. Someone's messing with me, with my life. Strange things are happening."

Jack narrowed his eyes and looked at Charlie. "Charlie, just back off for a while. Let's get together on this." He stepped toward Tike. "I'll tell her you were here," he said, his voice soft. "You call me. A day or two, we'll get everything sorted out." He reached out and gripped her shoulder. "You call me."

She turned to Charlie. "The cell phone bills. Did they come in the mail? Was there a reindeer drawn on them?"

"Proud of your work, missy?" He snorted, then looked away from her, down the hall. He started to say something but the light over Liz's room started flashing and nurses started running.

"Get out of here, Tike," said Jack as a nurse shoved him aside, pushing into Liz's room. "Just go."

She went.

She turned and walked around the corner toward the elevators, nothing to pack, nothing to take with her but what borrowed clothes she was wearing.

Brokerage accounts? Phone bills? Geneva?

Tike dug her keys out of her pocket as she moved down the hall. One of Jack's men caught up and handed her his parka. He looked her in the eye and gave a short nod, then turned quickly and walked off. She used her elbow to punch the button for the elevator, punching it again and again. When it arrived and the door opened, Ed Magnus got off, talking to another agent, then paused in mid-step when he saw Tike. He looked right at her and, without a word, walked on toward Liz's room. Tike slumped against the elevator wall as the doors closed. *Him, too?*

Downstairs she shrugged into the deputy's parka as she pushed through the side doors.

They believe it. They think I did something. That I caused this.

She struggled with the zipper as she came out into the hospital parking lot, bending her head into the wind. New snow blew, the jacket flapped open, the zipper unmanageable with her bandaged hands. She gave up and held it closed with her arms, the blowing snow stinging against her face.

I've been trying so hard. I just want a normal life. Like normal people. She trudged to her truck. The snow fell from her door as she struggled to unlock it, dropping the keys twice, her hands useless.

Why even bother. Why should I?

Finally the door opened; she crawled in. She leaned her head on the frigid steering wheel as she started the truck and cranked up the defroster. She could barely see out the windshield. Her whole body spasmed with cold and fatigue.

Without waiting for the engine to warm up, she put the truck in gear, shifting with her wrist, wiping both her nose and eyes with the sleeve of her coat as she backed out of her slot. Sheets of snow and ice and parking lot debris rattled and blew from the hood and windshield as she turned on the wipers for a vain brush across the glass, then headed for the exit and pointed her old Ford north, for home.

CHAPTER 48

Tike stepped into the kitchen of her farmhouse, shoving the door closed behind her with her foot. On the floor before her were piles of sodden rugs and warped strips of polished oak, her kitchen table pushed into the stairway, her chairs piled onto the countertops. There was black grease smeared in the kitchen sink, and a pile of sawn pipe ends on the floor around the overflowing trash basket. There were three bills taped to the refrigerator: plumber, LP service, fire department.

Tike went to the thermostat and turned it up to 65, then went upstairs to put on some of her own clothes. When she came back down, she stepped around the debris and tried to open a bottle of wine but failed, her bandaged paws useless. She found a can of beer instead and used a screwdriver to pop it open, carrying it to her couch. She parted the curtains and looked out the window; she could see Pepper outside. He gimped over from the barn and sat by the front wheel of her truck, his back to the house. When he was done ignoring her he'd come in. She hadn't spotted Nickel yet.

She closed the curtain and leaned her head back, putting her feet up on the coffee table, feeling the vibrations in her hands from the long drive.

I just want quiet.

All the way back she had tried to make sense of it. The morgue calls, the reindeer, the deposits. The false alarm. Now these other papers, at least according to Jack.

I don't get it.

She pulled the cell phone out of her pocket—Barry's, she realized—and put it on the table. She stared at it, tapping the tips of her wrapped hands together, then used her thumb to dial Magnus's number. She started to leave a message, then stopped. *Maybe I should get more information first.* What did Jack tell him?

She didn't know who else to call. She put the phone on the table and pulled a blanket around herself, closing her eyes. The house was dead silent.

———————

When Tike woke from her nap on the couch it was dark. She stumbled out of the blankets and turned on the lights. She went to the porch and dragged in the crate of mail that had accumulated since her last stop, on the way to the airport in Sioux Falls.

So long ago, she thought, shaking her head. She stepped back outside and called the cats. Pepper came running, ready now to acknowledge Tike. Tike gave him some scraps in the kitchen as she made a sandwich and put a pizza in the oven. She replaced the ketchup-splattered gauze on her hands with a dozen adhesive bandages.

By the time she smelled the pizza browning she could almost see the bottom of the crate. Most of the mail so far would go into the burn barrel in the morning, but she had come across a few checks, too, including one for the magazine story she finished the night before she went to Chicago to see Geneva and U.P. There were magazines, newspapers. Some Christmas cards. One from U.P. and Geneva, a big one from Pete Russell. Nothing from Nick.

No cell phone bill yet.

Near the bottom of the pile was a long white envelope with no return address. A Rudolph stamp, Chicago postmark. She picked up her knife to slit it open, then paused. She went to the kitchen and pulled out the pizza to cool, then dug around under the sink and found a mismatched pair of rubber kitchen gloves. She put them on as she went back to the living room, then used the knife to open the envelope, shaking it over the coffee table. A folded paper dropped out. It was a page from a cell phone bill. Her bill. She looked back at the envelope. *Definitely not from the phone company.*

She examined the bill, turning it over. On the back was a pencil sketch: a winged reindeer and a woman, side by side on a riverbank. She touched them with a gloved fingertip and shivered. *Meandash.*

The woman was Tike.

She flipped the page over again. The printed side was page four of her latest bill, a bill she hadn't found in any of her mail. She grabbed the mail crate and scrabbled through the few remaining envelopes; no phone bill.

She scanned through the outgoing calls on the single page before her, trying to recall the numbers. She got a pad and pencil and copied down several she didn't recognize, then started calling. The first three were a veterinarian, a Chinese restaurant, and a former editor. The fourth was busy.

The fifth, for a call made at 1:03 a.m., reached voice mail: "Hello, this is Roy McCall."

Roy? When did I call him at one in the morning?

"I'm not here right now," the voice said. "To reach the central Plum Island switchboard, dial zero..."

She dropped the phone on her lap and grabbed the paper, running down the list to the entry for that call: 1:03 a.m., seventeen minutes, Dec. 22. *No way.* She grabbed her calendar.

Dec. 22: The morning Roy announced the false alarm. *Before* he announced the false alarm.

And she made this call? Not possible. She thought back. What was she doing that night? Morning?

This is what Jack was talking about. "Calls," he had said—plural. What else had she—her phone—done? What was on the other pages of her cell phone bill? Tike snatched up the page and looked over the numbers again. The next entry after the call to Roy was a call to U.P.'s...at 1:21 a.m. *What?* She had never called U.P. in the middle of the night.

Have I?

Tike picked up the phone and dialed U.P. The phone rang twice, then a metallic voice came on.

This number has been disconnected. Please check the number...

She hung up and collapsed back onto the couch. *What have I gotten into?* She pulled off her gloves and dropped them on the floor. She looked at her hands, patched with latex rectangles of gauze and ointment, half of them peeling loose. She put her hands over her face. *I didn't do it. Didn't.* She closed her eyes, saw the lawyers, saw the deposition teams, heard the questions, smelled the courtroom, the police station. Tasted the bitter nausea, flinched from the cramping in her stomach. Pepper jumped onto her legs. Where was Nickel? She picked Pepper up and held him to her chest. *What have I gotten dragged into?* She bit her lip. *Dragged myself into.*

Pepper reached out and batted at a bandage on her face. She closed her good eye as her tears started to leak and flow and sting when they hit her raw flesh.

She turned into the couch, Pepper in her arms.

They were right. I can't cut it.

———————

The next morning Tike carried her mail debris and warped oak floor scraps to the burn barrel, her feet dragging. She stood watching the flames as they caught, the smoke drifting slightly away. She stood by the barrel, warming her hands, her insides numb, beyond warmth. She called for Nickel, but he still didn't show. After a while she walked over to the mailbox to put up the flag, letting the mailman know she was home.

She tugged on the metal flag, knocking away some ice so she could creak it into position. That's when she saw the snowy lump of debris on the ground. Flat and still. Night black fur. *Nickel.*

"Nickel," said Tike, her voice a cry, her knees folding, her heart collapsing. He was curled up under the bushes behind the mailbox, snow drifted over his legs, his yellow eyes and pink mouth open, his body twisted. Twisted bad. *How long has he been there?* Tike fell to her knees in front of him. *Was it a fire truck?* Or the plumber or the LP guy. Too much traffic. *How long did he stay alive?* She closed her eyes at the sharp cramp in her gut. *I could have been here. Saved him.*

Tike staggered to her feet, her mouth sagging open. She walked back to the burn barrel, poking at the flames, standing in the smoke until it burned down to embers. Cold and dead. She kicked over the barrel, knocking the ashes into the snow. She walked to the barn and dug out an empty feed sack. She took it to the mailbox and put Nickel inside. He was stiff. His tail wouldn't go in.

She tried to dig a hole but the shovel wouldn't go through the frozen ground. She went into the grove and put the sack between two trees and covered it with a pile of rocks and rusted tractor parts.

She went inside and locked the doors. Pepper watched her from the door to the kitchen.

She sat in her kitchen and tried to call Nick, but there was no answer. She left a message: "Hi Nick, hope you're doing fine. Things aren't going great. Maybe you could give me a call. They said you're gone. I hope you're okay."

Pepper came over and jumped on her lap. Then she broke. "It's Nicky," she said. She choked. "Our little baby. He's dead. I buried him Sort of. Our little Nickel. Where are you? Things aren't going well." Tike slid to the floor and lay there, gasping, her mouth slack with cries.

Pepper went to the door and howled.

———————

Late that night, as Tike lay on her couch, Pepper beside her, the house phone rang. Tike picked it up without opening her eyes. "Yes," she said. "What?"

"I've got a message from our friend, 12991," said a man's raspy voice. "He can't get to a phone now."

"What?" said Tike, sitting up with a wince, eyes open.

"Just listen. I only have a few seconds. I'm not okayed for calls. Our friend says be careful, there was a note at the scene, on Zack. He said it was a drawing of a reindeer. With wings."

"What?"

"Look, I'm just telling you what our friend said. I don't know what the fuck it means. That's your problem."

"Yeah. Thanks."

"And the last thing," he said, coughing. "Our friend said he got the rest of the police reports. The reindeer was drawn with Zack's blood."

He hung up.

———————

CHAPTER 49

At this particular moment, Heather was not thinking about her work at Plum Island, about viruses, about Yolanda, or about Roy. She wasn't thinking at all. She was just feeling, feeling the man in her arms, in her bed, in her warm softness. Later she would think about getting on the ferry, going to the lab, dealing with tests and tests and tests. Later.

But now she gripped Panko's smooth, slim waist and pulled it in to her. His skin was like butter, soft and warm. Creamy, pale, delicious butter. He was a tall, long-legged man, and surely outweighed her, but somehow felt almost dainty in her arms, which she could wrap completely around him. She worried about crushing him as they turned and rolled and gripped each other.

Heather didn't worry too much. That required consciousness.

"Heather? Heather?" The voice on the answering machine echoed in the room. Heather's round arm reached out from the covers and grabbed the phone. "Uh," she said into the receiver. "Yolanda?"

"Heather—thank goodness you're there," said Yolanda. "Why didn't you answer your cell phone?"

Heather closed her eyes and pictured her cell phone: downstairs, somewhere in a trail of clothing, starting with her purse (by the door), then her gloves (foyer), coat (living room), blouse (dining room), brassiere (hallway), panties (stairs), skirt (upstairs hall),...the shoes were next to the bed. She smiled and pulled the blankets up.

"Are you okay?" said Yolanda.

Heather poked her head up and looked at the clock, then jumped. *Late. Damn. Late late late.* She swung her legs out of bed, then reached under the bed, looking for her slippers. *Why was it so dark?* She looked

around the room. *All the curtains are closed. I don't remember doing that.*
"Oh hell," said Heather, turning on the light. "I overslept."

"Hey, don't worry about it," said Yolanda. "Calm down. Heather, it's
started. The strike—they finally made a decision last night."

Heather sat up. She snatched up her glasses from the nightstand and
put them on with one hand while adjusting the phone with the other.
"You're kidding." She looked at the empty pillow beside her and smiled.
There was a note on the dresser just beyond it.

"No kidding. We're striking. Can you believe it?"

"So...what does that mean for us? Now what?" Heather reached for
the note and crawled back under her warm bedcovers.

"Now we wait for them to come up with a decent contract, that's what."

Heather whistled. "We don't work? We don't even go in?" She
opened the note. The handwriting was Panko's odd spiderwork: *Thanks,
doll! You're fabulous.*

"Nope," said Yolanda. "Not until they call us back."

They agreed there was only one alternative: Shopping.

————————

The lab on the sealed third floor of the Plum Island main building was
very quiet. The only technical staff not on strike were on vacation. Some
visiting scientists still scuttled around in their labcoats, the Homeland
Security medallion embroidered on the pocket. They did the minimal
required steps on their experiments and left, stacks of reading under their
arms, loyal to their brethren in white.

By early afternoon, as Yolanda and Heather entered their fourth
antique store of the day in downtown Old Saybrook, eleven miles and a
ferry ride away, a lone figure roamed the third floor.

He used his own security card to scan himself into the secure BSL-3
area. He walked straight through, his street shoes sticking to the period-
ic adhesive floor mats, and entered the restricted tissue culture rooms
where Yolanda and Heather had done so many FMD assays.

He went into the central hood room. Here, Yolanda and Heather had
sat side-by-side, gossiping, each facing a glass panel, behind which their
gloved hands dealt and shuffled stacks of hand-sized sample trays filled
with debris and fluids sent in from farms and ranches and zoos and
national parks around the country.

The man went to the last hood and took a seat. He turned off the interior ultraviolet lamps which kept the stainless steel surface sterile during
down time. He turned on the unique fans which isolated the workspace,

making it a little island protected by a controlled tornado of sterile air. He reached through the blowing wall of air—like reaching through a waterfall—and pulled the gas burner toward the still center of the work-space. He pulled the lever to turn on the gas, and used the striker hanging on the wall to light it. The bunsen burner shot a six-inch blue flame straight up, untouched by the controlled tornado surrounding it.

The man rolled back his stool and went to each of the other seven hoods in turn, turning the gas lever on each.

He did not, however, light them.

He then worked his way up the hall, through the less-secure areas, opening the gas lever at each work bench. He also propped open the doors of the chemical safety cabinets—the red-striped cabinets, where alcohols and ethers were stored.

Exiting without pause through the shower-out facilities, his shoes leaving grit footprints on the tacky floor pads, the man entered the stair-case and descended until he faced the locked door of the second of three basements. Here, he could not use his own security card. However, he had Heather's, as Heather now worked in the second basement, ever since the unfortunate Jannssen test result screw-up.

He passed Heather's card through the scanner just below a sign: "North American Vaccine Bank." The scanner registered the use of Heather's card, and authorized access.

When the lock mechanism of the door clicked, the man opened it and went in, the lights automatically clicking on. This floor was also empty. There wasn't much for a scientist to do here, anyway, as the second base-ment was designed for frozen storage.

The man had only a few tasks; some of the prep work was already done. First he removed lids from some large tanks; creamy fog flowed out of each and rolled across the floor. As he did, he glanced upward at the sprinkler system, checking the locations of the sprinkler heads. The rest of the room was filled with massive stainless steel freezer cases with displays reading -80° C, plus or minus a few degrees. *Not for long.* He made his way down a long row of the freezers, throwing open the heavy lids, leaving each agape, then left the room without a glance.

Back at the staircase, he descended one more floor to the utility base-ment. Here he made one final adjustment to an installation left on a pre-vious visit before squeezing down a small alley behind the furnaces. On the wall behind the largest furnace was a small door, its handle freshly chipped free of rust. The man turned the handle and passed through the door, closing it firmly behind him.

The man whistled as he walked down the long emergency tunnel, using a small flashlight (printed with "Star of India Restaurant, Manhattan" in red lettering) from his pocket. The narrow beam would suffice until he reached the third corner, where, he knew, daylight from the exit would be adequate to guide the rest of the walk.

He should just make the next-to-last ferry.

The man drove his rental car away from the ferry landing, parked on the Old Saybrook waterfront, then lit a cigar as he sat to watch the ferry make its slow chug back to Plum Island.

Five blocks away, Yolanda and Heather were taking a break at the Swiss Bakery. Heather sat back in her chair, eclair in hand, and closed her eyes—antiques were exhausting.

Eleven miles away, across the water, on the third floor of the lab, the sole flame continued to burn. It was in its own little world in the hood, protected and insulated from the increasingly gassy air of the lab by the waterfall of purified air surrounding it.

Six floors below, a small timer—a relatively new addition to the wiring of the Plum Island utility basement—reached the finale of its scheduled program. The timer sent two signals. One traveled forty-seven feet to the emergency power controls. This didn't have any noticeable effect, as the emergency power was not on at the time. The signal assured that would not change. A short time later—0.014 seconds, to be exact—the second signal went eighty-two feet to the master electrical controls.

This did have an effect.

Six floors above, the waterfall of air, which separated the burning bunsen flame from the air of the lab, stopped, along with the lights and every other electrically-powered beeping, blinking, shaking or wiggling thing in the lab. The air of the lab flowed into the until-that-moment-sterile environment of the hood holding the flame. This took about 1.5 seconds.

Eleven miles away, Heather snapped open her eyes. *What was that?* she said, running to the door of the cafe, out to the street. *Yolanda, what was that?*

Five blocks from her, a cigar butt sizzled in the water as a rental car moved up Main Street, headed for the interstate.

CHAPTER 50

Clarissa Ivy stood in her bathrobe in the kitchen of her condo just outside the Washington beltway. She gripped her phone, cringing in the late morning sunlight pouring through the shutters. Her hair was snarled and sticking out from her head in great tufts that swung from side to side as she shouted.

"I didn't," she said, wedging the phone against her shoulder, wincing as she touched her cheeks with her fingertips. *Oh my God. It's worse.* She reached up and closed the shutters. "Of course not. Besides, I haven't sent out any press releases at all for two days...No, I don't know anything about it. I just got up." Clarissa looked at the clock in her kitchen. It was after 10 a.m. *How could that be?* "I've been, uh, asleep...Yes, I must have a bug or something. But you're serious—the island, the whole lab? Exploded?"

Clarissa sighed as she listened. "I know, this'll make things a mess...You can't tell who sent out the press release?...Okay, you keep handling the phones; I'll get to work on a press release to set things straight. What a disaster."

Someone knocked at Clarissa's door. She looked at the door, then scribbled more notes on her pad. "Right...right. Got it. My God, if we can't set this straight, if people think we did this, we're finished. Ruined," she said, putting down her pen, touching the side of her mouth, looking at her fingertips. *Wet. Blood?*

The pounding at the door got louder.

"Look. I have to go. There's someone at the door. Call me in fifteen minutes with an update, okay? I'm working from here today. I, ah, don't feel so well." Clarissa hung up the phone just as the door burst from its frame. She froze, one hand still on the phone.

"Clarissa Ivy?" Three men came through the ruptured doorway.

"FBI, FBI," shouted one, approaching her with his weapon raised. "Don't move, don't move." The other two men, wearing body armor, moved quickly into the small apartment, rushing the side rooms. Clarissa and the armed man stood frozen, facing each other, until the two men reappeared and gave an all clear.

"Miss Ivy, we need to look around," said the first man in a calmer voice. "Where is your car?"

"Garage," she said, her voice strangled.

"Please step toward the door," he said. "You need to come with us."

Clarissa tightened her robe around her waist and came toward him, stepping out of the dim kitchen into the bright of the living room. She staggered, and caught herself on the edge of the TV.

The men stepped back as she looked up, her face hot with fever. Blistered. She made the last steps toward them, holding out her hands. They were blotched with blisters and raw skin.

She sighed, her shoulders sagging. "I think I need help," she said. The men froze as her mouth opened, a trickle of blood coming out one corner, the exposed gums red and swollen.

Blistered.

Explosion at Plum Island disease labs

GREENPORT, NY — (7:35 p.m. EST, Jan. 6, CNN.com) Greenport Fire Chief Max Delansky confirmed the near-total destruction of the high-security national research and diagnostic lab for live-stock diseases, Plum Island.

"We've still got multiple teams on location and waterships off-shore," said Delansky. "The explosions occurred at approximately 4:05 p.m. today. Fortunately, most of the staff was off the island--they were on strike--and most employees have been accounted for."

He declined to say whether any bodies have been found.

The US Secretary of Agriculture, Dr. Tomas Irwin, announced an agreement with the Paris-based livestock disease organization, O.I.E., to help deal with the current FMD (Foot-and-Mouth Disease) crisis.

"As Secretary of Agriculture, I can authorize testing on the mainland at our alternate laboratory in Ames, Iowa," said Irwin. "However, the Ames lab is in a hot zone."

Instead, all samples will be shipped to Europe for testing. "The timing is not good," he said.

Dr. Irwin has set an emergency meeting of Department of Agriculture officials and advisors for 10 a.m. tomorrow in Washington, D.C.

From the January 7 National Enquirer:

Woman Gets Deadly Animal Disease

Thousands rush to emergency rooms

Lovely Clarissa Ivy is lovely no longer...and she's MAD.

"I'm a victim," she said from her hospital bed, her face wrapped in bandages and her hands cuffed to the rails. "Why me?"

From the January 7 Blue Mound (Wisconsin) Daily Reporter:

Capitol Resident Diagnosed with 'FMD-like' Illness

ATLANTA, Ga. (AP) — Officials at the Centers for Disease Control today confirmed a case of an unidentified FMD-like disease in a Washington, D.C., resident.

"We don't think it is FMD (foot-and-mouth disease)," said Dr. Donald Larson, head of the infectious disease division of the CDC. He pointed out CDC is not equipped to do the full testing that could have been done at Plum Island, destroyed yesterday in a series of explosions. "We did what we could," he said. "It appears to be two viruses: FMD, and another, which is actually causing the symptoms." It gives an "additional band in Western Blotting," he said.

Larson confirmed the individual had been exposed to authentic FMD, which does not typically produce symptoms in humans. "We're trying to determine the origin of her exposure to each virus," he said. "Neither is actually very contagious or is harmful to humans."

Tests are underway to determine the exact identity and level of infectivity of the second virus.

Individuals with characteristic symptoms (see sidebar) or who attended the Jan. 1st and 3rd MATA rallies on the Mall in Washington, D.C., are asked to contact their physicians or the CDC.

The CDC has also requested all individuals who have had contact with suspected FMD livestock cases to contact their physicians for more information.

FMD is a highly contagious livestock disease currently sweeping through farms and ranches nationwide, leading to the death of hundreds of thousands of cattle, swine, and other livestock.

From the January 7 Chevy Chase (Maryland) Tribune News:

FMD Vaccines get U.S. OK

WASHINGTON, D.C. (AP) — The US Secretary of Agriculture, Dr. Tomas Irwin, today authorized vaccination of US livestock against FMD (Foot-and-Mouth Disease).

"We're starting a 'vaccinate to live' program immediately," said Dr. Kurvin Gustadt, head of the U.S. Department of Agriculture vaccine division. "We are working with international partners to obtain an adequate supply of an FMD vaccine cocktail."

The USDA's national FMD vaccine stockpile was destroyed in the recent explosion at Plum Island.

Only one US company, Euvaxx, of San Diego, currently produces FMD vaccine.

"The circumstances are unfortunate, but we have FMD vaccine ready to sell," said Dr. Michelangelo Salt, CEO of Euvaxx. "We will also license our vaccine technology to suitable partners. We are in discussions now."

Gustadt said the loss of the Plum Island diagnostic capabilities was the primary reason for the decision. Plum Island specialized in diseases on the so-called international "List

A," he said, a ranking of the most significant infectious livestock diseases.

"Without timely and secure testing, it is not feasible to manage or prevent an outbreak of a List A disease in the absence of vaccination," he said.

Roy McCall, director of the former Plum Island facility, said review of alternative diagnostic sites had been underway before the explosion and has been accelerated.

"One option we've examined is to site the new facility in a series of former gold mines in South Dakota," he said. "This would be a sealed and stable environment, ideal for Plum Island work. We're saddened, of course, by the huge loss of the Plum Island facility, but looking forward to new opportunities to serve the interests of national security and the national economy."

McCall said the investigation of the Plum Island explosion has been slowed by island-wide decontamination activities of FMD and other diseases that had been studied or stored in the facility, and loss of power.

CHAPTER 51

Images of the explosion were broadcast over and over on the news. Tike watched, curled on the couch in her farmhouse living room, Pepper curled into the crook of her legs. More footage was added as excited tourists cradling video cameras found their way to the news outlets. Explosions and smoke, close-ups of reporters with the Statue of Liberty in the background. *Too familiar.* She shivered.

Just before midnight, while Tike and Pepper watched Letterman, she went to the kitchen to get another beer and saw the caller ID light flashing on the Princess phone. She checked the screen to see who had called at this hour.

A 927 area code? Where in the world is that? Just so she could have the satisfaction of yelling at someone for calling her so late, she called back.

There were two odd clicks, the sound of a transferred call, then a surprised voice: "Hello? Hello?"

"Hi," said Tike. "Did you page me?"

"Me? I'm just sitting here eating my peanuts. Are you paying for this call?"

"Excuse me?" said Tike. She pushed Pepper to the side and sat back on the couch, pulling a blanket around her knees.

"These phones are expensive," said the woman. "I've never used one. Although I visit my son and his no-goodnik wife at least three times a year. I'm sure she uses them all the time."

"I'm sorry, ma'am. Am I disturbing you? It must have been a prank."

"A what? I'm sorry, the stewardess was bothering me. You just can't get good service any more."

"Um...stewardess?" *What the hell?* Tike sat up straight. "Ma'am, did I call an airplane?"

"Well, of course. How else would I get to Des Moines?"

Get to Des Moines? Tike's stomach tightened. "Where are you flying from, ma'am?" she said.

"La Guardia, of course. I live in Manhattan, although it's going downhill. A crying shame. I just don't understand young people today. Disgusting. Those falling-off pants. And such a movie they showed tonight on the plane. Schlock. Who makes these films?"

After Tike disentangled herself from Seat 12F she put the cell phone in her sweater pocket. Then she went around the house checking the locks on the doors and windows. She turned out the lights and stood at the living room window, looking out over the empty farmyard. She saw the shadow of a cat move across the snow, fly up to the moon. She heard a strong gust of wind tug at the house; the old glass in the window bowed and distorted.

Something has to change. Tike was at the bottom, flat on her ass, looking up. What did she have left to lose?

Something had to change. It was time.

———

The next morning Tike got up early. She showered and put on fresh bandages, then called Ed Magnus while she sat at her kitchen table and poured some tea.

"Glad you called," he said. "Come back down to Des Moines."

Tike's stomach spasmed and she jumped to her feet. "You going to arrest me?" *Go ahead. I can take it. Fuck you all.*

He gave a short laugh. "Not yet. Take it easy. Come down here. I've got something interesting to show you."

Tike's knees folded and she dropped into her chair.

"Okay, I'll be there."

———

Four hours later, in Des Moines, she walked into Magnus's office.

"This is no piece of tablecloth," he said, pushing the red 12-inch square of thick fabric—the one she snagged from Barry's locked desk drawer—across the table toward her. "We're still going through the notebooks you brought out."

Tike picked up the soft, shiny cloth and stroked it with her fingers, turning it over. It smelled like dusty metal, and made a crackling sound when she twisted it. It was absolutely flat, with no wrinkles or creases. "What do you think?" she said.

He leaned his chair back and started a new piece of gum. He leaned forward again and put his hand out for the fabric. "It's unusual," he said. "The lab guys've never seen anything like it." He laid the fabric on the table and reached for her can of pop. "May I?" he said.

She waved him on.

He held the can of pop over the fabric and watched her as he tipped the can. The pop poured onto the fabric, nearly a full can. He set the empty can on the table. "Pick it up," he said, gesturing at the fabric.

Tike reached for a corner of the fabric and lifted it an inch. No puddle. She lifted the square halfway off the table. No puddle left on the table, and no drips. *What the heck?* The fabric was heavier now, but otherwise looked unchanged. She twisted it. It crackled. That was all. No dripping. She squeezed it between her fingers. Same result. She smelled it. It smelled like pop. Pop and dusty metal.

"What the hey?" she said.

"It's made of biologically-inert fibers with 100 micron pores," he said. "The pores are lined with electrical charges. You can't tell just by eyeballing it, but this sheet's been divided into quarters. One quarter is coated with BSA, another with fetal calf serum, another with RGD peptides. The other quarter is uncoated."

"The control," she said, shaking her head. "Oh man."

"Yep. The untreated quarter is like an experimental control. This little square of red material you brought us is basically laboratory-grade tissue culture plastic, but flexible enough to make into a nice suit jacket. The pores are just big enough for an embryo and the fluids to keep it happy. It's also insulating. Feel the temp. Your pop was nice and cold, wasn't it?"

She laid her hand on the dry-looking red square. The fabric was the same temperature as the tabletop.

"The larger particles," he said, "the embryo-sized stuff, would come out undented if you centrifuged at 500 rpm, but the liquid and smaller particles wouldn't come out unless you centrifuged at 25,000 rpm."

She picked up the fabric and snapped it like a whip. No splatters. She held the red square up with her fingertips. Nothing dripped; it didn't even look damp. She squeezed it between her thumb and index finger; it was dry. "You could load other stuff into it, too," she said, looking at the fabric as she spoke.

Back when Tike ran a biotech company with a lab full of people cutting and pasting DNA and making very secret (and profitable) engineered bugs, they had a joke about visitors: No scientists with long sleeves allowed to visit the lab. A nice clean cotton sleeve, they knew, could quietly dab up a hefty dose of DNA or a patented bug, and walk it right out the door. They kept loaner lab coats—long-sleeved—for the guests. And they watched who leaned where.

"DNA," she said. "You could load it with DNA. Or bigger stuff."

"Yep," he said. He looked her in the eye as he reached for the fabric. "Like viral particles. Lots and lots of viral particles. The guys calculated you could load this with about 10 billion particles per square inch. Not per liter or milliliter—per square inch."

Magnus paused as he held up the fabric. "We found another piece of this."

She lifted one eyebrow at him. "Yes?"

"Kip. Your dead co-founder of EmbroGen?" Magnus put the fabric in his pocket. "Kip had an identical piece of this fabric stuffed down his throat when they found him in Chicago. Floating." He got up from his chair. "Lunch? The cafeteria special today is lasagna."

They were silent as they walked down the hall toward the stairs. She cleared her throat. "Um," she said. "I need to talk."

Magnus was silent.

Fuck it. Don't be a sissy, Tike. Let's do it. She took a deep breath. "Things are happening," she said. "I don't know what's going on."

He turned his head and glanced at her as they walked, still not saying a word.

"I haven't told you everything." Tike was close to tears. "I don't know who I can talk to. But now I don't care. I just don't care."

He stopped walking and turned to her. They were at the end of a hallway, around the corner from the cafeteria. People walked by in groups, laughing. She could smell the lasagna.

Tike bit her lip. "I think I'm going to be in trouble," she said. "I've been getting things in the mail. Things that look bad."

"Like this?" He stopped and reached into his folder, pulling out a ragged scrap of paper encased in a plastic sleeve. "It was in Liz's pocket," he said, his voice quiet.

She took the scrap and held it to the light. She could make out a few phone numbers. She knew what they were: a veterinarian, a Chinese restaurant, a former editor, Roy McCall. It was her cell phone bill.

"Yeah. Like that."

————————

On the drive back from Des Moines, the landscape along Highway 4 empty around her, Tike pulled in to fill up at one of her regular small-town stops. She waved to the old guys having coffee at the tables in the corner, asked them about the weather, knowing they'd be happy to discuss her for the next half hour. *Seen her before. Nice old truck she's got. Clay County plates. Oh really? Been to the fair there. What do you think her husband does? She ain't got no ring. That so? Cattleman sticker on her truck window. No kidding.*

She got a can of pop and headed up the road. Two hours away from the farm her phone beeped.

Lompoc Federal.

"Something's happened," he said, rushing. "I don't understand how, but I've lost phone privileges for three months."

"You okay?" she said.

"Yeah, but this is worrisome. This is my last call. Someone's got some wire, to be able to do this. I've been clean, and it's not like I don't have my own support system." He coughed. "You got my other message? About Zack? About the blood?"

"Yes," she said.

"Good."

"I'm sorry," she said. "It's because of me, this stuff that's going on for you. Isn't it?"

"I don't know. But Tike. Be careful. I'll try to keep an eye out, but I have a feeling I'm going to be out of the loop for a while."

"I'll check on you, okay?" she said.

The line was silent.

"Okay?" she said. She looked at the screen of the phone.

Call Ended. She set the phone on the seat and put both hands on the wheel. It was twilight. She had to watch for deer on the road.

———————

When Tike drove into her farmyard it was after dark. Pepper sat in front of the barn door.

In Nickel's spot.

She went into the house and tried to find something to eat. She made a bowl of cereal and poured a glass of wine, finally able to manage a corkscrew. She ignored the blinking lights on the answering machines and the fax and the caller ID, and laid down on the couch in front of the TV.

Sometimes it was good to live a long way from everything.

———————

CHAPTER 52

The next morning Tike had a long shower, made some hot tea, and found some yogurt and a wrinkled apple in the stale refrigerator. She sat at her kitchen table eating breakfast and reading the police reports and hospital admissions in the *Spencer Daily Reporter*, looking for names she knew, circling errors and typos and AP style violations with a red crayon.

Pepper sat on her lap, more of a beggar than usual. Tike gave him some yogurt from her spoon. After she finished the paper she slung Pepper over her shoulder and went through her coat pockets to find her spare phone, a replacement for the one she lost at EmbroGen, and checked it for messages.

There was only one. This time, the morgue was in Chicago.

"Yes, Dr. Lexington—we've been expecting your call," said a woman's voice. "Professor Servid is on the road. He left directions to the seminar for you."

Tike scrambled for a pen, her mind racing. *Servid? What else: the genus Cervidae—the deer.* It was her reindeer man.

"Here we are," said the woman. "Tonight, 7:30 p.m., the university faculty lounge, 3287 West Seventeenth Street, seventh floor, Quimby—is that a town, or the university?" she said. "Well, it just says Quimby. Quimby, Iowa. Dr. Servid said he looks forward to seeing you and introducing you to his colleagues."

She signed off.

Bastard. No more. It was time for this to end. Tike punched in Magnus's number.

Faculty lounge? Right, she thought as she listened to Magnus's line ring. She'd go, but not to the faculty lounge. There was no lounge, no seventh floor, no university, no "3287 West Seventeenth Street" in Quimby. There wasn't even a Seventeenth Street in Quimby. There was only one street in Quimby—Main Street—and there were only four things on it: a gas station, a church, a diner with bad coffee, and a sign pointing down a gravel road. The gravel road curved along the river bank and went into a big cluster of trees, from which rose an endless snake of foul-smelling steam.

That's where he would be: At the operation behind the trees, at the headquarters of the largest employer in Quimby.

Saandval Rendering.

The phone picked up. "Magnus here."

"This is Tike. I got another one of those calls. But I have an idea."

By mid-day, Special Agent Magnus's sedan was parked in Tike's gravel farmyard. Tike leaned against the gold medallion on the door while he checked his digital recording equipment.

"It's going to be okay, Tike," he said, tucking the small device into a pocket within his kevlar vest.

She just shook her head and slumped. "I'm messed up bad, Magnus. This is a tough one."

He put an arm around her shoulder and gave her a rough squeeze and a clumsy pat. "We'll already be inside when you get there," he said. "I've got guys from Sioux City and Sioux Falls on the way. I'll send out the call when this reindeer guy shows. He won't get near you. Then we can try to straighten this mess out." He stood and turned to face her. "We can get this one, Tike. He's already got a little red laser dot on his forehead. Bang bang."

She laughed and wiped her face on her sleeve. "Put one on his ass, too, would you?"

"That's my girl." He looked her in the eye. "I'm here, Tike. You're going to be okay." He gave a crooked smile. "You outlived Zack, didn't you?"

She laughed. "That dumbass."

"There you go." He mussed her hair, got into his car, and headed for Quimby. She went back inside and brought out the trash, Pepper at her heels. It was a good day to burn something.

It had been dark for over two hours when Tike arrived at Saandval Rendering, a mile outside Quimby. She drove in slowly and parked by the truck scale. All the lights were on inside both buildings. She knew Magnus and his team were watching, but, as planned, none of them were in sight.

She turned off her car, hesitated, then got out and walked into the front building. "Hello? Mr. Saandval?" No one was in the reception area, so she headed toward Saandval's office.

Down the hall, a man walked out of the restroom checking his zipper, the sounds of a flushing toilet behind him.

"Pete? Pete Russell? What are you doing here?" Tike stopped in her tracks. *He has to get out of here. This could really mess things up.* Pete smiled as he approached from the restroom, waving with an embarrassed shrug.

Why is he here anyway? thought Tike, looking around the empty office. *Who's he meeting with?*

"Hey, how are you?" He smiled and reached for Tike's hands. "It's been too long. Too long. I mean it."

"But...why..."

"Shh," he said, placing his fingertip on her lips. "We're all alone."

"Pete, you shouldn't be here," Tike said, her voice a whisper. "I can't explain now."

"Tike," he said, his voice serious, his hands squeezing her shoulders, his pale green eyes looking into hers. "You don't know how difficult this was to arrange. But I had to see you. I can't get enough of you."

Oh shit. Tike's mouth went dry. *That's what Zack used to say.* "You paged me. You've been paging me. You've been calling from the morgues."

He closed his eyes and dropped his head as he blew out a breath, then gripped her shoulders hard. "What am I going to do? I'm done here, one of my best projects ever. A masterpiece. My bags are packed. I shouldn't even be here. But you—you're messing me up." He pulled her close and leaned into her. She could feel his breath in her hair as he spoke in a low voice, his chin on top of her head. "I can't believe I'm doing this," he said "I'm sorry."

Tike stood frozen, feeling the pound of his heart, the heat of his breath, unable to see, blocked by his arms. She strained to hear the sound of approaching feet. *Where's Magnus?*

"Pete, you need to let me go," she said, her voice muffled. *How could I get suckered again? It's Zack all over again. Damn it.* Her mind raced, choosing her words with caution. "This isn't...appropriate."

He loosened his grip and leaned back.

"You're a good guy Pete," she said, "but you've got to slow down, talk to somebody about this. Get a little more...perspective." *Damn it, where's Magnus?*

Pete was silent, watching her.

"Pete?"

"He's not coming, you know."

"What? What are you talking about?"

"Magnus. He's not coming. They went home. Like I told you, we're all alone."

"Magnus? What?"

Pete cleared his throat and shifted his shoulders—his hands still gripping Tike—and said, "Listen." He licked his lips, and a crooked smile came over his face, a smile that was now chewing gum, snapping it. "Listen," he said, but now it wasn't Pete.

It's Magnus. Dear God.

"Listen," he said, snapping his gum, now looking very serious. "X-Ray 7-3 this is Zebra 2-5. I'm 10-23 and we're no go here. Head on home. I repeat, no go at the Quimby plant. All teams report at oh-nine-hundred tomorrow."

"But where's Magnus? Where's Ed?" said Tike. *Oh hell.* "What did you do? Why?"

"Look, it's what I do. I control people, they do what I want; I make money, I move on. It's an art. I'm the best."

"But how are you making money here?"

He snorted and shook his head. "Exactly. I shouldn't be here. But you—I don't know." He let go of one of Tike's arms and rubbed his forehead, his eyes closed. "You confuse me."

Tike looked over his shoulder. *There's a side door. A fire door. I bet it's unlocked.* She lunged away, twisting out of his grip, throwing herself toward the door. He spun and slammed into her as she hit the door.

Locked.

"I can help you, Tike," he whispered into the back of her neck. "We're alike, you know, you and I. Always snooping around, always telling our stories, making big plans. You've got the perfect mind for what I do. We could work together."

"Leave me alone. I've got a life. Normal friends. I don't need you."

"Those are friends?" he shouted, and spun her around, pushing her up against the door. "They're not good for you. Magnus—you know he cheats on his wife? Nick the drunk. Liz the martyr—she sleeps around, too. Those are friends?"

"Yes, my friends. Mine."

He smiled and winked. "Sure," he said, then winced. "This damn plate." He pushed his forearm across Tike's chest, pinning both arms, then quickly put two fingers in his mouth to pull out an upper plate, which he slipped into his jacket pocket. He smiled again as he leaned back, perfect teeth shining in the lights of the reception area. Pete Russell's silver crown and chipped tooth were gone.

He shrugged. "Cheap party tricks. Good enough to get by. But what I'm really good at—I read people. I smell you, smell your fear, your desire. I know what you feel, better than you do. That's how I know." He tapped her chest. "I know what's inside."

He brushed her cheek with his fingertips. "You've got so much. People don't see it."

Tike bit her lip. *Zack used to say that.* She made her body relax in his grip, gave a small smile, tilted her head. *He'd say it right before he hit me. Bastard.*

"Better? Okay?" His arms opened wide and he stepped back. "Now. Let's wrap this up. I've got a plane to catch."

Tike ran.

———

Tike ran out the side of the reception area into the long hallway that connected with the other building. At the end of the hallway she slammed through the door into the noise and reek of the extruder room. The stench of hot raw dog biscuit was pouring from the machines as the paste churned and seethed, bone chips popping, a hundred years of scorched grease coating the hammering mixing tubes.

As she ran the catwalks past the extruders, she could see banks of lights going black behind her, one by one.

Not good. She plunged on, into the carcass rooms.

Into the deadstock.

She hoped someone, anyone—other than him—was in the plant. The sound and vibrations of the grinding and chopping increased as she moved deeper into the facility, but she had to get across the plant before the lights went out.

She almost made it. She was in the peeling room. She could see and hear the massive floor screw making its slow, infinite turns, the screw trench running the length of the room, dragging empty air into the chopper.

Then the last light went out.

Where is everyone? Then she pictured the guys she had seen here during the day, thought about the kind of guys who would work a night shift in the peeling room of a rendering plant, pushing and sliding foul peeled carcasses into the screw trench. *How much would it cost to get them to take a break? Twenty bucks? A foil of meth?*

The floor was slick with decayed blood and fluids. She tried to stay away from the screw, taking small steps. After a minute she could see a bit of light from cracks in the roof. She knew she had seen some knives hanging by the winch controls. She reckoned the direction to the winch and tried to circle the room to get there without getting pulled into the screw.

Twice she stumbled over cold stiff legs. Once she slipped and fell onto a swollen balloon of a cow; it ruptured with a small explosion and a spray of fluids. She staggered from the smell—and taste—and immediately vomited, then continued, no slower, no faster.

Then her face smashed into the steel pulleys of a peeling winch, the hook overhead piercing the hide of a large hog, still attached by a few scraps to a flayed carcass lying on the floor below. The thick, rusty hook, the size of her head and probably weighing over forty pounds, hung from the ceiling on an ancient chain as thick as her arm. She reached carefully for the wall, trying to remember exactly where she had seen the knives. She knew they were close.

She followed the dark wall with delicate taps, remembering how easily the knives cut the tough hides to start the peeling. She couldn't hear a thing, but she hoped she would feel the difference.

Her fingernails hit something resonant and she froze. With even slower movements, she traced the length of the knife with her shaking fingertips. She wrapped her fingers around the handle of the 10-inch blade and yanked it from its magnetic bracket. She slipped the rough strap of the heavy handle over her wrist. *You taught me this, Zack. You brought me here.*

Through the door she could see the probe of a flashlight coming her way.

"Tike, don't run. Where are you?" cried a high-pitched voice, barely audible over the gnashing of the chopper.

Pete. She thought of the calls. The reindeer. What else had he done? *Not-Pete. Who is this guy?*

Well, come and get me, bastard. Bring it on.

Tike returned to the suspended hog. With three short cuts, she released the dangling hide from the carcass. It fell to her feet.

The moving beam of the flashlight reached the door of the peeling room. She crouched on the floor, pulling the hide, hair-side out, over her head, retching as the fatty surface slid over her shoulders and neck. The floor below her was slick with rotted blood. She breathed through her mouth, unable to bear the staggering smell, watching the dark room through a gap in the hide.

Her stomach heaved; she fought the impulse to vomit. Something moved in the fatty material covering her neck. *Maggots?* Tike crouched, motionless. Pete stood in the doorway and probed the room with the blinding beam.

Then his light stilled, aimed at the floor in front of Tike. At something in the slick of decaying blood. Tike looked at the slick, at the patterns in it, the patterns directly in front of her. *Footprints.*

Mine.

She took a deep breath and gripped the seething skin with one hand, ready to pull it aside. Her knife was in her other hand. She watched through the narrow gap, saw the flashlight coming closer. Twenty feet. Fifteen.

Oh Liz. She saw her on the floor of the tank room, was pierced by despair and fear. *You'll never know it wasn't true, Liz. I didn't do those things, didn't betray you.*

Ten feet. Five. She saw the outline of something sharp and curved in his left hand, metallic reflections as he moved closer.

Nick, my Nick. My little Nickel. Nick slept, an Italian moon on the balcony behind him, his arm warm and safe over her hip. *We could have made it. Oh Nick.*

The glare of the flashlight pointed directly into the fold of her moving skin, into her eyes. She closed them, didn't want him to see their reflection.

"Tike?" He was nearly screaming, only yards from the crashing chopper and the grinding screw. "Terrible, isn't it? Such noise."

Through her eyelids she could tell: Pete turned off the flashlight.

Now or never. Go go go. She snapped her eyes open, still blind, and thrust the knife out between the folds of her skin cover, slashing at his legs in the dark.

The knife hit something solid and meaty. She withdrew it to make another plunge when he kicked, knocking her over. He kicked again, and she pushed to her feet, pushing the skin toward him, shoving it at him.

The heavy skin hit him and she pulled her knife back to stab through it. She slipped as she thrust, the knife tip catching on the skin and yanking out of her grip.

As he bent down to clutch his leg, the skin sliding over his shoulder to the floor, she saw his profile. The faint light was enough, her good eye recovered enough to see the outlines of the room again. She kicked at him, knocking him over, onto the slimed floor, then turned away, slipping.

She ran toward the big door, the one leading straight outside, by the scale.

My car. Just let me get to my car.

She stumbled toward the outline of the big door, high and wide enough to let trucks back in and dump their loads of deadstock, making her way along the trench holding the turning screw. It ended just beside the door. Light leaked in around the massive frame of the entrance; she could feel wind and snow blowing in as she got closer.

She glanced back, saw Pete's outline tall and moving, not far behind. She snapped her head back toward the big door, eyes wide to see through the dim, just as she ran full-force into an empty peeling winch. Her knees smacked into the wide iron hook at the same time her head rebounded from the thick chain. She staggered back a step, then slipped, trying to catch her balance, the edge of her boot heel snagging on the rim of something. The screw trench.

She fell in.

Tike slid backwards under the screw, feet first, twisting around as she slid, trying to match the curvature of the screw lip, her legs just fitting into the groove. Her arms scrabbled against the greasy floor as the screw slowly slid along the back of her legs.

Don't catch don't catch. Please don't let it catch.

She arched her back to keep her legs curled away from the screw, pressing them into the wall of the trench, her fingernails scraping along the floor, seeking handhold.

Sudden pressure started sliding along one thigh.

Dear God, please no.

A jagged prong on the screw snagged her pants and moved inch by inch down her legs, tearing the fabric, scoring her skin.

My boot, will it catch my boot?

Her hands moved faster on the floor, pulling up splinters, jamming them under her fingernails. The prong caught her left boot and the inexorable movement of the sharp prong continued, pulling at the boot, pulling at her foot. She wiggled her ankle, feeling the prong dig into her heel, yanking away, finally sliding her foot out of the boot until her bare skin, the top of her foot, pushed against the icy wall of the screw trench.

A light flashed in her face. She heard a metallic squealing sound as the screw shook and vibrated, slowing its rotation. Wet hands grabbed her arms and pulled, sliding her out of her slot, just as the metallic squeal sharpened and ruptured with a loud crack, and the screw sounds surged and returned to normal. She looked up at Pete as his wet hands started dragging her toward the big door.

And then what?

I don't think so.

Tike twisted her whole body, pulling out of Pete's hands, jumping to her feet and kicking at legs she knew were already damaged, turning and running the last feet toward the big door. There was a smaller door to the side, ajar; she slammed through it into the icy outdoors.

She came out of the thundering peeling room into the icy yard outside, one foot bare, plunging for her car, digging through her pockets as she ran, feeling for her keys.

Fuck. Her pockets were empty. No keys. *Did I leave them in the ignition?* She got to the car, reached for the door handle. Locked. Her wet hand froze to the handle; she yanked it away, the skin of her palm tearing.

She looked back, saw the smaller door slam open, saw an outline in the diffused moonlight, heard a voice.

"Tike." It was Nick. "Wait."

She froze. *Nick? Here? Thank God.*

Then a laugh. "Tike." Now it was Zack. *Dead dead dead. Dead guy.* "Wait, bitch. Shouldn't have done that."

Shit. She ran around her car and into the front building, back to the reception area where she had first arrived.

Phone. I need a phone.

She ran to the receptionist's desk and grabbed up the phone handset. No dial tone. *Shit.* She dropped the phone and ran down the hall to the offices.

Walkie talkies. A cell phone on a charger. Something something something.

She ran through one office after another.

Nothing. How about a gun? Letter opener? Something. Something. She ran, looking, running.

Then the lights went off.

"Tike?" It was Nick.

"Tike," said Pete, coming around a corner into the office area, wearing someone's tall rubber chore boots and heavy gloves. "Please stop. I just want to talk. You don't understand."

Tike jumped around a partition and dropped to the floor, curling under a desk, then reached back up and grabbed a heavy glass paperweight she had seen on the desktop. She slowed her breath, knowing it was fruitless.

How long do I have? What else can I do? Fire alarm? Tike replayed the images of the rooms she had been through. *Did I see any fire alarms?*

She watched through a crack in the desk front. She saw his profile come around the partition, his head distorted and bulging.

Night vision goggles? Yes. Shit.

He stopped, tucking his head down, looking at the base of the desk where she hid, then standing upright again. He leaned against the partition and spoke directly at her hiding place.

"You're ungrateful, Tike," he said. "You should be thanking me. After all I did for you. Not like Zack."

She stiffened. *How did he know about Zack, anyway?* Of course: The first year she met Pete at the Keystone Integrin conference was the year she left Zack. She had cried out her story over drinks in the bar.

"You were so fragile when we met," he said. "So bruised. I knew then I was meant to protect you." He sighed. "I watched over you. Someone had to."

Tike's mind scrambled, trying to remember the layout of the room. *Out the window? Where does the window go? Can I get to Quimby?*

"And you brought me FMD, Tike," he said. "You were obsessed. That impressed me. And you were so right. God almighty, I love trading commodities. These last nine weeks were a personal best." He laughed. "I'm thinking of writing it up for *Trader* magazine: 'How To Make One-Point-Four Billion Dollars In Nine Weeks With No Fucking Risk'." He started whistling.

Tike's eye throbbed, the bandage dangling. She pulled the bandage off, dropping it to the floor. Her foot was bleeding. She was dizzy and nauseated. She picked a squirming maggot out of her hair and sagged. *Who am I kidding?*

Tike thought about the other unknowns. Barry. Kip. "Did you steal the embryos from EmbroGen tanks?" she said.

"Oh please. I'm a trader, not a thief. I know the guys who did it, though; we've done some deals. Everyone loves my fabric." She saw his profile shift. "Look." The flashlight sparked on for a second, aimed at the lining of his jacket, held open with one hand, while the other shielded his eyes, behind the goggles. The lining was a distinctive red—it was the red cloth from Barry's desk.

"Russian, of course, an 'accident' by some underappreciated polymer chemists I bought years ago. But our little Dr. Kip reached out. He didn't like being number two on the EmbroGen totem pole, I hear. Wanted more. Nasty boys he hooked up with. Chicago boys, no class. Unprofessional. Once they understood what was stockpiled at EmbroGen, Kip and company didn't stand a chance."

He stood and walked toward the desk, closing the blinds, his profile disappearing into inky dark. "Enough about that fool. I was worried about you," his voice said. "You shouldn't have eaten the donuts."

"You watched me."

"Of course. I'm always watching." His voice was only inches away, on the side of the desk, whispering. "Hungry girl. Bad girl." He moved closer. "What should I do with you, Tike? I can't decide. This is so fucking confusing."

Tike gripped the paperweight, braced herself against the footwell of the desk. Thought about Liz. Nick. Her old house and oak floors and white lilacs and a world of her own. She hefted the glass sphere and waited. *Into his face. He's got to duck down. It's my last chance.*

The desk flew into the air and she fell sideways, off balance. Air—and something solid—rushed toward her head, then a blow that knocked her flat on the floor. As the pain exploded behind her eyes his knee landed on her chest, his gloved hands gripping her wrists, forcing them together, binding them with a tight strap. Her kicks only hit the desk, now on its side. He shifted his knees to her thighs and strapped her knees and ankles, then stood, his goggles in silhouette from the dim moonlight through the window, his hands digging something from his pockets.

She sat up, snatching at him with her tied hands, and gagged, the pain tearing through her skull, nausea ripping through her. Her vision telescoped down to a small ring and she shut her eyes, gasping as she collapsed back onto the floor, her pulse throbbing behind her face, her concussed brain taking command. He knelt beside her, causing her to retch again when he shoved his gloved hand into her mouth, forcing something bitter down her throat. She could taste old blood from the gloves. He slid a strap behind her shoulders and bound it across her chest.

He dragged her back to the din of the peeling room and snagged her chest strap on the hook of a peeling winch, then reeled her up, leaving her feet dangling. He disappeared from her narrowed view. The lights went on. The chopper and floor screw went still and she hung motionless, trying to think through the pain. Behind her, across the room, a chain rattled and metal pulleys squealed. She heard rollers moving along one of the ceiling tracks, moving toward her. *A second hook? Why?*

The sound stopped. Pete stepped into her line of vision, goggles gone. "Feeling better?" he said.

She did. The pain was softer on the edges, fuzzy. Warm. *What's happening?* The thoughts came on top of each other. *He gave me something.*

"Demerol. Rohypnol," he said, and sighed. "You should have just talked to me."

Tike wiggled her fingers. Tried to. They were sluggish already. He looked at them, nodding.

"Another few minutes," he said. "I'm almost ready."

He gripped her hips with his hands. She tried to buck away but her muscles were hers no longer; her pulse slammed into her skull with what effort she made. Pete turned her slowly and she came face to face with Magnus, hanging from a peeling hook, hands and eyes wrapped with duct tape, his face slack. Pete let go of her hips and she swiveled back, bumping into Magnus. As he came to rest against her back she could feel his heart beating, a slow tap. She closed her eyes. As she watched Pete step over to the knife rack she heard a sputtering behind her, a mumble. Magnus. She leaned back as best she could, moving an ear closer to his mouth.

Bang bang, he was saying. Talk talk.

Talk.

The recording device in his Kevlar vest. It must be on. She shifted back to center, her eyes on Pete. *Oh yes. We'll have a nice talk.* Her eyes shifted to the knives. *At least the tape will tell the story. My story. Fuck you.*

"Nice and quiet here," said Pete, studying the knives. "Quiet as a morgue." He plucked one, long and broad, from the magnetic strip and hefted it, holding the blade up to the light and squinting, looking along the blade edge, then put it back. He shrugged and pulled one from the holster at his waist. "I'm particular." He held the blade, engraved and blackened, to the light and nodded. He turned to her, shaking his head. "Zack wasn't good enough for you. Neither was Nick."

Tike froze. "What've you done to Nick?" Her words stumbled, her lips sloppy from the rohypnol. She tried to lick her lips but her tongue was loose.

He turned back to the knife rack. "What do you know about him, anyway?" He pulled a whetstone from a hook and gripped it in his palm, sliding the knife edge across the stone in long strokes. He put the whetstone in his pocket and turned to her. "How do you hook up with these people?"

"What did you do?" she said, softer. She closed her eyes. *Oh Nicky.* She opened them again. *Talk, you bastard. Tell them.*

"Oh Tike," said Pete, stepping closer. "This is really confusing for me." He checked his watch. "Five minutes. I hate to rush."

She tried not to move.

"Did you get my little gifts? You wanted to keep them, didn't you?" He held up his palm. "That's okay. You don't have to tell me. I'm sure they'll let you keep it all. And don't worry about me. I can write it off."

"Tell me about you, Pete," said Tike, trying to keep her voice clear, trying to breath, trying to think beyond the knife. "What's your story?"

"Hmmm."

"What's your real name?" she said, her words slurring.

He tightened his mouth. "No. I ask the questions." He slid the hooked knife under the fabric, then tilted it and ran it down her leg. Tike gritted her teeth as her skin split, but it was someone else's skin. There was no pain, just a strange sensation of sliding. She looked down and could see droplets of blood balling up on her greasy skin and rolling down her leg like tears.

"I shouldn't be here," he said, moving to the other leg. "You distract-ed me, almost messed up my plan. Four years of preparation, getting in position, getting doors to open. Four years." After a while he cut the tape on her numb legs and arms, then stepped back, his arms dropping to his sides, knife sliding to the ground, his breathing hard, his eyes closed. "If it was anyone but you." He took off his heavy gloves and stuffed them in a pocket. His voice was soft. "I did use you as a diversion. My little red herring. I am sorry I couldn't let you in on it."

Pete tilted his head and looked her in the eye. "My name? Does it matter? Wasn't I who you wanted me to be? We make a good team, don't we?"

He stepped behind her and walked away; Tike held her breath.

She heard him cross the room, then pause. *No. Keep going. Go.* His footsteps started again, got louder, then returned to her, his left hand cupping a thick smear of black machine grease.

He placed his hands on her wrists. "Just a little something to remem-ber me by." He moved his palms in small circles on her skin, then stepped back, silent. He squinted one eye and leaned close to speak soft-ly into her left ear. "I did something for you," he said. "I visited Zack."

Behind her, Tike felt Magnus shift, heard a low moan. *Bang bang.*

"I did to Zack what he did to you," said Pete. He stepped back, his face tight. "He deserved it, the bastard."

Tike was nauseated and cold. Her head throbbed, but there was no pain. Just a floaty feeling. Snow was drifting through the cracks in the roof. "I'm not doing so great here, Pete. I still don't understand. Why me? Why...everything?"

Pete stared, his face silent, then gave a half smile, gave her a soft kiss on her good eye and leaned up to her ear again.

"Don't worry about that," he whispered. "We're going to be fine." He stood back, his face calm, reaching out to stroke her cheek. "The skies are ours. We'll cross the river together."

"The river Meandash?" said Tike, her voice a weak scratch. "To the bone house?"

Pete smiled. "My smart girl." He nodded. "The old stories have old truth inside them. No different than your wooden crosses."

He looked into her eyes and stroked her cheek, speaking in a tongue she didn't understand. A snowflake fell on his lip and melted. Then he leaned back and sighed. "But we're just beginning." He walked away, out of her tunnel of vision. "You're not ready yet," he said, his quiet voice behind her now. "I have to go now."

The chopper and floor screw started. He pulled Magnus from his hook, jostling Tike. As she swayed on her chain a rattling noise came from the screw. She closed her eyes.

Pete returned empty-handed and stood beside her. He put his mouth against her ear, shouting against the noise. "I can't take you with me. Not this time." Tike opened her eyes as he stepped back and looked at his watch, wiping it against his sleeve. "Got to go," he shouted, pulling on his gloves. "I'm almost done. One more deal to close." He looked into her eyes, his face soft. "Sorry about your friend. He shouldn't have stuck around. He cared for you." He stroked her cheek and stepped past her.

A minute later, the lights went out and the machinery stopped.

In the blackness, Tike could feel snow fall on her slick skin. Numbness. The smell of the room shifted. *Smoke*? She saw light through the big doors. Not moonlight. Red and orange. *Fire*.

That's when she heard the sirens.

From the January 9 Sioux City (Iowa) Journal:

Fire Levels Quimby Plant, 2 Injured

SIOUX CITY, Ia. — Fire-fighting squads from three counties struggled to control a fire after a near-fatal accident at a rendering plant in Quimby last night.

The cause of the blaze, which leveled the offices of the 106-year-old facility, is still under investigation.

CHAPTER 53

The next morning Tike lay flat on her back, bandaged and wrapped, staring at the ceiling of a hospital room. She tried to wave away a fly, but her hand wouldn't move. It wasn't a fly, anyway; it was a voice.

"Magnus is in surgery," said the voice. It was a man in a suit. Magnus's partner? "They're trying to salvage his legs. But he cleared your ass anyway. We have it on tape." The recording unit was built into his Kevlar vest, he said. It almost wound up in dog biscuits, but Magnus's gun jammed the chopper.

She closed her eyes. *Bang bang. You'll be fine, Tike. We'll get him.* She could smell urine and disinfectant and hear nurses passing in the hall. Did Magnus have a wife? *Pete said he did.* She should know that.

"The recording was crap, but there's a crew working on it," said the agent. "Someone'll be coming in to talk to you."

She opened her eyes as he turned to leave. She raised her hand. "Liz," she said, her voice raspy. "Liz Thomas. Is she still here? How is she?"

"Lost an eye," he said. "She's in ICU."

"My fault," said Tike, tightening her grip on the sheets, turning her head to the side, away from him. "My fault. I need to see her."

He turned and left.

Tike focused on the pull of bandages criss-crossing her body, closing her eyes and turning her head to the wall, away from the agent who should have been Magnus. Away from the empty chair where a friend should have been sitting. *Magnus. Liz. Or...who?* Not many options.

She opened her eyes, blinking, smelling lilacs, roses. There were two bouquets on the bedside table. She could see the card on the roses: "*Get well. Good work. More later.*" It was signed by U.P., with a postscript: "*Back soon. Ask Gasparowicz for our new number.*"

Next to the roses was a bowl of lilacs. White lilacs. She reached out a shaking hand and turned the vase to see the note.

"Love from 12991. Wish I could be there."

She turned her head to her pillow, feeling her insides burn and tear. *Oh my dear one. So do I. At least you understand, know the truth. Love me anyway.*

The agent stepped back in the room and dropped some forms on the bed, telling her she needed to fill them out. "You'll do fine," he said, his voice rough, and walked out.

Ed Magnus had said that too.

Tike closed her eyes, smelling the lilacs. Her childhood, her home, her lilac hedges. *I'm playing in the hedges...*

After a blurry day of people coming and going, it was finally night. The lights in Tike's room were off. The hall outside was quiet; the air was cool.

She dozed and awakened. Someone was holding her hand. Cradling it, a smooth, warm, strong embrace cupping her limp, numb fingers. She tried to look but couldn't turn her head. Bandages. She moved her hand.

"Who?" Her voice sounded old. Felt old. Her eyes closed.

Someone stood, leaning over her, still holding her hand, and whispered in her ear, lips touching her, a quiet hand brushing her hair from her face.

"Quint worked for me, not for Jack. I was trying to watch out for you. But this guy was too slick, too fast."   She heard his voice catch.

He kissed her re-bandaged eye, her bruised cheek, her ripped fingernails. *Nick.*

"I couldn't risk calling you," he said. "I thought I had him. My unit's been tracking him for a year."   He put her hand against his cheek. "They approached me four years ago. Recruited me. Homeland Security, special assignments only. Only the managing editor knows. It was so hard, not being able to tell you. Talk to you. But it wasn't safe. And when you didn't answer my note, I wasn't sure what to think. Then I found you, too late." His voice cracked. "I thought you had left, with Magnus. Then I couldn't reach him. And then the fire." He whispered, "I thought I lost you."

His breath was rough, strained. *Nick?* Tike opened her mouth, but no voice would come.

"The recording," he said.   "It's the best lead on this guy we've ever gotten, ties him in to some of our other cases. We've been working on it since they found you. This guy. This...Meandash. He's slick. Smart. Very. Pete Russell—that's a new alias. We thought we might get a break, get a clue where he was going." He paused. "When you're ready, the team wants to talk to you. You're the only one who's ever seen him. And knows it. We don't even know what country he's from. The Saamis, the Meandash culture—they're scattered all over the world. Nomads." He took a deep breath. "They wanted me to come in, to go back to D.C. this year, run the unit, but that can wait," he said. "I want to be with you. Need to."

After a moment he pressed something into her hand. "Liz gave me this for you," he said. Dense, a sharp shape against her bandages. Crystal. *Swarovski*? A cat. *The survivor.* He spoke softly. "She wants to see you when you're ready. She said she needs a friend like you."

His warm mouth breathed against her ear, then whispered, weak: "So do I. Please forgive me. I'm here now."

She opened her mouth, licked her lips. "Maybe," she said, stumbling over the syllables. "Maybe okay." She opened her good eye as he dropped to his knees beside the hospital bed, burying his head in the tangled sheets over her bandaged belly. She stroked his hair as his shoulders shook, his hands twisting the sheets into knots. He smelled like sweat and horses and woodsmoke and warm nights and slow, cool mornings.

"Maybe okay."

———————

From the January 12 Grand Rapids (Michigan) Times:

FMD Found in N. Carolina Wild Deer

RALEIGH, N.C. (AP) — The Department of Natural Resources reported the first confirmed case of Foot-and-Mouth Disease in a wild deer found in the Putney Woods area.

"This is a crisis for our state economy," said Jervis Ralkins, DNR director. "FMD in the wild deer population will be a constant source of infection for our livestock. This is a disaster."

Ralkins said the DNR has started meetings with the Carolina Pork Producers to determine what measures, if any, can be done to continue pork production in North Carolina.

The three largest farrowing operations in North Carolina last year reported combined revenues of $587 million, primarily from sales of juvenile feeder pigs to grow-out operations around the country.

"We've been talking with the Department of Agriculture to determine whether we'll run a special season to do a complete cull of the wild deer population," he said. "This may not be feasible or effective, as our major deer territories are contiguous with those of four surrounding states."

He said DNR agents are now in the field collecting more deer to survey the level of infection in the wild population.

The origin of the viral outbreak remains unclear.

Reports of an infected bison in Yellowstone National Park are also under investigation.

From the January 21 Rahway (New Jersey) Star-Ledger:

Novartis to Acquire FMD Vaccine Company

Wilmington, Del. (AP) — Representatives of Euvaxx and Novartis today released a joint statement of intent.

"Our successful vaccine technology will help this country recover," said Dr. Michelangelo Salt, CEO of Euvaxx. "Novartis recognizes and appreciates this value, and brings marketing reach to the table."

Rhonda Morgenstern, Vice-President of Animal Health for Novartis Global, said Euvaxx will become a wholly-owned subsidiary of Novartis US. "Euvaxx and Dr. Salt have a positive vision for animal health," she said, speaking from Novartis headquarters in Basel. "Novartis is excited to share that vision."

Financial terms were not disclosed.

From the January 13 Boise (Idaho) Valley Post:

U.S. Meat, Dairy Exports Lose Status

CHICAGO, Ill. (AP) — The Department of Commerce today reported a permanent change in export status for US beef, pork, sheep, and goat products, including milk and cheese.

"US exports no longer hold FMD-Free status in international markets," said Francis Gulmondo, US Secretary of Commerce, in Chicago for the annual meeting of the International Association of Commodity Brokers. "This is a major hit. Our reduced trade status will cost us billions of dollars a year."

"With FMD now in wildlife populations, there is no hope the disease can be eradicated," he said. "We will not regain our preferred trading status."

He said the US is now in discussions with major trading partners and a Paris-based livestock disease organization, the O.I.E., to press for changes in FMD trade standards.

The U.S. Department of Agriculture has convened an emergency committee to study options for reimbursing farm losses, expected to top $9 billion before exports resume.

The Chicago Board of Trade opened two hours late due to adjustments in trading regulations.

From the January 15 Phoenix (Arizona) Desert Sun-Times:

CFTC, Homeland Security Investigate Manipulation of Commodities Markets

WASHINGTON, D.C. (AP) — Today the Commodity Futures Trading Commission disclosed an investigation into inappropriate transactions during the recent livestock disease outbreaks.

"We have assistance from key players within the commodities trading community," said Rafaela Curbanez, chair of the CFTC. "We're working with Homeland Security to track specific criminal events preceding and during the FMD (foot-and-mouth disease) outbreaks."

These activities, she said, included computer intrusion, falsification of financial documents, arson, and homicide.

CHAPTER 54

Pennti Ruottila stretched his long pale legs and arched his back with a quiver. He settled back into his low beach chair and scrubbed his heels in the black sand. A wide hat, from one of Pennti's favorite shops in Milan, hung over the top of his dark wraparound sunglasses, shielding his pale green eyes from the strong sun directly overhead. Pennti's watch alarm beeped and he reached into his bag for a small device with a back-lit screen. Numbers and Chinese characters scrolled across the screen; the Dalian was closing in 10 minutes. He watched the market action as it closed, made a few notes on a pad, then put the screen away.

Noisy little children ran by screaming; he couldn't understand a word. Pennti reached into his beach bag and pulled out a stack of magazines still in their plastic mailing wrappers. They were all a bit out of date; it took a while for mail to get to Pennti. Some were addressed to Pennti Ruottila, or Parker Roos. Or P. Ross or Panko Roskovich.

Or Pete Russell.

Some had come to a remote farm in Finland, others to a rented mail-box in Rahway, New Jersey, or La Jolla, California. Most ended up in a 17th century silver filigree box, dead center on a spalted maple desk behind a door engraved with an unusual crest—a winged reindeer, in flight over a dark river. The silent room was on the top floor of a bank in Basel, Switzerland.

Pennti flipped through his magazines, looking for one with a nice picture on the cover. Something colorful. Something lively, exciting, new.

Something...profitable.

He stretched his stiff knee and scratched at an ugly scar on his leg as he read. The long scar was still dark purple and thick. It cut through a tattoo of a double helix on his inner left ankle. Now the helix looked like a tornado.

He paused at a thick publication: *The Journal of International Entomological Research.* He stared at the cover photo of a very ugly spider, aiming a small red eye at the reader. The text under several of the sharp little spider feet read "Page 394. Novel Chemistry in New Kenyan *Nikomorphus* Species: Jackpot...or Nightmare?"

Pennti tapped a finger against the spine of the magazine and closed his eyes, his mind composing and sampling images, testing their ability to breathe and live. He saw, swirling together: a crying politician, a lock-box of currency, workers trudging into a diamond mine, stained maps of property lines. He saw people on stretchers, a woman—a beautiful widow—reading a newspaper headline, an expensive car pulling up to her door.

Pennti opened his eyes and read the cover text again: *Jackpot...or Nightmare?*

"Or both?" he said, his voice a whisper. Then he laughed. *Oh yes. Would that do it?* The equatorial sun bounced off his perfect teeth. He slit the plastic wrapper of the magazine with a sharp fingernail, clean and buffed smooth, and pulled it away from the glossy cover. A gust of wind whipped the plastic from his hand, into the air, down the beach, behind the children, toward the harbor. He watched it sail over the head of a couple walking hand in hand, leaning toward each other, sharing the sun. Pennti looked away. He turned to page 394.

Yes, that would do it.

Pennti had homework.

———————

From the September 19 Lake-of-the-Woods (Minnesota) Nine Lakes College Daily Trumpet:

Campus Calendar
This week:

Tuesday, 3 pm: Student Center, Vergstren Memorial Lounge. Meet the new visiting professor, biology department, Dr. Per Rasmussen. Slideshow of research on spiders in Africa. Coffee and cookies.

TECHNICAL NOTE

Foot-and-mouth disease has been called the most important animal disease in the world because it is highly contagious among cloven-hoofed livestock (such as cattle, sheep, goats, pigs, llamas and deer), and being free of this disease is critical to a country's global trade in animal products. The United States has been free of the disease since the 1920s. For more than 50 years, Plum Island Animal Disease Center (PIADC) has been successful in its mission of preventing and being prepared for the introduction into the U.S. of foreign livestock diseases, like foot-and-mouth disease. At PIADC, the U.S. Department of Homeland Security (DHS) and the U.S. Department of Agriculture (USDA) work together in the mutual goal of protecting America's livestock and agriculture.

PIADC develops diagnostics and preventatives for foreign animal diseases and also trains federal, state, military, and academic veterinarians and veterinary pathologists through its Foreign Animal Disease Diagnosticians (FADD) courses. These FADD school graduates are this nation's sentinels for foreign animal diseases and have learned how to recognize foreign animal diseases, take correct samples, and send to the appropriate diagnostic authorities. In addition, PIADC USDA and DHS scientists have performed groundbreaking state-of-the-art molecular research on many of the causative agents of foreign animal diseases in order to develop new prevention and control strategies. This research has led to the development of the first of a new generation of foot-and-mouth disease vaccines and antiviral therapeutics that, in collaboration with the DHS and private companies, are now in the first stages of commercialization.

Also, other laboratories worldwide are capable of diagnosing the disease, and in 2004, PIADC developed a portable diagnostic laboratory tool that can test for foot-and-mouth disease and other livestock diseases in other regional and state U.S. diagnostic laboratories (e.g., the National

Animal Health Laboratory Network). This is in the process of being validated. Most recently, a collaboration among DHS, USDA, University of California-Davis and Lawrence Livermore National Laboratories has resulted in the preliminary development of a candidate rapid diagnostic assay that tests for foot-and-mouth disease and six other similar diseases of livestock simultaneously. In May 2006, this interagency team demonstrated the candidate assay in a high-throughput capacity that allows for the processing of up to 1,000 samples within 10 hours using two robotic workstations and two lab technicians. This technology, too, continues through development and will shortly enter into the validation process.

ACKNOWLEDGEMENTS

Many people helped me get this book into your hands.

On the writing side:

The gang at the Santa Barbara Writers' Conference, especially Anne Lowenkopf, Leonard Tourney, and the night Pirates: Shelly Lowenkopf, Lorelei Armstrong, and Marcy Luikart, among others. Editor Greg Miller. John Walter and the other editors at Successful Farming and @griculture Online over the years including Betsy Freese, Mike Holmberg, Gene Johnston, Loren Kruse, Dan Looker, and Dave Mowitz. Barry Baxt, Jerry Jennings, Kristine Garland and the team at Plum Island Animal Disease Center. Shadi Ahmed El Aker, my host while I did book research in Dubai and Abu Dhabi. (Tike hits the road in Book Two.) Other advance readers of early and later drafts included Dick "Slider" Gilmore, Pam York, Jack Kerley, Jerry Perkins, Melanie Wilt, Ralph Scherder III, Sheila Ehrhardt, Frank Kutlak, Charlie Powell, Pam Smith, and Mark Leonard. Special thanks to Maureen Kampen, to Susan Reiter, formerly of the Centers Against Abuse and Sexual Assault, and to commodities broker Al Kluis.

On the practical side:

Kelly McCarty of the Iowa Great Lakes Small Business Development Center. Publicists Pat Higgins and Angie Weaver. Angie Mayer and Tim Frank at Emagine Marketing. Photographer Michael Fischer. Graphics and layout artist Jennifer Cizek. Bankers Denise Steffen and Dean Jacobsen. Kiana Johnson and the O'Brien County Economic Development Corporation. Accountant Sue Behrens. Diana Willits at Meredith Corporation. Jon Hjelm and Neila Rohan at The Acre Company. Linda Versluis at Staples.

The radio drama and audiobook team at Spencer (Iowa) Community Theatre, including director Curtis Dean, Roger Partridge, Rhonda Dean,

Mark Joenks, Wade Nelson, and composer Chad Elliott.

The flipbook team: Artist Rita Goeken and Flipologist Matt Pollard.

The braille edition: Braillist Jodene Ludden.

Plus, for additional reasons, Becky and Denny Winterboer, Larry Steffes, Jane Burns, Linda Lasure, Helene Baribault, Nick Williams, and Barb Doyen. Bruce Spence, Homeland Security-Certified Agroterrorism Master Trainer. David Hugunin, my first fan. Patrick Morgan, former officer of the Spencer (Iowa) Police Department.

This isn't an adequate 'thank you,' merely an acknowledgement that many people, more than are on this list, have helped me, and continue to do so. This means a lot to me.

I also thank you, who are reading this book.

ABOUT THE AUTHOR

Kate Iola writes about business and agriculture for publications including *Successful Farming* magazine, *New Ag International*, the *Sioux City Journal*, and the *Des Moines Register*. She lives in rural Iowa.